Haven's Light

Sequel to Haven's Key

Tia Austin

authorHOUSE®

AuthorHouse™
1663 Liberty Drive
Bloomington, IN 47403
www.authorhouse.com
Phone: 1 (800) 839-8640

Published by AuthorHouse 04/28/2015

ISBN: 978-1-5049-0938-9 (sc)
ISBN: 978-1-5049-0937-2 (hc)
ISBN: 978-1-5049-0901-3 (e)

Library of Congress Control Number: 2015906577

Print information available on the last page.

*S*hrill, eerie cries echoed in the darkness outside his window. Though the sounds were familiar enough to him, they still gave him the shivers. He heard them almost every day, far away in the distance, as the sun's light faded from gold to gray. Earlier and earlier, it seemed to him. Yes, he heard the sounds often enough, but on this evening, they had a different quality to them. He'd heard them seem desperate, or mocking, or even questioning. But tonight, they seemed... pleased. As if those bizarre unseen creatures were glad about what he had done, as though they were cheering him on. Was that possible?

A chill ran down his spine, but he was certain it was not from the cool air coming in through the open window. Well, what was done was done. He had studied long and he had studied hard, and at long last, he truly believed he had found the answer. He had recorded every myth or legend that he had read, written down every rumor he had been told. So many scholars, so many lifetimes, so many guesses as to where the long-lost city of Haven might be found, if indeed it truly existed.

What an inspiring possibility! Haven ...

He had pieced everything together over and over again, and finally, it all seemed to make sense. Yes, it seemed as though the way to Haven had been revealed to him at last! In ink, on paper, at the very least.

True, it had been no secret that the idea of Haven's existence had intrigued him over the years. And the voices that had spoken into his ears on the subject could also speak to others. So it had been no great surprise when the knock at his door brought guests who desired for themselves the information he had amassed.

As far as he was concerned, this information was priceless.

And his guests had paid him dearly to get their hands on it.

~ 1 ~

Brace breathed deeply, a breath of relief. He let the pure, clean air of Haven fill his lungs once again. He was home again at last – *Home!* Yes, Haven truly was his home now. How long had it been? Three months? *Yes, that must be right*, he thought. He had actually been living in the miraculous, long-lost city of Haven for an entire season. They all had – he and Tassie, Jair and Ovard, Arden and Leandra. And *Zorix*.

Three months, and the city of Haven continued to astound them with its beauty and mystery. Jair's unexplained knowledge of the red vine fruit growing in the Fountain Court, as they had come to call it, was only the beginning. He had discovered wonder after wonder, secrets that had long been hidden from the outside world. There was the stream of crystal-clear water flowing down from the mountains through a large grove of fruit trees, emptying into a deep lake just north of Haven's large stone gate. The water, they had discovered, brought renewed strength to anyone who drank it.

Brace could not forget the fact that Jair could somehow understand the ancient language written in the old books of Haven's library. And finally, there had been Jair's discernment about the glassy stones forming the walls lining Haven's main roads. A warm, comforting light emanated from the lightstones, as they all had noticed, which faded to darkness at the same time each night – at the *right* time, not strangely early, as it did out there, in the rest of the world. The evenings here in Haven were a slow, peaceful fade of the sun as it sank lower into the west, creating a vast sweep of color so much more vivid than any of them had ever before seen – pinks, oranges, purples and reds. It was breathtaking.

After the warm golden sun had fully disappeared below the horizon, the lightstones continued to shine out their pure, white light for nearly an hour until it too faded, giving way to the dark of night.

This darkness held no fear, they had discovered. No thoughts of night screamers plagued them, no fears of strange creatures crawling about in the shadows. The dark simply brought on a peaceful silence, in which they were able to sleep deeply.

The reverberating echo of the large gate filled Brace's ears as it closed tightly behind him. He gladly turned his back on it, letting the early morning light fill his vision. The sun was just peeking over the horizon, and the pure white glow of lightstones cast faint shadows on the road leading into the city. No one could have possibly slept through the creaking and groaning of Haven's gate; they would all know by now that he'd returned.

He had come and gone from the city three times since they had arrived. One of Jair's discoveries had made Brace's travels possible; how could he have gone at all otherwise? It was all for Kendie, who had waited at Milena's farm in Spire's Gate. They'd promised her they would come back for her when they found the way, and they knew how deeply she desired to see Haven for herself.

Of course Brace had to go back – *someone* did, and he had promised Kendie himself that he would come back for her. But it wasn't safe out there beyond the gate, beyond the mountains. They all knew it. They felt that they'd barely survived their first trip over the mountains in the dark and the icy wind, but what really weighed on them was the threat of the night screamers. Zorix had been attacked by one of them, after all, and they had feared for his life. None of them felt that it would be right sending Brace – or anyone for that matter – out alone to face those horrendous creatures, whether he knew the way or not.

One morning, Brace had come upon the sight of Jair standing beside one of the city's high roadside walls, deep in thought. He'd had the same faraway look in his eyes that Brace had become accustomed to seeing.

"What is it?" Brace had asked him quietly. "Making another new discovery?"

"It's the stones," Jair had told Brace that day, the slight frown on his face revealing his efforts to put together the idea that was forming in his mind.

"What are you talking about?" Brace asked him. "What stones?"

"The lightstones in the walls lining the streets," Jair explained. "It's not just the city – it's not the *gate* that keeps the screamers away. It's the light from these stones that does it."

"Are you sure about that?" Brace questioned him. Jair only looked at him, that same look he always had these days, whenever he was questioned about some new discovery he made, some new realization that came to him.

Haven't I been right often enough for you to believe me? that look said. Brace grinned and ruffled Jair's hair.

"Yes, I'm sure," Jair said with a laugh. "Don't you remember? The screamers wouldn't come near the city. They didn't even come into the clearing near the gate. They stayed hidden in the trees. I knew there was something keeping them away. It's the light. They live in the darkness; they won't come near the light!"

Jair's theory had been put to the test. Finding a few fragments of lightstones which, though broken, still produced light on their own, they waited until night had fallen, deep and dark. They gathered at Haven's gate – all of them together, even Zorix, who wouldn't let Leandra out of sight if he could help it. Brace held the pieces of stone cupped in his hands, their pure white light illuminating the air around him like the glow of a full winter moon. The light was beautiful, he admitted to himself. It was mesmerizing, but was it enough to keep the night screamers away, as Jair believed it would?

The main gate was opened, and Brace stepped out of the city, into the wide clearing. He could just see, on the other side of the open land, the dense forest that stretched out from the base of the high, craggy mountains. Brace could hear myriad cries of angry night screamers among the trees, and he looked back over his shoulder, reassuring himself that everyone was standing watch. They were just behind him inside the city, and it was a comfort – though a small one – knowing they would come to his aid in an instant if needed.

Taking a breath to steady his nerves and muttering *harbrost* to himself, he stepped farther into the darkness, clutching the broken pieces of stone in his hands. There were streaks of smoke darting through the trees, visible proof that the forest was crowded with night screamers. Brace almost lost

3

his nerve and turned back, but he trusted Jair's word. If the boy said that the light from Haven's puzzling glassy stones would keep the screamers at bay, then he chose to believe it could be true.

He pulled himself up to his full height, held the lightstone fragments higher, and took another step out into the darkness. Almost immediately, the shrieking creatures began to retreat, with anger in their wailing voices. Farther and farther away into the trees they went until Brace could no longer see or hear them. Beyond relieved, Brace looked back to see the joyful faces of his friends – the night screamers wouldn't come within his sight! He would indeed be safe from them, as long as he had Haven's light to protect him.

Safe. That meant that there was no reason, now, not to go back for Kendie.

And so the bits of stone had been secured onto a leather cord for Brace to wear around his neck, keeping his hands free. He had packed his bag full of the supplies he would need for the journey back to Spire's Gate, said his farewells to his friends, and set out. It was not a long trek, but it was a difficult one, over the mountains of bare, cold rock, fighting the strong gusts of wind and spending his nights alone, huddled against the mountainside in the dark.

Kendie had been overjoyed when she spotted Brace trudging across the land toward Milena's farm. He remembered now all too well how her face had lit up with joy, how she had called out his name and ran to him, embracing him tightly. How glad she had been to see him alive again – she told him how much she'd worried about all of them, praying that they would find Haven and be safe.

She had chattered on, as she often did, telling Brace how wonderful Milena had been to her; Buying her a new dress – *two of them!* – sharing her home with her, giving her a comfortable bed to sleep in, good meals to eat, and loving her more than she remembered ever having been loved, for so many years.

Kendie's joy increased as she nearly dragged Brace back to the farm, pulling him along by his hand and informing Milena and her farmhands that *he had returned!*

Milena, of course, had been very welcoming, making certain that Brace had several warm drinks and plenty of mouth-watering food as he told them all that he could about Haven, answering every question any of them asked until there was nothing left to be said. Brace told them about the healing fruit and the glassy lightstones, told them that the light they gave off kept the night screamers away, and that he was able to cross the mountains, safe from harm.

Kendie's joy at the thought of seeing Haven for herself had turned to sorrow when Milena told the girl that she wouldn't be coming with her.

"But why?" Kendie asked, bewildered. "Doesn't it sound wonderful?"

"I'm too old," Milena told her, gently taking her small hands in her own. "There is no way that my old woman's body can make it over those high mountains."

"Please, please come," Kendie pleaded with her tearfully. "Don't you think you could try? We'll be there to help you. Can't you try?"

Milena patiently endured, stroking Kendie's wavy black hair. Finally, she shook her head, a sad smile on her face.

"I'm sorry, my sweet," was all she had left to say, and though she was heartbroken, Kendie had no choice but to accept it.

Brace had wondered if the thought of leaving Milena behind would be enough to make Kendie change her mind, and not want to come back with him. He could see it in her eyes, the wavering between conflicting desires, but the elderly woman had taken Kendie's face in her worn, wrinkled hands and made her promise to go back with Brace.

"Haven is where you truly belong," she told her. "You go back there for me. I will always be in your heart, Kendie, and you will always be in mine. I'll take good care of Jax here, and he will live to be as old and as happy as I am."

Kendie finally smiled once again, thinking of the mule that had brought her from Meriton to Spire's Gate, pulling the rickety old cart. She had named the stubborn beast, after all, and she had grown very fond of him.

Brace had invited everyone on the farm to travel with him to Haven. Nav, the older of Milena's two "lads", as she called them, hadn't given the idea a second thought. No, he could not possibly leave, he had said. Milena needed him there on the farm. He couldn't leave his master all alone.

Dursen, the younger farmhand, had wrestled long and hard with himself about the idea. Torn between his desire to see Haven for himself and his loyalty to Milena, he had struggled about making the right decision.

Seeing that he wanted to leave but also to stay, Milena had given him her blessing, encouraging him to follow the others to what must be a place more wonderful than anyone could imagine. Eventually, settled with himself on the idea, and decided that he would dare to join Brace and Kendie.

And so, after the difficult climb over the rocky mountain pass, the three of them had found their way to Haven's gate – tired, cold, and sore, but unharmed – and they were warmly welcomed home by the others, who had been anxiously waiting for them.

Having come and gone once already, Brace continued to go out in search of anyone who had knowledge of the ancient city and had been longing for its safety, or, upon hearing of it, anyone who was willing to give up everything they had in the outside world in order to see it with their own eyes.

Now Brace was home once again, just having returned from his latest mission, and Tassie's face was all that he wanted to see. He'd had enough of dusty roads and dark mountain passages. And as wonderful as it was to experience the warmth and light of Haven once again, there was a place in his heart that could only be satisfied by Tassie, and none other.

Tassie – beautiful Tassie! Hers was the face that Brace always wanted to see first when he returned from his missions. Since he had gone and successfully brought back Kendie and Dursen, he had been put in charge of the task of bringing others into Haven. Ovard's studies had revealed that now was the time for a great return to the ancient city of their ancestors, and Jair was adamant that people be shown the way as soon as possible. With the sky getting darker and the night screamers working ever harder to keep people away, it was becoming evident that the longer people waited, the harder it would be to find their way to Haven safely.

Making his way down the wide, familiar main path into the city, Brace pulled off his heavy winter cloak. There was no need for such a thing here – the air inside Haven always, miraculously, felt exactly perfect, no matter how cold it may be on the outside. Brace tugged off his gloves and tucked them into his belt, flexing his fingers in the warmth of Haven's early morning sunlight. The skin on the back of his right hand still itched from time to time, but it was nothing compared to the throbbing pain that he'd had to endure after being marked with the marriage tattoo– he on his right hand and Tassie on her left. Ovard had done it for them, with one of Tassie's medic needles and the dark brown ink that Brace had purchased at the town of Spire's Gate the first time he'd journeyed from Haven.

Tassie is my wife, Brace thought to himself again. Sometimes he felt the need to remind himself of the fact; it seemed too wonderful to be true, and it was all still so new to him, the memories so fresh in his mind.

He remembered how his heart had been beating so fast as he waited for the marriage ceremony to begin, as he waited to see Tassie . . .

Standing in the Fountain Court with Ovard at his back, facing Arden, Dursen, and Kendie, who all stood before him, watching him wait; Jair standing at the entrance to the courtyard, where the wide street met up with the high, arched gap in the lightstone walls.

The sweet smell of red vine fruit filled the air, and the sun was warm on Brace's head. Why did he need to wait so long? The anticipation had been building, and now it was almost unbearable. When would he see Tassie enter at last?

He let out a breath to steady his nerves. This was her time, he knew, her time with Leandra. It was Tassie's moment to reflect on what was to come – this joining of two as one, and her life would never be the same. She would, at this moment, be sharing her deepest thoughts with only Leandra, who in turn would give her any wisdom she could share.

Brace had had his own time as well, earlier that morning, with Arden. Such was the custom, after all, for the soon-to-be-wed pair to meet separately with someone who had experienced married life, someone with whom they shared a deep bond of friendship. Brace had confided in Arden that, though he felt in his heart that this was right, his marriage to Tassie, he was plagued by insecurities. Tassie had never been with another man, and Brace had had plenty of past relationships, though they had been shallow ones at best. Despite all of his experiences, Brace felt that Tassie meant more to him than all of the other women, all added together. He wanted to be all that he could for Tassie – to care for her the way that she deserved, and to be the man that she wanted and needed him to be.

Arden had given Brace the same advice that Brace had once given to him —
just be there. Be there, Arden had told him. Be there when she needs you, in
body and in heart. Open your ears, your mind, your heart, to truly hear her.
Don't listen on the surface, Arden had told him. Go deeper.

Brace was fairly confident that he had grasped the meaning of Arden's
words, but even so, his heart raced in his chest as he stood waiting for Tassie.
What the women could be discussing, he had no way of knowing. What he did
know was that his hands were getting damp with sweat as he held them at his
sides, and he brushed them against the front of his shirt to dry them.

He caught Jair's eye, and the boy smiled, amused. Jair had seen what Brace
had done, and he realized how nervous he must be feeling. Brace took another
steadying breath, then he saw Jair look aside – Tassie was coming in at last!

Jair stepped aside and disappeared behind the lightstone wall as Leandra
briskly entered the courtyard, taking her place beside Arden, slipping her hand
in his.

Tassie would be the next to enter, Brace knew, with Jair at her side.
She had no father to present her as the bride, and with Ovard, her uncle,
leading the ceremony, Jair was the only one left who should walk Tassie to her
husband's side.

The air was still and silent as the two of them rounded the corner of the
wall and stepped into the courtyard, arm in arm, their shadows going on before
them. Brace held his breath. There she was at last, looking more beautiful than
she ever had, or so Brace believed at that moment. Her dress was one that Brace
had seen her wear many times – it was not a new one, worn for the first time,
as was customary. But the dark green of the fabric was perfect, he thought, as
it brought out the color of her eyes.

Dainty wildflowers had been woven into her braided hair, and they
framed her face like a halo of white, yellow and pale purple. Her cheeks blushed
pink as she came, with Jair beside her. All eyes were on her now as she walked
slowly past everyone toward Brace. He couldn't take his eyes off of her, even
if he had wanted to. She held his gaze, their eyes locked on each other's as she
slowly approached him, smiling her small smile, somehow seeming both shy
and flirtatious at the same moment.

Brace took a breath, swallowed, and managed a lop-sided grin in response
to her smile.

Jair leaned in to give Tassie a quick kiss on her cheek before stepping back, joining the others. The boy may have had an encouraging smile for him, but Brace did not see it. He kept his eyes on Tassie's face as she stood in front of him. When he took her hands in his, he realized that she was trembling slightly. Was she just as nervous as he was?

"You all right?" Brace mouthed the words, knowing she could understand while no one else would hear.

She nodded slowly, and her face blushed deeply.

Ovard stepped toward them, placing his hands on their shoulders and speaking their names aloud for all to hear. Sunlight glinted off of Haven's lightstone walls all around the Fountain Court, where they stood gathered closely together.

"We have come to this place," Ovard began, "to celebrate the union of our dear friends, Brace and Tassie, as they pledge their love and loyalty to one another, from this day on, until their lives should end."

Brace felt Ovard give his shoulder a squeeze, and he managed to pull his gaze away from Tassie's deep green eyes to look over at him.

"Do you vow to take this woman as your very own, and her only, for the rest of your days?" he asked, though Brace could see in his eyes that he already knew the answer.

"Yes, I do," Brace replied readily.

Ovard smiled, then turned and repeated the question for Tassie.

"Yes," she answered breathlessly, overwhelmed by the significance of the moment. With one simple word, she and Brace would no longer be two people leading separate lives. From this day on, and forever, they would be one. *They would belong to each other.*

Ovard took their hands, Brace's right, Tassie's left, and held them together between them, Brace's resting lightly on Tassie's. Brace felt the roughness of Ovard's callused fingers as he led them to repeat their vows: They would be true to one another forever and always, regarding one other as above themselves, living lives of honor and courage – of harbrost *– keeping their two hearts as one, no matter what the future may hold. As Brace repeated line after line, he meant each and every word, with everything he had in him. His only regret was that he had no name to give Tassie, no name of his own. He had no knowledge of who his father had been, or what name he would have given to*

9

Brace as his son. They had agreed that they would keep the name that Tassie had taken as her own so long ago – Ovard's name, Barrison.

No, Brace could not give Tassie his name, but he could give her something better – his life, and his heart, as much as he knew how.

When the last words of the vows had been spoken, Ovard held Brace and Tassie's hands together tightly. "Now," he said in a voice that everyone could hear, "you are no longer two, but one, for the rest of your days."

Brace kept his eyes on Tassie's face. Her beautiful, shy, smiling face. After a moment, he realized that everyone was still watching them silently, expectantly. Glancing at Ovard, Brace cleared his throat.

"Should I kiss her?" he asked.

"By all means, do!" Ovard replied, laughing and stepping back.

Brace held Tassie's hands tightly for one short moment longer, then let them go, taking her face gently in his hands and letting his lips touch hers – there, in the Fountain Court, in front of everyone.

Kendie's cheering broke the silence, and the others followed, clapping. Brace ended their kiss before he'd wanted to, and Tassie laughed as the two of them were surrounded by their friends, their family, congratulating them with their kind words of congratulations, with hugs and handshakes.

It all felt like a dream, a day that was etched firmly in Brace's memory. Tassie was his now, and he was hers, *no matter what the future may hold,* as they had vowed.

And in Brace's mind, the future stretched out before them, full of hope, and anything was possible.

Brace had left home three times, and now he came back alone. After bringing Kendie and Dursen back with him, he had returned to the farmlands of Spire's Gate and found others – a woman named Jayla, her husband Rudge and her brother Kalen. They had heard Kendie's stories about Haven and had readily joined Brace on his return trip over the mountains.

Now on this, his third journey, Brace had wandered along the outskirting farms of Spire's Gate, making his way east as far as the town, taking time to purchase a bundle of new paper for Ovard with some of the money Tassie had given him. No one there had paid him any mind. No one asked him any questions about where he'd come from or what he was doing in Spire's Gate. When he'd casually mentioned that he was heading west to get back home, no one had asked him what was out there, despite the fact that, as far as anyone knew, all that lay west of the farmland were jagged mountain ranges and wild, unfriendly forests.

Brace had considered going back to the city of Meriton, but what would he say to the people there?

"Do you want freedom?"

Freedom from what? They would likely ask. If he explained Haven to them, what would they think? Would they believe him, or would they think he was crazy? Brace was also concerned about Rune Fletcher, the innkeeper at the Wolf and Dagger. Kendie had been working under his charge – did the man think she had run away, or that the lot of them had taken her when they left? The last thing Brace needed was to have kidnapping added to his list of charges.

But, though alone, he was safely home once more, and Brace was full of relief. The opening of the enormous stone gate was always a noisy occurrence, so it was no surprise when the pale white light of early morning made Arden's form visible as he slowly approached.

The tall archer's pale blond hair was beginning to grow out once again, slightly, giving him back a bit of the dignity that he'd once had as a Royal Archer. His duty to protect the rest of them was less pressing now in this safe place, and he had been having a difficult time adjusting to life in Haven, thankful though he was to be living there at last. The peace and safety of the ancient city of their ancestors was a welcome relief after spending so long a time out in the wild lands, facing its many dangers, but Arden's restlessness had been easy to see. Now, he spent many of his days keeping up his hunting skills by tracking game among the massive trees of Haven's Woods, just beyond the farthest western streets of the ancient city.

"Welcome home," the archer greeted him, his voice low and his eyes half open.

"It's good to be back," Brace replied, taking note of Arden's ornate clothing. It was oddly disheveled, as though he had hurried to put it on without even looking.

Arden glanced down the wide road past Brace's shoulder.

"Alone?" he asked.

Brace nodded. "Not so lucky this time." He shrugged.

Arden let out a sigh. "Well, that's that. Can't be helped."

Brace nodded once again, further resigning himself to the journey's outcome. "I'm sorry I came in so early," he continued. "I was here, so I couldn't bring myself to wait any longer. I'm sure I woke everyone up with all the noise of the gate."

Arden smirked, running his fingers through his unruly blond hair. "All of us but one," he pointed out.

"Leandra didn't wake her?" Brace asked, mildly surprised.

"No," Arden replied. "It *is* very early. And she thought you'd rather be the one to do it."

Brace found himself smiling. "Tell Leandra thank you."

Arden clapped a heavy hand on Brace's shoulder. "I will. And we'll all be seeing you later, at the Main Hall."

"Right," Brace agreed.

Arden lifted his hand to wave goodbye, turning down the side road toward home. Brace watched him go for only a moment before he continued along the road to the small house that he shared with Tassie – it seemed he'd done this a hundred times. Stepping up to the door, he rested his palm on the worn surface for a moment. *My own home,* he thought. *Surely this will be a place that I'll never need to run from.*

There was no lock – no need for such things in Haven – so Brace simply pushed against the wooden door and stepped inside.

In the warm, dim glow of light pouring in through the windows, Brace could see that the main front rooms were empty. Laying his wool cloak on the small wooden table where he and Tassie shared their meals, he went into the bedroom and stood beside the bed where Tassie lay sleeping. He felt a twinge of regret at having left her alone all of those nights – *again*. She was safe here, of course, but just the same, he couldn't shake off his feelings of guilt.

Brace loved to gaze at Tassie's face while she slept. She was so beautiful, her long waves of dark hair falling around her shoulders, her eyelashes resting on her smooth, fair skin, her gentle mouth. She was so sweet, so *Tassie*, even while she slept.

Only once had Brace seen her looking troubled while she slept, the night after Ovard had finished work on the marriage tattoos that were now patterned across the backs of their hands – Brace's right, Tassie's left, cascading in ornate loops from their outer fingers down to and encircling their wrists. That night, three nights after their wedding, Tassie's brow was creased in a slight frown. Though she did not voice any complaints, Brace knew the pain she felt – he felt it as well. But it was well worth it, he told himself often, particularly after the swelling and redness had faded and he could see the markings as they were meant to be seen. In another year, they would have their other hand done to match the first. There was no mistaking it now, the fact of their union. Any stranger would only need to look at them and see that they belonged to each other.

Brace pulled off his boots and let them fall to the floor, thumping soundly in the still of the morning. He knew that the sound wouldn't wake Tassie – she couldn't hear anything, after all. He carefully lifted the bedcovers and slid under them, lying close to Tassie, his face near hers. He reached out to touch her hair, and she stirred slightly, then opened her eyes.

"Brace!" she said with a sleepy smile. "You're back."

"I'm back," he replied, then leaned in to kiss her. She kissed him in return, then moved in to snuggle against him, her head tucked under his chin, her arms wrapped tightly around him, her feet touching his.

"You're cold," she told him, but Brace didn't answer, he just held her closer. Tassie moved so that she could look at his face. "Did you bring anyone back with you this time?"

"No," Brace told her. "I don't think we'll get anyone else from Spire's Gate. I'll … I'll have to go farther out next time."

"And you'll be gone longer," Tassie said regretfully. Brace only nodded.

"You should take someone with you," she urged, as she did every time he left.

"Maybe I can now," Brace agreed. "Maybe Dursen can join me."

"I would feel better if you weren't alone."

Brace smiled ruefully. "You know I can take care of myself. But I don't like leaving you alone either."

Tassie ran her fingers along Brace's cheek. "Just as long as you always come back," she told him.

"Oh, I'll always come back to you," he told her. She smiled as he leaned in to kiss her again, pulling the blankets up over their heads.

~ 2 ~

Brace managed to get a few hours of sleep that morning before he finally, reluctantly, pulled himself out of bed. When he meandered into the front room, having washed and changed into clean clothing, he smelled before he saw that Tassie had fixed him his new favorite drink – hot spiced tea. He slid into his seat at the table just as Tassie saw him, smiled, and came over to give him a freshly poured mug.

"Thank you," he told her, resting his hand on hers. She lowered herself onto the seat beside him and leaned her head on his shoulder for a moment, taking his hand and letting their fingers slide together.

"I'm so glad you're back," she said, looking up at him.

"So am I," Brace replied, taking a drink of his tea. "Did I miss anything important while I was away?"

Tassie shook her head. "Not really. Rudge and Kalen are making great progress, getting the stonework repaired. Ovard is becoming more confident in his understanding of the ancient writings – Jair is proving to be a good teacher." Tassie smiled. "And Kendie wants to write a song about Haven."

Brace chuckled. "She would do that." There was silence for a moment while he sipped more of his tea. "How is Leandra?" he asked.

Leandra was as strong and bold as ever, even with her pregnancy progressing along so that her belly was beginning to show some roundness. She'd made it through the early months of relentless nausea, and Zorix had managed to as well. The furry creature had completely healed after being attacked by the night screamers, but on the days when Leandra was particularly ill, Zorix's color-changing fur had faded to a dull blue-gray, revealing that he must be feeling just as sick as Leandra had been.

"She is doing well," Tassie replied. "Everything seems fine with her and the baby. Arden has been really going out of his way to take care of her."

"That's good to hear."

Tassie smiled. "Leandra has told me that at times, it feels like *too* much."

Brace nodded, recalling the sense of melancholy that had seemed to be hanging over Arden for a time. Concerned, Brace had managed to catch him alone one day. Their friendship being what it was now, he knew he could speak with Arden about it – but not too bluntly. He knew that the archer would often shrug things off if he was questioned outright about what he was feeling. He would say it was nothing, that he was all right. In Arden's mind, whatever was going on around them was always more important than his own inner feelings, and he would keep them to himself unless he felt that they pertained to the situation at hand.

What Arden was thinking *did* matter to Brace, however. When they had first met, their relationship, if it could be called that, had *not* been on good terms. Arden had thought of Brace as being trouble, an unwanted nuisance, and Brace had seen Arden as cold, judgmental, and militaristic. What they knew of one another now went so much deeper than all of that. Life was complicated, Brace knew, and he had learned that this was true of individuals as well, Arden in particular.

So, one afternoon when Brace found Arden standing along the lightstone wall in the courtyard, he nonchalantly asked if he could join him.

Arden nodded. "You're welcome to."

Brace leaned against the wall beside him, looking down at a nearby stone bench, which had been repaired by either Rudge or Kalen – he could see the jagged line where the corner had once been broken off before the newly-made mortar had been applied to it.

"They've done good work here," Brace commented, indicating the bench.

"That they have," Arden agreed.

"Everything is coming along so well," Brace added, crossing his arms over his chest and leaning back against the lightstone wall, feeling its warmth flow into him. "You should be pleased."

"Oh, I am pleased."

"You don't seem it," Brace told him gently. "You seem ... let down. Is something wrong?"

Arden sighed and looked away for a moment. "Not really wrong," he finally answered. "It's only that..."

"Yes?" Brace prodded.

"Well," Arden replied, in a voice heavy with resignation, "Rudge and Kalen are doing what they know, what they've been trained to do – the stone work. Tassie is learning so many new things, how the plants here can heal; Ovard is learning the language. They are all doing what they know, what they love, what they are skilled at. But..." Arden shrugged. "I'm trained to protect, to defend. What do I need to protect anyone from, here?" He shook his head. "There is nothing. I feel like I don't have much of a purpose here."

"You hunt for game in Haven's Woods," Brace pointed out. "You're providing meat for everyone to eat. That's a good purpose."

Arden squinted into the distance. "Yes, that is," he admitted. "But I don't feel quite ... *fulfilled*."

Brace nodded, considering Arden's words. The sing-song voices of Haven's birds could be heard from far away, among the ancient trees in the orchard, which surprisingly – or not surprisingly – still bore plentiful fruit.

"Well," Brace began again, when the thought came to him, "not *everyone* here is doing what they've trained for, what they are skilled at."

Arden looked at him, momentarily confused.

"I'm not doing what I've been skilled at all my life," Brace pointed out, and Arden grinned.

"That you aren't, are you?"

"No," Brace replied, shaking his head. "I'm sure I'll never steal another thing for the rest of my life. But the point is, I'm learning a new skill, or at least serving a new purpose, by bringing people here. If I can do something new, you can as well."

"And what would that be, exactly?"

Brace shrugged. "Being a father," he told him. "The time will come before you're ready, I'm sure. But you and Leandra will have a little one who will need both of his parents to be there."

Arden nodded slowly, a look of heavy realization coming over his face. "Everything else will have to be put on hold then, won't it?"

"I think so," Brace replied.

Arden now no longer seemed melancholy – he looked downright fear-stricken. Brace chuckled and clapped him on the shoulder. "Don't start worrying, now. I know you'll be a good father."

Arden scratched the back of his head, where his hair was starting to grow out again after having been cut off to hide his identity as an archer. "I hope so," he told Brace. "I really have no idea what to expect."

Brace rose to his feet, patting Arden's shoulder once again. "Just take it one day at a time," he suggested. "Do what I'm learning to do. Just be there."

And so Arden had, as Tassie pointed out, become very attentive to Leandra's needs, or even her perceived needs. He still, out of necessity, made periodic hunting trips into the Woods, often accompanied by Jair, and sometimes by Leandra as well. She asserted that she wanted to feel useful as much as Arden did, and that he could use her help if – or when – he took down a deer or a large game bird.

Brace felt Tassie's hand touch the side of his face, interrupting his thoughts. "Where did you go?" she asked him, and Brace smirked.

"Just now?" he asked, and Tassie nodded.

"I was only thinking," Brace replied. "About Arden mostly."

"You should drink your tea," she told him. "You'll have to meet with Ovard soon, let him know that no one came back with you on this trip."

Brace obediently picked up us mug and emptied it.

"Are you hungry?" Tassie asked him.

"I am," he replied. "But that can wait. I'll go and meet with Ovard now. We'll figure out where I should go when I head out the next time."

Tassie's gaze fell to the table. Brace knew all too well what that downward glance meant. She had something on her mind, but was reluctant to share it.

He truly hated leaving, now. He hated leaving the peace and safety of Haven's walls, hated seeing the look on Tassie's face when he had to go. He hated making her worry. Although he had no more trouble with night screamers, Tassie was concerned with the possibility – no matter how slim it may be – that someone would recognize him as the wanted thief that he was. That idea worried Brace as well, he had to admit. But for the time being, he, along with the rest of them, felt as though he was the best person to spread the news of Haven's discovery. The rest of them were needed there.

He reached over and held her hand tightly until she looked up. "Tell me," he said.

"I don't want you to go out anymore *at all*," she told him. "I try not to worry, but I can't help myself. It isn't safe for you."

"I wear the lightstones," Brace reminded her. "The night screamers don't come anywhere near me."

"You know that isn't what I mean," she scolded. "If the wrong person sees you, recognizes you – they won't know that you're not that person anymore, no longer a thief. You wouldn't have a fair chance."

Brace absently ran his finger along the rim of his mug. "We're so far south, though," he pointed out. "I don't think anyone this far south would know that I'm a wanted thief."

Tassie shook her head. "You know there's always that chance."

Brace sat silently for a moment, then nodded. "You're right. I know there's a chance. I'll talk to Ovard. If Dursen comes with me, like we've talked about, I'll teach him what to do, what to say, and then *he* can lead these search missions." Brace was surprised when Tassie remained quiet – she didn't even smile. He lightly touched her arm so she would look at him again.

"Isn't that what you want?" he asked. "For me to stay here?"

"Yes," she replied meekly. "But I hate the thought that I'm making you give this up if you don't want to. The coming and going, I mean. If I'm taking that last little bit of freedom away from you, I'm worried that you might resent it. Resent *me*."

Brace shook his head, smiling a little. "Tassie, I'd give it all up in a heartbeat. If I want to travel, I'll walk out to Haven's Woods and spend the day out there."

Tassie studied him thoughtfully for a moment. "You really mean all of that, don't you?" she asked.

"Of course I mean it," he replied, just as there was a light knocking at the door. Brace looked aside, in the direction of the sound. "Someone's here," he told Tassie. "It's probably Kendie, here for her medic lesson."

"Oh," Tassie commented, remembering that the girl was coming. She stood and headed toward the door, but Brace rose and caught her hand, making her look back. He stepped close to her and kissed her, not too long, not too quickly. He loved the way she reacted whenever he kissed her unexpectedly – her cheeks blushed a rosy pink, whether anyone could see them or not.

Brace smiled. "I think I'll go and meet with Ovard now."

Focus, focus, *he told himself. More and more lately, he was finding it hard to keep his mind on his work.* What if I could see Haven for myself? *He often found himself wondering.* If what I've discovered really is the way, why couldn't I go there, see it with my own eyes?

The sound of the shrieking creatures, seeming gleeful the night he'd sold his secret, constantly plagued his thoughts. But why? What did it mean? What could those unseen beasts have to do with the legend of Haven, if there really was such a place, or with him, for that matter?

Maybe his memory was playing tricks on him. Maybe his ears had deceived him, and the creatures hadn't really sounded pleased at all.

Maybe there really wasn't such a place as Haven, and it truly was just a legend.

Maybe.

Just Maybe.

~ 3 ~

The sun shone full overhead, a perfectly round circle of vivid light, unbroken by any cloud cover. Brace felt its warmth flow over him as he made his way through the Fountain Court toward the Main Hall. A cool breeze swept across him as he entered through one of the high, arched openings in the wall around the courtyard. There was no need, during the fullness of day, for any visible light to emanate from the glass stone walls curving around him, but Brace knew it was there. It was always there, keeping the screamers away. No evil could ever enter this place, he knew. The light from the stones had protected him, though how or why exactly, Brace could not explain.

The courtyard was empty now, early in the day, and silence settled over him as he walked across the smooth cobbled ground. Only the distant echo of birdsong reached his ears. Everything came into so much more focus for him, Brace realized, when things were quiet like this. There were no distractions.

He passed by the red vine fruit growing along the inside of the northern walls, rooted in the narrow stretch of dark, rich soil that ran the length of the wall. He gently ran his hand along the large, square stones as he passed through the far end of the Court, leaving it behind him. The stones were warm as always, and it made Brace wonder – was the light from the stones *indeed* always shining, as he assumed? Or did it put itself out, like a snuffed candle, when it sensed that it was not needed? He had only seen the light in early morning and at dusk. And it certainly did not shine out at night. How did the walls *know* what to do? Brace chuckled at the thought, walls *knowing* something, anything. If this wasn't Haven he was contemplating, the idea would be completely absurd.

Just another question to ask Jair, he supposed.

Inside the Main Hall, Ovard was deeply engrossed in the yellowed pages of the ancient textbook that lay open on the table in front of him, so much so that he didn't look up, or even notice, when Brace entered and approached the back of the room.

"What is this word, *aduna*?" Ovard asked Jair, who sat on his left. "Mountain?"

Jair peered at the book, where Ovard's finger rested on the page.

"No, it's more like a heap, a pile," he replied patiently.

Ovard scratched at the side of his bearded face, frowning a bit. "Mmm," he murmured. "I was sure I'd gotten a better hold on those kinds of words."

"It's all right," Jair told him. "You were close."

Ovard grinned and patted Jair on the back, only then noticing that Brace had arrived.

"Ah, there you are at last!" He called out, standing and coming to greet him as he always did, with a handshake and a quick embrace. "Have you brought anyone back with you?"

"No," Brace replied. "Not this time." He couldn't help noticing the disappointment on Jair's face as he came to take a seat across from him.

"Not *anyone*?" Jair asked as Ovard sat beside him once again.

"I'm sorry, no. I tried. I think we'll have to forget about Spire's Gate, at least for a while."

Jair nodded, looking toward the main doors when he heard voices approaching. It was the first day of the week – the day set aside for everyone to meet and discuss important issues. Brace looked back over his shoulder to see the expected familiar faces: Arden, Leandra, Dursen, Rudge, Jayla and Kalen. Everyone was present but for Tassie and Kendie, due to the medic training session that the two of them were busy with. Tassie had mentioned that she didn't mind not attending the meetings from time to time. Never knowing who would speak next, or not knowing who to look at more closely, often left her missing half of what was said and feeling frustrated. It would be easy enough for Brace to fill her in on everything afterward. Zorix never went into the Hall for meetings either. There were too many voices, he had told Leandra, speaking and thinking – he could hear them all. He preferred to wait outside the main doors until they'd finished.

"Hello again," Arden greeted Brace cheerfully as he came up to the table, now looking fully awake.

"Hello," Brace replied with a smile.

"Welcome home," Leandra said as she leaned forward to give him a friendly hug.

"Thanks," Brace told her as she moved to sit between him and Arden. He couldn't help but glance at her slightly rounded middle. She wasn't showing her pregnancy too much just yet, but Brace noticed that she often rested her hand on her stomach, almost instinctively, as though that was as close as she could get to her child until she was able to actually hold it in her arms.

"Where are the newcomers?" Dursen asked, seated on Brace's right.

"There aren't any this time," Brace told him.

Ovard nodded, as everyone silently found seats around the long wooden table, letting the news sink in.

"So," Jair finally spoke up, "no more trips to Spire's Gate, then."

Rudge nodded solemnly, while Jayla gazed at the table's surface. Kalen sat quietly, his face not betraying any emotion, but Brace knew what they must all be thinking – they still had friends or family in Spire's Gate. Would *they* ever make it into Haven?

"We'll have to broaden our search," Ovard continued.

"I'd like to talk about that," Brace spoke up.

"Yes?" Ovard asked.

"Well," Brace began. "I know we've been talking about having someone travel with me on these trips – Dursen, if he's willing?"

"I'm willing," Dursen replied with a nod.

"This would be a good time to start coming along, then," Brace told him, turning toward Ovard and Jair, who sat across the table from him. "I was talking with Tassie this morning," he continued. "She's worried about me going out again, about going any farther than I have. She's worried that I could get into trouble."

"Why would you get into trouble?" Kalen asked.

Brace glanced in Ovard's direction before answering. "Well, I wasn't too great of a person before I came here," he explained. "I was … well, I was a thief. I'm wanted by the law, out there," he said, tipping his head to indicate the world beyond Haven's walls. "So, this would be a good time for Dursen to come with me, to see how I've been going about the whole thing, so he could ..." Brace paused a moment. "Well, so he could take my place from now on."

Brace waited in silence, giving everyone a chance to respond. Jair was the first to speak up.

"Would you do that, Dursen?" he asked the former farmhand. "Would you take Brace's place leading search missions? We could have someone go with you to help you, if you want."

Dursen sat there, wide-eyed at the thought of such responsibility. "I – I think I could do that," he answered. "I can try. I'm not really knowing how to go about it, though."

"Don't worry about that," Brace spoke up. "We'll go together on the next trip. You'll learn from me and then you'll be able to teach someone else. It's really not that hard. You just have to keep your eyes open for people who look like they'd want to come here."

Dursen chewed thoughtfully at his lower lip for a moment. "Sure," he said at last. "Like I said, I can try it."

"I'm sure you'll do very well," Ovard encouraged him. "Thank you for agreeing to do this."

Dursen nodded, smiling a nervous smile.

"Well then," Ovard spoke a little louder, "Jair, why don't you tell everyone what today's meeting is concerning."

Jair sat up straighter in his chair as he looked around the table at everyone. "All right – well, we've been looking at this book, Ovard and I have, and it tells about the way the ancients worked the gardens, how they did their farming." He stopped and took a breath. "We know about those empty places, where there are no buildings, just broken pieces of fence left around them. I think those are the gardens, or farming areas. We can plant things there," he told everyone. "We can grow our own food, like potatoes, or peas, or carrots, grain, corn, anything!"

Leandra smiled. "I love your enthusiasm," she told Jair, causing him to look away slightly in embarrassment. "Of course we can grow anything," she agreed.

"Right," Ovard continued. "But we need to have seeds to start the crops with. So, we need to decide what we should grow for our first crops. The seeds can be purchased on Brace's next trip out with Dursen. We also need to find out how much silver we can put together. If everyone gives a little, we should have enough for a decent start. Then we can plan out what to plant where, and ..."

"But don't forget," Dursen interrupted. "Ya can't plant the same crops in the same field season after season. Ya need to change them around, or you'll ruin the soil."

"Good point," Ovard told him. "Thank you. We'll be sure and do that, with your guidance." The older man turned his attention back to Jair. "Is that all for today, then?"

"Yes," Jair answered.

"How would you like to close today's meeting?" Ovard asked him.

"Well," Jair replied. "I guess I need to ask everyone how much silver they can give to get our crops started. Brace and Dursen will have to take it with them when they go out again next week."

"We have some we can give," Rudge spoke for himself and Jayla.

"So do I," Kalen added, as did Arden and Ovard. All told, they came up with 45 silver to buy potatoes, squash, peas and grain, which they all agreed should be their first crops. Brace sat quietly, knowing that he had nothing to give. He had spent every coin in his possession to buy an old cart and a mule, making travel easier while they were still searching for Haven. Now he didn't have one cent to his name, despite all his years of having taken whatever he wanted.

"Thank you everyone," Jair said as he pulled tight the strings on the leather pouch, which now held the silver coins. "Ovard, will you keep this with you until Brace and Dursen leave?" he asked.

"Of course I will."

"Thank you." Jair sighed, then smiled. "I guess that's it for today." He shrugged. "We can all go now."

Arden chuckled at the simple words that had ended the meeting, and everyone stood to leave. Kalen was the first to go; the man was always eager to get to work. He deeply enjoyed seeing broken things set right, and doing much of the repair work himself. Brace often wondered if the man was simply finding satisfaction in a job well done, or if he was working to try and forget about something, working to avoid having too much time to think.

As Brace rose from his seat, Jair ducked his head. "I'm not very good at leading meetings," he muttered.

"Oh, come now," Leandra shook her head. "We covered everything that needed to be said, and we made a decision together, did we not?"

"Yes," Jair admitted.

"Then you did more than well enough," Leandra informed him. "Don't doubt yourself, Jair."

The boy smiled. "Thank you."

Arden and Leandra took their leave, while Jayla remained at the Hall. She would stay and continue the process of reading and re-writing Haven's old books, working at Jair's side, who was teaching her the language just as he was teaching Ovard.

Rudge walked beside Brace as the two of them left the building together. Rudge seemed quiet, pensive, as he looked at Brace out of the corner of his eye, and Brace was uncomfortable under the apparent scrutiny.

"What have you got on your mind?" Brace finally asked, breaking the tension that was building up in his shoulders.

Rudge cleared his throat. "Well, truthfully, I was just wondering – were you really a thief?" he asked.

Brace hesitated briefly before answering. "I was," he admitted. When Rudge kept quiet, Brace's discomfort increased. What would the man think of him now? Would he no longer want to associate with him? Would he look down on him as a person of bad moral character?

"Well done, then," Rudge finally spoke.

"What's that?" Brace asked in surprise.

"Well done," Rudge repeated. "Turning away from your old way of life to come here," he explained. "It isn't easy, becoming a new person."

"Well," Brace replied, feeling relieved, "I wouldn't say I'm an entirely new person."

"But you have changed," Rudge stated plainly.

"That I have," Brace agreed. He let out a short laugh. "I often felt like I was being forced to change against my will," he told Rudge, who raised an eyebrow, then nodded.

"I think I know what you mean."

"And I'd go through it all over again," Brace added, "knowing that Tassie and I could be together. She always believed in me, even when I didn't."

Rudge nodded, his smile showing beneath his bristly moustache. "She seems to have a good mind about things, about life."

"She does," Brace agreed. "I really don't know where I'd be if I hadn't met her."

"Well, you're here now," Rudge told him. "And you've been married for ... how long?"

"Just two months."

Rudge nodded. "Jayla and I have been together for twenty years now," he said, "and if there's one thing I've learned, it's that both partners need to do their share of give and take. One person can't always hold the other one up, so to speak. One will need to be strong for the other at times, but the roles will be reversed at others." He shrugged slightly. "I suppose what I'm saying is, don't lean too much on Tassie to steer you right, or to be the strong one, the wise one. You will need to do the same for her when she needs it."

Brace blinked as he took in Rudge's words. "Thank you," he said at last. "That's very good advice."

Rudge nodded and gave Brace a pat on the back as they parted ways. "See you again soon, my friend."

Brace smiled briefly and waved him off.

Taking advice was still something that he was adjusting to. As a child, and a younger man, he'd avoided other people as much as possible. Even if he *had* been given any advice then, he was sure that he would not have been so quick to accept it. And *this* advice – about being strong for Tassie – this was something new, and he found himself dwelling on it. Tassie was strong in her own way, Brace had seen that. But he had also seen her feeling vulnerable and afraid. He'd been able to be there for her then, though he hadn't known any more than she had about how to handle the situation. If they were to encounter hard times, would he be able to make the right decision for them? He could be there for Tassie, that much he knew. He could be a shoulder to cry on if she needed one. But beyond that, Brace strongly doubted himself. Most of the decisions he'd made during his life had not been wise ones. Lately, he'd found himself relying on Tassie's wisdom to lead him in the right direction.

Well, he told himself, *all I can do is take each day as it comes, the same as anyone else.*

It was not a long walk from the Main Hall, and Brace soon found himself at home once again, the pale blue-gray stone walls of the house a comforting, welcoming sight. The thickly thatched roof and the stone chimney, the clear ancient glass of the windows – it was *home.* A home he would never need to run from, and that in itself was a miracle enough for him.

He pulled open the front door and came inside, his heart content, and found Tassie standing in the front room, at the table with Kendie. She was showing the girl how to properly wrap a bandage – not too loose, not too tight. Tassie had given herself over to letting Kendie practice on her whenever possible. At the moment, Kendie was winding a long strip of cloth around Tassie's hand and arm.

"Can you still feel your fingers?" Kendie asked.

"Yes," Tassie replied, touching her forefinger to her thumb. She smiled to herself. "I think I've taken it for granted, having clean hands. There was a time when my hands were so dirty, I thought they'd never come clean."

Kendie laughed. She looked over her shoulder and smiled when Brace entered, and Tassie looked up.

"Hi, Brace!" Kendie called out.

"Good morning, Kendie."

"Did the meeting go well?" Tassie asked him.

"Very well," Brace told her. "And you're looking well too, little thing," he told Kendie, who smiled.

"I'm not so skinny any more, am I?" she asked.

"Not at all," Brace agreed. Kendie had most assuredly been well cared for at Milena's farm. She had filled out a bit, and now her fair skin had a healthy shine; her wavy black hair was soft and thick, almost always kept in braids, never messy or unruly as it had been while she lived at the inn with Rune Fletcher.

"But," Brace said with a dramatic sigh, "I *am* going to get skinny if I don't get to eat some breakfast."

"Oh, I'm sorry!" Kendie exclaimed. "I'll come back later. Is that all right, Tassie?"

Tassie smiled. "That's fine," she told the girl, who scampered out of the house, calling out her goodbyes.

"You're such a tease," Tassie said to Brace as soon as the door was shut, unwinding the cloth from her hand. "You can't be *that* hungry."

"I'm near it," he insisted. "But let me help you," he added, recalling Rudge's advice. "I know how to make biscuits," he continued, seeing the doubtful look on Tassie's face. "You said the biscuits were good the last time I made them."

Tassie smiled. "They were … edible."

"Now you're the tease."

"Am I?" Tassie asked as she gathered up the rolls of bandages and other various supplies. Brace caught her hand, and she looked up, surprised.

"Let me help you," Brace told her again.

"What's gotten into you?" she asked.

"I just want you to know …" Brace began, but trailed off, unsure of exactly what it was that he was trying to say.

"To know what?" Tassie asked him.

"How much I love you," Brace said simply. Tassie sighed, smiled, and shook her head. She leaned against him, the bandages hanging loosely in her hands, and wrapped her arms around him. Brace did the same.

"I know you love me," Tassie told him. "You don't need to do anything to prove it."

This is real freedom, Brace told himself, stretching his arms over his head. Tassie still slept beside him, the early morning sunlight falling across her face. He turned onto his side to look at her. He had never thought in his life that he'd be married, that he would spend the rest of his life with *one* woman. His head still spun when he thought about it, but right now, he was happy.

The week was passing much too quickly for Brace's liking, and he wanted to soak up every moment. He felt torn between waking Tassie and just lying there beside her. There were things to be done, but for Brace, the most pressing was to spend as much time with Tassie as possible. He deeply appreciated the fact that Tassie was always there. He could see her whenever he wanted, so unlike the countless nights he'd had to sneak around to see whichever woman he had been involved with at the time.

There was nowhere he needed to run to. No reason to run at all. Brace basked in the enjoyment of simply being there, in Haven. Just living life one day at a time, going to sleep when it was dark – in his own home – and rising again in the light of morning. He enjoyed sharing his meals with Tassie, he enjoyed watching her work. He loved seeing the look in her eyes when she was completely wrapped up in a task, or when she was making some new medical discovery. Frankly, he liked who he was when he was around her. *This* was life as it was meant to be, he found himself thinking.

He had a home, a family, and friends, true friends that he never thought he would have. His days of running from place to place were over, days of trying to convince himself that he was free to do what he wanted, no matter how it affected anyone else.

Life had settled down now into a comfortable rhythm, and Brace was not at all ready for it to end. He was not ready for the interruption of leaving once again, and it was only a small comfort knowing that this would be the last time.

"Tassie," Brace said softly, fingering her hair. "Will you wake up?" He gently nudged her shoulder until she opened her eyes, blinking.

"What?" She asked. "What's happening?"

"Nothing," Brace replied. "I just wanted to see you."

Tassie smiled. "Good morning."

"Morning."

Tassie gave him a quick kiss, pulled back her hair and slid from the bed, her long nightgown falling around her ankles. Brace watched her as she washed and dried her face, peering at her reflection in the small mirror propped against the wall.

"What would you like to do today?" she asked, turning to face him.

"Just be with you," he replied.

Tassie smiled. "Well, I think we can manage that." She slipped into her dark green dress and pulled at the strings to snug up the front. "We could go out to the stream, to the orchard. Bring back fresh water and some fruit to eat."

"Whatever you want," Brace replied, grinning.

"You just dress yourself," Tassie told him. "I'll get breakfast going."

Tassie left the room, and Brace quickly pulled on his shirt and breeches, stuffing his feet into his worn boots and running his fingers through his hair. A quick glance in the mirror told him what he already knew – no beard. Apparently, not even Haven's healing fruit or strength-giving water could make him grow facial hair.

Breakfast was biscuits again, but Brace had no complaints. They were easy to prepare, and baked in no time on the low grate over the hearth fire. When the meal was finished and everything was cleared away, Brace and Tassie walked hand-in-hand along the road, making their way toward the orchard, each of them carrying an empty wooden bucket.

"Good morning, son!" Ovard called out from the door of his house as they neared it. "Good morning, Tassie," he added, lifting his hand in greeting.

"Good morning, Uncle," Tassie replied as Jair squeezed his way outside, smiling broadly.

"What are you doing today?" the boy asked, brushing his hair away from his eyes.

"Just going out walking," Brace told him. "You?"

"Reading," Jair replied. "More of Haven's books."

"Every question I could ever ask about life here is being answered," Ovard added.

"Sounds like an adventure to me," Brace commented, and Jair smiled. "I'm still waiting for you to tell me about yours."

"You'll have to keep waiting," Brace told him. "Most of my *adventures* should never have happened."

Jair's smile faded, and he nodded. Ovard gave his shoulder a squeeze. "I'm sorry, my lad, but I tend to agree. We're all making new stories for ourselves here."

Jair nodded, though he was clearly disappointed.

"Enjoy your day," Ovard told Tassie and Brace, nudging Jair in the direction of the Main Hall. "We will let you know what we find in the old books, eh?"

"Yes, please," Tassie replied. "I would very much like to know all about it."

Jair and Ovard went on their way, and Brace and Tassie continued on, passing the homes now occupied by Jayla and her family. Making their way down a narrow lane bordered on both sides by empty houses, Brace could see that the thatch roofing was still in need of repair, though it was clear that some work had already been done.

"Isn't it striking?" Tassie asked.

"What?"

"The view," she replied with a sweep of her hand.

Brace looked out into the distance, past the high stone gate and the clearing beyond it, past the tall evergreens toward the deep range of mountains jutting up along the horizon.

"It's hard to believe we climbed over them, isn't it?" Tassie asked.

"It must be a fading memory for you," Brace agreed, "but I've done it several times. I've become all too familiar with those rocks."

He smirked in Tassie's direction.

"I'm sorry you've had to go alone," she told him.

"I'm used to traveling alone," he replied. "It only makes me all the more grateful to come home."

Tassie smiled as they went on, hand-in-hand, as the stone-paved road faded into the gentle slope of grassy hillside leading toward the ancient orchard. A breeze blew across them, playing at Tassie's long brown waves of hair. The grass was green and slick beneath their feet, and the air had a sweet, fresh quality, and there was nothing Brace could compare it to. Birds flew high overhead, their musical cries filling the sky, unhindered by any cloud cover. If only Tassie could hear them, this moment would be perfect.

"Will you get the water," Tassie asked as they neared the still, cool lake, "or should I?"

"I'll get the water," Brace replied. "We'll put the fruit in your bucket."

Tassie waited as Brace made his way through the thick grass to the edge of the lake, his reflection peering back up at him, the wide blue sky above him. The water was cool and refreshing as it ran over Brace's hands, filling the wooden bucket.

What a truly peaceful moment this was! Although the two of them had begun getting to know one another on the long journey to find Haven, they had quickly discovered that married life was another story altogether. There had been many awkward moments over the past three months. Their attempts to work out their differences, or wondering whether they were of the same mind about something, anything, had caused many tense and frustrating days. Brace hoped this would not be one of them.

As he stood and faced Tassie, cool water dripping from his bucket, she slipped her hand around his elbow. "If we fill my bucket with fruit," she commented, "we will be able to share some with the others."

"Right," Brace agreed. "No need to hurry, though."

"Did you say something?" Tassie asked.

"I said, no need to hurry," Brace repeated. "I'm all right if we spend all day out here."

Tassie smiled. "I wouldn't mind that either." As they followed the stream farther up the hill, Tassie let go of Brace's arm and strode on ahead into the trees. Brace watched her as she ran her hand along the rough bark of a low branch before picking a piece of fruit, rubbing it on her sleeve, and biting into it.

"Perfect, as always," she reported, looking back at Brace.

"Why wouldn't it be?" he asked lightly, setting down the heavy bucket full of water. She smiled and began picking more fruit, putting it into her own bucket. Brace worked at her side, and soon the bucket was nearly full. Brace tugged at her sleeve.

"It that enough?" he asked.

"That should do," she replied, setting the bucket in the grass beside the first. She reached out her hand, and Brace took it in his own. "Come on," she said. "Let's go all the way up to the top. I love the view."

Brace gladly joined her, feeling the breeze grow in strength as they worked their way up the sloping hillside, through the gnarled old fruit trees to the highest point. From there, they could look down over the city, see the Fountain Court and the curved walls surrounding it, see the wide roads leading out from that central point into the city in straight lines, like bursts of light from the sun itself.

Brace pulled Tassie close, his arm wrapped around her, and she rested her cheek on his shoulder. "I never get tired of seeing this," she commented.

"I hope you never do," Brace told her. He gave her another long, quiet moment before taking her hand, leading her along toward the nearest tree and pulling her down onto the grass beside him. Tassie smoothed her dress over her boots and settled against Brace's side, taking his hand and letting their fingers slide together.

"You don't need to worry about me while I'm gone," Brace told her.

"But you know I will."

Brace gave her a lop-sided smile. "I know you will. But I've survived on my own all this time. I know how to keep from being seen when I need to."

Tassie's face grew serious, and she looked at him intently.

"What is it?" Brace asked her.

"I want to know more about it," she told him.

"More about what?"

"Your life. Before we met."

"You already know, Tassie. I stole things. I lied, I cheated. I ran away, over and over again."

Tassie shook her head. "I know those things happened. I just want to know … well, like Jair, I suppose, I want to hear your stories. All I know is what's on the surface. I don't know about any of the *moments*. Times when you were happy, when you were angry or afraid. I want to know your story."

Brace said nothing, running his thumb along the back of Tassie's hand.

"I'm willing to share my story with you," she told him. "Will you share yours with me?"

"Your story is a better one."

"Maybe." She paused, not taking her eyes off him. "But we do have one thing in common."

Brace looked up at her.

"Losing our mothers," she explained. "We were both so young when we lost our mothers. It can really change a person."

"It can," Brace agreed. "But you had Ovard to look after you."

"I still mourned," she told him. "She was my mother. My heart broke over the fact that I was away when she died. And Ovard, grieving for his sister, his wife, and his son. My cousin. I felt like I had failed them somehow, by wanting to go to town with Ovard. My goodbyes were so easy, so off-handed. I could never have known it was the last time I'd ever see any of them."

Brace nodded. "Neither could they. I'm sure they understood."

"But what about you?" Tassie asked. "Surely you had the chance to say goodbye to your mother. Didn't you?"

Brace shifted uncomfortably. Even after so many years, it hurt to think back to that time when he'd been so afraid, and felt so alone.

Tassie rested her hand on Brace's cheek. "Didn't you?"

"I..." Brace began. *I'm not sure if she heard me.*

The words were there, but he couldn't make himself say them. He shook his head. "It was a long time ago. I can't really remember."

"Can you tell me something?"

"What?" he asked defensively.

"Just something," Tassie replied. "Anything. About how something made you feel. What you remember about it."

"I don't want to think about any of that," he told her. "You're the one who told me I could be more than I was. I don't want to look back. I just want to look ahead, to the new life I have here with you."

Tassie nodded. "I can understand that, Brace, and I'm glad. But you can see why I'm asking, can't you? I know that you've been through some hard things, and you've made some wrong choices, and I know that you're brave and willing to change. Willing to risk letting people in even though it could hurt. I know you are able to truly care for others. But there is more to you, Brace. There is always more. I just want to know the rest of what makes you who you are. Can you understand that?"

Brace looked at her, at her deep green eyes, so full of intensity.

"I do," he told her. "I do understand." He sighed, his temper cooling. "What makes me who I am…" he thought aloud. "Right now, it's being here. In this place, with you, starting over. I know I could have gone on to Danferron, but who would I be if I was there? Who would I have become?" He shook his head. "That doesn't matter, does it? What matters is who I *will* be, now that I'm here in Haven. I'm not in Dunya, I'm not in Danferron. I'm in Haven. I'm with you. We both have a new life here. Isn't that what really matters?"

Tassie smiled slightly, though Brace could see it in her eyes that she was only letting it go for the time being. She wasn't completely satisfied.

"You're right," she said, putting her feet under her and standing. "That is what matters."

Brace pulled himself up beside her.

"We only have a few days left before you go again," she commented. "Let's make the best of them."

Brace nodded, taking her hand in his. He wanted to tell her he was sorry, but the words stuck in his throat. He couldn't tell her what she wanted to hear – what if he couldn't be the man she needed him to be? What if he just *couldn't?*

"Come on, Brace," Tassie said lightly. "Let's head back. We've got the fruit to share. And we've got the whole day ahead of us. Let's make it last."

Brace managed a crooked smile. "Lead on, my lady. This day is yours. I will follow you wherever you want to go."

The day before he and Dursen were scheduled to leave, Brace woke to find that Tassie's side of the bed was empty. Only mildly surprised, he stretched, sat up, and listened for a moment until he could hear her moving around in the kitchen. He sighed, half awake, considered lying down again, then decided against it. If this was to be his last day in Haven for a time, he wanted to make the most of it. He pulled himself out of bed, washed his face, combed his hair and dressed in the nicer of his two sets of clothing.

Checking his appearance briefly in their small mirror beside the stone wash basin, he made his way into the kitchen, stopping to stand in the doorway and watch. Tassie had been up for some time, he realized, and she'd been hard at work. She had made biscuits – a *lot* of biscuits. She had set aside a large portion of their dried meat and measured out small packets of Brace's favorite tea. One jar of preserves and several full of vegetables were on the table as well. At the moment, Tassie had her back to him, busily looking over her shelves of medical supplies.

Brace took in the view – so much food! She must be providing for him *and* for Dursen, he realized. Tassie pulled a small jar off of the shelf and turned toward the table. Seeing Brace in the doorway, she startled a bit.

"Oh," she said, being sure not to drop the jar. "You're up."

Brace nodded. "I am – and so are you; you have been for hours, from the look of things." He gestured toward the table.

"I couldn't sleep any longer," she explained, adding the jar to the supplies.

"What is that?" Brace asked, stepping toward the table, eyeing the jar in Tassie's hand.

"It's ointment," Tassie replied. "It helps relieve sore muscles. I know you and Dursen have a longer way to go this time, to get to Erast. And," she continued, turning back to the shelving, "here is something to use on cuts and scratches, and some bandages."

Brace watched as she gathered the things off of the shelf, arranging them on the table.

"All right," Brace replied nonchalantly.

"You may think it's too much," Tassie informed him, "but you never know if you'll need it. It's better to be prepared."

Brace grinned and nodded. "Right. You're the medic; I trust your judgment."

Silently, Tassie began gathering up half of the food and packing it expertly into Brace's pack. He sighed. He knew she was worried, but trying to hide it; trying to stay busy so she couldn't think about it. He knew she would rather have him stay here, but at the same time she had accepted the fact that he had to go, on one last journey. He could see every subtle change in her face, and he had learned what the changes meant. At least, *most* of them.

And he wasn't going to tell her not to worry, because that wouldn't stop her from doing it. Instead, he stepped up beside her to draw her attention. "What can I do to help?" he asked.

Tassie smiled a little. "You can go to Dursen's," she told him. "Tell him we have some things for him to take along on the trip. Tell him to bring his pack."

"I can do that," Brace replied, giving Tassie a quick kiss on the cheek as he headed out the door.

⁓

Dursen was more than ready to leave on the following morning. His pack was full, and he was anticipating the journey, anticipating the chance to experience something that would be a new challenge, a new adventure. He and Brace rose early, as did everyone else in Haven, wanting to see them off. The sky overhead was just beginning to grow light enough to see the faintly-lit roads by the time they had gathered in the Main Hall for the send-off. Kendie was there, still sleepy, but she had insisted that Leandra wake her so she could say goodbye.

"Have you got everything you need?" Ovard asked Dursen and Brace. Everyone stood around the Hall's large meeting room, or seated themselves at the long wooden table.

"I think so," Brace replied. "We've got the money for the seeds, and Tassie made sure we had enough food to last the whole trip down. She packed us some medical supplies as well, in case we need them."

"Do you have the map I gave you?" Ovard continued.

"Yes," Dursen spoke up. "It's in my pack."

"And the writing – the letters you'll need in order to get back in through the gate?"

"I've got that," Brace replied. "I haven't quite got them to memory yet. I'd hate to be locked out." He smirked and nudged Dursen, who grinned in response.

"How long do you think it will take you to get to Erast?" Jair asked.

"Not too sure," Brace told him. "Five days, six maybe."

Jair nodded. "I hope you can find people there who believe Haven is real."

"So do I," Brace agreed. He smiled light-heartedly. "We don't want Dursen to be disappointed on his first trip out, do we?"

"Just tell them you live there," Kendie advised. "Tell them you've seen Haven with your very own eyes, that you *know* it's real. They won't be able to say it's only a legend if you tell them you've been there."

"It seems so simple, doesn't it?" Ovard asked, and Kendie nodded firmly.

"We'll tell them all about it," Brace told her, "but it's up to them to decide whether or not to believe us. Sometimes people need to see things for themselves before they'll believe in them."

"Right," she agreed, even as Brace remembered that there had been a time when he himself wasn't certain that Haven would actually be a *real* place.

"So you have all you need?" Arden asked. "There's nothing else you might want to take with you?"

Brace thought a moment, catching Dursen's eye. "Is there?" he asked him.

"I don't think so," Dursen answered.

"Do you have the lightstones?" Jair asked.

"Of course," Brace told him. "Can't forget those."

Ovard looked Dursen and Brace up and down, and his expression showed a hint of doubt, as though he wondered whether their worn boots would hold together during the trip. "That seems to be everything, then, doesn't it?" he asked, knowing there was nothing to be done about their boots at the moment.

"I think it does." Brace turned toward Dursen. "Are you ready to do this?"

"Very ready," he replied enthusiastically. "I never been that far north. I'm wanting to see some new places as much as I'm wanting to help bring new people in here."

"It's time, then," Ovard told them. "Be safe. Be on guard. Watch out for each other. Remember, men's hearts are growing as dark as the night sky. You can't always be sure about who is trustworthy. Use good judgment." Ovard smiled. "And come back to us as soon as you can."

"And bring new people back with you!" Kendie added cheerfully.

"We'll do our best," Brace told her with a grin.

Leandra came forward and put her arms around Brace's shoulders in a friendly, almost sisterly hug. "Take care of yourself," she told him.

"I will," Brace promised. "You do the same."

Arden patted Brace firmly on the shoulder, then shook his hand. "I'll see you soon."

"Sure," Brace agreed.

As the archer moved on to wish Dursen well, Brace let his eyes fall on Tassie, where she stood nearby, trying to be brave. He winked at her, and she smiled and shook her head. Brace wanted to go to her, to hold her close one more time, but it was just at that moment when Jair stepped up in front of him.

"I'll miss you when you're gone," Jair told him.

"I'll miss you too, my boy," Brace said, ruffling Jair's hair. "Make sure you keep everyone in line while I'm gone," he joked.

Jair laughed, running his hand over his hair to smooth it. "I will."

Brace leaned toward Jair, turning his face away so Tassie couldn't read his lips. "And be there for Tassie for me, will you?" he asked. "I'll be gone longer this time, you know, and she worries. You're good company for her."

"I will," Jair replied solemnly. "I promise."

"Thanks. Really, Jair. It means a lot to me."

When the goodbyes and well-wishes were over, Brace and Dursen headed for the doors of the Main Hall, ready to leave. Only then did Tassie step up beside Brace, taking his hand in hers. He held it tightly until she finally looked at him.

"I'll be fine," he whispered, and she nodded.

"Here," she said, slipping something into his hand. Brace looked at – a small leather pouch, with silver coins inside, he could tell by the feel of it.

"I don't think we really need this," he protested, but Tassie shook her head.

"Take it, please. Just in case you need it."

Brace looked down at the small pouch in his hand, then back up at Tassie, and nodded. "All right," he relented. "Just in case."

Dursen was walking ahead of Brace now, looking back at him expectantly. "I'd better get going," Brace told Tassie. "The sooner I go, the sooner I can come back."

"Right," she replied, forcing a smile. Brace took her in his arms and held her close in a long, tight embrace. She wrapped her arms around him, and when she let go, Brace could see she was fighting back tears. Thankfully, Leandra noticed it as well, and put an arm around Tassie's shoulders.

"We'll be fine here," Leandra told Brace. "You show Dursen how it's done out there, will you?"

Brace nodded. "I'll do my best."

"Come on, Tassie," Leandra said gently. "Let them go. They'll be fine."

Tassie smiled at her gratefully, then allowed Leandra to lead her away, taking one last look over her shoulder at Brace, lifting her hand to wave goodbye.

"Ready?" Dursen asked.

Brace cleared his throat, pushing down his emotions, then turned toward his traveling companion.

"Ready," he replied. "Let's do this."

~

As Brace at last trekked his way up to the top of the first mountain peak, he turned back and looked across the forested land toward Haven's tall, wide, arched gate, standing closed against any foreign dangers. Dursen struggled up the rocky surface beside him, breathing hard.

"Is that all the farther we've come?" he panted, looking down the roughly sloping mountain.

Brace nodded, catching his breath. "That's it."

Dursen wiped his sleeve across his forehead, pushing his ash blond hair away from his eyes. "The gate looks small from up here," he commented.

"It does," Brace agreed. He gazed long at the smooth stone surface in the distance, knowing what – and who – was behind it, that he would be missing.

Although he knew he had to go on, what he wanted more than anything was to turn back. He never imagined he could ever feel so strongly about one person that he couldn't stand being apart from them. But, despite the fact that he hadn't yet known Tassie a year, he felt connected to her. Like part of himself was missing when she wasn't there.

"Get a good look at it now," he told Dursen. "Once we get down over this ridge we won't see it again for a while."

Dursen nodded and looked back toward home. "Don't see how you do it," he thought aloud.

"What?"

"Leave like this. Ain't so hard for me, I got no family there. But you – you got Tassie. How do you do it?"

"It isn't easy," Brace told him. "But it's easier knowing this will be my last trip." He forced a smile. "You're taking my place, remember?"

"Can't forget that."

"Come on, then," Brace said, shifting the weight of his pack. "Let's get going."

No matter how many times Brace had crossed these mountains, it never got any easier. There always seemed to be another peak, no matter how many they'd already climbed. Dursen was strong and fit from working many years as a farmhand, but climbing mountains was nothing like planting and harvesting crops. He seldom complained, but the going was slower than Brace had hoped. Night fell, and they had to make due with a small overhang as a roof, where they huddled together against the cold, hard rock. They managed to get a few hours of sleep despite only being partially hidden from the icy wind that howled overhead. Thankfully, the lightstones that Brace wore over his wool cloak did their part. During the hours when it was darkest, although the men could hear night screamers in the distance, they never once saw any sign of them. They would have no trouble there.

When morning came, they were stiff and sore, but knew they had to get going again. There would be no hot tea with this breakfast; they ate dried meat as they walked.

By the end of the following day, Brace and Dursen had finally crossed over the mountains and made their way into the flat land bordering Spire's Gate. From there on, the traveling was much easier, and Brace passed the time by giving Dursen pieces of advice.

"Pay attention to where we're going," he told him. "You'll have Ovard's map with you every time, but it's more important to remember your way. Look at the land around you as we go on. Get familiar with it."

Dursen took Brace's advice to heart – every bit of it. Brace taught him what he knew about traveling well: drink plenty of water, pace yourself, look for signs of animals in the area – ones that could be eaten or ones that could try to eat *you*. He pointed out familiar landmarks and showed Dursen where they coincided with the locations on Ovard's map. At night, Brace taught Dursen how to identify the groupings of stars, when they could see them, most of which he was already familiar with. They worked together gathering wood for fires to heat water for tea, and setting up their tents when they needed to get some rest.

The screeching of many night screamers pierced the air from some distance, every evening. Brace imagined that, just maybe, those beasts knew that he and Dursen had come from Haven, and they desperately wanted to get at them. He was relieved that the fragments of lightstones kept them away, though he was still unnerved by them, as was Dursen; it was plain on his face.

"You all right?" Brace asked him one night as they huddled around a small fire.

"Yeah, I'm fine," Dursen replied quietly, keeping his eyes on the low flames.

"They won't dare come near us."

"I know it."

A loud cry filled the air, and Brace grimaced. "Still, it gets to you, doesn't it? It does me."

Dursen looked up and nodded grimly. "Sure does."

"Have you been sleeping at night?" Brace asked, suddenly aware of how tired Dursen seemed.

"Well enough."

"*Have you?*"

Dursen shrugged. "I haven't been slowing us down any, have I?"

"No, we're making good time. But you can't let yourself get to the point of exhaustion, Dursen. We've got to go all the way back home once this mission is over, and we'll likely have someone with us who's counting on us to lead the way. We need to be at our best, for their sake as well as ours."

Dursen nodded. "I know all that. But we won't be hearing them screamers when we get to Erast, will we? I'd sleep better if it was quiet at night."

"We shouldn't," Brace replied. "I think they avoid the towns and villas, keep to the wild lands."

"I'd be relieved at that. I'll be fine, Brace. I just make myself keep going. I can sleep deeper when we get to Erast."

"All right," Brace replied with a nod.

What more could he say? It was what it was, and as long as Dursen was able to keep going, there was no need to worry over things beyond their control.

The sky was dark when he awoke suddenly in the night. His heart was pounding, and his face was hot and sweating. He sat up quickly, trying to calm his breathing. What had happened? He searched his thoughts for a moment, and there it was – the lingering memory of the dream he'd had. Strange black creatures had flown at him in the dark, though not attacking him. It was more like they'd been surrounding him, encircling him. But why? Were they angry at him, or trying to protect him from something? He threw aside his covers in frustration, wiping the sweat from his brow. This wasn't the first time he'd had such a dream. His sleep had been fitful for the past week at the least. He hadn't told anyone about the dreams. How could he? They wouldn't understand. But he couldn't help feeling that he knew the reason for the dreams that frightened him. He couldn't shake the feeling that he'd made a mistake. He'd tried telling himself that nothing would come of what he'd done, but he hadn't convinced himself. The thought of living the rest of his life with the secret hanging over his head often made him feel sick to his stomach, but what could he do about it? He couldn't tell anyone. No, that he could not do. Consequences, *he told himself.* I must live with the consequences.

When his heartbeat finally calmed, he lay down again and closed his eyes.

It's just the darkness, *he thought.*

Things would look better in the light of day.

A slight breeze pushed its way through the trees in Haven's sprawling orchard, making the leaves dance and whisper in the afternoon sunlight. Leandra's fair, straight hair blew loosely around her shoulders, while Tassie had pulled hers back out of the way and tied it with a wide ribbon. She adjusted the long leather strap that was slung over her shoulder, feeling the weight of the basket of fruit she'd been picking.

"Mine is getting pretty full," she told Leandra.

"So is mine," Leandra told her. "Just a little longer?"

"All right," Tassie replied with a smile.

"I can't believe how amazing this is!" Leandra exclaimed, reaching up to pick another of the large, soft, peach-colored balls of fruit. She brushed its surface with her palms, then bit into it.

It was delicious, Tassie had to agree. The juice was sweet, but not as thick and syrupy as the red vine fruit growing in the Court. And as far as she knew, this particular fruit did not have any special healing qualities. None that she had seen, at the least.

Tassie simply smiled, picked another piece, and added it to what was already in her basket.

"What should we do with all of this, what we've picked today?" Leandra asked her. "More canning?"

Tassie thought a moment. They'd already canned a fair amount of it over the last month or so. *No*, she said to herself. She wanted to do something different, something to keep her mind off of Brace's absence. She felt like she'd been doing well enough at that over the last three days, but she was grateful that Leandra had suggested going to the orchard. Getting outdoors always made her feel more at ease.

"Not canning," Tassie decided. "I think we should make a cobbler with this. I think there's enough here for everyone, don't you?"

Leandra smiled. "There's plenty," she said. "Cobbler sounds wonderful. I think we should get Jayla and Kendie to help us. It will be the ladies' treat to our men." Her smile faded a bit, hoping that the words she'd let slip out wouldn't make Tassie regret Brace's absence. If they did, though, Tassie didn't show it in the slightest.

"That's a wonderful idea," Tassie agreed.

"Jayla needs to take more time for this sort of thing," Leandra thought aloud. "She spends far too much time studying."

"She's very dedicated," Tassie agreed as she pulled a few more pieces of fruit from the branches just above her head. Then she smiled. "But I agree." She breathed in the cool, fresh air. "This …" she began, looking all around her, "is so wonderful. I can't find the words."

Leandra looked over her shoulder, in the direction of Tassie's gaze. The sun's light was soft, fading slightly in the west, and birds chirped and sang as they flitted among the trees growing in the orchard, all around them. Zorix scampered and sniffed at everything, his long tail flicking with interest.

The cool breeze on her face, the smell of the fruit all around her, and the sound of the wind in the branches all had worked a sense of magic, permanently fixing themselves in Leandra's memory. This, she thought, would be what home meant to her, for the rest of her days.

Leandra stepped up beside Tassie and linked arms with her. "It *is* wonderful. And so is seeing your smile."

Tassie ducked her head, feigning interest in her basket of fruit until Leandra gave her arm a slight tug. "Let's go find Jayla and Kendie," she suggested, "and get that cobbler going. I don't know about you, but I'm *very* hungry."

Tassie laughed. "I think you've been using that baby as an excuse lately to have extra helpings."

Leandra winked. "Just don't tell anyone, all right?"

The hearth-fired oven was hot as Tassie stood beside Leandra to look over the dessert. It was hot, yes, but the smell was delicious. Juice bubbled up in the large clay dish, and the edges of the cobbler were a deep golden brown.

"I think it looks perfect," Jayla said with a smile as she peered down at it.

"I agree." Leandra leaned over the cobbler and breathed in the aroma. She held a thick piece of cloth and gave one to Tassie. "Ready to serve it?" she asked.

"Very much," Tassie replied. "Kendie, go and tell the men that they don't need to wait any longer. We're coming."

"All right." Kendie smiled broadly as she hurried out into the main room of Rudge and Jayla's house, where all of them had gathered together.

"It's coming!" Kendie called out, and Jayla laughed.

"What is it?" Tassie asked, seeing her smile.

"The girl, Kendie," she replied. "She's so full of life."

"That she is," Leandra agreed. "Have you got a hold on this?" she asked Tassie. "It's heavy."

"Yes, I've got it," she answered.

"Let's go, then!"

Jayla hurried ahead of them as Tassie and Leandra hefted the hot dish through the doorway.

"There it is at last!" Ovard smiled as they came into the next room. "It looks as wonderful as it smells."

"I can agree with that," Rudge commented as Jayla sat beside him.

There were many words of thanks as the cobbler was served around the table, many comments on how delicious it tasted. Tassie sat beside Leandra and Arden as everyone cleaned every last bit of warm fruit and flaky bread from their bowls. She felt a little out of place, like part of her was missing, and really, it was. She forced herself to pay attention to watching the people around her, trying to catch what they were saying – it was too easy to drift away into her own thoughts.

Zorix sat close by Leandra, under the table, his front paws resting on her feet and his large ears pressed forward. His nose twitched as he waited for a bit of the cobbler, which Leandra gladly shared with him, letting him lick it right out of her spoon.

Ovard was discussing how the hunting had been going, off in Haven's Woods. There were deer out there, Tassie knew, and game birds of various sorts, as well as rabbits. It was likely there could be foxes or even bears, but she couldn't be sure. This was Haven, after all – a safe place. Didn't that include the wildlife? How safe would the animals be if they had to contend with predators? And now here *they* were, killing them for meat. It couldn't be helped though, could it? They needed meat to eat, didn't they? Should Arden be hunting in the lands on the *other* side of the gate? She wondered. The animals out there weren't a part of Haven, not as those in the western forest were, in Tassie's mind. But Arden wouldn't be safe out there, not without the light of Haven to protect him, the way it would protect Brace and Dursen. They could always break off a few more bits of the lightstone walls …

Tassie felt a hand on her arm. "Don't you think that's a good idea?"

She smiled a guilty smile. "I'm sorry, I wasn't paying attention. What is a good idea?"

"Storing up as much of this fruit as we are able," Leandra told her. "Whether Haven follows seasons or not, it would be nice to have some of it on hand to bake with from time to time, wouldn't it?"

"Yes, it would," Tassie agreed, trying to force more enthusiasm into her voice than she was actually feeling. She was sure that those who knew her well would be able to pick up on it, so she avoided their eyes, turning instead to look at the empty baking dish. "It certainly did all get eaten."

Tassie inadvertently caught Arden's eye, and he smiled sympathetically at her, then nodded, his way of telling her he knew that she was putting on a strong face. Blushing, she looked down at the table until she felt Leandra's hand on her back.

"Come with me," she said. "Let's get these bowls washed up."

"No, certainly not!" Ovard countered. "You have worked hard enough today, the four of you. Let some of us menfolk clear away the dishes."

"I'll help!" Jair volunteered, rising from the table.

"So will I," Kalen joined in.

Whether due to the desire to help or the shame they'd feel if they did not, all of the men rose and began clearing away their places, along with the empty baking dish, and headed for the kitchen. Arden hesitated at Leandra's side.

"Are you feeling all right?" he asked her. "If you're tired, I can walk home with you."

Leandra shook her head. "I'm fine, really. I can wait."

"All right," Arden replied, rising to his full height and stepping back from the table. "Thank you, Tassie," he added, holding up the empty bowl and spoon. "This was well worth the wait."

"You're very welcome."

He seemed to want to say more, but couldn't find just the right words.

"I know, Arden," Tassie told him. "Thank you. I'll be fine, and Brace will be all right, and Dursen. It's just hard getting used to at first, when he's gone. *Thank you.*"

Arden simply nodded and left the room.

"I enjoyed myself today," Jayla commented. "Thank you both for including me in this."

"Of course," Leandra replied. "You need some time away from your studies."

Jayla smiled. "Oh, but I've been learning so much," she told them as Kendie came closer, leaving her seat at the other side of the table.

"Like what, have you been learning?" she asked with deep interest.

"Just the language, mostly," Jayla told her. "It amazes me how young Jair can just look at it and understand it, as though he's been reading it all his life."

"It is a mystery, even to him," Leandra spoke up.

"There is so much about this place ..." Jayla's words drifted away.

"I'm sure that there is so much more we have to learn," Tassie agreed. "And we've got plenty of time to do it."

"Have you been helping Ovard rewrite the books?" Kendie asked.

"Yes," Jayla replied.

"What do they say?" Kendie sat expectantly waiting, eager to hear something new.

"Well, I don't know if it's really my place to share it," Jayla admitted. "That would be Ovard or Jair's decision, wouldn't it?"

"It would," Leandra agreed. "I'm sorry, Kendie."

Seeing the disappointment on Kendie's face, Jayla relented a bit. "There is one thing that I've noticed, though. Many times there is writing about Haven's light. The books say that the city is under the protection of Haven's light."

"We've seen that," Tassie said quietly. "The bits of stone that Brace wears around his neck keep the night screamers away."

"Right," Leandra agreed. "And they won't come near the city, even with the gate open."

"Yes, but …" Jayla hesitated.

"What?" Kendie pressed her. "You can tell us just a little bit more, can't you?"

Jayla shrugged slightly. "Well, it's hard to understand, but Jair says that the writings describe the light as being *alive*. I'm not sure what it means. We know the night screamers are alive, but … the light? It doesn't really make sense, does it?"

"Does it mean that the stones are alive?" Leandra wondered. "The light comes from the stones."

"But the stones can be chipped or broken," Tassie pointed out.

Jayla shook her head. "I don't know. Jair says that the *light* is alive. He doesn't really understand it either, he only tells us what the books say."

Kendie glanced toward the kitchen where she could hear the men talking as they cleaned. "He won't be upset that you told us, will he?"

"I don't think so," Jayla replied. "I know he plans to tell everyone what the books say, bit by bit. He's not planning on keeping anything from anyone."

"Well, that's something to think about, anyway," Leandra said as she stifled a yawn. She smiled. "Maybe I am more sleepy than I realized. I think I'll take myself and the little one home for some rest."

Zorix snorted from underneath the table, and Leandra smiled. "And you're tired too, my friend? What have you busied yourself with today?"

Zorix's ears drooped at the sides of his head, and his furry coat took on a reddish hue.

"What's he saying?" Kendie asked.

"Oh, I'm sorry, Zorix," Leandra said aloud, then looked up. "He says he gets tired easier these days. He says that he feels my body get tired from carrying the baby around, and it makes him tired as well."

"How far along are you?" Jayla asked.

"Six months," Leandra told her as she turned and rose from her seat. "I think Zorix and I both will need to make sure we get enough rest from now on until the baby is born. He can sense things about the baby," she added, almost to herself. "I wonder … will the baby be bonded to him, the way he and I are?"

She looked at Tassie as though she just might have an answer, but Tassie shook her head.

"I'm sorry, Leandra. I don't know anything about how that might work out."

Leandra smiled as Tassie stood up from the table to see her off. "No, that's all right. I was just thinking aloud." She gave Tassie a quick hug before heading for the doorway. "Are you coming, Kendie?"

"Sure," she replied. "I'm getting a little tired too."

"Run in and tell Arden we're heading back, will you? Tell him he doesn't need to hurry. We can see him when he gets home."

"I'll tell him," Kendie said with an amused smile, "but I don't think he'll wait. He still wants to watch out for you, even here in Haven."

"Oh, I know that," Leandra replied. "I think he will always be that way. It's all part of living with *harbrost*. He won't ever change when it comes to that." She looked over her shoulder toward the kitchen, where she could hear the men talking. "And I am so very glad of it."

~ *T* ~

Four days had passed since they'd left the mountains behind them, and still Brace and Dursen continued northward until they spotted a large strip of hazy gray along the horizon.

"What's that?" Dursen asked.

"Wayside Lake," Brace told him, "and the city of Meriton. It's just a few days east of us. We'll be keeping to the west, and go straight on past it."

"Meriton is closer than Erast?"

"Yes, it's closer."

"Well, why aren't we going there, then?"

"You can, some day," Brace informed him. "Maybe on your next trip. But I don't plan to ever set foot in that place again."

"Why not?" Dursen asked, his eyes heavy from want of rest.

Brace paused to gather his thoughts. "Well," he began, "you know what I was, once?"

"A thief?" Dursen asked softly. "I know. It took me so long to stop calling you Merron," he remembered aloud, "even after I learned your real name."

"Right," Brace agreed. "Well, I *was* a thief. I've never stolen anything from Meriton, but that place is the most dangerous for me right now, I think, in this part of the country. At least it *could* be."

"Why's that?" Dursen pressed.

Brace looked at him. "Hasn't Kendie told you her story?"

Dursen thought a moment. "Meriton," he mused. "That's where she come from, right?"

"Right."

"She ran away?"

"Yes," Brace answered. "But some people might not see it that way. To some, it could look like we – *like I* – helped her run away. Or even took her."

"That's so?" Dursen replied, in a near whisper.

Brace nodded. "The man's name is Rune Fletcher. He was Kendie's guardian, but he mistreated her. That's why she ran away. With *us*."

Dursen stood quietly, letting it all sink in. "I can see why you want to avoid the place."

"Any of us should," Brace told him. "Any of us who were there at the inn when we met Kendie. But *you* can lead a trip there; you'll have no trouble. There are a lot of hurting hearts in that city, I'm sure of it."

～

On and on they went, Brace leading while Dursen took in their surroundings. They crossed the land bordering the western edge of Spire's Gate farmland, eventually leaving it behind them. The ground rose and fell before them in smooth, rolling waves, strewn here and there with stones and large gray boulders. They were forced to work their way around them, and several times up and over or through them, always being sure to continue on northward. When evening fell, they made camp and slept, rising with the sun.

The night screamers became more distant as the two of them neared civilization. Brace was relieved at that, and Dursen as well. As they kept up their even, steady pace, with the mountains far behind them, Dursen seemed to be regaining most of the strength he'd had when they had begun their journey out of Haven.

Brace lingered now at their small fire each morning, giving them more time to eat and rest their weary muscles before starting off again. They had the entire day ahead of them; no need to rush off.

The morning air was cool, and the smoke from their fire drifted upward in lazy billows before being pushed away by a steady breeze. Brace reveled in the quiet, listening to the sound of dry, snapping wood, and watching tiny sparks jump upward, fading into ash.

Still, as peaceful as it seemed, he could sense something inside of him that would not leave him in complete peace. It felt almost like a warning, something he never felt when he was at home in Haven. It was a sensation that he was certain came from the knowledge that, out here, something unexpected could happen at any moment. The feeling was intensified on that particular morning, when Brace heard among the trees and brush, what sounded too much like the huffing and sniffing of some wild creature to possibly be anything else.

He looked over at Dursen, who was eyeing him in return. "Ya hear it too, don't ya?" he asked quietly.

"I do," Brace replied with a nod.

"What is it?"

"Can't say."

The two men sat in silence, straining to hear, but the sound had faded.

"Is it gone?" Brace wondered aloud.

"Maybe," Dursen replied. "Could be it's watching us, though. Likely it smelled our food."

Brace nodded, feeling a wave of fear run through him. He shifted his shoulders, trying to shrug it off.

"You …" Dursen began hesitantly. "You don't think it could be a dragon, do ya? You said you all had trouble with a dragon when you were on your way to Haven the first time."

"A dragon?" Brace asked, raising his eyebrows in surprise. "No, it couldn't be, not out here like this."

"Why not?"

"Well, look around. The trees are so spread out, and what brush there is isn't near big enough for a dragon to hide in."

Dursen nodded, obviously relieved. They ate in silence once again, hearing nothing that alarmed them any further.

"Don't know what we'd do if we ran into a dragon out here," Dursen muttered.

"Have you ever seen one?" Brace asked him.

"Only from afar off," he replied. "Gyaks, I've seen plenty of. Them and foxes."

"Gyaks?" Brace asked.

"Yeah, those lizard things. Almost like a dragon, ya know? But smaller, and no wings. They love to eat chicken's eggs. Milena didn't keep no chickens, but some of her near neighbors did."

Brace nodded and took another bite of hard, dry biscuit. "Do you ever wonder how Milena's been since you left?" he asked. "You and Kendie?"

"Surely, I do," Dursen replied heavily. "She loved that girl so deeply. She done the right thing, letting her go. She could never have crossed over the mountains with us, just no way. But she'd never have stopped us from going."

"No," Brace agreed. "She wouldn't have. And she is so far along in years." Brace hesitated before going on. "What do you think Nav will do, after she's gone?"

"He could keep the farm in Milena's place," Dursen guessed. "Or try to find work on some other farm."

"Do you think he'd try to get to Haven?"

Dursen considered the question. "Could be he might, but not alone. I think he'd want someone there to show him the way. He's just not the sort to go off alone like that."

"Too wise for that sort of thing?" Brace asked.

Dursen nodded in reply, just as the brush nearby began to rustle, and both of them froze.

"It's back," Dursen whispered. "What could it be, do ya think?"

"Well, it's no dragon," Brace commented, slowly standing and searching for something to strike out with if need be.

"Maybe it's …" Dursen began, but he was cut short when a large gray bearcat leaped out of the bushes, snarling.

Dursen scrambled to his feet as Brace startled and backed away quickly.

"Well, that's no dragon," Dursen panted, while the creature continued to snarl, baring its sharp white teeth.

"What does it want?" Brace asked.

"Our food, o' course," Dursen replied.

"I say let him have it, then!"

"*What?*"

"Not all of it! Just something! Give it *something*, and we'll run while it's busy eating."

"Right," Dursen agreed, jumping back out of the way as the animal came closer, swiping at him with long white claws.

Brace wondered what he would possibly do if the bearcat attacked, but Dursen was quick. He snatched a small bundle of dried meat from his open pack and flung it at the animal's face.

The creature flinched, then realized what it had on the ground in front of him, quickly biting into it.

"Perfect," Dursen said quickly. "Grab your bag and run!"

Brace wasted no time in obeying, leaving the bearcat and the last dying embers of their fire behind them.

After the bearcat, they encountered no other wildland creatures but for a few birds and burrowing ground squirrels. This was much to their shared relief, and eventually, Wayside Lake stretched out across the horizon as far as they could see, sparkling like diamonds in the sunlight. Dursen murmured in surprise at the sight of it.

"Is something wrong?" Brace asked him.

"No," he answered, almost in a whisper. "I just never seen anything like this in all my days."

"It's really big, isn't it?"

"Big, yes," Dursen agreed. "It don't seem real. It looks like ... magic, or something."

A steady breeze swept across the land, tossing their hair and whipping at their long wool cloaks. The surface of the lake was churning as well, each high point of water glinting white against the deep gray-green.

When Brace kept silent, Dursen spoke up again. "Ya don't seem as taken by it as I do."

"Well," he replied with a shrug, "I've been here once before." Brace tried to look at it as though seeing it for the first time. "I can see what you mean, though. It is pretty amazing."

"And quiet here, too," Dursen added. "Peaceful, like there really ain't any trouble in the world, you know?"

Brace nodded shortly, though he was all too familiar with how much trouble there really was, going on all around them. He'd been in his share of trouble, and caused quite a bit of it himself.

"Brace?"

"Hmm? What?"

"Do you think we'll have any trouble while we're out here?"

"Well, I hope we don't. I wouldn't think so." He paused, thinking. "I've never been to Erast," he continued, "so I have no idea what to expect when we get there. Not exactly. But I am sure of myself in one thing, at least. I know the look of hopelessness in people's faces when I see it. If there's anyone in Erast who will want to come with us to Haven, it will be the people who don't have a reason to stay. Or better yet, people who have a reason to get out."

Dursen nodded, understanding.

"So," Brace continued, "if we stick to talking to *those* people about Haven, quietly, and don't make ourselves too obvious, or a nuisance, we should be fine. I don't think we'll have any trouble."

"Sounds perfect to me."

Brace stretched his tired back and arms. "Have you had enough of the view?" he asked, gesturing toward the lake.

Dursen grinned. "Sure enough," he replied. "Let's keep going."

Continuing on, they crossed the land bordering the western edge of Wayside Lake. Their path turned and twisted through the large rocks, but they always kept the lake at their right. Two days passed before they had worked their way around the far side of the Lake, and by then they'd eaten all of the biscuits and preserves, most of the vegetables, and Dursen's black bean stew. They were left with only what remained of their dried meat and rationed water by the time they were near enough to see the Royal Road stretching out before them.

"There it is," Brace announced glumly when he saw it.

"What?"

"The Road. Civilization."

"You don't like it?"

Brace snorted, grinned, and clapped Dursen on the back. "I don't think *it* likes *me*."

Dursen let out a bit of a laugh. "You told me not to worry. Y'are not worrying now, are you?"

"Not exactly," Brace replied as he took a few steps toward the wide, dirt-paved road. "I'm just … cautious. I've been here before."

Stepping out into the middle of the Road, Brace looked down the length of it, feeling a familiar tightening in his stomach. *Watch your back,* the thoughts came on again. Caution, suspicion – how long had he lived under such things? Wondering if someone would recognize his face, even long after he'd moved on. Being on the Road on foot, in the full light of day, such as it was, reminded him of his vulnerability.

Well, he thought to himself, *this will be the last time. Just get through this, and you can leave it all behind for good.*

Fortunately, the Road remained empty for most of the day. The only traffic the two of them encountered was a fair-sized merchant's wagon pulled by two large mules and, several hours later, a pair of men on horseback bearing Meriton's crest, traveling eastward toward home. When the riders lifted their hands in greeting, Dursen responded while Brace kept his eyes on the dirt at his feet, trying to make himself appear as tired and disinterested as possible, hoping the men would overlook his rudeness. After they'd passed by and gone on a considerable distance, Dursen questioned Brace's actions.

"You didn't even want to look up at them?" he asked. "Did you want to be as invisible as that? Should I not have waved at them?"

"No, I'm glad you did," Brace told him. "It was good, what you did. They would have had reason to be suspicious if neither of us had greeted them. But I need to be more careful than most, remember?" He lowered his voice. "I am a wanted man – don't forget that."

"Ah," Dursen breathed. "Right. Sorry."

So it was, that when they finally reached the town of Erast, tired, dirty, and hungry, it was decided that Dursen would do most of the talking while Brace remained aloof and kept his eyes open. The former farmhand quickly worked up his boldness and was able to get directions to a small inn, as well as an outdoor eating arena, though sleep was what they wanted first and foremost. So, as the afternoon sky began its unnaturally early transformation into dusky darkness, the weary travelers shut themselves into their small, sparsely-furnished room, gratefully pulled off their dusty boots and cloaks, fell into their rented beds, and drifted off to sleep.

After a decent night's rest, they were feeling very refreshed – and very hungry. So, after leaving the inn early in the morning, they made their way through town toward the eatery they'd been told about the day before. Brace was relieved to find that Erast was nowhere near as busy or crowded as Meriton had been. They could walk along the streets with ease, not once bumping into anyone (or being bumped into, alleviating Brace's concerns about pickpockets). The villagers seemed to move around at a leisurely pace as they did their marketing. Many of the men, Brace knew, were loggers, as lumber was the city's main source of income. He could see some of those well-muscled men now as they went along. Most of them, he guessed, would be out in the forests to the west of town, working hard.

When they arrived at the eatery, however, Brace quickly saw that he hadn't been *quite* right in his assumption. Many of the men were still in town, breaking their fast, sitting around the many outdoor tables of the eatery. He and Dursen exchanged a glance.

"This here seems to be the busiest place in the whole town," Dursen remarked.

"You've got that right," Brace agreed.

"I think I see one empty table, if you still want to eat here."

"I think it's the *only* place in town," Brace replied quickly. "Let's get that table before someone else does!"

Dursen quickly led Brace to the small, weather-worn wooden table with its two short, empty benches.

"Right, so," Dursen spoke up, "you stay here and I'll go get the food?"

Brace smirked. "You've got it," he told him. "I'm sorry, but ..."

"I know, I know," Dursen interrupted with a shrug and a smile. "You've got to stay as unseen as possible, and I need to learn about doing all this myself."

"That's exactly it," Brace said with a sigh as he sat on one of the benches. "And keep your eyes open. You never know when you'll spot *just the right person*."

Dursen nodded in agreement as he walked away toward the eatery's main building. Brace sat alone, unobtrusively eyeing the crowded seating arena. A few families sat around some of the tables, but most of the seats were occupied by loggers, that was obvious enough. They were muscular, burly, for the most part unshaven men with scarred and calloused hands who ate as though they were starving, or in a hurry, or both. It was unlikely that any of them would give Brace the time of day, even if he bothered to ask them for it.

Brace sighed, turned his gaze to the weathered surface of the table, and waited for Dursen to come back.

"Um, excuse me," a gentle voice spoke, and Brace looked up to see a young woman standing at the far side of his table.

"Yes?" he asked, surprised.

"Well," she explained, "there are no empty tables here this morning, and frankly, you're the only man here who doesn't disgust me, so …" she shrugged. "Would it be all right if I sat here? With you? Just so I can eat my breakfast."

Brace glanced around at the crowded platform. "Sure," he replied. "You can join us."

"Us?" the girl asked nonchalantly as she sat, pulling a bread roll from the bag she carried.

"I'm here with a friend," Brace told her.

She nodded, chewing a piece of bread and brushing crumbs from the skirt of her lacy yellow dress.

"What brings you *here?*" she asked, distastefully emphasizing the last word.

"You don't like it here?" Brace surmised.

She shrugged and wrinkled her nose. "It's all right, I suppose. Its' just so … *the same*, every day. The men working, and coming here to eat. This is really the only public place to have a meal, so I come here too, on my break from work."

"What's work?" Brace asked casually, all the while thinking that good fortune seemed to have fallen into his lap, so to speak. Could this young woman be the sort who would want to go back to Haven with them?

"At the seamstress," she replied, pushing her wavy red-blonde hair over her shoulder, away from her face. "It pays well enough, but I start *so* very early in the morning. So I never eat breakfast at home any more, I always come here on my break. I work just down the road, so it isn't far. It isn't so bad, since I get off early in the day, after lunch."

Brace nodded, resting his chin in his hand. "Must be nice."

She shrugged, eating the last bite of bread and pulling a peach from her bag. "Sure, but then I've got the rest of the day with almost nothing to do," she told him, biting into the peach. "I usually end up going to my father's house and cleaning up his messes," she continued. "He's not a very tidy housekeeper."

"No mother?" Brace asked.

She shook her head. "She died when I was ten years old."

"I'm sorry," he replied. "My mother died when I was small; I know how it feels."

"Yes, it was a long time ago, but I still miss her at times."

"Couldn't be that long ago," Brace spoke up. "You don't look much older than eighteen."

The girl smiled. "I'm twenty-one, actually. Been pretty much on my own for the past four years, living day-to-day in this *nothing* place."

Brace sat up and looked at her, suddenly struck with a realization. She was exactly the type of girl he would have searched out, would have pursued, only a year ago. Her pretty face, her outgoing demeanor, her dissatisfaction with life in a small town. He could imagine himself flirting with her – she seemed a little flirtatious herself. This was all before *Tassie*, of course. Though Brace couldn't imagine, now, getting involved with any other woman, he still found himself taking notice of this girl's beauty, and he felt strangely drawn to her. It made him uncomfortable, left a bitter taste in his mouth. *Tassie is the only one for me*, he told himself forcefully. *Focus on why you're here.*

It was not so much the girl's beauty leading Brace's thoughts astray, but her discontent with life in Erast. Maybe she would be someone who would want to come to Haven. He had to tell her about it.

For Jair, Brace thought to himself. *For Jair's cause of filling Haven with people once again, and for the prophecies, of a great return to the ancient city of their ancestors. Not for me.*

"Do you mind if I ask your name?" he said aloud.

"Yara Blye," she replied readily. "What's yours?"

"Brace."

"Just Brace?" she asked. "No last name?"

"Honestly, I really don't know. As I said, my mother died when I was young, and I have no idea who my father was, so …"

Yara nodded, understanding.

"I've taken my wife's name as my own," Brace told her, and he noticed a hint of disappointment flash across her face. Yes, he was married. And the realization of the fact disappointed her. He decided to ignore it, and went on. "You don't really enjoy living here much, do you, Yara?" Brace asked pointedly.

She wrinkled her nose and shook her head.

"Well," Brace began, knowing he was treading unpredictable waters, "Where I'm from – I'm sure you'd like it there. It's a pretty amazing place."

Yara leaned forward in interest. "What's amazing about it?" she asked.

"Well, it's not exciting, like life in a big city, but it's really … miraculous," he told her. "There is fruit growing there that can heal any injury, and nothing evil can ever enter the city."

"Evil?" Yara asked. "What do you mean?"

"Nothing harmful," Brace explained. "It's a perfect place."

"If it's so perfect, why did you leave?" she asked suspiciously.

Brace sat back in his seat. "For this," he told her, spreading out his hands. "To try and find anyone who might want to go back with me. With *us*. There are eleven of us there now, but the city is so large – there's room for anyone who wants to call that place their home."

Yara sat quietly for a moment, eyeing Brace as though looking for any sign that he might be joking, or lying. "What's the name of this place?" she asked.

"Haven," Brace told her. "It's an ancient city, where our ancestors lived thousands of years ago. Have you ever heard of it?"

She shook her head. "Where is it?"

"To the south-west of here," Brace replied. "Over the mountains. Not too far away, really. It took my friend and me only about a week to get here from there."

"And you expect people to just up and leave their homes when you tell them about this place?" Yara asked, incredulous. "To go and live there, just like that?"

"Some already have," Brace informed her. "It's well worth it."

She thought a moment. "So you're inviting me to come back with you?"

"You're more than welcome there."

Surprised, Yara sat back in her seat. "You're really serious about this? You're not joking with me?"

Brace shook his head solemnly. "I'm not joking with you."

Yara turned her head and gazed into the distance, as though she was seriously considering going with him. *Could she be?*

"I know it's not an easy decision to make," Brace encouraged her. "My friend Dursen and I are planning on staying here for another day.

You should be able to find us right here ... In case you do decide to come with us."

She turned back toward Brace again, and smiled a little. "Right."

Brace smirked. "You don't think I'm crazy, do you?"

"Crazy?" she asked. "No. A little odd, maybe, but not crazy."

"You'll think about it, then?"

She nodded absently. "I'll think about it."

Brace shrugged. "That's all I ask."

~ 8 ~

Kendie hummed to herself as she cleared away her plate and cup from the table, placing them in the large wash basin. She turned back to the table where Leandra still sat with Arden.

"Are you through?" she asked. "I can take your plate for you."

"That's all right, Kendie," Leandra told her. "I can take care of it."

Kendie smiled, and seeing that Leandra's plate was empty, she picked it up. "I don't mind doing it," she said, almost chiding. "I like helping you," she went on as she worked at the dishes. "Since you're going to have the baby, you shouldn't have to do too much work. Besides, I'm used to it, and I like to be busy. I like helping. And when you have the baby, I'll be able to help you then, too."

Kendie paused in her chattering when she heard Arden chuckle. She turned back to look at him.

"I'm doing it again, aren't I?" she asked with an apologetic smile. "I'm talking too much."

Arden grinned and shook his head. "You definitely keep things lively," he told her.

"I really can't help it," Kendie went on. "When I get excited about something, or I know a lot about something, or I really *care* about something, I just can't help talking about it. It's like it's all up there in my head and I just have to let it out!"

"That's part of what makes you who you are," Leandra told her with a smile. "And you know we love every bit of you."

Kendie dipped her head in embarrassment. "I love being here with you too," she told them. Her eyes shone, and her smile broadened. "I really can't wait until you have the baby!" she exclaimed. "It will almost be like having a little brother or sister, won't it?"

"Sure enough," Arden agreed.

"You'll make a wonderful sister," Leandra told her.

"You'll be great parents, too," Kendie returned the compliment. "You're both so *good*, and patient, and ..." Kendie stopped when she saw the look that passed between Leandra and Arden. "What?" She asked in alarm. "Is something wrong?"

"No, nothing's wrong," Leandra spoke up quickly. "It's just that ..." she hesitated until Arden gave a little shrug and a nod. "Well," she continued, "I have to admit, we have had some doubts."

"About what?"

"About being good parents," Leandra replied. "I'm sure no one ever feels completely sure of themselves. Well, neither of us really knows what to expect, being the parents of a new little one."

"I don't have much experience with small children," Arden added.

Kendie's eyes grew serious as she turned toward Arden. "Oh, I *know* you'll be a good father," she informed him. "You live with honor and courage. Those are two of the best things in the world to live by! And so is love, and I *know* you'll love your baby."

Arden managed a smile, directed first at Leandra, then at Kendie. "Thank you," he told her. "That really means a lot to me, what you just said. Thank you, Kendie."

Kendie smiled, threw her arms around Arden's neck, and kissed him on the cheek, taking him by surprise. "Of course," she told him. "It's all true!"

Her words were followed by a sudden, loud, unexpected bang coming from somewhere outside the house. Kendie gasped as Arden flinched, and she tightened her grip on him. Zorix leaped up from the corner where he'd been resting, his fur instantly turning a bright, vivid red. Leandra was startled as well, and they all sat still for a moment, staring at one another.

"I've heard that sound before," Arden said optimistically as he rose from the table, Kendie clinging to his arm.

"You're right," Leandra gasped. "It's the gate! It's opening!"

"Brace and Dursen can't be coming back," Arden commented, "not this soon. Could it be – more people are arriving, just as we did?"

"There's only one way to know for certain," Leandra replied. "Let's get there, now! No matter who is at the gate, it's what we've got to do!"

Arden hesitated only for a moment, then hurried toward the door, all but dragging Kendie along behind him; she wouldn't let go of him. "I'm getting scared!" she called out.

"It's all right, Kendie," Leandra told her, pulling her away from Arden. "Whoever it is, they'll be people coming in, like we did – they must have the key, the way in. They must be descendants of the remembrance keepers, like Jair is."

"Are you sure?"

"It must be ..."

"Then why is Arden taking his bow?" Kendie asked in alarm.

Arden turned back just before going outside. "Just in case," he told her.

As they hurried down the main road toward the enormous stone gate, they were joined by Jair and Ovard, Rudge, Jayla and Kalen, all wide-eyed and alarmed.

"So you've heard it as well," Ovard greeted them.

"Can't have missed that," Arden muttered as they pressed on.

"We have newcomers ..." Ovard's voice trailed off, not knowing what else to say, or what to expect.

"Where is Tassie?" Jair asked in alarm.

"At home, most likely," Leandra answered. "She wouldn't have heard the noise."

Satisfied, Jair looked ahead as they neared the far eastern edge of the city. Just around the corner of the next wall, they would be able to look out through the gate, which they could already see was standing wide open.

"I can't believe this is really happening," Jair remarked. "I want more people to come to Haven, but I never expected it to be like this!"

"I don't think any of us did," Leandra agreed as they turned the corner and stopped just before the open gate, staring into a group of faces that looked just as surprised as they were.

"Welcome," Ovard called out at last, breaking the silence.

"Is this Haven?" a haggard voice came from the crowd.

"Yes!" Jair replied, stepping forward. "It really is Haven, you've found it." He paused, not sure what else to say.

"Where have you come from?" Arden spoke up.

73

"Danferron," one of the men answered, looking worn and weary, as they all did. "A long way from here – but that can wait. Can you help us, please? One of us has been injured badly, and he desperately needs help!"

"What happened?" Leandra asked, coming closer.

"I'm not sure, exactly," came the reply. "Some sort of strange creature … it happened at night. We never really saw it …"

Leandra's face grew somber. "Say no more," she told the man. "Where is he? Bring him inside, and come in, all of you. You've found your new home here. Come in where you'll be safe."

The mass of dirty, tired, and fearful faces – men, women, and one small child – made their way through the open gate and into the light of Haven, eyes wide with awe. Two of the men turned aside and struggled to half carry, half drag their injured companion through the city gate. Leandra came forward as soon as she realized how badly off the man was.

"Here," she said. "Put him down for a moment. Let me see him."

The men obeyed, gently lowering him to the ground at the edge of Haven's main road. He was very limp, his eyes lightly closed, his skin pale and clammy.

Jair looked down at him, then turned to Ovard. "Tassie can help him, can't she?" he asked. "But she's not here …"

"Zorix!" Leandra called out, and he quickly ran to her side. "Go for Tassie. Bring her here."

Zorix sat still a moment, staring wide-eyed at the wounded man lying on the ground, surrounded by his friends.

"Now, Zorix!" Leandra scolded. "He's been hurt by the night screamers, just like you were."

Zorix gave Leandra one quick glance, blinked, then hurried off in obedience.

"What can we do for him?" one of the women asked fretfully.

Leandra remembered, all too well, how quickly Zorix's health had faded after he'd been attacked. "How long ago did this happen?" she asked.

"Late last night," a man replied. "Hours ago."

Leandra nodded. "Just keep him still for now, I've sent for our medic. Keep him warm."

One of the men nearest his injured friend removed his outer coat and carefully draped it over him.

"What is your friend's name?" Leandra asked.

"Daris."

"Daris?" Leandra spoke softly to him, touching his arm while everyone stood around helplessly. He didn't respond in the slightest.

"What's taking so long?" one of the older men complained.

"Tassie will get here soon," Arden asserted. "She has just what your friend needs to heal. She will be able to help him."

The moment was tense – they could all feel it. The small boy in the crowd of newcomers began to whimper and clung to his mother's arm.

"Leandra!" Tassie's voice called out at last. Leandra looked back to see her running toward them, accompanied by Zorix, who bounded ahead of her. "What is going on here? Zorix was making such a fuss, jumping up and down, turning in circles …" Tassie stopped abruptly, her eyes taking in the large group of people.

"It's the newcomers," Ovard told her. "One of them is hurt – attacked by a night screamer."

Tassie nodded, glancing around at all of the new faces. "I grabbed anything I could think of," she said, patting the side of her medic bag. "I knew something had to be wrong." She paused a moment to catch her breath. "Where? Who?"

"Here, this man," Leandra told her, gesturing.

Tassie turned toward the tightly-packed group. "Everyone, please get out of the way," she told them forcefully, and they spread out, making room for Tassie to kneel at the man's side. She leaned over him, hoping to feel his breath on her cheek. It was faint, but he was still breathing. She immediately opened her medic bag and pulled out the bottle that she'd filled with juice from the large red fruit they'd discovered – the very ones that had saved Zorix's life. She pulled out the stopper and, gently opening the man's mouth with her free hand, poured in a few drops of the thick red juice.

"What is that?" the man standing at Daris' feet asked impatiently. But Tassie wasn't looking in his direction – her eyes were on her patient.

"It will help him," Leandra spoke up. "Trust me."

Satisfied that Daris had swallowed the juice, Tassie looked up. "Let's get him to the clinic," she directed. "We need someone to carry him there."

The wounded man's companions exchanged a few quick glances, unsure if any of them were strong enough to carry his tall frame.

"I'll do it," Arden volunteered, pushing his bow into Jair's hands. He put a hand on Tassie's shoulder to get her attention. "Go ahead of me," he told her, "open the clinic door, and get the place ready."

As Arden struggled to lift the man into his arms, Tassie turned to go. "Thank you!" she told Arden as she hurried off. "I will!"

"Someone get the gate closed," Ovard advised.

"I've got it," Rudge volunteered, working his way through the bewildered crowd to press the gate's closing mechanism. Everyone startled a bit as the gate lurched and began working its way closed, but their eyes remained fixed on what they could see of Haven – the wide, smooth street before them, the faint glow of light from the high stone walls, the city spreading out before them, mysterious and unknown.

While Arden, with Daris in his arms, struggled his way down the main road after Tassie, Jair eyed the group of new arrivals curiously. He knew he should say something, but he had no idea what. Finally, he cleared his throat, drawing a bit of attention from those closest to him.

"Well," he began. "Wel – Welcome to Haven," he stammered. "My name is Jair. How – how did you find your way here?"

No one answered at first. In a moment, a woman came forward, her red-brown hair tousled around her shoulders. "It was me," she spoke up. "Or, rather, it was this." She reached up and touched the gold chain she wore around her neck, then held out the pendant. "This shows the way here," she continued, then shrugged a bit. "And here we are." She also seemed to be at a loss for words.

"You came from Danferron?" Jair asked, and she nodded.

Jair took a step closer to her. "Can I look at it?" he asked, pointing at her gold chain.

"Yes," the woman told him. As Jair stepped up to peer at the necklace, she took note of the markings on his face. "You ..." she began, and Jair looked up at her. "You have the way as well?"

Jair nodded solemnly. "Yes. My ancestors were remembrance keepers. Yours must have been, too."

"I received this when my grandfather died," the woman told him. "For years I didn't know what it was, or what it meant. When it was explained to me – to us, my husband and I – we knew we had to come back here. I'd heard stories about Haven growing up, and I knew I wanted to see it for myself."

Jair simply nodded.

"Who explained its meaning to you?" Ovard asked.

The woman looked back toward the rest of the group, and one of the men stepped forward - the man who'd been impatient about getting help for Daris.

"I did," he spoke up. "I've studied for years, and was able to discover what the writings meant. The map was easy to follow after that."

"May I?" Jair asked again, gesturing toward the woman's necklace. She quickly, easily, pulled the chain off over her head and placed it in Jair's hand with a tired smile.

He gazed at it, mesmerized. "This isn't Haven's language," he said aloud.

"Haven's language?" someone asked.

"No," the impatient man spoke up. "It's the old way of speaking, from Danferron's days long passed."

"Well," Ovard addressed the group. "You've made it here, and you are welcome here. Why don't you all come with us into the city? You must be tired, you must be hungry. Come and rest, get cleaned up. There will be plenty of time to discuss these things later."

"And what about Daris?" a young woman asked timidly. "Where is he? Will he be all right?"

"Why don't you all come this way," Ovard suggested. "There's a large courtyard where you can all have a place to sit down. And you can see your friend Daris, at least some of you, at the clinic."

"I'm going there," the woman told him.

"I am as well," a man spoke up, the one who had interpreted the meaning of the necklace.

"All right," Ovard responded, taken back a bit by his bluntness. "Come with me, everyone."

Following Ovard's lead, the tired and bewildered group of new arrivals made their way down the road leading into the heart of Haven, leaving the world behind them.

~ 9 ~

Dursen looked over the canvas sacks full of seed once again to be sure they were secure. "Don't want none of the seed escaping," he commented.

"I'm sure they were fine the first two times you checked them," Brace chided good-naturedly.

"We're going an awful long way," Dursen defended himself. "We don't want to waste anything."

"Oh, I know," Brace conceded. "I agree with you there."

He smiled disarmingly, and Dursen relaxed. "I'll be glad to get back," he said. "The folks here aren't too friendly. Can't blame them, really, but *still.*"

Brace nodded, helping Dursen pack away their purchases, in preparation for the trek back to Haven. "They really do want to mind their own business, and have others do the same, don't they? To have *us* mind our own business."

"They hardly even put up with us being here," Dursen agreed. "I only really talked to one person, and he shrugged me off. Maybe I didn't do it right."

"You did fine," Brace told him. "I heard what you were saying. You told him just enough, and you weren't too bold. You said the right things. I don't think he believed you, and that isn't your fault."

Dursen half-shrugged. "I suppose not."

"Don't worry yourself," Brace encouraged. "You'll get better with time and practice."

"So that's it then? We're leaving at last?"

Brace looked back over his shoulder, toward the window, where he could see the street leading farther into town. "Not just yet," he said. "I think we have one more thing to do before we go."

"What's that?"

"Stop by the eatery." He turned back to look at Dursen's confused face. "I was able to talk to one person as well, don't you remember?"

"That girl?" Dursen asked. "You haven't seen a glimpse of her since you talked to her."

"I know," Brace admitted. "But I did tell her where she could find us. I'd hate to not be there, one more time, before we go. In case she made the decision to join us. It wouldn't be right."

"All right, then," Dursen agreed. "One last time."

~

The outdoor eatery was just as crowded as ever when Dursen and Brace arrived, but there was no sign of Yara. Brace stood, scanning the tables, but there were only the usual loggers and an occasional family gathered there on that particular morning.

Standing beside him, Dursen cleared his throat. "Uh, Brace?"

"What?"

"I need to use the privy."

"That's fine," Brace told him. "I think I'll wait here for a bit longer. I want to give her a fair chance. You go ahead, and meet me back here."

Dursen nodded. Brace could tell that he thought it was a waste of time, looking for Yara, but he was deferring to Brace's leadership. Brace made himself a mental note to speak with Dursen about having patience. Since he would be leading these trips in the future, the young man needed all the good advice he could get.

A few tables emptied only to be filled again quickly, and Brace kept waiting. He wasn't sure if he really expected Yara to show up or not – she had seemed curious, but noncommittal, and Brace still wasn't sure if she really believed what he'd been telling her. He sighed. Well, at least he'd done what he could.

Above the constant noise of voices, Brace could hear a bit of a commotion from somewhere behind him, but he thought nothing of it until one voice called out above all the others.

"You there!"

Brace turned to look, wondering who the angry-looking man could be talking to.

"Yes, you!" he went on, taking Brace by surprise; he was looking right at *him*. "What's this I hear you've been telling my daughter about? Some miraculous city?"

The man was thick and burly, not too tall, but the look on his face was menacing.

"I have been talking to her about it, yes," Brace admitted. "Have I done something wrong?"

"What miraculous place is this?" the man asked with a sneer.

"It's called Haven," Brace explained. "It's a perfect, wonderful place. I've just come from there myself."

"And where exactly *is* this place?" It was clear that he didn't believe a word Brace was saying to him.

"South. Over the mountains."

"So you thought you could just take my daughter away with you?"

Brace blinked in surprise. "Not take her, no! Only if she wanted to come. And not only her – Haven is for everyone. Whoever wants to come is welcome."

The burly man crossed his arms over his chest. "I don't believe there is any miraculous city," he informed him haughtily. "What I think is that you're trying to trick my daughter into coming with you to a brothel or some such thing. That's what *I* think."

"No," Brace asserted. "I'm not coming from any brothel. I'm not trying to turn your daughter into a tramp!" He held up his hand so the man could see his marriage tattoo. "I'm a married man!" Brace glanced around, and there were many pairs of eyes on him, and on his accuser. He didn't like the way this was going, but no one seemed at all ready to get involved, or come to his aid. Why would they? He was no concern of theirs.

But the angry man didn't seem to notice at all, or didn't care to. "I've seen your kind around here too many times," he went on. "Been hanging around my Yara too often, and I've had enough. It's time to teach you a lesson. At least *one* of you." He gestured with his arm, and Brace saw two men come up behind him, staring at Brace from under their scowling eyebrows.

"You don't need to do this," Brace protested. "I didn't come here to harm anyone, to take anyone away if they didn't want to come ..."

Brace's explanation was cut short when the man suddenly punched him on the side of his face. For half a second, Brace stood still in shock. Then anger overtook him, and he rallied to hit the man back, but the other two thugs grabbed him and threw him to the ground, hitting him with their fists. As he tried to fight them off, he could hear Dursen calling out.

"What's going on here? Stop this! *Stop!*"

But the men paid him no mind, and Brace's attempts to defend himself were unsuccessful – there were too many for him to fight off. As it became more and more difficult to fend off their blows, he simply folded his arms across his face and waited for them to stop.

~ 10 ~

Arden, grateful not to be carrying the man any farther, lay Daris down on the bed that Tassie had readied in the clinic.

"How is he?" Tassie wasted no time in asking.

"There's no change," Arden breathed.

Tassie nodded and pulled a blanket up over Daris' legs. She looked him over, laying her hand on his forehead briefly. "He's very hot," she commented, thinking aloud.

Arden and Tassie both startled when a small group of people suddenly burst in through the clinic door – Arden at hearing them, Tassie at seeing them.

"Daris?" one of the men called out, looking quickly around the room, then eyeing Daris where he lay on the bed. "Is he going to be all right?" he blurted out.

"I'll do all that I can for him," Tassie answered, then turned aside to scan the shelves of supplies.

"What was that, what you gave him out there?" the impatient man asked gruffly.

"She can't hear you," Jair informed him, from where he stood near the door. "She's deaf."

"A deaf medic?" he asked, incredulous. "How on this earth does she –"

"Tassie is very good at what she does!" Arden snapped. "And she's the only medic we have here, so you either accept her help, or you don't."

The man blinked in surprise at having been reprimanded.

"Come on, Brodan," the man standing behind him said quietly, taking him by the arm. "Let's go on out of here, let them work. *Trust* them."

The impatient man – Brodan – silently allowed his friend to lead him outside, and Arden shut the door after them. Jair sat beside Tassie, where she was dissolving a bit of powder into a clay mug full of water. She kept her gaze on the motion of Daris' chest rising and falling with each breath, slight though it was. Retrieving her jar of red juice, she poured a few more drops into his mouth.

"He's still breathing," she said to no one in particular. "But he's so hot. Arden – will you soak a rag in cold water and bring it to me?"

Arden nodded. "I will." Finding a cloth rag on one of the shelves, he submerged it in the basin full of fresh water, while Tassie carefully poured a bit from the clay mug into Daris' mouth and watched as he swallowed.

Jair rested his hand on Tassie's arm, and she looked at him.

"How is he, really?" Jair asked. "Did they get here in time for us to help him – for the fruit to help him, the way it helped Zorix?"

"I don't know," Tassie replied. "His breathing seems very weak. How does it sound?"

"It sounds bad," Arden answered truthfully, holding out the wet cloth. Tassie took it from him and folded it across Daris' forehead. She sat quietly for a moment in thought before turning back to Jair.

"Everything here is so perfect," she said, almost in a whisper. "People aren't supposed to die here, not like this. This sort of thing can't really happen here, can it?"

Jair looked from Daris to Tassie, wide-eyed with worry. "I don't know," he told her. "I really don't know. I hope not."

Arden stood by helplessly until he heard the door open again. He turned to look, and Tassie followed his gaze. Leandra peered inside, forcing a smile. "How is he?" she asked.

"The same," Tassie replied.

Leandra nodded. "That's good. He has a few more visitors. Is it all right if I let them in? They only want to see how he's faring," she added, seeing Tassie's reluctance.

"That's all right," Tassie relented. "You can let them in."

With a nod, Leandra opened the door all the way and gestured kindly for the visitors to enter. A young woman with short blond curls came inside, followed by an older man. The woman's eyes were red and puffy; Tassie could see that she'd been crying.

"I think I'm needed elsewhere," Leandra told Tassie, who nodded in response.

"Come on, Jair," Arden directed as Leandra stepped outside. "Let's get back out there. Tassie will be all right for a bit, and Daris is in good hands. There are a lot of others who need to be seen to."

Tassie nodded at Jair, letting him know that it was all right. He took one last look at Daris, his eyes full of concern as he followed Arden outside.

As the door slowly closed, the older man was the first to speak, looking across the room at Daris. "He's sleeping?" he asked.

"Yes," Tassie replied. "But he's more than asleep, really. Something is keeping him from waking."

The blond woman sniffled and gazed at Daris' face. "Is he going to be all right?"

"I think so," Tassie told her. "I think that you all got here in time."

"What was that red liquid you gave him?" the man asked.

"It's from the fruit that grows here," Tassie explained. "We realized that it had healing qualities when we all arrived here ourselves. You see, one of us had been bitten by the screamers."

"Screamers?" the woman asked nervously.

"Oh, I'm sorry," Tassie apologized. "That's what we've been calling those … *things* that come out at night. It's because of the noise they make, so I'm told. I've never heard them myself."

"Because you can't hear," the woman spoke again, kindly. "We know – she told us. Leandra told us."

Tassie nodded and smiled. "My name is Tassie," she introduced herself. "I haven't been introduced to any of you, I'm sorry."

"My name is Essa," the woman replied quietly. "This is Lomar."

"Hello, Essa, Lomar."

The old man nodded, then let his gaze fall on Daris once again. "Shouldn't he be improving by now?" he asked. "Haven is a place of miracles, isn't it?"

"Miracles, yes," Tassie agreed. "But the juice needs time to work through his body. It isn't … *magic*."

Lomar nodded in understanding. "Well, I can see that you've stayed on top of things here, so I will leave you to it."

"You can come in and see him any time," Tassie let him know. "I'll stay with him until he's well enough to leave."

Lomar gave Tassie another nod, then turned away, leaving Essa standing alone, nervously biting at her lip. Tassie could easily see that she wanted to stay.

"Would you like to sit here with me for a while?" she asked, and Essa nodded eagerly.

"Yes, I would, very much, thank you!" Essa quickly stepped across the open floor and pulled up an empty stool, placing it beside Daris' bed and sitting down to look at him closely.

Tassie studied Essa's face, noting the way she gazed at Daris, as though she desperately wished that he'd open his eyes and look up at her.

"You really care for him, don't you?" Tassie asked.

Essa glanced at her, then nodded.

"You love him?"

"Yes, I do," Essa replied earnestly. "He's – well, he's the only person who really knows me. He understands me." She smiled a bit. "He makes me feel safe."

"You are very safe here," Tassie remarked.

"Oh, I'm sure I am," Essa agreed. "But I feel safer when I have Daris beside me." A far-away look came into her eyes. "When that creature attacked him, I was so *scared*." She looked at Tassie. "I thought he might *die*."

Tassie nodded. "I don't think you'll need to worry about that, not now. He's healing. Slowly, but he is healing."

"He's always been the brave one," Essa mused. "The one who encourages everyone else, who wants to look after others." She rested her hand lightly on his, looking down at his still face.

"Well, you can help me care for him a bit," Tassie suggested. She rose from her seat, wet the rag once again in the basin of water, wrung it out, and then handed it to Essa. "He's still a bit warm," she explained in response to the question on Essa's face. "This will help keep him cooler."

Essa smiled uneasily as she took the cloth and spread it over Daris' forehead. He stirred at her touch, but didn't wake.

"How long will he sleep?" Essa wondered aloud.

"It's hard to say," Tassie replied. "When Zorix was bitten, he didn't really sleep as much as just … lie there. He didn't want to move; it hurt too much."

"Do you think that's what Daris is feeling?"

"Possibly," Tassie had to tell her truthfully. "It could be that the effect is different on people than it is on animals like Zorix. I'm sorry, I don't know."

Essa nodded slightly.

Tassie rested her hand on Essa's, and she looked up at her. "We will take care of him," she encouraged her. "We'll take care of him together."

~

Not far away, Ovard had gathered the frightened, weary travelers into the large round Fountain Court. The sweet smell of vine fruit helped to calm them, it seemed, as they were at last able to seat themselves on stone benches around the open courtyard. Most important now was their need for water, which was provided by the stream, clear as ice, cascading down through Haven's Orchard.

Ovard and Leandra made the rounds, along with Rudge, Jayla, and Kalen, going to each newcomer in turn, doing all they could to try and help them start to feel at home there. Most of them had clothing that was worn and scuffed, as well as cuts and bruises, smudges of dirt on their hands and faces, and an exhausted glaze over their eyes.

It was important to Ovard to introduce himself to them, and to learn their names in return. He hoped that he would be able to remember at least most of them.

The woman who wore the gold pendant – the map to Haven – introduced herself as Shayrie, her husband as Nevin, and their teenage children as Persha and Gavin. The woman and her small boy were Zora and Trystan, who shyly but firmly informed Ovard that he was now six years old, not five. Ovard smiled.

The older man was Lomar, the younger was Berrick; then there was Worley and his wife Dorianne. Essa had gone to stay with Daris at the clinic; the bold, impatient man was Brodan, and the man accompanying him was named Stanner. There were so many of them that Ovard felt his head begin to spin in the effort to remember them all. *Well, that will come in time*, he told himself.

He was greatly relieved when Jair and Arden finally come to join them. "How is the young man?" Ovard asked him.

"All right, I think," Jair answered. "Tassie gave him more of the red juice, and something to fight off his fever."

Ovard nodded. "Well, he's in very good hands. Let's see what more we can do for the rest of our guests."

Jair looked around at the small crowd of people seated around the Court. Some gazed in awe at the lightstones of Haven's city walls, some huddled together trying to encourage or comfort one another; others appeared to be lost in their own thoughts, too exhausted to be sure what they thought of finally having arrived at Haven – their long-sought-after destination.

"They're not guests," Jair replied suddenly, looking back at Ovard. "They live here now. They need to have a home here, a place where they can settle in and feel safe, and get some rest. Don't you think that's what we should do now?"

"I think that sounds perfect," Ovard agreed.

Jair was every bit the welcoming host as he and Ovard gathered up the weary travelers and led them through the streets once again, pointing out the homes that were unoccupied and allowing them to choose wherever they wanted to settle. There was still a bit of work to be done, as none of the empty homes had any real bedding as of yet. The tents that they had brought along provided cloth for making mattresses; soft grasses and leaves were gathered for the filler. The stream was visited several times as the new arrivals filled their mugs, canteens, and washbasins. They were all eager to return to a sense of normalcy, with a roof over their heads and a bed to lie down on.

Ovard breathed a sigh of relief when everything settled down once again. So much had happened so quickly, so unexpectedly! But the air was quiet once again, and he was ready for a bit of rest himself. *Not sleep*, he thought, *just time to breathe, and to think*. And he wanted to record the happenings of the day – this was not an event to be forgotten. With the last of the new arrivals settled in at last, he turned toward home himself.

When he noticed Jair standing near the wall across the road, looking rather dejected, he stopped.

"Is something wrong, son?" Ovard asked. "Are you feeling all right?"

"I'm fine," Jair replied, trying to smile.

Ovard was not convinced.

"Tell me what's troubling you," he pressed as he put an arm over Jair's shoulders and turned him toward home.

Jair sighed. "Well, it's not a big thing really," he began. "It's just … that necklace that Shayrie has. It shows the way to Haven from where she lived."

"Yes?" Ovard prompted.

"It isn't really fair, is it?" Jair complained. "I mean, she has the map on a chain, and I have to wear it on my face. *Forever!* Why couldn't my parents have *given* me something that showed the way, something I could take off the way she can? Why did they need to have me *marked?*"

Ovard ran his hand over his short gray beard, as he often did when considering his words before speaking them. "It was the choice they made, Jair."

"But *why?*"

"Believe me, Jair, your parents did have a reason for doing what they did."

Jair walked on in silence, then regarded Ovard with a curious expression. "Do you still remember that day?" he asked. "When they gave me up?"

"I do."

"Will you tell me about it? Why couldn't they keep me? Why did they give me to you and Tassie? Did you already know them before you took me in?"

Ovard smiled ruefully. "So many questions," he remarked. "But I can't blame you for that. No, I did not know your parents before they put you into my care. I only ever spent that one day with them."

Jair was quiet a moment. "Can you tell me why? Why they couldn't keep me, why did they have me marked with the way to Haven? And how did they know the way to Haven to begin with?" He sighed. "I have a thousand questions, Ovard. I guess I can't ask them all right now, can I?"

"Not all at once, my boy," Ovard replied as they reached the door of their home. He opened it with ease – there were no locks on Haven's doors – and Jair followed him inside.

"Why don't you sit down?" Ovard suggested, a resigned heaviness in his voice.

As the two of them took their seats at the table, Jair looked at Ovard with anticipation.

"I'm afraid I can't answer all of your questions, Jair, but I'll tell you what I can."

Jair nodded. "Please."

"Your parents knew about Haven's existence," Ovard began slowly. "Your father was a descendant of the remembrance keepers. But, you might have guessed that yourself?"

"Yes," Jair replied. "I thought either my mother or my father must have been."

"Your father was," Ovard repeated, "and when he came to me, he told me that he'd been visited by a prophet. He said he'd been told that the time was coming for a great return to Haven, and that you, Jair, would play an important part in it all. The prophet warned your parents that because of who they were – and because of who *you* are – in time, things would become very dangerous for all of you. Your parents feared for your safety, Jair. All they wanted was to keep you as far away from danger as possible."

"But if they didn't know you, how did they know to leave me with you?" Jair questioned.

"The prophet who came to them was a man I'd met a few times over the years," Ovard explained. "He told your parents that you would be safe there with me. You had already been marked, Jair. Your father knew that anyone from the larger cities where you had been living could more easily have recognized your mark for what it was. He knew that it would not be safe to remain there."

"Where were they from?"

"A country far, *far* north of Dunya," Ovard told him. "Your parents knew that your little map – the way to Haven – would still be accurate, even from where they found me. They told me their story, and how they knew that I could be trusted to do what was best for you."

Jair slowly shook his head. "I don't remember them at all."

"You were not yet three years old," Ovard informed him. He smiled. "You were so small, so curious, so adventurous. Tassie took a liking to you right away. It was all we could do, the two of us, to keep you out of mischief." He chuckled at the memory.

"What happened to my parents, then?" Jair asked, almost in a whisper. "What did they do? They couldn't go back, if they thought they were in danger too. And they didn't come here, to Haven. Where did they go?"

Ovard shook his head. "I'm sorry, Jair. That, I honestly don't know. They – well, they planned to come back for you, when you were old enough to understand it all, when you were old enough to travel. They wanted to come to Haven, Jair. They wanted to come here with us."

"But they never came," Jair thought aloud.

"No," Ovard replied.

"When I was old enough," Jair repeated Ovard's words. "How old did they want me to be before they traveled with me?"

Ovard's face grew solemn. "Ten years," he replied gravely.

"But that was three years ago," Jair said quietly.

"I know, son," Ovard replied. "I have no idea where your parents went when they left us, or what could have happened to them. I'm sorry, but I just don't know."

Jair nodded solemnly. "Thank you for telling me." He eyed Ovard closely – the man seemed tense, uneasy, as though he had more to say but wasn't sure if he should say it.

"What?" Jair asked. "There's something else, isn't there?"

"It's something that the prophet told your father," Ovard replied. "He said that you were a very special child. You are not only a descendant of remembrance keepers. You are also the closest living relative to Haven's Overseer."

"Overseer?" Jair asked in surprise. "What does that mean?"

"The Overseer ..." Ovard shrugged a bit. "Well, he was the closest to what we would call a king, in our time, in our way of thinking. The prophet said that, in the days of departure from Haven, the Overseer entrusted his own brother as the first remembrance keeper. And you, Jair, are his direct descendant. That makes you not only Haven's key, but Haven's ruler as well."

91

Jair's eyes grew wide. "So I'm supposed to be the new Overseer?" he asked. "No matter who comes here, it's supposed to be me, out of everyone else?"

"It appears that way," Ovard told him.

Jair was speechless for a moment. "Maybe that's why I seem to just know things," he voiced his thoughts. Then he looked up at Ovard suddenly. "You won't tell anyone, will you?" he asked.

"Tell them what?"

"About me being the Overseer. I feel like everyone already expects so much of me. I'm not ... well, I'm not *great*. I don't know how to be a king. I'm just doing the best I can."

Ovard smiled wisely. "You are doing a fine job of it."

"Still, you won't tell them?"

Ovard considered Jair's question. "No, not at the moment. But some day, Jair, there may come a day when I will need to tell them. To tell everyone here that *you*, as young as you are, are their rightful ruler. The people will need to know. Some day, they will need to know."

~ 11 ~

"Brace! Brace? Are you all right? What happened? Why were they hitting you?"

He could hear Dursen's questions, and the worry in his voice, but all Brace could think about was the way his head, his face, and his body ached where the men had pounded him with their large, strong fists. He managed a bit of a groan in response.

When he felt a hand touch his shoulder, he flinched, pulling his arms up over his face, an almost involuntary reaction.

"Easy now," said an unfamiliar voice. "I'm not going to hurt you."

Brace relaxed a little – the man's voice sounded friendly enough. He managed to open his eyes, although his right eye was nearly swollen shut. When his sight came into focus, he could see the man who had spoken to him, kneeling beside him.

No beard, Brace thought. *He's not a logger, from the look of him.* Somehow, that was a small comfort to him – he'd had enough of loggers.

The man's thick, black hair was brushed with a bit of gray at the temples; his build was not as large as most of the men Brace had seen in Erast, either, and his eyes were as kindly as his voice.

"Are you all right, then?" the man asked.

Brace took a breath. "I don't know," he groaned.

"Let us help you," he offered. "Torren, Ben, let's see if we can get him to his feet, slowly. Gently."

"I don't know why this happened," Dursen told the men as they gathered around. "I just went to use the privy, and when I came back, they were beating on him."

"It's all right now," the first man replied. "We'll get him out of here, get him fixed up." When he touched Brace's shoulder again, he didn't flinch.

"Can you stand?"

"I think so," Brace managed.

"We'll help you."

Brace closed his eyes, concentrating on every move he made, wanting to avoid causing himself any more pain. He tried to push himself up off the ground, but a shooting pain ran across his side, and he gasped.

"Here now," another voice said. "Let us do that."

Brace felt several pairs of hands take hold of his arms, and under his arms, firmly but gently, and they somehow managed to get him to his feet.

"All right?" a voice asked. Brace opened his left eye again, and slowly nodded.

"Here," Dursen spoke up, coming into Brace's limited vision. He was holding out his handkerchief. "Your lip is bleeding," he explained.

Brace accepted the small cloth and held it to his face as the kind strangers slowly half-walked, half-carried him away from the crowded eatery.

Finally, gratefully, Brace stumbled in through the doorway that the kindhearted man held open for him. His side ached and his head throbbed, and he relied heavily on the other men's strength to keep him on his feet as he entered the house.

"Ronin, what on this earth?" a woman's voice asked in surprise.

"This fellow ran into some trouble down at the eatery," the man answered. "He needed help."

Brace heard no reply, but he felt himself being led aside and gently lowered to sit down on what must have been a bed. He kept his eyes closed – he couldn't open the right one anyway – and held Dursen's handkerchief to his lip.

"Right," the woman finally replied, seeing what condition Brace was in. "What should I do?"

"Bring some water and a rag to start with," Ronin suggested. Brace felt a hand on his arm, and he managed to look at the man who sat beside him on the quilt-covered bed.

"Let's have a look at your lip." Brace let his hand drop to his lap, still clutching the blood-stained piece of cloth.

"That's a bad one," Ronin commented, "but I believe that I can fix it up for you."

"Can you?" Brace mumbled.

"I have a bit of experience as a medic," Ronin said nonchalantly. "I'm not formally trained, mind you, but the men in this town do have their share of mishaps working out there among the trees. Many of them would rather come to see me for minor injuries. I suppose I'm less intimidating than the real thing. I don't cost near as much, either."

Brace could hear a touch of humor in Ronin's voice as the woman – his wife? – brought a small, fat pitcher of water and a clean cloth. *Well*, Brace thought, *he doesn't seem worried. Does that mean that I feel worse than I actually am, or is he only trying to ease my mind?*

Ronin held the cloth to Brace's bleeding lip while the woman peered at his swollen eye, and Dursen and the other two men watched with varying degrees of concern from across the room.

"That's quite a gash," Ronin spoke again. "It will need stitching up."

"Can you do that?" Brace asked him.

"I can," he replied as he rose from the bed and returned with a jar of blue-tinted liquid and another cloth. "Go ahead and lie down. The gash is deep, but small. It won't take long."

Brace steadied himself on the bed, putting all of his weight on his hands as he pulled his legs, one at a time, off the floor and onto the faded quilt, then slowly leaned back with a groan to lie flat on the bed. He hadn't quite gotten his head onto the pillow, and though he didn't particularly care at the moment, the woman came and gently arranged it under his head while Ronin soaked the fresh cloth in the bluish liquid.

"I'll get something cold for your eye," the woman told him in a voice as caring as Ronin's.

"Here," Ronin said as he placed the saturated cloth onto Brace's lip. He could feel the liquid seeping into his wound, but it only stung briefly, mildly, and then he couldn't feel it at all. He watched as Ronin produced a fine needle and even finer thread.

"This really won't hurt any," he said as he carefully removed the wet cloth from Brace's lip.

"You're sure?" Brace mumbled.

"Absolutely."

All the same, Brace shut his good eye tightly as Ronin's hands came near his face. He waited, but felt nothing. Had the man not done anything yet, or could he actually *not* feel it?

"There now," Ronin said only a moment later. "That's done. Feel anything?"

Brace looked at him again, surprised. "No," he replied. Ronin smiled.

"How ..." Brace began, but Ronin waved his hand.

"Don't talk unless you must. Let yourself heal. What else hurts? Show me, if you can."

Brace rested his hand on his aching side, and as the woman returned with something cold wrapped in thick cloth, Ronin went to work, gently pressing his fingers into different places along Brace's ribs until he winced.

"That's the spot, there," Ronin said aloud, almost to himself. "Can you breathe easily? Take a full breath for me."

Brace obeyed, but stopped short.

"That hurts?" Ronin asked, and Brace nodded.

Ronin felt along Brace's ribs again, more gently. "I don't think anything is broken, just bruised."

Brace felt a hand touch his shoulder, and he turned slightly to look. "Hold this on your eye," the woman told him. "I'll bring some ice for your side as well."

"Go ahead and get some rest," Ronin told him. "Does it hurt anywhere else?"

"No," Brace mumbled. *Not as much as what you already know about,* he added in his thoughts.

"All right then. Here, eat this."

Brace looked to see Ronin holding out what looked like a small square of caramel. "What is it?" he asked.

"It will help ease your pains, and help you rest," the man told him. "You can chew it." He placed it into Brace's palm, and without a second thought, Brace carefully placed it into his mouth. It was soft, and he could chew it easily; it almost dissolved before he swallowed it.

"There now," Ronin said as he rose from the bed. "Don't worry about anything. You're safe here. You can sleep if you need to."

Brace nodded slowly, his eyes feeling suddenly heavy. Whatever that thing was he'd eaten, he was certain that it was making him sleepy. As he felt himself drifting off, the pain in his head and his side subsided to almost nothing, and he breathed a sigh of relief.

~ 12 ~

he Main Hall was more crowded than Jair had ever seen it. Ovard had insisted that every single person in Haven be invited to this particular meeting, but now, over the constant din of voices, Jair could hardly get his own thoughts settled down.

"All right, is that everyone?" Ovard spoke up over the constant murmur of sound.

"All but Tassie, Essa and Daris," Arden informed him. "Brodan tells me that the rest of his people are here."

"*His* people?" Ovard questioned. "Aren't we all Haven's people now?"

Arden tipped his head in assent. "Yes, I suppose that's so," he muttered.

"What's wrong then?" Ovard asked quietly.

Arden leaned in close to Ovard, and spoke softly in his ear. "That man Brodan is getting on my last nerve," he confided. "He is by far too impatient and bold."

Ovard rested his hand on Arden's shoulder. "I agree with you there, my friend, but let's give him time to settle in here. Perhaps he'll do better once he's adjusted."

Arden grunted in response as Ovard turned toward Jair, who sat beside him, facing the large group that had gathered upon request. "I think it's time you started the meeting, my boy."

Jair nodded, his eyes wide at the idea of speaking to so many people at once. Standing, he gathered his courage. "Hello, everyone!" he called out, and the crowd began to quiet themselves. "Thank you for coming here, to the Main Hall, I mean. I hope you all are getting used to your new homes. We're – I'm – glad you're here." He paused and took a deep breath. "I've just been having this dream lately, not a *real* dream, but – I just really want to see Haven get full of people, like it was so long ago. I want it to be what it should be. It's a refuge, and I want people who need a refuge to be able to come and live here." He shrugged a bit. "So I'm glad you're here."

There were a few encouraging nods, smiles, and thank-you's, and Jair, emboldened a bit, went on. "So, I know it's been two days, not very long, but I would like to know what everyone is good at – skilled at. There aren't very many of us here yet, and there are so many things that need to be done here. We've already started fixing things up – Rudge and Kalen are repairing the stonework – but there is so much more to be done. There is an orchard, and there will be gardens soon, we're clearing the land. When Brace and Dursen get back with the seed, we'll need to start planting. We'll have our own food to eat, so we won't need any from out there." Jair nodded his head, imagining the vast, dangerous land that was the rest of the world, as far as he was concerned.

"We want to get so we can take care of ourselves here," he went on. "We don't want to need anything from out there, if we can do anything about it. So …" he glanced aside at Ovard, who nodded, encouraging him to go on.

"So," Jair continued, facing the small crowd of new faces, "I just wanted to let you all know what needs to be done, and see what any of you are willing to do to help. Maybe Tassie could have some help at the clinic, or people could go hunting in the Woods with Arden. Anything, everything," Jair summed up. "We just need to know what everyone can do, or what they would like to do to help get things going here, to be organized." He glanced again at Ovard, who smiled encouragingly.

"May I ask a question?" a man's voice came from the crowd.

"Uh, sure," Jair replied tentatively. "What's your name again, please?"

"Stanner," the man replied. "My question is just, how do you know that Haven is intended to be a refuge?"

"Oh, it's in the writing," Jair explained. "On the wall in the Fountain Court. It says that Haven is a refuge for anyone who comes here with a pure heart."

"A pure heart?" Lomar asked warily.

"Yes," Jair told him. "I think it means that you come here not wanting to cause trouble."

"What, then?" Brodan asked. "If someone does cause any trouble, will they be considered of impure heart and banished from the city?"

"No!" Jair exclaimed. "That isn't what it means at all. It just means that your reason for coming here is to live in peace, and not to try and take over, to claim the city for yourself. It only means that you've come because you want to leave the rest of the world behind. I know sometimes people do things they shouldn't. Haven's books have ... rules ..."

"Guidelines," Ovard assisted.

"Yes, guidelines," Jair repeated, "in case anything does happen, if people are arguing or something. It's all in the books, about how to have people work things out."

"How to make amends to each other," Ovard added. "It's all very straightforward, and very fair, all with the goal of helping us keep the peace with one another."

A bit of an uneasy silence filled the Meeting Hall.

"None of you have come here to cause trouble, have you?" Jair asked in alarm.

"No, of course not," Worley answered quickly.

Several agreements came from other members of the small crowd.

"I do have one question, though," Lomar spoke up. "I'm just wondering how you can read that writing. No one else seems to be able to read it."

"Well, I just can," Jair explained, at a loss as to how better to put it. "I'm teaching Ovard and Jayla how to read it. Everyone will know how, as soon as -"

"But how do we know that it really says what you're telling us?" Brodan demanded, leaving Jair speechless.

"Why would Jair lie to us?" Arden demanded, standing. "What would he gain by deceit?"

No one had any response; several eyed Brodan as though they either feared what he'd said, or feared what the repercussions would be because he'd dared to say it.

"Jair is the most honest person among us," Arden continued, "as far as I can tell. He cares about Haven and the people who come to live here more than I ever thought possible. If you don't learn anything else here, you must learn that Jair can be trusted to tell the truth. *Always.*"

There were many nods of understanding, approval, and respect, as Brodan looked down at the floor. Jair gave Arden an appreciative glance before addressing his audience once again.

"He's right," Jair continued. "I wouldn't lie to any of you. There are so many things about Haven that I just sort of discovered, that I know somehow. But there are still a lot of things I don't know, I'm sure. And there are a lot of things we can do to make Haven as beautiful as it can be. As it used to be. And since Haven is your home now, I thought you'd all like to do what you can to help fix it up. That's all."

"Er..." one of the men stuttered, "I'm sorry to seem bold, but.. well, say I was to bring someone on to help me. What would I do to pay him his wages? I don't think any of us would be able to do that..."

Jair shook his head adamantly. "We don't need to worry about any wages. We don't need money here. We just need to have food to eat and a place to live. The only thing we need money for is to bring in supplies to get everything started. Once Haven is built up the way it should be, we won't need money for anything. The work that people do won't be for pay. They'll be doing it because they want to. Because they care about the city. They care about their home."

There was silence for a moment, until finally, Nevin stood. "I would like to help."

Shayrie joined him as their children looked on. "So would I," she added.

One by one, to Jair's delight, many of the others stood as well, offering their hands. A single sheet of thick new paper was laid out on the table, and as the meeting came to a close, Ovard recorded the skills that each person spoke out, sharing in what ways they would be of help in Haven's restoration. Some were willing to work the gardens or orchard, others to continue repairing the homes and walls, even the great stone fountain. Dorianne volunteered to help teach the children, though she questioned what they would need to know in this new and amazing place.

With the meeting adjourned, everyone filed out of the Main Hall into the bright light of day. Jair was relieved and exhausted at the same time, so he did not notice, at first, young Gavin standing just outside the doors as Jair passed by him.

"Hey there," Gavin said, startling Jair a bit.

"Oh – what?" Jair stammered.

Gavin shrugged. "I just thought you'd like to have some fun," he explained. Seeing Jair glance questioningly at Ovard, he went on. "You *can* have fun here, can't you? I mean, you don't have to work all the time?"

Ovard smiled. "No, we don't work all of the time," he told him. "Jair, how would you like to take a break and just enjoy yourself? You've more than earned it."

"Well – all right," Jair stammered, as though he wasn't sure he remembered how to simply play, and not act as the responsible leader that he was expected to be.

"Go along then," Ovard prompted him. "Be a boy for a while. There is plenty of time left for you to be a man."

Jair smiled. "Thank you!"

"Come on," Gavin urged. "Will you show me what's what?"

"Sure," Jair replied with a grin, allowing Gavin to pull him away from the Main Hall.

"Let's go!"

Jair followed Gavin down the main road away from the Hall at first, then the older boy stopped. "Where should we go?" he asked. "Where do you go for fun?"

"Well," Jair began sheepishly, "I really haven't had a whole lot of time for fun since I got here. I've had to be in charge ..."

Gavin shook his head in dismay.

"I do like to go to the orchard," Jair went on. "That's a nice place."

"Let's go to the orchard, then," Gavin suggested. "Anything that isn't work."

Jair smiled. "All right." He led the way through Haven's streets toward the grove of fruit trees that grew near Haven's gate.

"How old are you?" Gavin asked as they walked side by side.

"Almost thirteen."

"I'm fourteen," Gavin informed him.

"You have a sister, don't you?" Jair asked.

"Yes," Gavin replied. "Persha. She's sixteen. She's not a lot of fun," he remarked. "She spends too much time by herself, thinking about things. And she's not good at taking advice either, you just wait and see. She wants to do her own thing."

"Really?" Jair asked intently. What little he'd seen of Persha had left him thinking only of how beautiful she was – clear, gray-blue eyes, her soft smooth hair. A little aloof maybe, but that made her all the more intriguing.

"Sure," Gavin replied, oblivious to Jair's uncommon interest in his older sister. "So where is this orchard of yours?"

"This way," Jair replied, waving him on. "It's not far."

The two boys passed through the large round Fountain Court and cut away to the left, then to the right through an opening in the glassy stone wall. Continuing on to the left, they eventually came to where they could see the shining, translucent waters of Haven's lake, with the orchard just beyond it.

"You didn't say there was a lake," Gavin commented in surprise.

Jair shrugged. "Sorry."

"That's really great," Gavin remarked, gazing at the lake's surface as they neared it. "Can you swim in it?"

"I think so," Jair replied. "I haven't … I don't think anyone really thought of it as a place for swimming."

"What's it for, then?"

"Getting water," Jair replied meekly. "And for fishing, and for drinking, and washing, and –"

"And swimming," Gavin said firmly. His face grew solemn for a moment. "It was really hard," he said, "crossing the mountains and everything. Leaving home. We went on and on, so far …"

"I know how it must have been," Jair replied. "It was like that for us too."

Gavin smiled once again. "But this is home now, isn't it?"

"It is."

"Well, I'm glad to be home," Gavin told him. "And I want to go for a swim. Don't you?"

Jair smiled in return. "Sure I do."

Gavin pulled off his roughspun shirt in one quick, easy motion, then kicked off his shoes. "Come on! Bet I'll be the first one in!"

Grinning, Jair followed suit, shedding his extra clothing. "We'll see about that!" he called out, running after him. His heart was glad at the thought that he had found a friend again at last.

~ 13 ~

How long he slept, Brace had not the slightest idea. Had he been dreaming? In his memory, he had been surrounded by – what were they? Wolves, ravens? No. Men. *Loggers*. Angry loggers, pounding him into the ground. He took a breath, glad to be awake, but not glad of feeling a heavy ache from head to toe. His mouth felt dry, and his head was throbbing. Brace stirred a bit, realizing that he was covered with another quilt, and that someone had removed his boots. When he managed to look out through his left eye, the first thing he saw was Dursen, seated in a chair by the foot of the bed, eating a bowl of soup.

"He's awake," Dursen announced, and several faces suddenly appeared as his caretakers came to stand beside the bed. There was Ronin, and one of his friends; Brace had heard the man's name spoken once, but he had no memory of it. There was also the woman again, and beside her stood a young girl, whose amber-colored eyes were wide as she looked at him with concern.

"What?" Brace asked, feeling disoriented. "Who – where?"

Ronin smiled and gently patted Brace's knee. "It's all right," he told him. "You've been asleep for almost three hours. This is my home, and you are welcome to stay here as long as you need." He rested his hand on the woman's shoulder. "This is my wife, Lira," he introduced her, "and my daughter, Ona."

"And your name is Brace," the girl spoke up.

"How …?" Brace tried to speak again, but his mouth was dry and pasty.

"Your friend Dursen told us," Ronin explained. "These are my friends here," he went on, gesturing into the room. Another man stood up from somewhere and joined the others as they looked on. "This is Torren and Ben-Rickard," Ronin introduced them.

"Call me Ben," the third man replied with a smile.

Brace nodded slightly. "Water?" he asked, his voice scratchy.

"Of course," Lira told him.

"Can you sit up a bit?" Ronin asked as Lira hurried away for a glass of water. It was a struggle, and it made his side ache, but Brace managed to sit up enough to accept the glass that Lira held out for him, and he drank it gratefully. Glancing at Dursen, Brace could see that he was eyeing him with concern.

"Did he tell you anything else?" Brace asked. Dursen's face revealed that he *had* said more, and he wasn't sure if he should feel guilty for it.

"He told us that you were on a mission of sorts," Ronin answered as everyone returned to where they'd been seated around the small room, eating what must be their midday meal. "He said you were trying to find people." Ronin's voice was full of questions.

Brace looked at Dursen again.

"I think we can trust them with this," Dursen remarked. "Look how much they've done for us already."

Brace considered the situation a moment, then nodded slightly.

"I don't even know what happened back there," Dursen pointed out. "Why those men attacked you."

"It was a misunderstanding," Brace answered.

"Was it about that girl?" Dursen asked, and Brace nodded.

"What girl?" Lira asked.

"Yara," Brace told her. "I asked her if she wanted to come back with us. Her father took it the wrong way. He thought I wanted her to work as a whore."

The room was silent for a moment.

"Come back where?" one of the men – Torren – asked. "Where are you from?"

Again, Brace looked at Dursen, his eyebrows raised in a question.

"Well, I didn't tell them all of that," Dursen informed him. "You're still the leader on this trip, after all. I didn't want to say anything that you wouldn't have wanted me to say."

Brace looked out at the curious, expectant faces. "Tell them," he instructed Dursen, then leaned back against the pillow.

Hesitantly, Dursen cleared his throat. "Well," he began, "we were sent out to find people who might want to come back with us," he told them again. "We're from a place called the Haven. It's an ancient city, but we found it."

Brace waited along with Dursen to see how everyone would respond. Ronin and Lira looked at each other. Ona appeared openly curious, and the two men seemed surprised.

"Haven?" Ben-Rickard asked. "Do you mean that the place truly does exist?"

"I thought it was only a legend," Torren agreed.

"It very much does exist," Dursen informed them. "It's real, and it's beautiful and amazing. We thought someone from Erast here might want to go back there." He spoke more boldly now, seeing how the men had reacted. "Brace told the girl, Yara, all about it, and we went back to the eatery today to see if she would be there, looking for us. We were going to leave today," he added regretfully.

"So, Yara wasn't there?" Ronin surmised. "But her father was?"

Brace nodded. "Him, and two other men."

"Three against one isn't a fair fight," Ona spoke up.

"No, it isn't," Dursen agreed.

"But – Haven," Lira redirected the conversation. "You've been there, and seen it with your own eyes?"

Dursen nodded eagerly, almost spilling his soup. "You've heard of it too?"

"A little," Lira replied. "I wasn't sure it was a real place either."

"So it *is* real," Ben-Rickard said aloud to himself. "Fascinating."

"It's *home*," Brace said when the room was quiet. "I just want to get back home."

"And you will, soon," Ronin encouraged. "But give yourself time to heal. No sense traveling with bruised ribs and only one good eye."

Brace sighed in frustration, but he knew that the man was right. *Tassie,* he thought. *Don't worry, not too much. I am coming home, as soon as I can.*

"Would you like something to eat?" Brace heard Lira ask him, but his eyes grew heavy, and before he could answer, he drifted off to sleep again, with the glass of water still in his hand.

~14~

Tassie stood near the window looking out into the bright light of day. Out there, everything seemed so cheery. There was even a large violet-colored butterfly flitting around, searching for a flower to land on. Yes, things outside were bright, but inside the walls of the clinic, things were tense and dreary. Daris still lay on the bed, his breathing labored, while Essa sat at his side, keeping constant vigil. Many of the others had come to check on Daris' well-being, but Essa had never left him since she'd come in through the clinic doors.

Tassie watched Essa from where she stood, realizing how fragile the woman seemed, both physically and emotionally. Her shoulder-length curls were disheveled and tangled, but she either was unaware or simply didn't care. Her focus was completely on Daris, as it had been for the past three days. Tassie had grown accustomed to reminding her to eat, and she hardly slept.

She deeply wished there was more she could do to speed Daris' healing and ease Essa's fears, but she was at a loss. She'd found the wound on Daris' shoulder, where it was obvious that he'd been bitten, and she had cleaned and dressed it, checking its condition quite often. The infection that had begun to set in was finally clearing away, much to Tassie's relief.

Pulling herself away from the window, Tassie looked down at her patient. She had become quite familiar with his face – she could easily see now when he was sleeping peacefully and when he was hurting and in need of more attention.

His face looked different now, she thought. As though he wasn't sleeping as deeply as he had been. Could it be …?

"Essa," she said softly. "I think he might wake up."

Hope flashed in Essa's eyes. "Do you?"

Tassie nodded. "Try to wake him, gently."

Essa placed her hand on Daris' arm and softly called his name. "Wake up, Daris," she pleaded. "It's Essa. Please wake up." She gently shook his arm. "Can you hear me? *Wake up.*"

Daris moaned and opened his eyes.

"He's awake!" Essa announced joyfully.

Tassie came a step closer. "Daris?"

He looked at her, blinked, and looked around. "Where am I?" he asked hoarsely.

"You're in the city of Haven," Tassie informed him.

"Essa?" he asked, looking over at her.

"Yes, I'm here," she replied, wiping away a tear of relief.

"We made it?" Daris asked.

"Yes, we made it! And it's a wonderful place, Daris. It's so full of light, and so peaceful. Just wait until you see it for yourself."

He reached up slowly and touched her face. "Did everyone make it here?"

"Yes, everyone," she told him. "We've all been worried over you. We've been here for three days."

"Three days?" he repeated in disbelief. He rested his hands on his chest, blinked again, then looked at Tassie. "And you are?"

"My name is Tassie," she answered. "I'm the medic here. My friends and I have been living here for several months now."

"Really? So we weren't the first ones here ..."

"No," Tassie replied. "Before you and your friends came, there were eleven of us. Your group has more than doubled our numbers."

Daris ran his hands over his face. "Is this real?" he asked. "This really is Haven?"

"It really is," Tassie said with a tired smile.

Daris lay quietly for a moment, thinking, while Essa held his hand and gazed at his face. "Those creatures," he muttered. "I only remember that we were getting attacked by those creatures. One of them came right at me."

"You were bitten," Tassie informed him. "But we have fruit growing here that heals wounds. I've been giving you the juice to drink. I think — well, I think it saved your life."

He nodded. "I think you're right."

"How are you feeling now?" Tassie asked him.

"I've been better," he told her. "I'm thirsty."

"I'll get you some water."

Essa leaned closer to Daris. "I'm so glad you're finally awake."

He smiled faintly at her. "So am I. I'm sorry that all this happened. I was trying so hard to fight this off, but it was too much for me."

"I know. It's all right now. It wasn't anyone's fault. It just happened. We were all so scared for you."

"I'll be all right, I think," he said as Tassie returned with a mug of water.

"You'll need to sit up a little to drink," she told him. "Can you?"

"I think so." With help from Essa and Tassie, Daris managed to sit up and, one sip at a time, he drank all of the water in the mug.

"That's plenty for now," Tassie said as she accepted the empty mug from Daris.

"I'm sorry," Daris began, "but … your voice. It's different. I haven't heard anything like it."

Tassie gave him a bit of a smile. "It's because I can't hear," she explained. "I was taught how to speak by feeling and seeing."

"Amazing," Daris said in a whisper.

Tassie nodded slightly. "There are many different sorts of miracles in this world. But yours is still working itself out. You need to lie down again, get some more rest."

With Essa's assistance, Tassie helped Daris to lie down comfortably. He winced, rubbing at his shoulder.

"Does it still hurt?" Tassie asked him.

He nodded. "Everything hurts."

"I'll get you something for that."

It took time, getting a blaze going in the open fire pit at the far side of the room, and time to heat the pot of water resting on the metal grate over the flames. With her back to them, Tassie was able to give Daris and Essa some privacy, a chance to talk among themselves. Every so often, she looked back over her shoulder to see them gazing at one another's faces, speaking words that she couldn't hear and did not try to read on their lips.

Just as steam began to rise from the water, Tassie filled the mug once again, adding a measured amount of the medicinal powder that she'd set aside. When she came back to stand beside the bed with the mug of hot, pungent liquid, she could see that Daris was in obvious discomfort.

"Here," she told him, resting her hand on his arm. "Sit up a little, one more time. Drink as much of this as you can. Be careful – it's hot."

Daris obeyed and managed to drink half of the mug before he had to lie down again.

"That's fine," Tassie encouraged him, putting the mug aside and bringing the jar of thick red juice over to his bedside. "Here," she said again. "One last thing, and you can rest."

Daris opened his eyes as she removed the lid and held the small jar out to him.

"Drink a little of this. It's almost like syrup," she said when he grimaced. "You won't need to sit up. I just need to pour a bit of it into your mouth so you can swallow it."

Tassie tipped the jar until enough of the juice had dripped out to cover his tongue. "That's plenty," she told him. "You can swallow now."

"It's very sweet," Daris commented when his mouth was empty. "What is it?"

"It's from a fruit that only grows here, as far as I can tell," Tassie replied.

Daris nodded, his eyelids growing heavy.

"You can sleep now," Essa told him, sitting as close beside him as she possibly could. "We'll watch over you."

He managed a tiny smile before he closed his eyes against the lingering pain.

"You will feel better soon," Tassie tried to encourage him. "The hot drink I gave you will help ease the pain, and you can rest again."

Essa leaned over him and kissed his cheek. "I'll be here when you wake up," she whispered.

As Daris finally drifted off to sleep once again, Essa fought to keep from crying. "He really is going to be all right, isn't he?" she asked.

"Yes, I really believe he is," Tassie answered. "Believe me, I wouldn't lie to you about this."

Essa nodded. "I'm sorry," she said, wiping away her tears. "I just didn't want him to see me crying. I hate for him to see my tears."

Tassie went to Essa's side and put an arm around her. "It's all right," she said. "He's going to be all right."

"I just love him so much," Essa sniffled.

Tassie decided that it was time to re-direct the woman's thoughts a bit. "How long have you known him?" she asked.

"How long?" Essa seemed surprised at the question. "Umm ... I think it must be ... two years, maybe."

"How did you meet?"

"At a market," Essa answered quickly. She smiled, blushing. "I was selling jars of apple butter from my family's farm, and he stopped and bought some. I kept to business, but he was so friendly. I remember thinking how *kind* his eyes were."

Tassie smiled encouragingly when Essa paused.

"Well," she went on, "the next week he came back to buy more. I really didn't think that one person could go through an entire jar of apple butter in a week, but I didn't say anything. I was glad to see him again. He was so easy to talk to, we talked about anything and everything, or nothing really, I don't know. Then he came back about an hour later, and he'd brought me flowers. Pink snapdragons." She smiled. "I don't know if he noticed how I shied away from him at first, but if he did, it didn't seem to matter to him."

"Why did you shy away from him?"

"Well," Essa began, her eyebrows coming together in a crease, "I have a hard time trusting," she explained quietly.

"Why is that?" Tassie asked gently.

Essa lifted the cloth from Daris' forehead, refolded it, and replaced it. "I was married once," she explained, with reluctance in her voice. "It turned out to be a mistake. A *terrible* mistake. At first ... well, it wasn't so bad. But after a few years, it just kept getting worse."

"What do you mean?" Tassie asked, though Essa seemed unsure whether she wanted to say more.

"He was cruel to me," she replied. "I was living in fear, of him and everyone else, it seemed. I had thought, before, that people could be

113

trusted." She smiled ruefully. "I learned otherwise. But, one night I managed to get away from him while he slept. I didn't know what else to do, but to run back to my family's farm. They took me back, of course. I was hurt, though, inside and out."

"What became of your husband?" Tassie asked her, amazed that she had been able to get away.

"He's gone," Essa replied shortly. When she said no more, Tassie nodded. None of that mattered now, after all. Essa was safe here in Haven.

"But you found that you could trust Daris?" Tassie asked, redirecting the conversation once again.

Essa nodded. "Oh, yes! He really seems to always be able to tell when I'm uneasy, even when I try to hide it. He's just always *there*, he doesn't even need to say anything. He just makes me feel safe. We – well, we want to get married. I am brave enough to try again, I think."

Tassie laid her hand on Essa's. "You will be able to get married," she told her. "Daris will get well, I'm very sure of that. Don't worry."

Essa forced a smile. "I'll try not to." She let out a breath. "You are married, I see," she observed, gesturing toward Tassie's hand. "But I haven't seen a man here with that same pattern. Is your husband …?"

"He isn't here just now," Tassie explained regretfully. "He's gone out again, with Dursen. They're searching for anyone who might need to call Haven their home. This will be his last trip, though, and I'm grateful for that."

"How long have you known him?"

Tassie grinned a bit. "Less than a year."

"Really?" Essa asked in surprise. "That's not long."

"No," Tassie agreed. "But somehow, we just knew it was right. He's right for me, and I'm right for him."

"Does he make you feel safe?"

"Not in the same way as you and Daris. But he makes me feel … not alone. Even when he's not here, he's still in my thoughts, and in my heart." Reflexively, Tassie laid her hand on her heart, where the leather starflower Brace had made was still hidden under her clothing. *Come home soon, Brace,* she thought. *I really do miss you. I need you to be here.*

Sensing that Essa was still looking at her, Tassie forced a smile. "Would you like to get something to eat?" she asked. "You must be hungry."

"All right," she replied tentatively. "But I don't want to leave him."

"We'll only be gone for a moment," Tassie reassured her. "We'll bring the food back here to eat it."

Essa nodded. "Daris has been there for me so many times," she thought aloud. "I don't know what I'd do without him."

"I understand," Tassie replied.

Oh, Brace, she thought, looking toward the window, with daylight pouring in. *I'm so tired. I miss you. Please come home soon.*

~ 15 ~

Brace peered at his face again in the small framed mirror. *Well, that's better anyway,* he thought. Four days had passed, and his face was beginning to look like his own once again. The skin around his right eye was still swollen and bruised a dark purple, but at least he could see out of it. His lower lip was also swollen, bruised, and tender, the stitches very visible, but the ache in his side was manageable. He didn't want to wait any longer. If he and Dursen left today, they could be home in another eight days. He just wanted to get out of Erast and home to Tassie. He tried to convince himself that his face wouldn't look quite so bad in eight more days.

He hadn't set foot outside of Ronin's home since he'd been brought there. Ronin, his wife Lira and daughter Ona were very kind and caring people who went out of their way to be sure that Brace was as comfortable as possible. They tended to his injuries, made sure he had plenty to eat, and often asked if he was getting enough sleep. Torren and Ben-Rickard, the other men who'd helped bring Brace to the house, stopped in from time to time as well, to visit.

When Brace announced that he was ready to leave, Ronin reacted in surprise.

"Are you certain?" he asked, concerned. "Your ribs are still healing."

"I know," Brace told him, "but I just want to get back to my wife. I've been gone longer than I planned. She'll worry."

"She'll worry when she sees what shape you're in, I'm sure."

"That can't be helped now. I'll be getting home nearly a week late as it is. No. I'm ready to go. I'll be careful."

Ronin made no reply, but he seemed ill at ease.

"You don't think I should leave yet?" Brace asked him. "I'm all right, really. My ribs don't hurt like they used to, and I have the medicine you gave me."

"No, that's not exactly it," Ronin replied. "I do think you're pushing things a bit, but I'm sure you'll be fine. What I'm really thinking is that I'd like to come with you."

"Come with me?" Brace was incredulous. "But your family …"

"We would all like to come," Ronin explained. "We've discussed it many times since you told us about Haven."

"You have?"

"While you were asleep," Ronin said with a guilty smile.

"I see. And you're all sure about leaving?"

"I believe so. Would you consider waiting one more day before you leave? So we can be sure we're in agreement, and get ourselves ready to join you?"

Brace sat down gingerly on the bed and rested his hands on his knees. *One more day*, he thought. Well, he would be past time getting home already, what was one more day?

"It *is* all right if we come, isn't it?" Ronin asked him.

Brace looked up. "Of course it's all right," he replied. "That's why I came here in the first place." He sighed in resignation. "All right. I can wait one more day. Is that enough time?"

"We'll make it be enough," Ronin answered, smiling.

"Make sure you pack light," Brace warned him. "And dress warmly. We will be going over the mountain ranges to the south."

"Good advice. Taken. Anything else?"

"Can't think of anything," Brace replied after considering the question.

"It's very kind of you, to say the least. Agreeing to wait, and taking on five extra people …"

"Five?" Brace asked in surprise.

"Oh, I'm sorry," Ronin apologized. "Torren and Ben-Rickard would like to come as well. They have fewer reasons to stay than I do. Is that all right?"

"It's fine," Brace replied. "Just, no more surprises, please?"

Ronin smiled. "No more surprises."

"How will it be for your daughter, crossing the mountains?" Brace asked, thinking of twelve-year-old Ona.

"She'll be all right," Ronin replied, assured of his answer. "She's strong in body and in spirit."

Brace nodded. "All right, then. One more day."

⁓

By the following afternoon, Ronin and Lira's small house was full of people and provisions. Torren and Ben-Rickard had been informed about the imminent departure, and the two men had quickly gathered together the supplies they would need, along with a few personal belongings. No matter how meager they were, it was at least a small piece of the life they would be leaving behind.

The two of them had gathered at Ronin's home, along with Brace, Dursen, and the three family members who found themselves suddenly deciding to leave their home and their villa behind them. Although they had prepared for this moment, it still was difficult, and Ona shed a few tears.

"It's going to be all right," her mother encouraged her, though her emotions were plain on her face as well. "We'll have a *new* home – a wonderful, amazing place to call home."

"I know it," Ona replied, trying to be brave. "But I have to leave my friends behind. And I think I'm just anxious about leaving." She sniffed and pushed her tears away.

Brace looked at her from where he was seated in a creaking wooden chair, arranging the contents of his pack once again.

"Your father says that you're a strong person," he told Ona, and she frowned, wondering if he was scolding her for crying. "Do you think that people who are strong or brave ever feel sad, or anxious?"

She bowed her head. "I don't know," she muttered.

"Well, I can tell you for certain that they *do*."

Ona looked up, her face a mixture of surprise and confusion. "They do?"

"Of course," Brace replied. "I know a man who is very strong, very brave, but he can also be sad, or afraid, or anxious at times."

"Yourself?" Ona guessed.

"Me? No, I wasn't talking about myself." Brace became aware that he'd gained everyone's attention, and they were all listening while they packed. "I wouldn't necessarily say that I'm very strong either," he admitted. "*Stubborn* is more like it."

Ona smiled a little.

"I was talking about a friend of mine," Brace continued. "But my point is, feeling sad or anxious doesn't make you weak. I think you're a strong person if you can understand what you feel and go on anyway. That's what I was getting at. Don't ever be ashamed to admit you're feeling afraid. Goodness knows I wasted enough years doing just that."

Lira stood behind her daughter and rested her hand on the girl's head. "Thank you," she said, smiling at Brace appreciatively. "That's good advice for all of us." She glanced around at the house once again. "This is really it. We're truly leaving."

"Don't think of it as leaving," Ben-Rickard spoke up. "Think of it as *going*. Haven is a real place, and we're actually going there!" His eyes had a far-away look to them. "It will be the adventure of a lifetime."

"That it will be," Dursen interjected. "And I don't know about the rest of you, but I'm more than ready to get going."

So, go they did, all seven of them, with full packs and high expectations. It was fortunate, in Brace's mind, that Ronin's family lived near the edge of town. That being the case, they only had to pass by a few dwellings before they started down the hillside just outside of town. That was perfectly all right with him. He believed that he could live the rest of his life without setting his eyes on another logger, at least not one from Erast.

The sun was low in the sky, and unnaturally pale, reminding Brace anew of the battle that was being waged all around them. His longing to be back on the other side of Haven's gate grew stronger, but he knew that he had to pace himself. His ribs still ached, and they all had a long way to go.

"Are you all right?" Ronin asked him.

"I'm fine," Brace bluntly shrugged off the question.

Ronin seemed slightly taken aback by Brace's gruff response.

"Sorry about that," Brace apologized. "I'm told I can be moody at times. Did I ever thank you for everything you did to help me?"

Ronin smiled kindly. "Yes, you did. You needn't concern yourself, though. It was my pleasure."

"I'm sure the men in Erast will miss having you there to treat their injuries."

"Well, they have other help there. I wouldn't worry about them."

"Oh, I won't," Brace said quickly. "Believe me, I won't."

"Wait!" a voice rang out suddenly, reverberating across the landscape. "Wait for me!"

Everyone turned to look back in surprise at the young woman who stood, breathless, at the top of the hill.

"Who is that?" Torren asked.

"That's Yara," Brace said, surprised. He had honestly never expected to see her, ever again, and he wasn't completely certain now whether he was glad that she had found them.

"Wait!" she called out again, running down the slope toward them, clutching a large handbag. "I want to come with you," she gasped when she had caught up with them. Her eyes scanned their faces until she recognized Brace, despite his bruises.

"I heard about what they did to you," she said, taking a step closer. "My father and the other men. I'm *so* sorry."

Brace shook his head. "He was just trying to protect you. He thought I was …"

"I know what he thought. That doesn't make it right," Yara insisted. She took a moment to catch her breath. "I've been trying to find out what happened to you, where you'd gone. I finally found someone in town who'd seen where you'd been taken. I've made up my mind. I want to go back with you."

Brace studied her determined face for a moment. "Are you only leaving because you're angry with your father?" he asked her.

Yara blinked in surprise. "That's not the only reason," she told him defensively. "But does the reason really matter? You said that this Haven place was for everyone. Well, I want to come. I *can* still come, can't I?"

Brace managed a lop-sided grin. "Of course you can still come. This wasn't your fault, Yara. I hope you aren't blaming yourself."

She took a step closer to Brace, wincing at the sight of his battered face. Then she nodded. "As long as you're all right."

Brace turned away from her, away from the sympathetic scrutiny he found himself under. "I will be," he answered simply. He looked around at everyone, but they were looking to *him*, he realized, for leadership. Was this how Ovard had felt, he wondered, when he'd been leading the group and trying to find the way to Haven? Well, at least this time, Brace knew the way.

"Well, it looks like now there are eight of us." He turned back toward Yara. "Do you have everything you'll need in that bag?"

She nodded exuberantly. "I do. I'm not going back for *anything*."

"Good." He nodded toward her handbag. "That's not the best thing to have when you're crossing over the mountains," he informed her.

"I'll just have to make it work," she told him. "It's all I had."

At least she'd dressed for travel, Brace thought. Her long gray coat appeared to be made of wool, and her boots looked sturdy enough.

"All right then," Brace addressed the group. "Ready to go on?"

"Very ready," Ronin replied with a smile.

"I'm very glad you found us," Lira told Yara, stepping up beside her.

"Thank you," Yara replied quietly.

Brace looked back at her, the wind pushing at her long red braid, pulling loose long strands of hair and swirling them around her flushed face. The look in her eyes betrayed her feelings – that she was worried, and not quite sure what she might have gotten herself into. She was welcome to join them, of course, though Brace felt himself pulling away from her, at least inwardly. She was beautiful, and real, and here. And Tassie was not. Though Brace had sworn to be true to Tassie alone, for the rest of his days, he felt something trigger in his mind at having Yara so near, and a chill ran across his shoulders and down his back. It worried him, how easy he realized it still was, to feel this pull toward attractive young women. Yara could come back with them to Haven, of course, but he would do his best to keep his distance from her.

"Don't worry," Brace told her. "We'll take it one day at a time. We'll all stay together, and we'll help each other on."

Yara smiled appreciatively. "All right, then. I'm ready. Show us the way to Haven."

~ 16 ~

The morning sun was clear and bright as always, untainted by the strange hazy darkness that hindered its light outside of Haven's walls. Daris blinked as Tassie and Essa led him out through the front door of the clinic. Essa held lightly to his arm, as he was still a bit weak and unsteady on his feet.

"Everyone has been waiting for you," she told him, even as he caught sight of the small group of people who stood in the road before him.

"Good to see you again, Daris!" Stanner called out to him, coming close to embrace him gently.

"And you," Daris replied.

One by one, the others greeted him – the elderly Lomar, kind-hearted Nevin and Shayrie, and steadfast Brodan, who avoided Arden's gaze, either out of sheer disregard or a sense of shame at his past behavior, the archer couldn't tell. Ovard, Jair and Arden, along with Leandra and Kendie, had joined them as well, to be there on Daris' first day of truly experiencing the sight of Haven.

"This is so beautiful," Daris breathed in amazement, gazing out at the city around him. "It's so full of light! And the smell in the air is sweet."

"It's the fruit that grows in the Fountain Court," Tassie explained.

"The fruit that helped you heal," Essa told him, her voice full of gratitude.

"There is so much more to see," Stanner went on. "There is an orchard, and woods, and the gardens ..."

"But we're still clearing the land there," Brodan spoke up. "They're quite a mess at the moment."

"And the Fountain Court itself," Ovard added, seeing Arden frown slightly. "It's been named for the large stone fountain there, though we haven't quite discovered how to get it flowing again. When we do, it should be quite beautiful."

"I'd love to see that now, even without the water," Daris commented.

"Do you have the strength for that?" asked Essa.

"Just enough, I think," he replied.

"It's this way," Stanner told him, gesturing with his arm, smiling contentedly.

It was a slow procession toward the courtyard, and as they went along, Daris took in everything with silent reverence and amazement. When the large round courtyard opened up before them, Daris breathed in the sweet aroma of fruit that filled the air.

"This is the healing fruit," Essa told him, pointing to where it grew up the high surface of the lightstone walls. Tassie stood and watched them, very pleased at how well Daris' condition had improved.

"It's wonderful," Daris said softly, taking it all in. He reached out to touch the stone wall beside him, then stared in awe at his fingertips when he felt the soothing warmth.

"There is the fountain," Nevin pointed out.

The large gray fixture stood tall near the center of the open area, the cracked stonework of its base fully repaired, but silent still, with no water flowing through its three tiered levels of curving, ornately carved stone.

"We've tried pouring water into the reservoir," Ovard commented, "but it all just runs down into the ground somehow. We can't see how to get it going. Not *yet*."

"It's still very nice to look at," Daris replied, suddenly seeming very tired.

"I think it's time we took you back to the house," Tassie spoke up.

"A house?" Daris asked.

"Yes, it's all yours," Jair told him. "It only needed a bit of fixing up. It's all ready for you now."

"Thank you, all of you," Daris addressed the group. "Thank you for coming to meet me. It's so good to see you all, and to be out of that bed."

"You're still going to need rest," Essa told him firmly. "Tassie says that it will take you some time to fully regain your strength."

Daris smiled at Essa, just as Zorix stepped up before him and gazed at him curiously.

"Well, what is this?" Daris asked.

"He is a lorren," Leandra replied. "He is with me."

"Why is he staring at me, then?" Daris asked, amused.

Leandra was silent a moment, hearing from Zorix, then explained what he had on his mind. "He was also bitten by the night screamers, as we call them," she said quietly, the memory still all too fresh. "He knows what you must have been feeling these past few days; he's felt it too."

Daris nodded. "Hello, little thing. It seems you and I are quite the fortunate ones, aren't we? To have survived?"

Zorix turned to face Leandra once again, and she laughed softly. "He is very pleased with you," she told Daris. "He appreciates the way you speak to him. He understands so much more than most people think."

Daris smiled, then leaned heavily against Essa, who struggled to support his weight.

"I'm all right," he said as Tassie hurried to catch his other arm. "I just haven't got much strength left."

"That's enough for today," Tassie said firmly. "He needs to lie down."

"I'll go on ahead and open the door for you," Stanner offered, then marched down the street, not needing any response. As Daris was slowly led away from the Court, the rest of them began to disperse as well, full of joy and relief.

Jair was just turning to leave with Ovard when Gavin stepped up beside him.

"Hey," he greeted him.

"Hello," Jair replied.

"Are you doing anything now?" Gavin asked. "I'm itching to do something."

"Well, I was going to help Ovard with the old texts ..." Jair began, stopping when he saw the disappointment on Gavin's face.

"Why don't you go on with your friend for a while?" Ovard suggested. "Your teaching can wait."

"Are you certain?"

"Of course," he replied. "It will give my memory a bit of stretching, to see if I can remember the words on my own."

"All right," Jair agreed, "if you're sure."

"He's sure," Gavin said quickly, as Ovard grinned and turned away. "Where do you want to go this time?"

"To the orchard again?" Jair suggested.

"No, I want to see something different."

Jair thought a moment. "Well, Haven's Woods isn't very far. Have you been out there yet?"

"No," Gavin replied, his interest piqued. "What's out there?"

"I don't know everything that's out there," Jair admitted. "I've only been there a few times, hunting with Arden."

"Let's go and find out!" Gavin exclaimed. "Which way?" he pressed.

"Follow me!"

The boys reached the shaded forest within the hour, leaving the sound of quiet voices behind them, to where the only sounds to be heard were the melody of bird song and the breeze sneaking through feathery evergreen branches high in the trees.

Jair gazed upward to where the sun streamed in from above the deep green of the treetops, while Gavin looked around as though he was searching for something.

"What are you doing?" Jair asked. "What are you looking for?"

"Oh, I don't know," Gavin muttered as he sat dejectedly beneath a large evergreen.

Jair came and sat beside him, the rough bark of the tree firm against his back. "This isn't really what you wanted, is it?"

Gavin shrugged. "It's not what I'm used to. Back home, my friends and I had the whole city to run around in. There was always something different to see, always something different going on. This place is so … quiet."

Jair sat for a moment, considering Gavin's complaint. The air was so still, and cool in the shadows, a slight damp that Jair could feel on his skin. The fragrance of the soil that had been crushed under their feet surrounded them, and if he strained to listen, he could pick out the distant calling of some large birds. It all seemed so soothing and peaceful, but he realized how, to Gavin, it might seem dull.

"Have you had some adventures living in the city?" Jair asked him. "Will you tell me about it?"

"Tell you what?" Gavin asked.

Jair shrugged. "Anything interesting."

Gavin thought for a while, staring off through the trees. Then he grinned. "Well, there was this one time," he said, his voice full of mischief.

"What?" Jair prodded. "Tell me!"

"All right," Gavin said as he settled in to tell his tale. "One day, some of my friends and I were walking around and we came by the back door of some shop, and it was open. Well, there was no one around, so we looked in and saw a jar of snuff reed."

"What's that?" Jair asked.

Gavin stared at him, incredulous. "You don't know what that is?"

"No," Jair replied meekly.

"Well, it's this stuff that makes you feel free and happy when you chew it," Gavin explained, fully engrossed in his story once again. "And, no one was looking, so we took some of it and ..."

"You *stole* it?"

"Only a few pieces," Gavin replied defensively. "Anyhow, we took some and went off with it until we found a quiet street. We hid behind the corner of an empty building."

"And you chewed it?" Jair guessed.

"Oh, we chewed it," Gavin boasted.

"What did you do then?"

Gavin smiled. "It was so funny – everything seemed funnier, you know. We were just joking around, and my friend Dane started acting like he was King Veryn and was leading his men on the Fool's March." Gavin laughed. "I guess you would have needed to be there to see it, but it was hilarious."

Jair laughed. "I can imagine what it must have been like."

Gavin stood up, put his hands on his hips, and puffed out his chest. "All right, all of you!" he called out in a deep voice. "I am King Veryn, and I say we're going to take the city by force! All of you! Every last one of you, get ready! Let's march!" Gavin stomped around, through the trees, and Jair sat watching him, laughing, his heart light. Gavin disappeared behind the nearest tree, then hopped back into view and bowed grandly. He laughed as he sat down next to Jair again, leaning his back against the tree trunk.

"How many of your friends were there?" Jair asked, amused.

"Six, I think," Gavin replied. "It was funnier then, too. Dane was marching on top of this brick wall. But – it was so funny at the time – he lost his balance and fell off!"

"Really?"

"Yes, and we were all laughing so hard until we realized that he'd broken his arm, but even then it was hard to stop laughing. Even Dane was laughing!"

"Even though he broke his arm?"

"Yes, even then," Gavin replied. "Laughing *and* crying."

Jair pictured the scene in his mind, and couldn't help laughing about it himself.

"Have you ever done anything like that?" Gavin asked him.

"No," Jair replied, suddenly feeling sheepish. "My life was pretty dull until we set out to find Haven. I had some friends, of course," he added, "but Ovard would never have put up with me chewing snuff reed, even if I had known what it was. He's very firm about things like that."

"Is he your grandfather?"

"No, he took me in when I was really small."

"Oh," Gavin replied, nodding. "So," he went on, "those marks on your face – that's what showed you the way to Haven, like my mother has on that necklace she wears?"

"Yes," Jair replied darkly.

"What's wrong?"

"Well, I just wish I didn't have these markings, that's all. Ovard says that I have them for a reason, so I try to just forget about it. I guess it doesn't matter so much, now that we're here. There aren't so many people who will wonder why I have them, to look at me strangely."

"Is that why they put you in charge of things?" Gavin wondered. "Because of your markings?"

"Sort of," Jair replied. "There's more to it than that, I think."

Gavin's face turned thoughtful. He seemed ready to ask a question, when a voice rang out through the trees.

"GAVIN! Are you out here?"

"Uh-oh," Gavin muttered, getting to his feet. "That's my sister, Persha. Yes, I'm here!" He shouted in return. "I'd better get back," he told Jair.

"I'll come with you," Jair spoke up. "I should go back too." He followed Gavin out of the Woods and found Persha standing at the far edge of the city, facing them, her hands on her hips.

"You've done it now," she told her brother. "Mam and Dad have no idea where you are, you know. We've been looking all over for you."

"What's all the worry about?" Gavin asked with a shrug. "It's not as if anything bad could happen to me here. I can't get lost, you know."

Persha turned and started to walk away. "I'm not going to waste time arguing with you," she muttered.

"Wait!" Jair called after her, and she looked back. "It's my fault really. I'm the one who said we should come out here. I'm sorry."

Persha smiled a little. "It really wouldn't have mattered where you said to go. My brother has a tendency to sneak off without permission." She cast a harsh glance at Gavin before gesturing for him to follow her. "Come on, I need them to see that I found you. *Again.*"

Gavin half-smiled at Jair before hurrying after his sister. "I'll see you again soon."

"Sure," Jair replied distractedly. He just couldn't get it out of his mind – the image of Persha's beautiful face was stuck with him once again.

~ 17 ~

"I've never been on this side of the lake before," Ona commented, looking across its windswept surface. "Erast is so far away, I can't even see it."

"We've got a lot farther to go yet," Dursen told her. "Soon you won't even be able to see the lake neither."

"Is it really, really far?" she asked in dismay.

"Not terribly far," Brace joined the conversation. "We've already been going on for two days. It might take us another four. Five, maybe."

"To get all the way to Haven?" Ona asked.

"That's right."

"It's not so far away," she mused. "It's so strange. Haven is so close, and no one ever really talks about it. Only like it's a child's story."

"That's so very true," Dursen agreed.

"Take your time, Brace," Ronin admonished him. "Haven will be there when we get there. Don't aggravate your injuries."

Brace nodded assent as he stood among the rest of the group, looking back at the southern edge of Wayside Lake. A long, blue-gray smudge across the horizon, its constant motion was mesmerizing, for Ona in particular. Brace appreciated the sight of it, that was certain, but he did not enjoy it. The lake was tied too closely in his mind with Meriton, the city that nestled up against it. To him, Meriton meant the Wolf and Dagger Inn, and Rune Fletcher, and his own unpleasant memories rising to the surface.

No, he found no real pleasure in the sight of Wayside Lake, though he would not prevent the rest of them from getting a chance to admire it.

131

"It's so pretty," Ona commented, while Brace took the opportunity to get a drink from his canteen.

"I thought so too, when I first saw it," Dursen agreed. "And it's so big."

Ona smiled up at him, the wind pushing her straight, sandy hair into her face.

The sun was actually fairly bright today, Brace noticed, picking up a scent of lake water on the breeze. The sky was clear of any clouds, and the air was very cool. He would have expected to see red and orange leaves skittering across the dry ground, but there were no trees in the area to bear them. The land was open and rolled along lazily, though as the group continued farther south, they would need to travel through the many large stones and boulders which were scattered haphazardly across the landscape.

Brace allowed a moment to pass, then turned his back on the lake. "Is everyone ready to go on?" he asked.

"I'm ready," Dursen replied quickly. The others agreed with varying degrees of eagerness. Ona hung back a little, taking in one long, last look at Wayside Lake before turning away.

The going was steady for a time until they were forced to slow down their progress, picking their way through the rocks. Brace gritted his teeth against the ache that was spreading across his side.

"I don't remember these rocks being so big on the way through here the first time," he grumbled, working his way between two of the large boulders. All of the going in and out, over and around, was wearing on him. They had just begun their travels, and already he was doubting his body's ability to go on at the rate he'd hoped.

He glanced back over his shoulder, wanting to be sure that everyone was following him, then stepped around a large boulder that towered above his head. Attempting to step over a smaller rock, his boot slipped and his foot hit the ground, jarring his bruised ribs. He winced as pain shot up his side, and he slumped against the tall boulder. Ronin hurried up to him.

"Are you all right?" he asked in concern. "What happened?"

"I slipped," Brace gasped, holding onto his side. He took a few breaths. "Maybe you were right," he said as more faces appeared from around the other side of the large rock to peer at him in concern. "Maybe I shouldn't have tried to start out yet."

"You did well enough yesterday," Ronin pointed out. "I think we just need to slow down a little. I know you're anxious to get home, but I think that being in a hurry will do you much more harm than good."

"I agree," Brace sighed.

"Let's rest here for a while," Ronin suggested to the group. "Our guide needs a break."

No one complained about having to stop, though Dursen's face was an odd mixture of concern and disappointment – he wanted to get back home as quickly as possible, Brace knew. Almost as strongly as he did.

Brace slowly, gently lowered himself to the ground, sitting on the sparse yellow grass and patchy dry soil in the shade of the tall boulder that loomed over him.

The others joined him, glad to remove their cumbersome packs for a while and to drink some water from their flasks. Brace groaned as he stretched out his legs, his back against the boulder. He noticed Yara standing a short distance away, eyeing him in such a manner that he knew she pitied him. Not wanting to deal with any pity at this particular moment, he averted his gaze. He wasn't able to forget, though, that he was still Ronin's patient – the man wouldn't leave his side.

"Did I tell you that my wife is a medic?" Brace asked him, making forced conversation.

"No, you didn't," Ronin replied with a grin. "That's fortunate. And I'm sure she is more skilled at her work than I am."

Brace shifted into a more comfortable position. "Well, you're good enough at it," he told him. "You seem to care about people just as much as she does. Maybe the two of you can share your knowledge with each other."

"I would like that." Ronin opened the pack that sat on the ground at his feet. "On that subject, I think that now is a good time to remove your stitches."

"Already?"

"It's been six days," Ronin reminded him. "That should be long enough."

"If you say so."

Ronin smiled again. "I do." He carefully searched through his supplies, then dipped a rag into a jar of liquid and held it out to Brace. "Here," he told him. "Hold this on your lip for a while."

"What is this for?" Brace asked as he followed Ronin's instructions.

"It will numb your face," Ronin replied. "It won't take long."

Brace sat in silence with the rag pressed against his face, watching the others as they ate a bit of food or simply sat gazing into the distance. Ben and Torren were deep in conversation, while Yara slowly paced back and forth, her brown leather boots scuffing against the rocks.

"That should be long enough," Ronin spoke up. Brace took the rag away from his face as Ronin moved closer to him. "Don't worry. You shouldn't be able to feel this any more than you did when I put them in."

Brace closed his eyes and, sure enough, Ronin was finished in no time, and he hadn't felt a thing.

"Done," Ronin told him, tossing small bits of thread onto the ground and returning his tools to his pack.

"Tassie will be eager to know what that was, what you used on my face," Brace told him.

"Tassie? Your wife?"

"Yes. She'll take any medical advice or new knowledge that anyone will give her. She just soaks it all in so fast."

Ronin grew pensive. "Will we need any of this knowledge, when we are in Haven?" he wondered aloud. "Will people ever get sick or injured there?"

"That's a good question," Brace told him. "I don't really know. But it doesn't do any harm being prepared, in case the need arises. How does my face look?"

"It's healing well," Ronin replied. "I can't say whether or not you'll have a scar. But you should be looking much better by the time you get home."

"When *we* get home," Brace corrected him. "Haven will be your home as well."

"Right," Ronin agreed. "How is your side feeling?"

"It's been better, but it's been worse."

"I think we should rest a little longer."

Brace nodded reluctantly. "You're the medic. I'll follow your advice."

Ronin picked up on the regret in Brace's voice. "I'm sure your wife is missing you as much as you're missing her."

Brace managed a smile. "It still sounds odd, sometimes, for me to call Tassie my wife."

"You haven't been together long?"

"Only about four months now."

"Is she pretty?" Ona spoke up; she'd obviously been listening in on the conversation.

"*Very*," Brace told her.

"What does she look like?"

"Well," Brace began, easily picturing Tassie's face in his mind. "She has long, wavy brown hair and green eyes. Deep eyes, like she knows something no one else does. She can't hear," he explained, "so she really does see more than most people do, I think. She pays more attention."

"She can't hear?" Ona asked, surprised.

"No. But she can see what people are saying, and she can speak." Brace smiled to himself. "I think she's the best thing that's ever happened to me."

"I can understand that," Ronin agreed, winking at Lira, who sat nearby, her long gray-blue dress cascading over her bent knees. She shook her head at him, smiling.

"My flask is almost empty," she told him. "I think some of us should go back down to the lake and fill up while we're here. Will you come with me?"

Ronin cast a glance at Brace, who nodded at him. "I'll be all right. I'm not going anywhere."

"All right," Ronin agreed. "I'll come along."

"Good," Lira said as she stood, holding her flask in her hands. "Torren, will you come with us to get water?"

Torren managed to pull himself away from his conversation with Ben. "Sure, I'll come."

"Ona?" Ronin asked his daughter. "Would you like to come along?"

The girl looked around at Brace, Dursen, and Ben-Rickard, as well as Yara, who would all remain there, in the shade of the towering boulders.

"I'll stay if it's all right," she answered. "I'll be safe here."

"That's fine," Lira replied, and she, Ronin and Torren loaded themselves up with everyone's water flasks before they trudged their way back through the boulders toward Wayside Lake to fill them.

There was a bit of awkward silence as the rest of them sat, unmoving, on the arid dirt under the fading afternoon sunlight.

"I'm sorry we're taking longer than I'd planned," Brace said, loud enough for everyone to hear.

"It isn't your fault at all," Dursen spoke up. "It can't be helped."

"It's *my* fault," Yara said forcefully. "I know you told me not to blame myself, but if I hadn't said anything to my father about you, this never would have happened. You wouldn't have been hurt. It is my fault."

Brace sighed. "If it's anyone's fault, Yara, it's your father's. Can we just forget about all of that? I'm trying to. Everyone, please just let it go. I'll be fine, eventually. I've been in fights before. I'll be fine."

Yara sat, considering Brace's words, her arms wrapped around her knees, which were tucked up to her chest. Her long, braided red hair blew over her shoulder in the steady breeze.

"All right," she finally agreed, softly. "I'll try and forget about it."

"Thank you." Brace closed his eyes and leaned his head back against the boulder.

"You've been in fights before?" Ona asked him, and he looked over at her.

"Yes, but I don't think I've ever been beaten this badly."

"Why did you get into fights?"

"Well, I was a troublemaker," Brace admitted. "I probably started a few of those fights myself. Or I could have at least prevented them."

Ben sat, listening in silence, while Ona eyed Brace suspiciously, as though she suddenly wondered if she had a reason not to trust him.

"He isn't like that now," Dursen told the girl.

Ona looked at Dursen, then at Brace, and nodded. "Why did you say that you aren't strong?" she asked him. "You seem strong to me."

"Do I?"

She nodded. "You're badly hurt, but you don't complain."

"Well, complaining doesn't do any good," Brace replied.

"You make a good leader," Yara spoke up.

Brace laughed, then winced. "I'm not a leader," he told her. "In fact," he added, "Dursen is more our leader now than I am."

Dursen's eyes widened in surprise. "What? That's not supposed to be till next time ..."

"Well, you need the practice," Brace pointed out. "And I'm not exactly in the best shape right now, am I?"

Dursen fidgeted uneasily.

"You'll do perfectly fine," Brace encouraged. "You remember the way back, don't you?"

"Yes."

"That's the most important thing. Just make sure you pay attention to what everyone needs," he advised. "Food, water, rest. We'll get there."

Dursen still appeared doubtful.

"I believe in you," Brace told him. "I never would have asked you to do this if I didn't believe you could."

Finally, Dursen nodded. "All right. It can't be too much harder than it was getting to Erast, right?"

"Not too much," Brace replied.

"Tell me something about Haven," Ben-Rickard spoke into the silence that followed.

Brace looked over at him, where he sat in the shadows. "Like what?" he asked.

"Anything," Ben replied. "I've only ever heard legends about the place. I'd like to hear something that's true."

"Well..." Brace began. What to say? There was so much! "There are walls made of stone there," he went on, "that make some sort of light on their own. You can see it a little during the early morning, but it's more noticeable in the evenings. It's a ..." Brace searched for the words. "It's almost a glow," he continued. "A warm glow."

"It *is* warm," Dursen spoke up, as Ronin, Lira and Torren trudged back into sight, listening to the conversation without interrupting. "The walls are warm." His eyes had a faraway look in them, and Brace knew how much he wanted to be back inside Haven, back where it was peaceful and safe.

"They are," Brace agreed. "The light fades at night, so it's dark enough for sleep." He pulled at the cord he wore around his neck. "All but these," he told them. Ona leaned closer, interested. "These are broken pieces of stone from Haven's walls. They still put off light, even at night. It keeps the screamers away."

"Screamers?" Yara asked, disconcerted.

Brace suddenly realized that he'd forgotten to warn everyone about the fearsome creatures that came out, screeching, after dark.

"They won't be able to get near us," Dursen told them. "The light from those stones keeps them away. Ya don't have to worry about them."

"They want to keep people out of Haven," Brace explained. "The screamers do. But Dursen is right. We may be able to hear them in the distance, but they won't likely get close enough for us to even see them. They hate the light."

"That's a relief," Ben commented, trying to ease the heaviness that had settled over them.

"I'm sorry I didn't tell you all before now," Brace told everyone. "I'd honestly forgotten about those things. Like I said, we won't have any problems with them as long as we have the lightstone pieces."

Lira knelt beside Brace and handed him his flask, dripping wet. "It's good water," she told him. "It's been purified; we can all drink it."

Brace took a short swallow. "Thank you," he told Lira. "It's cold and wet – just the way I like it."

She smiled. "You're quite welcome. I believe you about the light from the stones, and I'm not afraid of the night creatures. When you went to Haven the first time, Brace, you didn't have those stone pieces, did you?"

"No," he replied. "We certainly did not."

"And you made it there. *So will we.*"

~ 18 ~

Arden wiped the sweat from his brow as he gathered another bundle of sticks and brush into his arms. Looking out over the wide, flat stretch of land that was the southwestern garden, he could see that the rest of the workers were getting weary, as he was, sweating under the midday sun. They had all been hard at work nearly half the day, and the worst of the tangled mess had already been cleared away. What was left would now require digging, to pull out the long, snaking roots.

He tossed his armload of debris onto the high, hot fire, where Ovard and Stanner kept watch over the flames. Nearly half of Haven's population was here at this overgrown patch of land; most of the others were working on clearing another of the gardens, to the northwest. Leandra and Kendie, accompanied by Zorix, were keeping busy making trips to bring water from the stream running through the orchard, keeping the thirsty workers well watered.

Arden let out a breath as he rubbed the sore places in his lower back.

"Are we just about ready to quit for the day?" Ovard asked, kicking a wayward branch back into the fire.

"I think so," Arden grumbled. "This is taking longer than I'd hoped. I really don't like stopping in the middle of anything, but I can see that we'll need to."

"Everyone has been doing their part, and they've been working hard," Ovard commented. "Haven't they?"

"They have," Arden told him. "That Brodan, though. His grumbling grates on me to the last of my patience."

Ovard grinned. "And are you a man of great patience, Arden?"

"I'm trying to be," he answered grudgingly. "Stanner is apparently a long-time friend of Brodan's," he went on. "He says that the man doesn't mean any harm, that's just his way. He tells me it's because Brodan wants everything to be the best it can be, and the best for everyone concerned. I don't know. That may be the case, but he wears on me."

"You're holding up well," Ovard encouraged him. "How about the rest of them?"

"They seem to be in good spirits," Arden told him. "That one, there ..." He pointed toward the right side of the plot of land. "What is his name?"

"Worley," Ovard remembered.

"Yes, that one. I'm not sure about him, exactly. He seems odd. I've seen him several times, daydreaming or some such thing. Sometimes it seems that he's looking at the sky, as though he's expecting to see something. I asked him about it once, and he told me that he's just so amazed by the light coming from the glassy stone walls that he can't get enough of the sight of them."

"And you think he isn't telling the truth?" Ovard questioned him. "Weren't we in awe of Haven's mysteries when we first arrived?"

"We were, yes," Arden had to admit. "Do you think I'm being overly concerned?"

"Not at all, my friend. I appreciate your insight. I prefer to give these people a fair chance, without judgment, but that does not include turning a blind eye where there is the possibility of some trouble."

Arden nodded in agreement.

"Helloooo!" a familiar voice called out from the road, a short distance behind them.

"That's Leandra," Arden said, relieved. "A perfect time to stop for the day." Stepping away from the snapping flames, he turned in Leandra's direction and lifted his hand high in greeting. Leandra and Kendie waved in return, then Arden faced the garden once again, were everyone was still hard at work.

"Break for water!" he called out. "We're stopping for the day! Job well done, everyone. You've more than earned some rest."

Cheers and sighs of relief filled the air as everyone gladly turned away from their work. There were many tired but contented faces as Leandra and Kendie came closer, pulling the small wheeled cart that Kalen had recently built.

"Here everyone, here's your water!" Kendie called out gleefully.

The flasks were doled out to their proper owners for the third time that day, and everyone was relieved at the refreshment.

"Look, it's the rainbow kitty!" Little Trystan pointed at Zorix, who bristled indignantly. "He changes color," the boy went on. "I've seen him do it!"

Leandra laughed as the anger Zorix felt turned his fur a brilliant blue right before their eyes.

"See!" Trystan exclaimed. "He changed color!"

"He does that," Leandra told him brightly. She leaned in closer to the boy and spoke quietly. "He's not very happy about being called a *cat*, though. He's a lorren, and very proud."

"A lorren," Trystan repeated in awe as Zora, his mother, took his hand and pulled him out of the way.

"Come along, Trystan. There are people waiting to get a drink."

"Adorable boy," Leandra thought aloud as Arden stepped up in front of the cart beside her, a smile growing on his face.

"Your eyes are shining," he told her softly.

"Are they?"

He nodded. "You look so happy."

"I *am* happy," Leandra replied, looking up at Arden's face. Kendie giggled, inadvertently drawing their attention.

"I'm sorry," she said, grinning. "I just really like it when you look at each other that way."

Leandra smiled at Kendie's comment as a tired and dusty Brodan approached them.

"Water?" he asked abruptly.

"Yes, of course," Leandra replied, moving out of the way so that Brodan could retrieve his flask. A quick nod was the only sign of thankfulness he gave before walking away.

Arden watched him go, his jaw clenched tightly in displeasure.

"Don't let him upset you so much," Leandra told Arden as she stepped close to him once again.

"What cause does that man have to be so contrary?" Arden demanded, while Kendie looked on in dismay.

"He's done no harm," Leandra pointed out.

"No, not directly," Arden admitted. "Still, I'm not pleased about his attitude. He …"

Arden stopped when Leandra touched her finger to his lips. "I know," she told him. "Can you let it go, for now? He's mellowed a bit, I think. Just give him time. I'm sure he's had a hard life. Being here can change anyone for the better, you know that as well as I do."

Arden's face softened a bit as Leandra moved her hand away to rest it lightly on her rounded belly. Arden placed his large hand over hers. "Our baby is getting bigger," he commented quietly.

Leandra smiled. "Don't I know it," she agreed. "Every day, it seems."

Kendie joined them, leaning against Arden's side. "I'm tired from all this walking back and forth through the city," she murmured. "Can we rest for a while?"

"That's a very good idea," Leandra firmly agreed. Arden glanced back over his shoulder toward the garden. Those who had been working were either heading home or resting themselves, talking and drinking fresh water from their flasks.

"We're done here for the day," Arden spoke up. "Are you feeling strong enough to head back to the house?" he asked Leandra, who nodded.

Arden turned toward Kendie. "Why don't you ride in the cart?" he suggested. "I can pull you."

Kendie smiled as she climbed into the back of the cart. "And Zorix?" she asked.

"Sure, Zorix too."

Zorix leaped up into the cart and rested his paws over the edge, quite content, as Leandra took Arden's hand in hers and they turned toward home.

⁓

Behind them, Ovard stood watching over the burning brush heap, waiting until every bit of flame was extinguished before he would leave.

Jair looked out at the vastly improved garden, smiling contentedly, startling a bit when Gavin appeared suddenly beside him.

"Hello there!" the older boy greeted him. "Is your work done here?"

"For today it is," Jair informed him. "It's not quite ready for planting yet."

"Neither is that other one," Gavin said distractedly. "It looked about the same as this one does when I left it."

"Are you finished there for the day?" Jair asked, a bit surprised that Gavin had shown up again so quickly.

"Sure," Gavin replied. "Can we go and do something again?" he asked. "I'm tired of working."

"I don't think so," Jair said, shaking his head. "I really need to be at the meeting we're having in a little while. We're going to report on how the work is going, and keep on with the planning for other things we'll start doing. A lot of people said they could help. I *need* to be there," he stressed, seeing Gavin's frown. "I'm sorry."

"Well, *I* don't need to be there, do I?"

"I suppose not," Jair replied.

"You're the only one here who's any fun to be around," Gavin complained. "Can't you let Ovard lead the meeting?"

"Well, Ovard says that I'm really the one who should lead," Jair explained. "He's only there to help me when I need it."

"Didn't he tell you to be a *boy* when you can, and not a man all the time?"

Jair hesitated. He really did want to go off with Gavin, and stay away from all of the responsibility that often overwhelmed him. But so many people were counting on him!

"No, Gavin," he finally spoke. "I can't. Not this time. I'm sorry."

"Oh, fine then," Gavin complained. "I can find something to do on my own."

He marched away, across the wide open land toward the streets and walls of the city, leaving Jair standing alone and feeling conflicted.

He was silent as the last of the burning brush was extinguished, silent as he cleaned himself up in preparation for the meeting; it wouldn't do to be covered in dirt and sweat when he had to stand up in front of all those people.

Each person in attendance had been working hard all day, and they were tired. Jair got right to the point, thanking everyone for their efforts and listing the few remaining tasks that still needed leadership. Ovard recorded the names of those who volunteered to fill the positions, and then everyone was dismissed to get a good meal and a long night's rest.

The Main Hall emptied quickly after the meeting, and Jair breathed a sigh of relief as he stood beside Ovard at the front of the room. All he wanted to do now was go home, eat something, and burrow into his own bed and dream. He looked up when he noticed Nevin and Shayrie approaching the long table, and he knew something wasn't right from the looks on their faces. Sleep would need to wait.

"I'm sorry to be a bother," Nevin addressed them, looking in particular in Jair's direction. "But have you seen Gavin this evening?"

Jair felt his face redden. "I did," he admitted, "just after we finished at the southwest garden. He wanted me to go off somewhere with him, but I told him I had to come to the meeting."

"You haven't seen him since then?" Shayrie asked, concerned.

"No," Jair told her. "I don't know where he went, either."

"He was told to meet us here," Nevin explained.

Shayrie sighed. "I'm so sorry," she addressed Ovard. "He's been wandering so much lately, I hope he isn't causing any trouble."

Arden, overhearing the conversation, came closer unobtrusively to listen, and Leandra followed him.

"Oh, I'm sure he isn't causing trouble," Ovard replied nonchalantly. "There isn't much harm that he can do here."

"But we have no idea where in Haven he's gone to," Nevin pointed out. "He's got to learn to stop wandering off."

"If he doesn't get back from wherever it is he's gone, when the light from the stone walls fades, he might not be able to get back home in the dark." Shayrie sounded more frustrated than worried.

"I can help you look for him," Arden offered. He turned toward Jair. "Where do you think he might have gone?"

"Well," Jair replied, considering the question. "The last two times we went off, we went to the orchard and the Woods. He may have gone to one of those places, since he knows how to get there. But he might have tried to find some new place. I don't know." He shrugged helplessly.

"Let's put together two groups," Arden suggested. "I'll lead one to the Woods and Ovard can lead one to the orchard. Three in each group should be sufficient."

"I'll go with you," Leandra volunteered, but Arden shook his head. "You've done enough for today. You need the rest." Leandra almost protested, but relented, knowing he was right.

Very few remained at the Hall, so the two groups were quickly formed, consisting of Arden, Shayrie and Berrick heading for the Woods, while Ovard, Nevin, and Jair would search the orchard.

Jair kept his thoughts to himself as they passed through the city streets during the last remaining hour of daylight. He wanted Gavin for a friend, but how could he be in two different places at the same time? How could he be Haven's leader – its *chosen* leader – and still go off at odd hours to play around?

He wished that Gavin would understand. He wasn't even certain if Gavin liked it here inside Haven, if he even wanted to be here. What would they do when they found him – *if* they found him? What would they say? What would *Gavin* say?

They hadn't gone far into Haven's orchard before Nevin spoke up. "There he is!"

Jair looked up to see Gavin sitting in the high branches of a nearby tree, eating a piece of fruit.

"Gavin!" the boy's father demanded, and Gavin startled when he saw the three of them approaching. "What were you thinking, going off like this? Get down from there!"

Gavin dropped lightly from the tree, landing on his feet.

"There wasn't anything going on that concerned me," Gavin defended himself. "What's the problem?"

"The problem is that you're always disregarding where you should be, and when," Nevin told him, grabbing his arm. "You've got to stop this."

"How did you even know where to find me?" Gavin turned an accusing stare in Jair's direction, and Jair dropped his gaze.

"That's of no concern to you," Nevin informed him. "I'm not going to put up with this type of behavior any longer. You're not only causing an inconvenience to me, but to everyone who has taken the time to come and look for you. You're not doing right by anyone."

"It was really no trouble," Ovard spoke up, attempting to diffuse the situation. "We were all glad to help."

"Just the same, Gavin," Nevin went on, "you've got to stop doing this, running off and not telling anyone where you're going. You're not a child any longer. You've got to start doing your part around here."

Gavin's jaw clenched in defiance.

"Let's just get back now, shall we?" Ovard suggested. "It will be dark soon. We're all tired; we've worked hard and had a long day. I'm sure things can be worked out tomorrow, when it's a new day and we're all freshly rested."

Nevin mellowed a bit at Ovard's words, but Gavin remained obstinate as they left the orchard behind, glancing again at Jair icily.

Well, that's over, Jair told himself. *I can forget about being friends with Gavin now.*

Ovard seemed to know what Jair might be thinking, and he put an arm over his shoulders. "Come on home, Jair," he said gently. "We will work this out."

Jair nodded, though he doubted there was anything left to work out. But he knew he could not be two people at the same time. He had to choose between being a carefree child and being Haven's Key, Haven's chosen, Haven's leader. Given the two options, the choice was clear to him. There was no going back. He had been called to Haven, he knew. He felt it in his heart, and more than anything, he felt a strong desire to fulfill his purpose. It was in his blood, he supposed, but more than that. Haven was in his heart and his mind constantly. It was as though Haven's light itself flowed through him, and he felt that he could never again be separated from it, or he would be left in complete and utter darkness.

If only Gavin could understand.

~ 19 ~

The wind whipped at their backs as they approached the base of the mountains, taking one careful step after another, preventing themselves from being pushed forward faster than they intended to go. Brace could see, as he looked up, the narrow gap where the pass cut through the high rocky peaks, and he turned toward the others.

"It's there," he called out over the wind. "I can see the pass!"

Torren stepped up beside him and leaned toward him. "Are you sure you want to do this now?" he asked in Brace's ear. "We could make camp here tonight."

Brace shook his head, shivering in the cold. "I know of a good place where we can stay for the night, just over this ridge. We'll be out of the wind." He looked at Dursen, who nodded in approval, slightly hunched over, holding his cloak tightly around himself.

Heavy gray clouds billowed overhead, hiding the sun from view. It was getting close to evening, Brace knew. If they were going to make it up and over the first mountain ridge before dark, they would need to go on now, and not waste any time discussing it. He waved everyone in closer to him so they could hear without his having to shout over the wind.

"Let's all decide now," he advised. "We either camp down here or wait until we get over this peak, where it isn't as windy. We don't have any time to waste. What do you choose?"

A moment passed while everyone looked at each other, at the darkening sky, and at the mountain itself.

"Can we get over that before it gets dark?" Yara asked.

"If we go now, we can."

"I vote for going on ahead," Ronin spoke up. "If there's less wind on the other side, it won't be so cold."

"Dursen?" Brace asked, facing him from under his hood. "What do we do? You are in charge now."

Dursen took one quick glance up at the hard gray stone before them. "I say we go on. We need to get some rest, and it's too cold and windy down here. I don't think anyone is too tired. Ona?"

"I think I can do it," the girl answered from where she stood, huddled between her parents. "As long as it's not too far."

"It won't be that far," Dursen replied. "Just over this one peak."

"Right, then," Brace spoke up. "Is everyone ready?"

"Will you be able to do this?" Ronin asked him. "How are your ribs feeling these days?"

"Much better," Brace replied. "I'll be fine."

He hoped that would be the truth. The land hadn't risen in much more than a slope since they'd left Erast – climbing around on a rocky mountain pass would be considerably more difficult, he knew. But he was feeling fairly confident that he was physically able to handle it by now. They had been traveling for six days, and he'd had almost no pain in his side for the last two.

"All right," Ronin said with a hint of doubt in his voice. "Let's go then."

Dursen led the way only after Brace gestured for him to go on ahead. Ronin, Lira and Ona followed him, then Yara. Brace went along behind her, with Torren and Ben-Rickard taking up the rear.

The mountain rock was cold and hard on their hands when they grasped it for balance, treading up the steep path. The way ahead of them was wide enough for two to walk side by side along the flat, smooth rock, free of scrub brush or brambles. The wind at their backs was like ice, though – Brace could feel it through his clothing, and he was sure the rest of them could as well.

On and on they went in silence, with the howling wind filling their ears and chilling them to the core. Brace wondered how the girl, Ona, was faring. If she was frightened, she kept it well hidden, huddled deeply beneath her wool cloak as she went along beside her father.

As they reached the steepest part of the pass, Yara was directly in front of Brace. He could see that she was struggling with her handbag, which to

Brace looked heavy and clumsy. She stumbled several times, but managed to keep going.

Brace grumbled to himself about it, then tried to distract himself. *Tassie*, he said to himself. *Just think about Tassie. I'll be coming home to her soon, at last!*

A gasp and the sound of stone clattering against stone caught his ear, and he looked up sharply. Yara was fighting to get a better hold on her bag when her boot dislodged the rock she'd been standing on, knocking it loose and throwing her off balance. As the rock ricocheted past Brace down the mountainside, Yara stumbled backward and fell, letting out a scream of fear as she and Brace collided. He felt a shock of pain in his side, but managed to keep his arms locked firmly around her waist, keeping his footing at the same time. Yara's bag bounced once, then skidded to a stop against an outcropping of rock at Brace's side.

"Are you all right?" Brace asked, holding on to her tightly. She was breathing hard and shaking.

"Um – yes. I think so," she replied, her voice trembling.

"Are you hurt?"

She thought a moment. "No, I'm not hurt. Are you?"

Brace grimaced, but standing at Yara's back, she could not see his face. "No."

Everyone had heard Yara's scream, and now they all stopped and looked in her direction from where they stood.

"Can she go on?" Ben called out, his voice carried forward on the wind.

"Yes," Brace answered, not sure if he'd been heard. He spoke into Yara's ear. "It's not much farther," he told her. "We're almost to the top of this. It won't be so hard, going down the other side. It shouldn't be so windy there, and we'll be able to rest."

"All right," she said, holding tightly to Brace's arms. "My bag!" she exclaimed. "Where's my bag?"

"It's right here," Brace told her.

"Please get it. I need it!"

"It's all right," Brace said firmly. "I'll get it, but I need to let go of you first. Are you steady on your feet?"

"Yes," Yara replied, her voice calming.

"All right then, I'm letting go." Slowly, Brace moved his arms away from Yara's waist. He pulled her heavy bag off of the ground and handed it to her, wincing.

"Thank you," she said as she took it by the handle.

"Just keep going," Brace prodded. "It's getting colder and darker."

Without another word, everyone continued on over what remained of the craggy peak, and finally, made their way carefully down the other side. The wind was indeed less fierce, blocked by the high wall of mountain, and they were able to pull their wool blankets from their packs or put on extra layers of clothing before they all huddled together for added warmth.

"I'm sorry," Yara said as everyone pulled bits of food from their packs to share. "I'm sorry I screamed. I just – I thought I was going to fall."

"You did fall," Brace pointed out, making himself as comfortable as he could on the cold, hard rock, wrapping his arms around himself. "You fell into me."

"I'm so sorry," she said again. "Did I hurt you?"

"Not enough to apologize for," he told her. "Don't worry about it."

"I just couldn't hold on to my bag," Yara rambled on nervously. "I didn't want to lose my bag. I'm sorry, I made a fool out of myself."

"Calm down, Yara," Ronin told her gently. "I think you're in a little bit of shock. Fear of falling down a mountain would do that to anyone. Just take some deep breaths to steady your nerves. And eat something," he added, offering her a piece of dried meat.

She accepted it, and ate it slowly, taking deep breaths.

"We've got a lot more mountains to climb yet, haven't we?" Torren asked.

"Yes, we do," Dursen answered truthfully.

"Isn't there something we could do, then, so Yara doesn't have to carry that bag? Can't we do something to it so she can pack it on her back?"

"I don't think we have any rope or leather ties, do we?" Ben asked.

"Will we be pitching our tents again between here and Haven?" Lira wondered aloud. "Even though we're going over bare rock?"

"That's a possibility," Brace answered, "but not very likely. Why?"

"Well, I was just thinking. We won't need the tents once we get to Haven, will we?"

"No."

"And if we aren't going to pitch our tents on the hard, uneven ground, then we could use the leather ties from our tent to make Yara's bag into a pack for her. Couldn't we do that, Ronin?"

"Of course we could do that," Ronin replied.

"You would do that for me?" Yara asked.

"It's my pleasure," Lira told her.

Yara managed a smile, though she ducked her head. "Thank you," she said quietly.

"We're not going to use our tents at all?" Ona asked, surprised and concerned.

"We're only a few days away from Haven's gate," Dursen told her. "We might not need to use our tents, if we can find out-of-the-wind places like this one to rest in."

Ronin nodded. "Yara can use our leather. It seems she's more in need of it than we are, for the time being."

In the silence that followed, the wind's high-pitched wailing could be heard high above their heads as it ran through cracks in the hard, smooth stone. Brace thought, though he wasn't certain, that he heard the sounds of night screamers mingled with the howling wind. No one around him seemed to take any notice, though. They all looked so tired and worn, their eyelids heavy, as though they could easily drift off to sleep despite the cold.

He felt the same, but there was a question playing on his mind. "Yara?" he asked quietly, hoping that no one else would take notice.

"Yes?" she asked, looking up.

"Why did you want your bag so badly?" he asked her. "What do you have in there that's so important to you?"

She hesitated, pulling the collar of her wool coat more tightly around her neck. "You'll think I'm being irrational," she muttered.

"You don't know that," Brace replied. "Try me out."

She looked at him for a moment, debating whether to tell him. "All right," she said finally. "I have some of my mother's old things in there along with my own. Two dresses, a book and some jewelry. I know, you wonder what need I'll have for those things where we're going. But I *wanted* them. I know I seemed all right about growing up without my mother, but I still miss her. These few things are all I have left of her." She looked at him again. "You probably don't understand."

151

"No, I do," he replied. "I don't have *anything* left of my mother. Only memories, and I have only a few of those."

Yara sat in silence for a moment. "Thank you," she finally told him. "For understanding."

"It's no problem," Brace replied, trying to huddle deeper inside his cloak. "Try and get some sleep."

"It's so cold," she muttered.

"It is that," he agreed. He sighed, leaning his head against the rock wall at his back. In his desire to keep his distance from her, was he being too hard? he wondered. Was he being unkind? He let out a sigh. "You can lean against me if you want," he told her. "We'll both be warmer that way."

"Are you sure I won't hurt you?"

"You won't. It's my other side that's bruised, anyway."

"Well, if you're sure it's all right."

"I'm sure."

Yara moved across the small space of rocky ground between them, leaning her side against his and resting her head on his shoulder.

"Thank you."

"It's fine," Brace muttered. It was pleasant, he thought, the feel of her nestled against him. He couldn't help but wish that it was Tassie, there with him. His side ached a little, and his head was throbbing from the cold, making him more aware that his bruises still hadn't faded. What a sight he must be, and they'd be back in Haven in a few days. What would Tassie think when she saw him? That she was right in not wanting him to go?

Well, one thing was a comfort. Whether the night screamers were out there or not, Brace knew that they wouldn't come any closer. And he was just as tired as the others were. He needed to sleep.

This is the last time, Tassie, Brace promised her in his thoughts. *I promise, this is the last time I'll leave you. I'll be home soon, and I'll never leave Haven again.*

~ 20 ~

Kendie sat down with a thump, and Leandra looked up in surprise. Zorix startled, grumbling about the noise, as he'd been trying to sleep. Kendie rested her chin in her hand, her elbow propped on the table, and she was frowning, something that she rarely did.

"What's wrong?" Leandra asked her, stroking Zorix' fur.

Kendie sighed. "I don't know."

Leandra smiled wisely. "Yes, you do. Tell me."

Zorix stood up, stretched his legs and his long thin tail, yawned, and turned in a circle before he curled up again with his back to them.

Kendie let her hand drop to the table. "Well," she said meekly, "it's about Jair."

"Jair?" Leandra asked in surprise.

"Yes. It's just ... well ..."

Leandra reached across the table and held Kendie's hand. "Tell me," she encouraged her.

Kendie smiled, then blushed in embarrassment. "I just don't like how he's always looking at Persha. I've seen him a few times, like after meetings or at work days, clearing the gardens. It's as though, when she's there, he can't even see anyone else."

Leandra laughed and shook her head. "Jair is growing up, Kendie. He's starting to notice girls, that's all."

"I know," Kendie agreed. "I just – well, I just wish he'd notice *me*."

"Really?" Kendie's comment took Leandra off guard – she'd never spoken about anything like this until now.

153

"Yes," Kendie replied. "I know I'm not tall and pretty like Persha, but – well, I guess I just thought maybe Jair would want to marry me someday, when we grow up. And," she continued with a spark in her eyes, "Persha doesn't think she *needs* a husband! I heard her say it once. She said she doesn't think she needs a man to look out for her; she can look out for herself. Besides, Jair isn't a man, he's still a boy, isn't he? Even though he's nearly thirteen?"

"I think Jair is a little bit of both," Leandra told her. "A little bit of a boy, and a little bit of a man." She smiled and squeezed Kendie's hand. "But there is something you should know. A lot of boys, when they start to think about girls differently, really take notice of the older ones at first. It isn't really love, it's just interest. Persha is sixteen, isn't she?"

Kendie nodded.

"That's what I thought. So you see, Kendie, Jair may think of Persha as a pretty young woman, but I'm sure that Persha thinks that Jair is just a child. This won't go anywhere, I'm sure. Just let Jair have his time. He will come to his senses."

"I'm eleven years old now," Kendie thought aloud. "That's not too young, is it?"

"Too young for Jair?" Leandra asked. "No, two years' difference won't matter. But ..." She tugged at Kendie's hand to get her attention. "You are still very young to be thinking about love and getting married. So is Jair. Wait a few years. Be a girl for as long as you can. You'll have to be a woman for a lot longer."

Kendie smiled and nodded in understanding as the front door to the house pushed open. Arden entered, his quiver of newly made arrows strapped across his back, his bow in hand. Zorix looked up, frowning, and deciding that trying to nap in the middle of the day was pointless, he came over to join them. Leandra turned to look at Arden, running her hand along Zorix's back.

"Did you have a good hunt?" she asked.

"Good enough," Arden replied, tiredness in his voice. "Berrick and Kalen were with me," he said as he unloaded his gear in the corner near the door, carefully hanging his bow on the wall. "That was fortunate, since I managed to take down an elk. A big one, too. It took all three of us to bring the meat back. It's being smoked now."

He turned away from the wall and looked at them. "What's been going on here?"

"Not much," Leandra replied, releasing Kendie's hand. "Just a bit of woman talk."

Arden smiled a tired smile. He stepped over to the table in his long, easy stride and sat down on the wooden bench next to Leandra, who put her arm around him.

"What sort of woman talk?" he asked. Leandra looked over at Kendie, one eyebrow raised.

"Nothing, really," Kendie told Arden. "It was about me. I've just been thinking about things, that's all."

"Ah," Arden replied, running his fingers through his chin-length blond hair. His tone of voice revealed that he was glad he hadn't been part of the conversation.

"What's it like?" Kendie asked suddenly. "Being married?"

Arden looked at her in surprise, then at Leandra.

"What's it like?" Leandra repeated. "Well, it's wonderful, really. Having someone you love to share your life with. But it's not all dreamy and flowers and kisses. Not always. Is it?" she asked, looking at Arden, waiting to hear what he would add.

"Not always," he agreed. "You need to care about the other's needs just as much as your own. Or more than your own."

"But you have someone you can tell all of your secrets to," Kendie stated. "And someone who loves you all the time, no matter what."

"To be there for you when life is hard," Leandra agreed.

Kendie smiled. "And to have a baby with."

Arden laughed softly in surprise. "Yes, that too."

Leandra laid her hand on her stomach. "The baby is moving around again," she told them. She took Arden's hand and placed it where hers had been. "Can you feel that?"

Arden was quiet for a moment as he waited intently to feel any movement. "Yes," he said at last. "I did feel it."

Leandra smiled at him, then turned and looked at Zorix. "What's that?" she asked him, then looked down at her belly.

"What is it?" Kendie asked, concerned. "Did Zorix say something?"

Leandra looked up and smiled. "Zorix can sense what the baby's feeling. He says that the baby wishes there was more room to move around."

Kendie smiled, delighted, while Arden gazed pensively at Leandra's round belly.

"Can he tell if the baby is a boy or a girl?" Kendie asked, giggling.

Zorix snorted indignantly, and Leandra laughed. "Unfortunately, no," she answered for him. "We'll have to wait for that."

A loud, deep noise reverberated suddenly through the air, startling each of them. Arden stood up quickly when he recognized the sound. "That's the gate!" he announced. "That must be Brace and Dursen. They've finally come back!"

"Kendie, go and get Tassie, she's at the clinic," Leandra told her, standing up beside Arden.

"I'll bring her to the gate!" Kendie said as she ran from the house.

Leandra took hold of Arden's hand as they went out the door in the opposite direction from Kendie. Zorix hurried on ahead of them as they passed by the still overgrown land of the southeastern garden and cut through the opening in the wall bordering one of the main streets into the city. They were the first to arrive at the large gate, which now stood wide open before them.

"It's them, isn't it?" Leandra asked. "I can't believe we're doing this again ..."

"I know what you mean," Arden agreed. It had been less than three weeks since the last time they'd heard the gate open unexpectedly. "Yes, it *is* them! I see Dursen!"

"Oh, thank goodness," Leandra breathed as several heavily-dressed figures emerged into the warmth of Haven's light. Hurried footsteps pattered down the wide road toward them, and they looked back to see Ovard and Jair, Rudge and Jayla hurrying toward them. Kendie and Tassie were farther off yet, but coming quickly to see who was entering through the gate.

"Arden!" Dursen greeted him, pulling off his hood. "It's good to see your face again!"

"Yours as well," Arden replied, clapping him on the shoulder.

"We have newcomers," Dursen announced as Jair ran up to him and stopped a few steps away, with Ovard right behind him.

"You're back!" Jair exclaimed. "We've been worried about you."

There were seven people now, standing around behind Dursen just inside the gate.

"Welcome, everyone!" Ovard exclaimed. "And welcome back!"

"Brace?" Tassie called out as she ran toward the gate with Kendie at her side. "Is Brace there?"

"I'm here." Brace reluctantly stepped forward, out from behind Ronin, so that Tassie could see him. He couldn't hide his condition from her any longer, and he desperately wanted to hold her in his arms.

"Brace!" Tassie gasped, seeing his bruised face. "What happened?" She ran to him and wrapped her arms around him tightly.

"I'm all right," Brace told her as she looked him over, not letting go of him. "We had a little trouble in Erast." He tried to smile, but he was so relieved at seeing Tassie once again, and being safe inside Haven at last, that he was too full of emotion to joke around. He held Tassie close and breathed in the smell of her hair. "I missed you," he told her, but she was wiping away her tears and didn't see.

"He's going to be fine," Ronin spoke up, and Ovard stepped forward to shake his hand in greeting.

"Welcome," Ovard said once again. "Have you come from Erast?"

"I have," Ronin replied. "We all have. This," he said, gesturing, "is Torren, Ben-Rickard, Yara, my wife Lira and my daughter Ona. My name is Ronin. I was able to look after Brace for a bit before we left. He is only bruised, it's nothing more serious than that."

"Thank you for your kindness. My name is Ovard, and this is Jair, Arden and Leandra, Rudge and Jayla. And Tassie, Brace's wife."

A few faces peered around the walls of Haven's main streets, but no one else felt brave enough to come all the way to the gate, or felt it wasn't their place to intrude.

"Who are those people?" Dursen asked in surprise when he saw them.

Ovard smiled. "We've had some excitement of our own here while you were away."

"Where did they come from?" Brace asked, taking note of them. "How did they get here?"

"Don't worry about all of that right now," Leandra told him as Arden moved aside to close the gate. "You all look like you could use some rest."

Tassie clung to Brace's side as the group followed after Ovard, who led them down the main road into the city. When they came to the point in the road where they would separate, Tassie gently pulled Brace toward home, leaving the others to go on and find a place of their own to settle into. Brace caught Yara's eye as she went on with the rest of the group; she seemed reluctant for them to part ways, but Brace was too tired and sore to acknowledge her. She would be fine with the others.

"There are many empty homes," Ovard was telling everyone. "You can choose any of them that you like."

Brace ignored what Ovard was saying; it didn't concern him in the slightest. He kept his eyes on Tassie's face, even as she looked up at his. Leaving the group behind, she led him down the familiar road leading to their front door.

"Are you sure you're all right?" she asked him. "Your face..."

"It looks worse than it feels."

"What happened to you, Brace? I've been so worried. You've been gone so long."

Brace sighed. "Can we talk about this later? I'm exhausted."

"Of course," Tassie replied. "Do you want to go straight home?"

"I think Dursen can handle the meeting with Ovard for me. He did well enough bringing all of us back here."

"And he can lead the missions from now on," Tassie stated firmly.

Brace managed a laugh. "Yes, he certainly can do that."

~

Tassie insisted that Brace not do anything for himself that evening. She examined his bruises, made him hot tea to drink, and helped him out of his dirty clothing, reacting in surprise and dismay when she saw more bruises on his side. But he didn't try to explain, and she didn't ask. She knew he would tell her when he was ready.

Brace did not see anyone else after coming home, other than Leandra and Jair, when they stopped in briefly to see how he was. Jair was concerned about Brace's appearance, but glad to have him back; Leandra hugged him gently and told him to get some rest, and they would see him again soon.

Tassie made soup for them to eat, refusing to let Brace do anything to help her. Brace felt useless as he sat at the table, feeling the throbbing ache in his side. He said nothing, shifting in his seat to try and ease his muscles. Tassie did not speak a word as she heated the soup and brought it to the table in small, steaming bowls.

"Thank you," Brace told her, resting his hand on hers.

She managed a hint of a smile in reply as she sat down at the other side of the table. Tassie was often a quiet person, Brace knew that well enough. But this silence felt wrong. She was tense, Brace could see that. She was keeping her thoughts to herself, just below the surface. Mercifully, Brace thought. Exhausted as he was, talking about what was already obvious to the both of them would have been too much to bear. Instead, he was left with this heavy silence.

Tassie hesitated before picking up her spoon and taking her first bite of soup. She seemed to be feeling the tension as well, but was at a loss as to how to break it. She seemed to be waiting for Brace to say something, anything, but he didn't know where to begin.

He tapped his spoon on the side of his bowl absently as he searched for something to talk about.

"You saw all of the people we brought back?" he began when Tassie looked up at him.

She nodded. "I did," she replied. "Your mission was … successful."

Brace nodded. "It was, at the end." He was struck with a realization. "If I hadn't gotten injured, I don't think we would have brought anyone back."

Tassie frowned a bit, waiting for Brace to explain.

"Ronin and Lira took care of me," he went on. "And their daughter Ona. Ben and Torren helped a little. If I hadn't been hurt, Dursen and I would have left, just the two of us. We hadn't really been able to talk to anyone about Haven while we were there, not until we were staying at Ronin's home."

Tassie nodded slowly as understanding sunk in. "But there was another," she pointed out. "You mentioned five people, but you brought back six."

"Oh, yes," Brace replied. "That's Yara. She joined us on the way out of town." He left it at that, bringing another spoonful of soup to his mouth.

Again, Tassie nodded.

"They are good people, all of them," Brace told her. "We'll be glad to have them here, Tassie. Ronin has medical training," he continued, hoping to catch her interest. He saw in Tassie's eyes that he had succeeded, at least a little.

"The two of you can share knowledge," he went on. "I already told him about you. He would like to talk with you, if that's all right."

"I would like that," she replied, her voice less strained. "Thank you."

Brace grinned in response, a smile that now came more easily. "Dursen did well enough getting us back over the mountains," he said casually. "He will do well enough from now on, I think, leading the missions."

Tassie nodded appreciatively.

"But you have new people here," Brace added, recalling the faces he'd seen peering down the road toward the gate. "Who are they? Where did they come from?"

"They are from Danferron," Tassie replied. "They came on their own, shortly after you left. Shayrie has a small map of her own, showing the way here from there."

"Shayrie?"

"Her ancestors were remembrance keepers. She brought others with her, but you will meet them all soon enough," she told him, taking another bite of soup. "Have you had enough to eat?"

Brace glanced down at his soup bowl, which was all but empty. "I have," he told her. "It was perfect. Thank you."

"I think you should get some sleep, then. You look so tired."

Brace nodded in agreement. "I think you're right."

Tassie cleared away the soup bowls and spoons while Brace got himself into bed – the first thing Tassie had let him do on his own. He had just gotten seated on the bed, pulling the covers over himself, when Tassie appeared in the open doorway.

"Are you all right?" she asked.

"I am," he replied. "Thanks."

"I was thinking I would just go over to the clinic for a moment," she told him. "I think I have something there that will help with your bruises. I won't be gone long."

"I'm fine, Tassie. Go ahead, on to the clinic. I'll be all right on my own for a few minutes."

Tassie smiled briefly. "I'll be back in a moment."

Brace laid all the way back onto the bed as Tassie went out the front door. How soft the bed was! Had it always felt this way? He sighed in relief. He was surprised that he'd forgotten how it felt, how he'd taken it for granted. All of it – everything about *home*. The air was warm, and a faint light cascaded in through the open window. There was no icy cold here, no wind howling across jagged rock. In fact, the only thing Brace could hear at that moment was the sound of his own breathing as he lay his head on his pillow.

He had almost drifted off to sleep when he heard Tassie's footsteps coming across the floor. "You're back," he said when he saw her standing in the doorway.

"I found what I was looking for," she told him. "Are you feeling all right?"

"More than all right," he replied as she came to sit on the bed beside him. "I'm sorry I was gone so long."

Tassie shook her head, smiling a little. "That doesn't matter now. The only thing that matters now is that you're back, and you're safe."

"Right," Brace agreed tiredly as Tassie slid under the bedcovers, still wearing her dress, and lay close at his side. "I hope you weren't too worried," he said as her long brown curls fell over his shoulder, and she gently lay her arm across him.

"It's all right now," she told him. "Just go ahead and get some sleep. We can talk again in the morning."

Brace hardly had time to nod in response before he closed his eyes and slept.

When he awoke, the room was dark; no light came in through the windows. He was confused, disoriented for a moment before he realized that he was at home in his own bed, in Haven, and it was fully night. He wondered briefly what had woken him when he heard a soft noise coming from the far side of the room. Was someone crying?

"Tassie?" he spoke into the darkness. "Fool," he scolded himself. "She can't hear you." He sat up in the bed and fumbled in the dark until he managed to light the lamp on the table beside the bed. A soft warm light bounced across the walls of the small room. Tassie was sitting beside the window with her back to him until she noticed the light, then turned to look. She had been crying, Brace could see that well enough.

"What's wrong?" he asked her. "Come and tell me. I'm fine, really, Tassie. I'll be all right," he said as she came back to the bed. At some time in the night she had changed into her nightgown, Brace noticed, but he must have been sleeping soundly and not noticed her moving at his side.

"I'm sorry I woke you," Tassie sniffled as she left the window to sit again on the bed beside him. He gently pushed her hair back away from her face.

"Don't worry about me," Brace scolded. "Tell me why you're crying."

"It's a lot of things, really," she said, wiping at her eyes. "I've missed you, yes, and worried about you. But it's more than that. Brace, when those people got here from Danferron, one of them had been bitten by a night screamer. He was a lot worse off than Zorix was, and I didn't know if he was going to live or die. I've been at the clinic every day with him and Essa, the woman who loves him. She's been so distraught. So fearful for him, for Daris. He's all right now, thankfully, but I've just had to try and forget about how worried I was about you. I had to keep going for Daris and Essa; everyone was relying on me, I couldn't let them down. I just didn't realize how tired I was, how afraid I was."

"Afraid of him dying?"

"Well, yes," Tassie answered, "but I also saw how fearful Essa was when she thought about losing Daris, and it made me think about what it would be like if I lost you ..." She shook her head. "I just couldn't ... And then when I saw your bruised face ..." She looked away.

Brace touched the side of her face, and she turned to look at him. "I'm sorry," he told her. "I wish I'd been here to help you. You're strong, Tassie, but you don't have to be strong all the time. And you don't have to be strong alone. No one can be as strong alone as they are when they have help."

Tassie wiped away a tear and smiled. "You've learned a lot while you were gone," she told him, a bit of the familiar spark returning to her eyes. She glanced down at his bruised side. "When will you tell me what happened to you?"

Brace sighed. "I'll say this much – I learned never to invite loggers' daughters to come away with you without explaining things to the father first."

Tassie nodded in understanding. "I see." She rested her cheek on Brace's shoulder. "I'm sorry."

She couldn't see his face, he knew, so she wasn't expecting a response. He lay down on the bed and put his arms around her, holding her close until he could tell by the sound of her breathing that she had fallen asleep.

~ 21 ~

There were so many new faces, so many new names to remember! A gathering was held in the Fountain Court rather than the Main Hall. There was more room there for everyone to get acquainted. The small group of people who had come back with Brace and Dursen was warmly welcomed, even by those who had arrived in Haven while they'd been away.

Odd, Brace thought. *It's as though they've been here for a year, instead of almost a month.* Men and women, old and young, even children – one of them *very* young. Haven seemed to be a different place than it had been when he'd left. Not terribly different – just more crowded. Brace would have felt like just as much of an outsider there as Ben and Torren must be feeling, if Tassie hadn't been at his side, or if he hadn't seen Arden's face among the many others.

There were many introductions on both sides, but Brace wasn't really trying to keep up. With time would come familiarity, he knew. There was no hurry.

"Oh, Brace," Tassie's voice intruded on his thoughts. "I want you to meet Essa and Daris."

Brace looked to see two smiling faces standing before him. "It's good to meet you, Brace," Daris told him, shaking his hand lightly. "Tassie is a very good medic; she saved my life."

Brace could see Tassie out of the corner of his eye, shaking her head.

"Yes, she really did," Essa agreed. "And she's a wonderful person. You must be so glad to have her as your own."

165

Brace nodded, smiling at Tassie and taking her hand in his. "I'm very glad. And I'm glad you're feeling better, Daris. Tassie told me what happened. You're very … fortunate." He had thought to say *lucky*, but Ovard's insistence that no one's life was governed by luck had stuck with him. Brace still wasn't completely convinced of that, but he was beginning to wonder if Ovard could be right.

When the gathering began to dwindle, everyone returning to their homes or activities, Brace noticed Yara lingering nearby. She was eyeing him, and he knew she wanted to speak to him. She was hanging back, though, seeing Tassie beside him, a fact for which he was grateful. Still, it would be inconsiderate of him to not introduce them, and now seemed to be the best time for just that.

"Tassie," Brace said, giving her hand a squeeze. "I think there's one more person you should meet."

"All right," she replied as Brace led her in Yara's direction. Yara smiled awkwardly as they approached her.

"Tassie, this is Yara," Brace introduced her. "Yara, this is my wife, Tassie."

"Hello," Yara greeted her with a friendly nod.

"It's good to meet you," Tassie replied. "I hope the journey here from Erast wasn't too difficult. I know how hard it is to climb over the mountains."

Yara glanced at Brace before answering. "Well, it could have been worse," she answered. "Brace didn't tell you anything about it?"

"No, nothing," Tassie told her. "He hasn't really said anything about the whole journey. I think it's just too soon, he hasn't really had the time." She looked questioningly at Brace, but he shook his head.

"There's nothing more to say, Yara. We went to Erast and brought back who would come with us. That's all there is to say. Leave the past where it belongs. You're here now. It's a new start."

She smiled again and gazed down at her hands for a moment before looking up again. "You're right. Thank you. I'm glad to meet you, Tassie. I hope that we can be friends."

"Of course," Tassie replied.

When Yara had gone on her way, Tassie looked at Brace with a question in her eyes.

Brace wanted to leave the past in the past, just as he had told Yara to do, but Tassie deserved to know more than he'd told her. "Yara blames herself for what happened to me," he explained. "She's the *logger's daughter.*"

Tassie frowned for a moment, then realized what he meant. She nodded. "Oh, I see."

"It's over, though," Brace told her. "I just want to forget about it."

Tassie wrapped her arm around Brace's elbow. "I'm sure it will be easier for everyone to forget once your bruises fade."

Brace smiled ruefully. "You're right there," he agreed. "Please keep me away from the mirror until then."

The informal gathering had ended quickly, much to Brace's relief. It wasn't until nearly everyone else had gone that Dursen finally came over to speak with Brace.

"Thank you," he told him.

"For what?"

Dursen shrugged. "For everything. For letting me come with you. For teaching me, and giving me a chance to lead. I never done anything like that before. I never thought I could do it. Now, I believe I could do it again, even without help."

Brace smiled. "I know you could."

Their conversation was brief and to the point – Brace couldn't speak for Dursen, but *he* was still tired. Deeply tired. Tassie picked up on it easily, and she led Brace back to the house for a light meal before allowing him to get back into bed, where he quickly fell asleep once again.

～

He awoke slowly, gently, in the full light of day. His body and mind were still heavy with sleep as he rolled onto his back and looked around the room. The fog slowly cleared from his head, and he wondered how long he'd slept. It had been light when he fell asleep, and it was light still. Maybe two hours, he thought. But he felt rested, finally.

When he had dressed and wandered into the front room, Tassie smiled at him. "Hello again," she greeted him from where she sat at the table.

"Hello," Brace replied, running his hands through his hair. "Thank you for letting me sleep. I feel much better. Can I help you with dinner this time?"

"Dinner?" Tassie asked, amused. "No. Breakfast, maybe."

"What?" Brace asked. "Breakfast?"

"You slept a day and a half away," she told him. "You must have needed it."

"A day and a half? Really?"

"Really, but it's all right. You haven't missed anything. We're just carrying on, though people have been asking about you."

"They have? Who?"

"Ovard and Jair, mainly. Arden, Leandra, Dursen." She paused. "Yara."

Brace scratched at his head, a bit surprised. "Yara? Really?"

Tassie nodded wordlessly, but he could easily read her face.

"There's nothing between, us, Tassie," he told her firmly.

She studied him for a moment. "I know that," she finally answered, her voice quiet.

"I was there for her, that's all," Brace explained. "On the way back from Erast, she almost fell when we were climbing the mountains, and I caught her." He shrugged. "She needed a friend, and I was one. That's all it is, Tassie, I promise."

Tassie's smile was slight, but her eyes were honest. "I know it is. I just can't help wishing that I had been there with you in her place. She had your company when I was missing it."

"I'm sorry."

Tassie shook her head. "I'm being unfair," she said, standing up. "*I'm* sorry. Can we forget this? I feel silly …"

Brace sat back in his chair. "Don't feel silly. I missed you too."

She smiled again, then remembered. "There is a meeting with Jair today," she told Brace. "I think we should go, if you're feeling well enough."

"Well, I'm sure I feel better than I look."

She tilted her head at him, a silent reprimand.

Brace grinned. "I'm fine. We can go, but can I get something to eat first? I'm *empty*."

⤳

Brace was overwhelmed at the many warm greetings he received when he arrived in the Main Hall with Tassie later that morning. Hugs, light claps on the back, and many expressions of how glad they were that he'd gotten enough rest and was up and around again. A few even told him that his bruises didn't seem quite as dark as before, but he didn't quite believe *that*.

The meeting that day mainly concerned the gardens, and the seeds that Brace and Dursen had brought back with them. Two of the three plots of land had been completely cleared and were ready for planting. Dursen, Rudge and Kalen were put in charge of overseeing the planting and care of the gardens. Tassie surprised Brace by speaking up, sharing her opinion that Haven needed chickens, or rather, the eggs that they would produce. She pointed out that they couldn't wait until the crops were ripe before they had decent meals to eat. Many agreed with her, and Nevin suggested that they have a few goats as well, for the milk.

Daris agreed, pointing out that the goats would be able to eat the brush that had overgrown the remaining garden, making clearing an easier task. Ovard, as always, deferred to Jair to make the decision, something that the boy was getting used to, though he still took it as a serious responsibility.

There was money enough to spare for goats and chickens, it was determined, though there remained the question of who would go for them, as well as the task of bringing them back over the mountains.

"Goats won't be much of a problem," Dursen spoke up. "I sure don't know about chickens, though."

"I really think we need to try," Leandra joined the conversation. "There are even more people living here now. We need to be able to provide for ourselves."

"We can't keep going out and buying things either," Brodan pointed out in his usual gruff manner. "Eventually, the money is going to run out. We should start trying to trade for what we need, or sell some of our excess crops, if we have any to spare."

Brace was caught off guard by the man's directness. Who *was* he, to speak so boldly? He couldn't help but notice the way Leandra laid her hand on Arden's arm, or the way the archer's face had clouded over with displeasure.

"That's a good idea too," Jair spoke up quickly. "But someone's going to have to leave again. We don't have any crops to trade or sell right now, but we can get the chickens and the goats. Dursen, can you go this time, like we planned?"

"I can," he answered. "I have a bit of skill with goats and such."

"I know you just got back …"

Dursen shook his head. "I don't need much time before I can go again. Brace showed me the way. It's getting awful cold out there, though."

"All the more reason to go sooner rather than later," Ovard pointed out. "It's getting close to winter out there – we don't want to you to cross the mountains in the snow."

"Right enough," Dursen agreed. "But where exactly should I go? Can't really buy goats there in Spire's Gate. The animals there are needed by the farmers."

"Go to Meriton," Ovard advised, though there was reluctance in his voice. "It's the nearest large city, with traders coming in from the Royal Road almost daily. You should be able to find anything you need there."

"But someone should go with him, if he's going to bring back animals," Rudge asserted. "That's too much work for one person."

He was right, Jair knew, but who would be the one to do it? There were many more people now to choose from, but who would be willing to leave Haven? Most of them had just arrived, after all.

Jair's eyes fell on Gavin's face, seated in the back, looking bored and distracted. Didn't he say that he missed having some excitement in his life? He was young, but he could help Dursen, couldn't he?

"What about Gavin?" Jair asked aloud, and the boy was suddenly paying attention.

"What?" he asked in surprise. "You want me to do *what?*"

"Dursen needs the help," Jair told him. "I think you could help him." He looked at Gavin's parents. "If that's all right with you."

Nevin and Shayrie faced one another for a moment, then silently agreed; Jair could see it on their faces.

"I think it would be a good idea," Nevin spoke for the both of them.

Gavin remained silent; Jair was grateful that at least he had the sense of respect not to argue right in the middle of a meeting.

When the important matters were decided on and settled, everyone was dismissed. Dursen and Gavin would leave in three more days. Jair hung back, at Ovard's side, as the Main Hall began to empty. He was unsure about facing Gavin – would he be offended? Would he be angry?

If Ovard was aware of Jair's uncertainty, he didn't show it. Eventually, knowing that he could not hide in the Main Hall for what remained of the day, Jair made his way toward the main doors, where Gavin stood waiting, his face solemn.

Jair tried to smile at him. "I hope you're not angry," he began. "I thought you'd like to have something to do."

"I understand, sort of," Gavin replied with a shrug. "I don't know about the goats, and crossing the mountains again, and all, though."

"I think you can do it," Jair told him, "or I wouldn't have asked if you could."

"You're not just trying to get me away from here?" Gavin asked, an edge of bitterness in his voice. "To keep me out of trouble, like my parents are?"

"No, it's not that," Jair replied feebly.

"Sure," Gavin remarked as he turned away. "If you say so."

Jair frowned in dismay, wondering if he'd made a wrong decision. When he felt Ovard's hand on his shoulder and saw the look of admiration in his eyes, the feeling dwindled a bit. "You made the right choice, Jair. I believe this will turn out for the best."

"But I think I've lost him as a friend," he objected. "I know I needed to keep up with my responsibilities, and Gavin can be a bother, but I liked having him as a friend. That's not wrong, is it?"

"Not at all," Ovard replied, then thought a moment. "Gavin may be older than you are, but I think you have more wisdom. He will be more of a friend, I think, if he gains some wisdom of his own."

"Do you think he will, while he's on the trip with Dursen?"

"I certainly hope so," said Ovard pensively. "But I think, more than anything, the boy needs to decide whether he wants to stay here, or to leave. The world has too much of a hold on him, I think."

Jair could only nod in silent agreement.

~ 22 ~

Life carried on, as it often does. Dursen and Gavin departed on their quest for goats and chickens, after having met with Ovard and Gavin's parents. Jair was not sure exactly what was said between them, but when the two of them left, Gavin was very somber.

Jair tried to put on a brave face for the rest of them – they needed him to be *here*. He couldn't let his mind wander away with Gavin. And Dursen may have left again, but Brace was still here, and Arden and Leandra, and Ovard, and all of them. So many of them! Faces and names that he knew by heart, and those that he still had to be reminded of. And whether he was prepared for it or not, they were all looking to *him* for guidance.

Fortunately, many important decisions had been made at the last meeting, and now quite a few people had tasks that they themselves could oversee without Jair's direct involvement. The newest delegated responsibility fell to Dorianne, who had volunteered her time to head up a school of sorts for the growing number of children living in Haven.

Today, for the first time, Kendie, Ona, Jair and little Trystan gathered together in one of the larger, formerly unclaimed buildings that nestled up against the walls surrounding the Fountain Court. Ovard had been firm that Jair participate in the classes, something that he really did not mind doing. This felt much more familiar to him than leading meetings and teaching Ovard to read Haven's ancient language, something that he still found strange that he could perfectly understand.

Persha had insisted that, at sixteen years old, she no longer needed any schooling. She would now spend her days training with Arden, learning how to use the bow. The girl had already developed a sense of respect for

Leandra, who had, even so far along in her pregnancy, taught her some self-defense skills.

Dorianne wasted no time in informing the children that she was not a "real" teacher, and that this school would not be like the others that they may be familiar with. Many of the things that were taught in other schools, she told them, they would have no use for here. She wanted Haven's school to help them learn about things that pertained to their new life in Haven.

"I never been to school yet," Trystan informed her.

"Well, that's fine," she replied with a friendly smile.

"Neither have I," Kendie admitted. "I used to work at an inn."

"Can you read?" Dorianne asked.

"Only very little."

"Well, we'll have reading lessons, then, for the two of you. Jair? Will you teach us all some of Haven's language as well?"

"I can do that," he replied. "I've been teaching Ovard and Jayla for a while."

"Very good! We can have reading, and language, and working with numbers; I think that's important anywhere. Is there something that any of you have special knowledge about, that you can share with us? Or something that you'd like to know about?"

Trystan shrugged while the others looked at each other for a moment.

"I would just like to know where everything is here, and what everything is," Ona finally spoke up. "The rest of you have been here longer. I haven't really gotten to see anything."

"Well then," Dorianne suggested, "why don't we begin our first class with a tour of the city? What do you think Ona should see first?"

"The orchard!" Kendie replied enthusiastically. "That's the next best thing to seeing the Fountain Court, and you've already been there, haven't you?"

"I have," Ona replied. "The very first day we got here."

"Shall we all go and see the orchard, then? Maybe Jair can tell us something special about it."

"I don't know if there is anything special about the orchard," Jair admitted. "So far, it seems like they are just ordinary trees. But the fruit tastes really good!"

~

Brace watched as the group of children, accompanied by Dorianne, made their way through the courtyard. He nudged Tassie, who stood beside him, picking more red fruit from the vines that clung to the stone walls. "I wonder where they're off to."

"Learning about one thing or another, I'm sure," Tassie replied. She placed two more large pieces of fruit into the cloth bag that Brace held open for her. "I think that's plenty for now."

Brace nodded as he twisted the bag and tied it shut. Tassie had used up a fair amount of the juice she had stored, giving it to Daris as he'd been healing from the night screamer wound. She had also insisted that Brace have a bit of it himself the first few nights after he'd gotten back, saying that it would help speed up his recovery. She was right, of course. Much of the ache in his side had ceased altogether, though the discoloration on his face had remained the same. That would need to fade in its own time, they had realized.

Ronin had appreciated the time he was able to spend with Tassie; he learned far more from her than he knew she could ever learn from him. Daris was completely healed now, and he and Essa were spending so much time together, everyone was sure that a wedding would not be too far in the future.

"Are we heading back now, then?" Brace asked Tassie as he held the bag in one hand, reaching for Tassie with the other.

"Yes," she replied, slipping her hand into his. She glanced back over her shoulder where a small group of men were persistently looking over the stone fountain. Rudge and Nevin were filling Ben-Rickard in on all the work that had been done, and everything they had tried in order to get the water flowing again. The fountain had become so important to them, as it had to everyone – a beautiful structure that, if they could get it working, would be a symbol of Haven's restoration. An easily seen reminder of the glory that Haven had once held, and would again, if they all worked together in reviving the beauty that lay hidden under ruin.

None of the men at the fountain noticed that they were leaving; they were all too engrossed in their task.

"Do you think they'll ever get it working again?" Tassie wondered. "I would so love to see it."

"They won't give up easily," Brace replied. "It really amazes me still," he said after a moment of thoughtful silence.

"What does?"

"How they all just get right down to work. Everyone, working at something. I've never seen so many people who are willing to do so much hard work, coming together like this for the same purpose."

"Of restoring Haven?"

"Yes. No matter who they are or where they've come from, everyone just comes together so easily. Ben-Rickard is one of the newest arrivals, and look at him. He wants to help out with anything that he possibly can."

"He has a good heart," Tassie mused. "Doesn't he?"

"He seems to. So does everyone who came back with us from Erast." Brace shook his head. "I didn't think I was going to be bringing anyone back from that place. It couldn't have worked out better, could it?"

"Better?" Tassie asked. "It could have gone better, yes. But it could have been worse."

"It could have," Brace agreed, knowing that she wasn't talking about the people, but the journey itself. About what had happened to him while he was away.

Tassie gazed ahead, her long brown hair falling in soft waves over her shoulders. Brace tugged at her hand to get her attention.

"You're thinking about something," he told her. "What is it?"

She hesitated a moment. "Were you afraid, Brace?" she finally asked. "I know that you've been through a lot of hard times, but do you still get frightened? When the men came after you ...?"

"Sure," Brace replied. "I was afraid, but I remember being more angry, really. There was nothing I could do to make them listen, to make them hear me. But I don't think it would have helped. They already had it set in their minds to give me that beating."

He shrugged, seeing Tassie's frown.

"You're doing that again," she told him.

"Doing what?"

"Not really talking."

"What happened, happened, Tassie. I don't see the point in talking about it."

"I don't mean that you need to tell me exactly what happened to you," Tassie challenged. "What I mean is, I care about what's on your heart."

"I just don't like bringing up what's past," he pointed out. "I'd rather look forward than back."

Tassie softened, hearing the frustration in Brace's voice. "Our past makes us who we are in the present," she said quietly. "Whether it's years past or something that just happened, it stays with us."

Brace shook his head. "I'm *fine*, Tassie. *Really*. I see what you're saying, but I'm strong enough to take what happened in Erast. There's nothing left to say. I just want to go on and do something new. I'm not planning on going on any more searching missions, remember? There's got to be something important that I can do right here inside Haven."

Tassie regarded Brace in silence, and he began to feel uncomfortable. At times like this, Brace felt like she could see right through to his heart and his mind, as though she was searching for something new, something that he hadn't told her.

Finally, she smiled. "You can do something important," she told him. "Today, you can help me get the juice from this fruit into jars."

Brace smiled back, relieved. "Yes, I can do that."

A sudden shouting startled Brace, and he flinched.

"Everyone, everyone! You've all got to come and have a look at this!" Kalen rushed into the courtyard from the southwest entrance.

Brace pulled Tassie to a stop, nodding in Kalen's direction.

"What is it?" Rudge asked in surprise. "What's going on?"

"It isn't a bad thing," Kalen explained breathlessly. "It's just unexpected."

"Well, what is it?"

Kalen shook his head. "You've got to see it for yourself."

Brace glanced at Tassie. "He want us to see something. Shall we follow them?" He nodded toward Rudge, Nevin and Ben, who were leaving the courtyard after Kalen.

"Of course," Tassie replied quickly.

Kalen lead them back toward the southwest garden, which he explained that he had gone to look after, but he would not tell them any more than that. They reached the plot of land very quickly, and it became quite obvious what had gotten Kalen so excited.

Green shoots of leaves were coming up out of the soil at regular intervals all throughout the growing area, each of them a good five inches tall.

"How long ago did we plant these?" Rudge asked in surprise.

"Three days ago," Kalen replied. "I didn't expect to see anything growing here yet; I only came to water the soil."

"This is amazing," Tassie said quietly as she knelt on the ground to touch the leaves.

"It is," Kalen agreed. "At this rate, we'll be able to harvest the potatoes in less than a month."

Tassie smiled up at Brace, who stood behind her, just as bewildered as the rest of them.

"Isn't it wonderful?" she asked.

"It's unbelievable," he replied.

"No," Ben spoke up. "Not unbelievable. If this could happen anywhere, it would happen here. When you think about it, it just makes sense, doesn't it?"

Everyone was quiet as they took in Ben's words. He was right – there was water here that gave strength, fruit that healed injuries, and stones that gave off light. Why not soil that caused crops to grow quickly?

Tassie stood and smiled. "Dursen will be quite surprised when he comes back, won't he?"

"You can be sure of that," Brace agreed.

Would there be no end to the mystery of this place, Brace wondered? He gazed up at the clear blue sky and the towering evergreens in the distance, and felt the comforting warmth in the air. He hoped there would be no end, he thought, to making new discoveries of the miraculous nature of Haven. His life had taken him so many places, but never had he thought it possible that a place like this could exist!

I'm sure I don't deserve all of this, he thought. *I don't deserve to be here, and I don't deserve someone as wonderful as Tassie. If I was meant to be a part of life here, as Ovard believes, I can only wonder why? I could never do enough good here to make up for all of the mistakes I've made.*

Well, whatever the reason – chance or fate, Brace was more than grateful as he took Tassie's hand.

"Come on," he said. "Let's go tell Jair about this. He'll want to know."

~ 23 ~

Gavin hefted the weight of his pack on his shoulders as he gazed out across the wide, open landscape. He couldn't believe he was out here again, especially so soon after having arrived in Haven. He looked back over his shoulder at the high, rocky mountains that he and Dursen had spent the last few days crossing. Cold, dark, dreary things. How could Jair have done this to him? Weren't they supposed to be *friends*? And he was older than Jair! How could it be that he was expected to take *orders* from him?

No one understood him. No one cared about what he wanted. What if he decided he didn't want to come back? He could just stay in Meriton. No one needed him, there in Haven. Maybe they would be happier without him...

"Are ya coming?" Dursen called from farther ahead.

Gavin sighed and turned toward him. "Yes, I'm coming."

He trudged along dejectedly for a long while, with Dursen close at his side. Neither of them spoke, and while Gavin kept his eyes on the ground, he could see Dursen alternately looking all around him, and glancing at Gavin as though debating whether or not to try and speak to him.

Finally – Gavin wasn't sure how many hours later – Dursen stopped and removed his pack, letting it drop to the ground.

"Let's stop here for the day."

Gavin looked around. Dry, flat land, low brush. No trees.

"Why here?" he asked. "It looks the same as every place else."

"It feels like the right time for it," Dursen replied. "We need to get ourselves ready for dark."

"What do we need to do?" Gavin asked begrudgingly, dropping his own heavy pack.

"Gather brush to make a fire," Dursen replied, "and get the tent set up."

Gavin nodded.

"Why don't you bring an armful of branches and such?" Dursen suggested. "I'll do the same."

"Fine," Gavin replied, wandering toward the nearest bush and struggling to break branches off with his bare hands.

"How on this earth do you expect me to get any firewood?" he demanded. "This is impossible to break off."

Dursen looked up from his work.

"Just break off the twigs and such," he called out in response. "And pick up anything you find laying around."

Gavin grumbled inwardly as he snapped smaller twigs off of various bushes, tucking them under his arm. When he came back to the place where they had left their packs, Dursen was already crouched on the ground trying to get a spark from his flint. Gavin let the branches tumble from his arms into a messy heap, and Dursen looked up in surprise.

"Do ya know how to get a fire going?" he asked.

"Of course I do. Don't you?"

Dursen grinned up at him. "I do. But I'd like to see you do it. Maybe y'are better at it," he added with a smirk.

Gavin sighed and got down onto his knees, holding out his hands. "Give me the flint. I'll get a fire going."

Dursen handed over the small knife and smooth flint stone and watched Gavin work. Soon, a bit of flame caught on the brush, and the two of them added twigs and branches until they had a healthy, snapping fire.

"Now what?" Gavin asked, handing Dursen his tools.

"Now we get the tent up," Dursen replied. "Then we'll eat."

"Why did we start the fire before we put the tent up?"

"It gets dark quick out here," Dursen replied. "The fire will help keep wild animals away."

Gavin looked around at the wide, open land all around them. But for the mountain ranges in the distance, and tall, narrow Mount Spire away off to the right, there was nothing out here. Gavin realized how exposed they were. There was nothing here to take shelter in but their simple canvas tent.

"Will we be safe out here?" Gavin wondered aloud.

"Safe enough," Dursen replied, loosing the rolled-up tent from the outside of his pack. He noticed that Gavin seemed concerned, looking all around for any hint of the wild animals Dursen had mentioned.

"They shouldn't come too close to here."

"What? Who?"

"Wild beasts," Dursen explained. "They'll be drawn to water, and the lake is still a two days' walk from here. There's not much to worry over."

Gavin nodded wordlessly.

"Come on then," Dursen instructed. "Help me get the tent up. Grab a hold of that side, there."

Gavin obeyed, pulling the tent out flat and smooth while Dursen fitted together the support beams and raised the top.

When the tent began to lean to one side, Dursen called out from inside the tent.

"Gavin! Pay more attention! Get the sides straight, peg the corners into the ground. Put some effort into it."

Gavin hurried to secure the corners while Dursen adjusted the roof. When Dursen emerged from inside the tent, Gavin stood in the gathering darkness, his arms crossed stubbornly across his chest.

Dursen sighed. Was this trip going to be *harder* with the boy along, rather than easier, as it was meant to be? He sighed again, letting out some of his frustration.

"See now?" he asked. "It's so much easier when two people work together."

Gavin only nodded.

"Are you hungry?" Dursen asked.

"Sure."

"Let's eat, then." Finding his pack, Dursen opened it and pulled out a small bundle of bread and smoked rabbit.

"It ain't much," he commented as Gavin joined him near the fire, "but it'll keep us going."

Gavin silently pulled his own meal out of his pack and bit into it, staring at the flames. Gray dusk gathered along the horizon, slowly pushing its way upward into the evening sky, and coolness settled over the land. Dursen added more branches to the fire, glad that they wouldn't need to keep it going all night. The lightstones he wore around his neck would keep away the beasts that would cause them the most harm.

He rubbed his arms to ease the chill, and watched as Gavin tore off bits of smoked meat to chew them without ever looking up.

"I know ya didn't really want to come on this mission," Dursen told him, and Gavin raised his eyes to look at him.

"Y'are angry," Dursen added. "Aren't you?"

Gavin shrugged.

"I know y'are angry. You feel like you've just got to work all the time, so they told me. But, try not to think of this as work you've got to do. Try to think of it as an adventure. Ya like that sort of thing, don't ya?"

Again, Gavin shrugged.

Dursen chewed his bread in silence.

"No one ever asked me if I wanted to leave," Gavin said quietly.

"Leave Haven?"

"No. Leave Danferron. Leave home. As soon as my parents were told what my mother's necklace was all about, they just decided to leave. They never asked Persha or me if we wanted to go to Haven."

"Persha don't seem to mind."

"Well, I *do*."

"I'm sorry for that," Dursen told him. "In a few years, you can be on your own, and then you can decide where you want to stay."

Gavin was quiet, but Dursen noticed his expression change. Was it haughtiness that he saw, as though Gavin knew something he hadn't shared, or did he feel that he was already old enough to decide such things for himself?

"What are ya thinking?" Dursen asked heavily. "What are ya planning to do?"

Guilt played on Gavin's face now, and he gave no answer.

"Y'are thinking you could stay in Meriton," Dursen guessed. "Aren't you?"

"Maybe," Gavin admitted. "I've been thinking about it."

"And leave me to come back with all them animals?" Dursen confronted him. "That's why y'are here on this trip, ya know that? To help me bring them back over the mountains. Would you just leave me to do all that work myself?"

Gavin frowned down into the crackling flames. "I only said I was thinking about it."

"Well, you just keep on thinking," Dursen told him gruffly. "Y'are not the only person whose wants should be considered. Y'are not just one person, all to yourself. Y'are *part* of something. Y'are part of Haven now. And y'are part of your family, and part of this mission. If you leave it – no matter what it is – you'll leave an emptiness, you'll leave a hole where you were needed, or loved. And someone else will always be left to suffer for it."

Gavin fingered what remained of his meat, sitting in silence as Dursen's words, and the cold and darkness of night, settled over him.

"Right," he finally spoke. "But like I said, I haven't decided anything." Biting the meat in half, he pushed both pieces into his mouth and chewed them. "It's dark," he said after swallowing. "I think I'll go to sleep now. If that's all right with you?" he added smugly, standing.

"Do what you want," Dursen replied in defeat. "I can't stop you."

He kept his eyes on the orange glow of firelight as Gavin trudged off toward the tent, stepping over scrub brush. He noticed when the boy hesitated, glancing back in his direction, before disappearing inside the tent. Had he felt remorse at his words? The boy wasn't *all* bad, Dursen thought. There was hope for him to make the right decision. He only needed to see that *he* wasn't the only one who mattered.

Jair had said that Gavin complained about having to work so much, that he wanted to play around. That he was tired of always being told what to do. He wanted to make decisions for himself.

Dursen sighed as he fed the last branch to the flames. He did not want to be just another someone giving Gavin orders, directions. But how could he let Gavin have the chance to make his own decisions if he couldn't be trusted to do what was best? If he wanted to be treated like a man, he had to act like one, and part of being a man was taking on your own share of the work, and not leaving your traveling partner to do all of the hard work alone.

Dursen absently fingered the strand of lightstones he wore, hearing the screeching of night screamers in the far distance. How could he let Gavin know that he respected him while not letting him get away with being irresponsible? If he was too hard on him – or too easy – Gavin just might decide to stay in Meriton. How would Dursen manage to get all the way back to Haven alone, with goats and chickens? Wild creatures would be drawn in by the smell of the farm animals. And the mountains – how would he manage, getting back over the mountains?

Well, he could only do what he could do. The rest of it would be up to Gavin himself, to make the right choice. What could Dursen do other than just try and lead him in that direction, and wait to see how it would all play out?

~ 24 ~

J air was completely amazed at the rapid growth of the crops – this was very unexpected, and very good news indeed! Haven's people would not need to strictly ration their food for nearly as long as they had thought. Relief was on every face, Jair's in particular. Brace knew the boy desperately wanted to be a good leader for Haven's people. He did not want to let them down, or for them to lack anything they needed.

A change had come over Jair, Brace could see it. He remembered the days shortly after they had met – how Jair had wanted Brace to stay with them, how he had wanted to hear Brace's stories, most of which he had never told him, even to this day. Jair had seemed so much a *boy* then – kind-hearted and innocent. Brace was sure that Jair's heart had not changed, but much of his innocence had been replaced with wisdom. Instead of curiosity, Jair's expression usually now revealed that he was deep in thought, sometimes oddly so, as some new realization came to him, some new mystery of Haven was revealed to him. He almost seemed haunted at times, Brace thought. He'd seen Jair wandering slowly through Haven's streets, letting his hand slide along the walls of lightstone, a far-away look in his eyes.

There were times when Brace wanted to ask Jair what was on his mind, but he felt as though he would be intruding.

So much had changed! Change could not be stopped, Brace knew that well enough. He had been changing along with everything else. This was nothing new to him – his life had been full of change. New faces, new cities, new villas, new challenges. He was familiar with all of it. And then he had truly begun to change when he had met Leandra in the wildlands. Leandra and Arden, and Tassie – all of them.

He smiled to himself now, when he remembered how he had disliked their company at first; how they had grated on him. Arden in particular – and Zorix. But now, Brace felt deeply connected to each of them, in a way that he had never thought he could feel about anyone after losing his mother.

Although Brace had become accustomed to a life in which he was no longer alone, there were days when he felt overwhelmed by it all. Attending meetings, remembering new faces, new names, and working out his relationship with Tassie – sometimes it felt like too much. He needed to withdraw from it all, to pull away so that he could have some quiet, where he could think and recover his inner strength and a sense of himself, of who he wanted to be.

On those particularly exhausting days, he often found himself out walking through Haven's streets toward the homes that still remained empty, sometimes going as far as Haven's Woods. He found that he had made a habit of it, a regular enough habit that Tassie no longer wondered what he was doing or where he'd gone. On those days when she couldn't find him, she now knew he'd simply gone off for a long walk.

A few days had passed since Kalen's discovery about the quickly growing crops, and Brace now found himself heading off into the empty western streets of Haven, toward the Woods. He seldom ever planned on these walks; they just happened. He would step outside for some fresh air, and before he knew it, he would just start walking.

He noticed today that the weather in Haven had changed, but only slightly. Despite the rapid approach of winter and the cold winds blowing across the mountains, Brace could only feel a slight cool in the air now, as he ambled through the empty streets.

He breathed out, a sigh of relief. *Quiet* – that was what he needed right now. He'd begun to feel like his head was spinning, so much had been going on. His journey to Erast, being beaten, needing time to heal, meeting new people and coming back home again, only to find that there were more new people in Haven who had arrived on their own while he was gone. Then there had been the strain of having to explain to Tassie what had happened, and knowing how much the whole thing had upset her. He only needed a bit of time to take it all in, to let it all settle over him, and he would soon be back in Tassie's arms once again. No matter how overwhelmed Brace got to feeling, no matter how much he wanted to get away from it all, after spending as much as half the day alone, he was always eager to get back to Tassie. If he found himself feeling down, or doubting himself, her smile would always lighten his mood. And she was always there to listen if he wanted to talk, giving advice only if he asked for it.

Although he felt that he knew her well – her quiet kindness, the way that she could be bold if the situation called for it – he was always learning something new about her. How she was embarrassed when he kissed her in public; how she loved to close her eyes and feel the sun on her face; that she preferred yellow flowers over red ones. Along with everything else, Brace appreciated the fact that she understood him, no matter what mood he was in, even when he was frustrated or if he blurted out something he shouldn't have said. She understood when he needed time alone.

Brace stretched his arms over his head, glad that only a slight ache remained in his side, and that he could now easily take a full breath without wincing. The sun was bright, the air was cool, and a peaceful silence filled his ears. He could feel his mind calming, his muscles relaxing. Yes, this was just what he needed today.

He could hear the clumping of his worn boots on the stone-paved street as he passed another empty house – there were so many! How many people could Haven hold? he wondered.

Movement caught his eye, just past the uninhabited stone house. He stopped abruptly, tensing for a moment. *What was that?*

"Hello?" he spoke into the silence. "Is someone out here?" In two quick steps, he rounded the corner and saw Yara standing with her back against the wall.

"Yara?" he asked.

She looked up in surprise, then quickly turned away.

"What are you doing out here alone?"

"Nothing, really," she replied. She sniffed, then wiped her hands across her cheeks.

Brace hesitated. If she'd been crying, it couldn't be about nothing. Maybe she just wanted to be left alone for a time, as he did. But then again, maybe not.

"Are you sure it's nothing?" he asked her.

She looked at Brace for a moment, then shook her head. "You'll think I'm being silly," she told him.

"You've said that once before," Brace pointed out. "You were wrong then. Don't you remember?"

Yara nodded through her tears.

"So, what's wrong?"

"It's just that – oh, I don't know. I think I'm just lonely. I don't know what I expected things to be like, coming here. It all happened so fast, coming in through the gate and everyone getting separated. I haven't had the chance to say a single word to you, for so long. There are things I've wanted to tell you, Brace."

Brace shook his head, feeling the tension returning. "There can't be anything between us, Yara. You know that."

"No, Brace, it isn't really like that. I mean, I do *like* you." She smiled. "When I first met you, I noticed how handsome you were. And how friendly." Yara laughed softly, drying her cheeks with her sleeve. "A little strange, but nice." Her smile faded. "I do like you," she repeated. "If you weren't married ..." She shrugged.

Brace rubbed absently at the back of his head. Yara's words made him feel uneasy, but he had already known, or at least suspected, that she might have feelings for him.

"I hope ..." Brace began, trying to put his thoughts together, "I hope I didn't make you feel like I was leading you on, when I invited you to come to Haven with me. You ..." he paused, unsure whether or not to go on.

"What?" Yara urged him gently. "I what?"

"Well, I thought you were beautiful, right away, when I first saw you."

"I *was* beautiful?"

"You are," Brace admitted. "Yara, I've been with a lot of girls in a lot of different places. Young and pretty and outgoing, just like you. When I saw you, that's the first thing that came to my mind."

Yara stood quietly as she let Brace's words sink in.

"But you still invited me to come back?" she asked him. "Even though you have Tassie? You weren't afraid you would feel ... tempted?"

Brace let out a long breath. "Maybe a little," he admitted. "But I love Tassie, with all my heart. I would never sneak around behind her back."

"I would never want to come between you and Tassie," Yara told him quickly. "I can ... *forget* ... about feeling attracted to you, Brace, but I can't forget about feeling alone. Everyone is so busy doing important things, and they already have their friends or their family. I don't have anyone." She stopped and took a breath. "I'm telling you this because – well, I feel like you're the one I *should* tell. You're the one who invited me here, after all. And ... I know you care."

Brace sighed and leaned against the wall. "I do care that you feel alone. I'm sorry about that. Maybe I could ..."

"Please don't tell anyone what I said," she interrupted. "I don't want them to try and make friends with me out of pity."

He nodded. "I can understand that."

Yara sighed, half smiling. "I actually feel a little better. I think I just needed to talk about things for a bit."

"Still, I am sorry, Yara. I know how it is to be surrounded by people and still feel alone. I know we're all busy here, but don't give up. Don't ... well, don't hide. Keep trying. You're easy to get along with. You'll make friends here. Trust me."

Yara nodded and tugged at the hem of her dress. "And you and I?" she asked. "Can we at least be friends? I'd like to think that I have at least one friend here already."

Brace found himself hesitating. Could he be a friend to Yara? He still felt less than at ease around her; he still felt attracted to her, despite his will. But maybe his will was strong enough.

"I think we can be friends," he told her.

She nodded and smiled sheepishly. "You were going somewhere. I must have interrupted what you were doing. I'm sorry."

Brace shrugged. "No problem. I've got nothing but time." He stood up, away from the stone wall of the house. "Are you all right now?"

"I'm fine," she replied, standing beside him. "You're looking much better too. Your face, I mean."

"Thanks," Brace replied shortly. "I'm feeling all right these days." He nodded toward the street at his side. "I just need to go for a walk, clear my head a little."

Yara nodded. "I'll let you get back to it."

"Right." Brace turned to go on his way, then looked back. "As long as you're all right. And remember, don't hide. There are a lot of good people here. You'll be welcomed by them, I know you will."

Yara nodded. "Thank you, Brace. You're a good friend."

Brace only nodded in response, lifting his hand to wave in parting.

Yara's face flitted in and out of Brace's thoughts over the next hour, as he went on his way toward Haven's Woods. Though he enjoyed the quiet solitude, thoughts of Yara weighed on him. Why did he have to keep thinking about her? *He loved Tassie.* Could his own mind be warring with itself? He had never felt it so strongly, struggling to choose one decision over another.

He was in the middle of trying to shrug off the memory of feeling her leaning against his side on the cold dark mountain, when his path came across Ben-Rickard, who was heading back toward the city.

"Hello there," Ben called out, waving.

"Hello," Brace replied, trying not to sound frustrated at having his solitude interrupted once again.

"Nice day, isn't it?" Ben went on as he came closer.

"Always is, here," Brace pointed out.

Ben chuckled. "True. What brings you out this way? Just walking, as I am? Enjoying some peace and sunlight?"

"Exactly," Brace replied. *I'd prefer to do it alone,* he added in his thoughts.

Ben looked up at the sky, a pale blue and streaked with soft white clouds, light strokes of an enormous paintbrush. "This place is wonderful," he thought aloud. "I can't thank you enough for bringing us all back here."

"Well, I didn't do it alone," Brace reminded him.

Ben smiled. "Of course. I'm thankful to Dursen as well. Haven is more beautiful than I could have imagined. I'm so thankful to be able to call this place home."

Brace nodded in response. "So am I," he told him, resigning himself to the fact that he wouldn't have his day of quiet after all. "For the longest time, I didn't feel like I deserved to be here," he confided. "Sometimes I still feel that way."

"No?" Ben replied. "I can see that, I surely can. I often feel that way myself."

"You've done more work here than I have," Brace pointed out. "You've been a big help, to so many people."

"Well," Ben humbly tipped his head, "I'm more than glad to do it. I don't think I could ever completely show how grateful I am to be here, to have Haven as my home."

"I know what you mean," Brace told him. "I haven't done much since I came back from Erast."

"Well, you've been healing," Ben said with a shrug. "And you've done so much already, bringing people back, that I don't think anyone expects too terribly much of you at the moment."

Brace nodded. "Well, I promised Tassie I wouldn't go out on any more missions. I think she needs me to just be *here* for a while. We've only been together for a few months."

Brace kept it to himself, about the possibility of encountering trouble due to having once been a thief, and now a wanted man. Ben-Rickard may find out eventually, but there was no need to bring it up now.

"Do you suppose I would be permitted to go out on these missions someday?" Ben asked.

"At the rate you're going, you could be leading them yourself," Brace replied. "So many people here look up to you."

"That isn't the reason why I help," Ben protested.

"I know it isn't," Brace told him. "But you're so quiet, and humble about everything. That only makes people look up to you more, I've seen."

Ben smiled. "Well, I've spent all morning out here, enjoying the Woods," he said, gesturing back toward the city. "I think I should be getting back. Are you going on?"

Brace sighed. "No, I think I'll get back as well."

Today would not be the day, he thought, to spend a long while alone. He had tried, and been interrupted twice. Maybe that was enough thinking about things. Then again, maybe he would try again tomorrow. He had to come to terms with himself, as far as Yara was concerned. He had to get it all straight in his mind. He hadn't made a mistake, he tried to convince himself, by inviting her here. That was what he'd been sent out to do, after all. How could he have known what it would lead to? Now she wanted him to be a friend to her, and he had no idea whatsoever of how to do it. When had he ever been just a friend to any girl? He wished he could just forget all about Yara, about her pretty, freckled face, about the way she made him feel. The only person he wanted to think about was Tassie, and being her husband. He didn't want this tension in his life. True, he hadn't done anything to deserve having peace in his life, but was that so much to ask for? Haven had allowed him to come here, hadn't it? Or even chosen him to come here? Couldn't he just live in peace?

~ 25 ~

The bright blue flags bearing Meriton's crest flapped in the breeze flowing up from Wayside Lake, a welcome to any visitors, while at the same time, the thick gray walls of stone surrounding the city seemed to warn everyone to keep out if they planned to cause any trouble there.

"Well, there it is," Dursen told Gavin as they stood outside the rear gate. A bell rang from some tower inside the city, signaling *what*, Dursen had no idea, but the sound carried out to them, along with the clamor of voices and iron-shod hooves of horses on the cobblestone roads.

"You've never been here?" Gavin asked.

"Never."

"How do you know we'll find what we've come for?"

Dursen shrugged. "We'll ask around."

"Right," Gavin replied with a nod.

The southern gate of Meriton stood wide open, guarded by only two men. There was very little traffic here; it was the northern gate, close to the Royal Road, where most people came and went. Meriton was a trade city, Dursen knew – goods were bought and sold there, coming from all over the country of Dunya and beyond. Crops grown on Spire's Gate farms were often sold there as well, in season. If goat herders from up north were in the area, they would be likely to find some of their animals for sale in the city.

Dursen glanced aside, trying to read the expression on Gavin's face. Here the boy was, on the outskirts of a large city once again. Isn't this what he had wanted? Dursen expected him to be happier about it. Instead, he seemed pensive. Maybe he was beginning to take Dursen's words to heart, about being a part of something important, beyond simply doing whatever he wanted, when he wanted to do it.

"Ready to go in?" Dursen asked, eyeing the steel armor of the guards. If they stood here like this for too long, the guards might become suspicious and give them trouble.

"Yes, I'm ready," Gavin replied without a moment's hesitation. The boy walked on ahead of Dursen and waved a greeting at the still, silent guards as they passed into the city.

What boldness, Dursen thought. *He's acting right at home here already.*

Dursen followed Gavin closely, crossing several streets as they went deeper into the city. Looking around at each person they passed, at each mule-drawn cart and each shop open for business, Gavin seemed to be absorbing it all into himself. Soaking it all into his consciousness, becoming a part of it. Frankly, Dursen couldn't see what there was about the place to be so drawn into. It was dirty, and noisy, and crowded. He would much rather be surrounded by trees and sky and hillsides.

"Well, then?" Dursen asked, trying to pull Gavin back.

"What?"

"Are you with me on this? Ya *do* remember why we're here?"

"I remember."

"Right. Good. Well, it's too late in the day to get the animals and head straight back. I say we find a place to sleep and look for them in the morning."

"All right."

Dursen nodded, glad that for now at least, Gavin was agreeable. He had no idea what was where in the sprawling city, so of course he couldn't lead the way to an inn. The only such place he knew of in Meriton was the inn that Brace had told him about. What was it called? The Dagger? *The Wolf and Dagger*. Dursen had not forgotten, though, that Kendie had spent most of her childhood working in that place. He remembered the anger in Brace's expression when he had spoken of it. What kind of a man took advantage of a little girl, making her wait on tables and serve ale? No, Dursen decided. He would not pay the likes of such a man to stay in one of his rooms, no matter how comfortable the beds were. He would find another place.

"Are ya hungry?" he asked, feeling a growing emptiness in his own stomach.

"Hungry enough."

"Let's find some place to eat first then," Dursen suggested, peering down the side streets for any sign of an eating establishment, memories of what had happened in Erast briefly flitting through his mind.

"Know what I always did when I wasn't sure where to go?" Gavin offered.

"What's that?"

Gavin smiled. "I followed my nose. Come on."

Well enough, Dursen thought, keeping in step behind the boy, who crossed another cobblestone street, then paused, looking to the right and left. He continued on straight, heading north toward the heart of the city. The way became more crowded as they went along, but Gavin kept on, undeterred, until he noticed a group of people gathered at the corner, in an open square.

"What's all that about?" Dursen wondered aloud.

"I don't know," Gavin replied. "Let's go find out."

"Are ya sure that's wise?" Dursen asked, but Gavin was already hurrying on ahead, and all he could do was follow after him. As they neared the back of the crowd, Dursen could hear lively music playing, and when he peered between the heads of the onlookers, he spotted several men playing reed pipes or stringed instruments.

"Street performers," Gavin told him cheerfully. "I always stop to watch them. This is just music – it's good, but sometimes there are jesters, doing tricks or balancing acts, like in a circus."

"I see," Dursen replied, unimpressed. He stood in silence for a few moments, forcing himself to allow Gavin a bit of time. They weren't in *that* much of a hurry, after all.

When the tune finally ended and the audience applauded, Dursen stepped closer so Gavin would hear him over the noise.

"Are ya through here? Ready to find some food?"

"Sure," Gavin replied, his expression flat.

"Which way, do ya think?"

"Not far from here, maybe," he replied, looking up and down the road as he had done earlier. "Maybe this way," he suggested, gesturing toward the right.

"Are ya following your nose?" Dursen asked lightly.

"No," Gavin replied. "Just my instincts."

"Fair enough."

Gavin strode confidently down the cobbled street past buildings of various sizes, constructed of varying colors of brick or stone. There were shops selling clothing, tapestries, clay pots and leatherwork, some of what Dursen could see was quite impressive. But the gnawing in his stomach reminded him that what they needed was *food*. And not just smoked meat and dry bread. He'd had enough of that over the past four days, and he was starting to feel weakness in his limbs. They needed a good meal – two good meals – in order to build up the strength they would need to get home again.

Passing another row of shops, Dursen noticed that the streets were becoming less crowded as they made their way east through the city.

"Where are we going?" Dursen asked, stepping up beside Gavin. "It looks empty out here."

"I'm following my nose," Gavin replied. "I smell food. Don't you?"

Dursen breathed in through his nose and caught a faint whiff of what he was certain was seasoned broth. "I do smell it. But where's it coming from?"

"We'll find it."

Dursen had no choice but to take Gavin's word for it, and no real reason not to trust him. And if it turned out they couldn't find what they were smelling, they could just go back the way they'd come and Dursen would ask for directions. Simple as that.

A cottager leading a mule down the street toward them gave them a curious look as he passed, and Dursen felt a wave of insecurity sweep over him and settle in his stomach.

"Where is it y'are leading us?" he asked, when Gavin stopped and nodded at the next street heading north.

"Right here," he replied simply.

Dursen stepped around Gavin and peered up the shadowed street, lined on both sides by shops that looked empty and forgotten. The smell of food was indeed stronger here, though, and as he looked, Dursen could see that there were people gathered in the street, among what appeared to be makeshift tent shelters and steam rising from cookpots over coal fires.

"This …" Dursen began, unsure what to say, "this ain't an eatery. I don't know if we'll be intruding here."

"It won't hurt to ask," Gavin insisted, and the unease in Dursen's stomach doubled, though he couldn't be sure he wasn't simply reacting to the aroma of food cooking.

"Just be careful about it," Dursen advised. "In fact, let me do the talking here."

Gavin frowned slightly, but took a step back. "Fine. I'll follow you."

"Right," Dursen replied with a nod, breathing in to gather his resolve.

Ambling slowly up the narrow road, his eyes darted around at the several people closest to him. They were dressed heavily against the cool in the air, though he could see as he came closer that their clothing was worn, shabby, or stained.

The thin, bony man on Dursen's left raised a thick, grizzled eyebrow at him as he approached.

"Are you lost?" he asked in a gravelly voice.

"No," Dursen replied. "No, we ain't lost. We're just hungry, looking for a place to eat, and we found our way here. I hope we're not intruding."

Another man from slightly farther in peered at them from behind the hood of his black wool cloak.

"Travelers?" he asked suspiciously.

"Yes," Dursen replied, sensing that Gavin was feeling unsure now as well, standing at Dursen's elbow. "We're only travelers, hungry ones. We aren't meaning to come in where we're not welcome," he added quickly. "We only thought …"

"What's this, now?" a woman's voice cut him off. "What's going on?"

A young woman emerged out of the shadows, her long dark hair falling down over the shoulders of her shabby gray wool coat. She peered at the two of them with curiosity, but not with hostility, much to Dursen's relief.

"They's hungry," the first man informed her, pointing a bony finger in their direction.

"Are they now?" she asked, smiling a little.

"We don't want to cause no trouble," Dursen told her, and she shook her head.

"It's no trouble," she replied. "I have some extra to spare. Follow me."

Following the young woman down the narrow, shadowed street was an uncomfortable thing, Dursen thought, as the two men eyed them with distaste.

"Here," the woman announced, moving aside to sit before a small fire and a steaming iron cook pot. She pulled one blanket off the smile pile she'd made into a seat, spreading it on the hard ground across from her.

"Are ya certain ya don't mind?" Dursen asked her. "Really, we were looking for an eatery ..."

The woman tipped her head at him. "If I minded, I wouldn't have invited you."

Dursen nodded appreciatively as Gavin settled close to him on the blanket.

"What's in your pot?" the boy asked quietly.

She smiled. "Fish," she replied. "I hope you're not against eating fish; I'm afraid it's all I have."

"We've got nothing against fish," Dursen told her. "Have we?"

"No," Gavin replied. "Nothing."

"Good," the woman replied, stirring the bubbling liquid with a wooden spoon. "I lost my bowl last week," she informed them. "Or rather," she added, raising her voice, "I think someone must have *stolen* it!" A moment passed in silence as she glared up and down the narrow street. "So," she said, looking again at Dursen, "we'll need to take turns eating it right out of the pot. I hope you don't mind."

"That's all right with me," Dursen told her, and Gavin shook his head.

"Good then. My name is Nerissa. Who might you be?"

"I'm Dursen," he introduced himself. "And this is Gavin."

Dursen couldn't help but notice the woman's beauty. She had large, dark eyes and a mouth that seemed always ready to smile, and he found himself drawn to her despite the fact that Gavin was fidgeting nervously beside him, distracting him.

"Are you all right?" Dursen asked him.

"I'm fine. I was just wondering," he said, looking at Nerissa, "do you all *live* here?"

She smiled. "Yes, we do."

"You've got no other place to go?"

Nerissa shook her head. "This is it, I'm afraid."

"Why?"

"Gavin," Dursen scolded. "Don't be so nosy, ya hear?"

"It's all right," Nerissa told him. "It's just the way things are, that's all."

Gavin chewed pensively at his lip.

"Where are you two from?" Nerissa asked.

"Watch yourself, there, Niss," someone called out from farther up the road. "Don't get too friendly with those two or they'll be wanting more of you than just yer food."

"You just shut your mouth, there!" she shouted back. "These men aren't like that at all. Are you?"

"No, ma'am," Dursen replied quickly. "Er, *miss*. No, we're not like that."

Nerissa studied him for a moment, only glancing at Gavin, whose face was drawn with worry.

"I knew you weren't," she said. "Please, call me Nerissa."

"All right," Dursen replied with a nod. "Nerissa. Thank you for being willing to share your food with us. Ya didn't have to. I could pay you ..."

"Hush," she snapped. "Don't say that." She glanced quickly back and forth down the crowded, narrow road, but everyone was intent on their food. "Keep your money where it is," she added in a whisper. "Don't let anyone know you have any."

Dursen's face paled. "Right," he responded.

"So, Dursen," Nerissa said casually, lifting the wooden spoon to her lips. "Where *are* you two from?"

"I'm from Spire's Gate originally," Dursen answered as she handed him the spoon. "Thank you," he muttered before going on. "Gavin, he's come from Danferron, that right?"

Gavin nodded. "That's right."

Dursen drank a spoonful of the fish soup, surprised at how tasty it was.

"Right," he said, passing the spoon on to Gavin, who hesitated before trying the soup. "But we've both just come from the same place," Dursen went on. "We were sent to find goats and chickens to bring back home with us."

"Where's home?"

Dursen hesitated. This was not officially a search mission, but that didn't mean they couldn't spread the word, did it? Jair would be disappointed if they'd had the chance to tell someone and had kept quiet about it.

"It's a place called Haven," he replied. "Ever heard of it?"

"No," she replied, accepting the spoon back from Gavin. "What is it?"

"It's a city," Dursen replied, aware that he'd gained attention from more than just Nerissa. "It's an ancient city, where our ancestors lived. It's a special place, hard to explain. It's full of light, really. And it's safe. Only those who want to live in peace there can even get in. We only left because we need the animals. We're trying to build up our provisions."

"Do many people live there?" Nerissa asked, as the people around them began to inch closer in curiosity.

"Not too many," Dursen replied. "People are only just starting to come back there. It's been empty for so long."

"Why?" The thin old man asked.

"Can't say, really," Dursen told him. "People just left it. But they're coming back now, anyone who wants to. Y'are all welcome to come back with us, too."

"This a real place you're talking about?" someone asked from the shadows.

Dursen shivered in the cold of evening, pulling his cloak tighter around himself. "Yes, it's a real place. Anyone is welcome to come with us. There are homes a plenty there, just for the taking. There's fruit that heals your sickness, and water that gives ya strength. And it's *never* cold there," he added, taking another bite of soup.

"It don't sound possible," an older woman spoke up.

"It is," Gavin informed her, finally speaking. "It's real."

Dursen looked at Gavin with admiration, but the boy shrugged. "It is a real place."

"How do you get there?" the hooded man asked. "I never heard of it, nor seen it on any map."

"It's just over the mountains, south of here," Dursen told him. "Gavin and I are leaving as soon as we get what we come for, and anyone can come with us who wants to."

"A safe place?" Nerissa asked. "A warm place, full of peace?"

"Aye," Dursen replied. "All that and so much more."

A far-away look came into her eyes, and Dursen knew he'd gotten to her. What did she have to stay here for, after all?

"Over mountains?" the old man asked. "Pah. I can't cross any mountains."

"You wouldn't be doing it alone," Dursen told him. "You'd have help."

"I think you're daft," the hooded man asserted.

"No, sir, we ain't crazy," Dursen argued. "It's a real place, and if you'll come along you can see it for yourself."

People began to drift back into the shadows, turning their backs, but Nerissa was looking at Dursen intently.

"You're really telling the truth, aren't you?" she asked.

"Couldn't be more so."

She nodded slowly. "I would like to come with you, then. I don't know why, but I believe you. You've got honest faces."

"Y'are more than welcome to," Dursen told her gladly.

"Did you say you came here looking for goats?" she asked.

"Yes, goats and chickens. Have you seen any for sale here lately?"

"I have," she replied, plunking the spoon down into the cookpot. "Come over here with me for a moment."

Dursen followed her, with Gavin right behind him, as she stepped around the others all the way to the end of the road, in the opposite direction from where they'd come. "Two more streets up that way," she said, pointing. "That's where the herders sell their animals." She pulled aside her long dark hair and tugged at a cord around her neck, drawing up a small pouch. Taking it off, her back to the road behind her, she removed two silver coins. "Will you buy a goat for me?" she asked, offering Dursen the money. "Since I'm coming with you, I think I'd like to have a goat of my own."

"How did you get that?" Gavin asked her, surprised.

She regarded him with one eyebrow crooked. "Men don't only come to me for food," she replied simply, and Gavin ducked his head.

"I'm sorry."

"I'll get you one, it's no trouble at all," Dursen said quickly, accepting the coins.

"Thank you," she replied, wrapping her arms around herself against the cold wind snaking down the dark, narrow road. "Will you be looking for a place to stay tonight?" she asked.

"Yes, we were planning to," Dursen told her.

Nerissa looked back down the crowded street for a moment, then turned back toward Dursen. "You're welcome to stay here," she said, "with me. I've got extra blankets. You can each have one to yourself, no strings attached. You can save your money that way."

"Are ya sure that's all right?" Dursen asked. "All the others..."

"Don't worry about them. If you're with me, they should leave you alone."

"Well," Dursen replied, unsure, "let me talk with Gavin here a bit? He's got a say in the decision."

"Of course," Nerissa replied with a smile. "You know where to find me."

Dursen watched as she strode back down the street, disappearing into the shadows. Turning back toward Gavin, he raised an eyebrow. "Well? What do ya think?"

"You mean, do I want to sleep *here*?" he asked.

"That's what I mean."

Gavin glanced back down the road hesitantly.

"I thought you loved life in the city," Dursen gently chided him. "I thought you were even considering staying here."

"This is different," Gavin protested. "I've never ... Well, I've never been around street people. I've seen them, sure, but I've never met any, and I've *never* thought about staying the night with them."

"Do they scare ya a bit?"

"Yes," Gavin admitted. "But they scare you, too. I saw it on your face."

"Y'are right there. But I trust Nerissa. She seems different from the rest of them."

"You *like* her," Gavin challenged. When Dursen couldn't say anything to refute the fact, Gavin crossed his arms and leaned back against the side of the empty building.

"Do you think..." he began, then stopped.

"What?" Dursen asked.

"Do you think it's true, what she said about how she earns her money?"

"Well," Dursen replied, scratching at the back of his head, "if I was her, I wouldn't say a thing like that if it weren't true."

"I never knew it could be like this," Gavin muttered. "To me, living in the city has always just meant fun, and freedom. I never thought..." he shrugged.

"Not wanting to stay so much now, are ya?"

"Maybe not."

Dursen rested his hand on Gavin's shoulder, smiling. "I knew you were a smart one," he told him, but Gavin still frowned.

"Well," Dursen said with a sigh, "what do you say about staying the night here? It'll save us some money, sure enough. And we'll stay warm enough, what with our bed rolls and a little bit of Nerissa's kindness."

Gavin considered it a moment, then nodded. "All right," he replied. "We can stay there. I'm sorry for what I said about you liking Nerissa."

Dursen smirked. "Well, you weren't so far off on that," he admitted, and Gavin managed a smile.

"Let's get back," Gavin suggested. "If we make it through tonight, we can get the goats first thing in the morning. Maybe we can buy Nerissa some breakfast before we leave."

"That sounds perfect."

Gavin sighed. "I just wish I knew how to sleep with one eye open."

~ 26 ~

"Pull back harder," Arden instructed Ona as she held up the smaller wooden bow, ready to fire an arrow.

"Like this?" she asked, her muscles straining.

"That's right," Arden replied with a nod. "Let it fly."

Ona's arrow fell far short of her intended target – deer hide stretched over a frame of tied branches, backed by a bundled mass of brush gathered from one of the patches of farmland. She frowned, but Arden only smiled and told her to try again.

Dorianne had approached him earlier in the week and asked him if he would come and teach archery skills to the children at the school. He had hesitated only a moment before agreeing to help. He had already been training Persha; there was no reason why he couldn't try and teach the younger ones as well.

Ona hurried to retrieve her fallen arrow, then returned to her starting position.

"You've got it," Arden encouraged her. "Elbows higher. Pull all the way back."

"It's hard to hold it still while I aim," Ona commented, firing the arrow once again. It sailed farther that time, but still missed the target.

"Better," Arden told her when she turned toward him, a look of disappointment on her face. "You can try again later. Jair, why don't you take a few shots?"

"Sure," Jair replied. Trystan jumped up and down as Ona handed Jair the bow.

"I want a turn! I want a turn!" he exclaimed enthusiastically.

"You'll get a turn," Dorianne told him. "Come and stand over here with me. Don't get in the way of the arrows."

Trystan obeyed glumly as Jair readied himself to shoot.

Kendie stood close beside Ona, and the two girls watched everything Jair was doing. He checked the position of his feet, held his elbows up, then stood still for a moment. The way he looked around made Kendie wonder if he had heard something. A heartbeat or two later, however, he took another look at the target, aimed, and fired.

Jair's arrow pierced the deer hide and lodged into one of the branches, just to the upper left of center.

"That was a great shot!" Kendie told him, her voice carrying across the flat, treeless stretch of land that would some day be the southeastern garden.

Jair looked back at Kendie and grinned. "Thanks," he replied.

"Well done," Arden spoke up. "You've remembered some of what I've taught you, I see." He turned toward the other youngsters. "Who thinks they can tell me what Jair did differently?"

"He's stronger," Ona stated.

"Possibly," Arden told her. "But there's more to it than that."

"He was looking around," Kendie added.

"What was he looking for?"

"Umm …" Kendie thought. "Was he trying to block out distractions?"

"That would be a good thing to do," Arden replied, "but I don't think that was the case. Jair? Why don't you tell us what you did?"

"I was checking for any wind," Jair said as he readied another arrow. "Can I try one more time?"

"Go on ahead," Arden told him with a nod.

"He's really good at this," Ona whispered in Kendie's ear as Jair took aim a second time.

"He's good at a lot of things," Kendie whispered back.

Ona smiled. "Do you *like* him?"

Kendie smiled and nodded, and Ona giggled.

"Shh!" Kendie whispered. "I don't want him to know."

"Why not?"

"Well … I don't know. I guess I *do* want him to know, just not yet. And I don't want him to hear us talking about him."

"Right," Ona replied knowingly.

The girls stood in silence while Arden showed little Trystan how to hold an arrow to the bow and point it toward the target.

Jair came to stand closer to the girls, where they waited out of the way. Kendie looked over at him and smiled, and he smiled back.

"You'll try next, won't you?" Jair asked her.

"Sure," she replied, "but I don't think I could be as good as you are."

"I think you could," Jair told her, and she felt her face blush pink.

"Really?"

"With practice, I know you could."

"Thank you," Kendie replied softly.

Jair watched as she responded to Arden calling her to take her turn.

Strange, Jair thought. Kendie was acting strangely. He'd never seen her face flush that way, at anything he'd ever said to her.

Maybe she just felt nervous about using the bow with all of them watching her. It was perplexing, and the thought of it kept coming back to him throughout the day, as he continued working with Jayla and Ovard in the Main Hall.

It wasn't until he heard the rumbling of the gates that the thought of Kendie blushing left his mind. *The gate* – that meant that Dursen had returned, and hopefully Gavin as well.

To prevent the possibility of unnecessary chaos or confusion, Arden and Leandra, along with Brace, Nevin, and Shayrie, had been put in charge of meeting any new arrivals at the gate. If Ovard and Jair were not otherwise occupied, they would go as well.

Today, Jair wasn't sure if he was glad he was free to see to the gate or not. Would Gavin be glad to be back, if he *had* come back, or had he enjoyed his time away so much that he would want to leave again? Would he still be harboring bitterness against Jair for suggesting that he leave in the first place?

Jair kept his doubts to himself as he accompanied the others down the main road toward Haven's gate. As they neared it and Ovard called out a greeting, Jair looked closer and saw four people and several goats waiting just inside the city.

Four?

Dursen and Gavin each held the end of a long rope, onto which several goats had been tied. A young woman with long dark hair stood nearby, with a large leather pack strapped to her back, quite full and apparently heavy. The fourth was a man with long, stringy hair and scruff on his chin, also carrying a full pack.

"Welcome back!" Ovard greeted them. "And who have you brought with you?"

"This is Nerissa," Dursen introduced with a tired smile. "She's come back with us from Meriton."

"Welcome to Haven, Nerissa."

"Thank you," she replied, shifting the weight of the pack.

"And this is Jordis," Dursen said, turning toward the man standing behind him.

"Welcome," Ovard repeated.

Jordis nodded in response, his gray eyes taking in the sight of new faces. "Thank you."

"Here, let me take that," Berrick offered, stepping toward Nerissa.

"Thank you," she said again. "But carefully – it's full of eggs."

"Eggs?" Jair asked, finally looking away from Gavin's tired yet mellow expression.

"Chicken's eggs," Dursen explained as Berrick took on the weight of the pack. "They're wrapped in some special cloth to protect them and keep them warm. They should be hatching in the next few days."

"There are two dozen eggs," Gavin spoke for the first time. "Nerissa has one half, and Jordis has the other. And we had ten goats, but one of them got loose during the night, somewhere in the mountains."

"Those things can happen," Ovard replied. "But you've all made it back safely! That is what truly matters. Come inside, everyone, and get some rest and something to eat."

Together, they unloaded the travelers' burdens – Jair leading one group of goats and Ovard the other, while Arden carried Dursen's pack. Nevin took Gavin's load as he and Shayrie held their son in a long embrace.

The small group was led toward the Main Hall, through the large, round Fountain Court, where they could rest on solid stone benches and eat red vine fruit to regain their strength. They would soon go on to the Hall for Dursen and Gavin to recount the events of their journey and introduce the newcomers, who could then refresh themselves and find a home to call their own.

Brace watched the reactions of the new arrivals as they took in the sight of the lightstone walls. Along one stretch of the curved stone walls surrounding the courtyard, there were etched in large letters, words of greeting in Haven's ancient language, and Nerissa was particularly interested in them.

"What is this?" she asked, lightly touching one of the letters.

"That's Haven's greeting," Jair told her. "It's in an ancient language. It says, '*The City of Haven. This city of refuge is open in welcome to all who will enter it with pure hearts. May all who find themselves within these sacred walls find peace and safety, for years upon years upon years, even until the end of all time.*'"

Nerissa smiled, looking back at Dursen, but Jordis rubbed nervously at his chin, looking all around him as though troubled. Brace found his reaction curious, but knew that he himself had been bothered by the words at first hearing them, and it was easy to see that Jordis must be as well. He made a mental note to himself, as he went back to the house for Tassie, to talk with the man about it some time, but not now. Tassie would want to be at this meeting.

He glanced at his reflection in the small mirror in the bedroom as Tassie readied herself. His face was almost completely back to its normal appearance; only his left eye showed faint yellowish bruises, and a scar was forming on his lower lip where Ronin had put in stitches. *What a relief,* he thought. The last remaining signs that he'd ever been through that beating were almost gone. Maybe he would start to feel more normal.

What is normal now, for me? he found himself wondering. *I wish I knew. Well, there's no time to sit around and wonder about it now,* he told himself. *Dursen's waiting.* This had been Dursen's first experience leading any mission, after all, and Brace wanted to hear how things had gone.

Tassie walked hand-in-hand with Brace over the short distance from their home to the Main Hall. She was staying so close to him these days. Not in a needy way, not so much, Brace thought. No, it was more like she was being ... protective, or possessive, or some such thing. The thought made him smile. Tassie, protective of *him*? Did she think someone here in Haven would try and do him any harm, would try and steal him from her?

His smile faded. Steal him ... *Yara*? She wouldn't, she had said she would never want to come between them. But it might feel that way to Tassie. Maybe she didn't actually think Yara would *try* to get Brace's attention, but that Brace's mind might simply wander in Yara's direction. And truthfully, it had.

They were too near the Main Hall now to discuss it. It would need to wait until later, though Brace preferred to avoid the subject completely.

Brace wasn't sure whether he was surprised, but more than half of Haven's population was in attendance that evening. The Main Hall was more crowded than he was comfortable with, but he kept telling himself that he could deal with it. He owed it to Dursen, to hear about how his first trip as leader had gone, no matter that he'd only had Gavin to look after.

They were late, it seemed, as Dursen was already standing at the front of the room, with Gavin nearby. Brace slipped onto a bench in the back, and Tassie slid in beside him.

"Well, once we got into Meriton," Dursen was saying where he stood in front of the long wooden table, "we found a goat herder who was willing to sell us some of his animals. It surprised me, really, that it didn't take long to find what we needed."

"Meriton is such a busy place," Tassie commented quietly, in Brace's ear. "I'm not surprised. Are you?"

Brace shook his head. "No, I suppose not."

"But," Dursen went on, "we were told that it would be easier to take eggs over the mountains rather than the chickens themselves, seeing as we had no cart nor cages."

"We got two dozen of them," Gavin added, "thinking some of them might break, or might not hatch at all."

"That's very good thinking," Ovard told him, and Gavin nodded solemnly in response.

"We didn't waste none of our money to stay at any inn," Dursen went on, catching Brace's eye.

Brace nodded and gave him a lopsided grin in response. Dursen must have remembered what Brace had told him about the Wolf and Dagger, about Rune Fletcher and his harsh treatment of Kendie, making her want to run away.

"You didn't stay at an inn?" Ronin asked in surprise. "Where did you stay, then?"

"Well …" Dursen hesitated, but Gavin nodded for him to go on.

"We stayed on the street. It was an old empty lane, rather," he continued, hearing a few mutterings of surprise. "The buildings there were empty, but when we passed by, there were all these people."

"Standing around on the street?" Jair asked.

"Standing around?" Dursen asked. "No. They lived there. That was where we met Nerissa." Dursen turned and looked toward the dark-haired woman who had come back with them, sitting near the front of the crowded room, with Jordis beside her. She smiled and waved awkwardly as everyone glanced her way.

Dursen cleared his throat and went on. "So, anyway, we told the folks there that we came from Haven and we were getting ready to go back, and that they were more than welcome to join us."

"Most of them didn't really believe us," Gavin spoke up, leaning his chin in his hand.

"That's right," Dursen agreed. "Most of 'em didn't. Nerissa was the only one who stuck with us, at first."

Dursen smiled in Nerissa's direction once again.

"Jordis decided to come the next morning. And that was that," Dursen finished with a shrug. "We found the goats, carefully packed away the eggs, and we left. There's nothing more to tell."

In response to Ovard's nudging, Jair thanked Gavin and Dursen, welcomed Nerissa and Jordis, then ended the meeting. Soon enough, everyone began to disperse. Dursen lingered, standing beside Nerissa, while Gavin simply walked out. Jair quickly excused himself and hurried out of the Main Hall, catching up to Gavin just outside the open front doors.

"Gavin! You came back," Jair blurted out, and Gavin turned and looked at him in surprise, as people continued to pass them by on their way out of the Hall.

"I did," he replied. Shayrie and Nevin were standing nearby, but when they looked back and saw Jair, they quietly went on their way, leaving the boys to talk.

Jair shrugged. "I was a little surprised. I thought you might like it out there, in the city."

"I did, at first," Gavin replied. "It felt more like home, like what I was used to."

"Did you ever think about *not* coming back?" Jair asked quietly.

"Maybe a little. But I knew they needed my help getting the goats and the eggs over the mountains. And…"

"And what?"

Gavin looked around, but by now, nearly everyone had left the Main Hall and had cleared away. Everything was quiet.

"And I saw how it was for the people we stayed with, there in the street. I've spent a lot of time in big cities, and I've been all over them, but I've never known what it could be like, not for them. For people without a home."

"What was it like?" Jair asked him. "I've never lived in a big city."

"Well, it was… really hard. They were hungry and dirty and cold. They barely had enough of what they needed, and the little bit of money they did have – well, it was awful, what some of them had to do to earn it." Gavin paused. "It was just awful."

Jair was curious to know more, but at the same time, he didn't want to ask.

"Nerissa was one of them," Gavin went on. "She said she hated it and wanted to leave. She wasn't going to let any mountains stop her from going, now that she had been given the chance."

"I'm glad for her," Jair responded. "And I am glad you're back, Gavin. I was worried you would be too angry to talk to me today."

Gavin managed a grin. "I'm not angry, not anymore. Actually, I'm sorry for how I acted before. It was hard work, traveling with Dursen. And even harder on the way back, with the goats and all. But I felt like what I was doing really mattered, you know?"

Jair nodded.

Gavin nudged Jair with his elbow. "I still think you need to take time and have fun, though. You're working too much."

Jair smiled. "I know, you're right. I can talk to Ovard, and we'll try and make time for fun. Just so it's not at the wrong times anymore. All right?"

"All right." Gavin covered up a yawn. "Well, I don't know about you, but I've been busy the last ten days. I'm tired. I think I'll go get some sleep."

"Right," Jair replied. "I'll see you again tomorrow."

As the two boys parted ways, Jair looked back over his shoulder. "Good night, Gavin!" he called out. "It's great to have you home!"

~ 21 ~

Brace's boots scuffed the stones lining the road toward home. He had finally begun to feel useful again – Rudge had allowed him to help with his stonework repairs, applying mortar and such. No climbing any ladders, but it was something, and Brace felt satisfied.

He was ready to go home, to rest, and to see Tassie. He stifled a yawn, brought on by the warm sun and the quiet, fresh air. He didn't think much of it when he noticed someone sitting on a bench outside the next house as he approached. Not until he realized who it was – Jordis. He was a quiet, solitary sort, Brace had noticed from the very beginning. His slightly unkempt hair and the stubble on his chin gave him an odd look, along with his piercing gray eyes, as though he wanted people to stay away from him.

Brace recalled the expression of alarm in Jordis' eyes when Jair had read the words of Haven's welcome, three days earlier. Brace had let it go for a time, assuming that he only needed to get settled in, but Jordis remained solemn and distant.

And now here he was, sitting alone. Again.

Was there anything he could do to try and ease the man's mind?

Well, he could certainly try.

Brace approached slowly, clearing his throat to alert him to his presence. Jordis turned to look, his long thin hair hanging down around his chin. Brace was struck, at that moment, by the way Jordis' eyes seemed to reveal a deep heaviness. How long had he carried alone whatever burden he bore, Brace wondered?

"Hello, Jordis," Brace greeted him, and he responded with a hesitant nod.

217

"My name is Brace," he continued.

"I remember."

Well, Brace thought with a hint of sarcasm. *He can speak.*

"It's a fine day," he said aloud. "I hope you don't mind my saying, but I notice you spend quite a lot of your time alone."

Jordis frowned slightly, straightening his broad shoulders and resting his hands on the knees of his worn breeches.

"And what's that to you?" he asked.

Brace hesitated. He hadn't wanted to irritate the man. He could feel himself getting defensive, so he took a breath to settle himself.

"I just want you to know you aren't alone. Or you don't need to be. I know you must have your reasons. Believe me, I understand. I can see that you've got something weighing on you. And…" Brace paused, taking a small step closer. "And I wanted you to know that I think I might know what's troubling you."

"And how would you know that?"

"I saw you," Brace replied, "when Jair read those words in the Fountain Court. I saw you react, pull away."

Jordis looked aside, his expression blank.

"I think I noticed," Brace went on quickly, "because I was bothered by those words as well, when I first came to Haven. 'The pure in heart', that's what got to me. I told myself that I'd never really been pure in heart."

Jordis looked again at Brace hesitantly, his face softening slightly.

Encouraged, Brace continued. "I thought, since I wasn't pure in heart, that I didn't really belong here. I even thought about leaving."

There was silence for a moment as Brace leaned his shoulder against the side of the house, an arm's length away from where Jordis was seated.

"What stopped you?"

Brace managed a grin. "Tassie," he replied. "My wife. I can always count on her to talk sense into me."

Jordis raised an eyebrow.

"She told me," Brace explained, "that no one is ever free from having made mistakes, and no one ever has motives that are exactly what they should be. That isn't what the writing means. 'The pure in heart' are those who come to Haven simply wanting to make it their home, to live peacefully and not cause any trouble. You have no reason to worry."

Jordis sat in silence for a moment, then slowly shook his head. "I don't think I deserve this place. It's too good for me."

"I often feel that way myself," Brace told him. "But it isn't true. Haven is for everyone, regardless of past mistakes."

"I've hurt people," Jordis went on, looking at Brace intently.

"So have I," Brace replied gently, but Jordis shook his head.

"Not like me."

Brace chewed pensively at the inside of his lip. What could he possibly say to ease Jordis' mind? Anything at all?

"Well," he began again, "you probably do have reasons for feeling like you should leave. I did. But I also had one very important reason to stay. I guess the only advice I can give you is to find that one reason for yourself. But," he added before turning to leave, "think about this. Jair believes that everyone who sets foot inside Haven's gate is *meant* to be here. And that includes you."

Jordis gazed out across the street, then looked up at Brace. He nodded. "Thanks."

"No trouble," Brace replied. "If you ever need a friend, I'll be here."

Jordis smiled a small smile. "Thanks." He rubbed at his chin. "How did you get your bruises?"

Brace grimaced. "Hopefully the last fight I'll ever be in," he told him, "though I don't think I got any punches in, myself, this time."

"A fight?" Jordis asked. "Here?"

Brace laughed. "No, not here. In Erast. I went on a trip with Dursen just before he went and found you in Meriton."

Jordis nodded. His face had begun to soften, Brace had noticed, but now his eyes clouded over, and he looked down at his feet.

Brace cleared his throat. "I'll let you be. I really should head home myself. Just remember what I said, will you? I'd like to be a friend to you."

Jordis looked up. "I'll remember," he replied in a low voice.

"Right, then," Brace said as he backed away. "Try and enjoy the day."

Enjoy the day, Brace chided himself. Couldn't he have thought of anything more fitting to say? The man had something weighing on him; that was clear. But he wouldn't try to pry it out of him. He certainly would not. No, Jordis would need to decide himself if he ever wanted to talk to anyone about it. He would hate for Jordis to leave Haven now that he'd come here. There was simply no reason for that to happen. Well, he had done his part, at least for now. Anything else would just have to wait.

~ 28 ~

Jair was very excited when, a few days later, he told everyone he wanted to hold another meeting. When Brace asked him what it was about, he shook his head, saying he would need to come to the meeting to find out. He wanted to tell everyone all at once.

Jair didn't seem particularly *happy* about the news he wanted to share, but he was unmistakably stirred up. The Main Hall was full when Brace arrived, with Tassie beside him. He caught Arden's eye, and could see that the archer was on edge himself. The air in the Hall bristled with expectation, wondering what Jair would possibly be wanting to tell them.

"All right, everyone," Ovard called out informally. "All right, please, find a seat. This won't take long, but it is monumental news."

The room quickly grew quiet as everyone settled down. Ovard looked back toward Jair, who stood behind the long table, a thick book laid open in front of him.

"Jair?" Ovard asked. "Why don't you just get right to it? Tell them what you've found."

Jair nodded. "All right," he said, nervously running his hand through his hair. "Well, I found this book in Haven's library," he began. "It's about the time when people started leaving Haven, so long ago." He stopped and looked around, but everyone's eyes were fixed on him, waiting for him to continue.

"So," he went on, "it says that people thought they wanted to go and settle in other areas, to spread out and find other places to live. They had been living in Haven for … well, forever, but they wanted to see what was out there, beyond the gate. The overseer let them go, but he made some people 'remembrance keepers', and gave them things they could use to make maps showing the way back. He wanted them to be able to come home again if they wanted to. They went out all over, the book says, and they found that even though the land wasn't quite the same as it was in Haven, it was good enough to live in.

"They started making towns for themselves, and a long time passed, and more people wanted to go with them. Some stayed, and some left, and it got to where all of the people in Haven were growing older, and dying out. The people who were left were saddened because they started to feel like everyone else had forgotten about their home, and they would never come back. They wrote it all down in this book, in case someone did come back. They wanted them to know what had happened and how they felt about everyone leaving."

Jair looked up again. The room was quiet, as though they'd all been holding their breath.

"And there's more," Jair stated. "Not in the book, but something Haven told me."

"Haven told you?" Torren asked.

"Yes, sort of," Jair replied. "I can get these … thoughts, or ideas of things, and I know it's the city that's telling me." He paused, but no one spoke, so he went on. "Well, Haven told me more about it. About what happened after people had left the city. Thousands of years passed, and when the city was empty, with no one living here, things started to change. Not here – nothing has changed here. Out there, things started to change. There are those black creatures that come out at night, that live out in the wilds. Well, they just all of a sudden *were*. They didn't exist before, I think, but after people had been living outside of Haven for so long, the black things just appeared. It's because people's hearts were changing. They used to be pure of heart, like the words say in the Fountain Court, but they started becoming selfish or hateful.

"The more people's hearts grow dark, the worse the screamers get. That's what I call the black creatures – screamers. They get worse as people get worse. And so does the sky. It's getting darker too. I'm not sure if the sky is changing because of the people, or if the screamers are doing it, or if the dark sky is making the screamers get stronger. I don't know. But it all goes together, and the screamers are trying to stop people from coming back to Haven. I know that for certain, if nothing else."

Jair stopped, and the room was completely silent for a moment.

"How..." Ben-Rickard began, "how does Haven tell you these things?"

Jair shrugged. "It's mostly pictures that come into my mind. Not so much in words. Sometimes it's words, but mostly it's pictures. It's like the city knew what I was reading about in this book, and that I had questions, and it wanted to explain things to me. People are supposed to live here," Jair went on. "They never should have left. The night screamers wouldn't even exist if people hadn't left Haven."

"But if they're only meant to live here," Zora began, "why does the rest of the land even exist?"

"I don't know that," Jair answered. "I guess people were given the chance to choose if they wanted to stay or to go. And a lot of them chose to go."

"And Haven was forgotten," Ronin commented heavily.

"For a lot of people, it was," Jair replied. "But we have to tell them about it. We have to help them get back here. If the night screamers want to stop people, we have to help them. We can be stronger than those beasts, since we have the pieces of lightstones to take with us whenever we leave. They can't hurt us if we take the light with us."

A sense of awe filled the entire room. Brace felt it so strongly. He couldn't help but stare at Jair in wonder – he was only a boy! To be given the privilege of having Haven speak to him! What an amazing thing.

Everyone was so full of wonder and astonishment that they had no more questions. They simply sat, taking it all in. Having nothing more to say, Jair dismissed them, promising that he would share with them as soon as he knew anything more.

The mid-afternoon sky was warm and clear as Brace left the Main Hall with Tassie at his side.

"That was unexpected," Brace commented aloud.

"Sorry?" Tassie asked, looking in his direction. "Did you say something?"

"Oh, I just said, that was all so unexpected."

"It was," Tassie replied. "I'm sure I missed some of what he said, but I caught enough to know what it was all about. It all makes sense, doesn't it? About the sunlight, and the night screamers, and everyone leaving Haven."

"Yes," Brace replied. "It does."

The two of them walked on in silence for a moment, until Brace heard someone behind them calling out his name. He turned to look, and Tassie did the same.

"Hello, Ronin," Brace greeted the man as he came strolling closer. "How have you been?"

Ronin smiled. "I was going to ask you the same thing. You're looking well."

"All thanks to you," Brace replied, but Ronin waved him off.

"I was glad to help. Are you feeling better these days?"

"I am. Much better."

"Good to hear. And Tassie," Ronin continued, tipping his head in greeting. "You must be glad to have him back."

"Very glad. Thank you for being there to help him when … when I couldn't," Tassie stammered. Brace slipped his arm around Tassie's slender shoulders.

"It was no trouble at all."

Ronin turned to Brace once again. "This is a truly amazing place you've brought us to. Hearing what Jair had to tell us just now – it's a lot to take in. But I can't ever thank you enough for bringing us here – you and Dursen."

"You don't need to thank us for that," Brace replied quietly. "Haven doesn't belong to us – it belongs to everyone. We only showed you the way."

Ronin smiled kindly – was there any other way for him to be, than *kind*? Brace wondered.

"Have you seen much of Yara lately?" Ronin asked unexpectedly, and Brace felt his muscles tighten.

"Uh – not too much," he replied. "Have you?"

Ronin shook his head. "I'm sorry to say, no. Haven't seen Ben or Torren too much either. Those two certainly made themselves right at home. But we haven't been here long. There will be time for us to catch up with each other, I'm sure."

Brace nodded, trying to force himself to act nonchalant, despite the mention of Yara's name.

"There will be that," he agreed.

"Well," Ronin went on, "it was good to talk with you, at least for a moment. And you as well, Tassie. I hope you both have a pleasant evening."

"Say hello to your family for us," Tassie replied, waving as Ronin turned away.

"I will do that."

They walked the rest of the way home in silence. When they reached the front door, Brace held it open for Tassie, then followed her inside.

"Are you thirsty?" Tassie asked him as he closed the door behind them.

"Um – sure," Brace replied.

He stood and watched, from the far side of the table, while Tassie filled two clay mugs with water they'd collected from the stream. She smiled as she handed Brace one of the mugs, but her smile was slight. She had noticed, Brace was certain, the way he had tensed up at hearing Ronin ask about Yara. But what could he say, now? What would Tassie make of it, that tension?

He remained standing as he slowly drank his water, and watched Tassie gather up the glass jars she'd emptied and cleaned earlier in the day, before the meeting. She found a piece of cloth and began to wipe away any remaining moisture from the jars' outer surfaces.

Brace swallowed his last sip and set the mug down on the table, trying hard to think of something he should be doing right at that moment, but coming up empty.

Tassie looked up from her work. "What's wrong?" she asked tersely.

Brace shook his head. "Nothing."

Tassie was silent a moment, running a cloth along the outside of the jar. "It's Yara, isn't it?" she asked, her voice quiet.

"What?" Brace was quick to answer. "What do you mean?"

"I noticed how you tensed up when Ronin mentioned her," Tassie replied simply.

Brace felt heat rising in his face, but he was unsure whether he was more frustrated at the fact that she *had* noticed, or self-conscious about himself, about the fact that Yara did make him feel uncomfortable.

"I just," Tassie went on, "I just wonder if something …"

"Nothing happened!" Brace interrupted, shaking his head.

Tassie lifted the jar, ran the cloth along the bottom, then set it aside.

"No ..." she replied, but Brace could hear an edge of doubt in her voice.

"Tassie," he began, but she had looked aside. He reached out and caught the corner of the damp cloth, which she held in her hand, and she faced him once again.

"Nothing happened, Tassie. *Nothing.* I've told you everything. You don't think I'm lying, do you?"

She shook her head. "Not lying, no. But I've seen the way she looks at you, Brace. And I see how you are when she's around, or when someone mentions her name. You don't react that way when people talk about Zora, or Essa, or Persha."

"Nothing has happened between Yara and me," Brace insisted, "and nothing is going to happen. All right? That's the end of it."

Tassie pressed her lips together in a firm line, but she kept her eyes on Brace, not looking away.

"I'm not saying that anything really happened between you and Yara," she went on. "But there's something you're not telling me."

"Forget about it," Brace replied, his voice firm.

"I can't, Brace. I can't just forget. I think there's something wrong, and I just want us to talk about it."

Brace looked away, leaning his hands on the rough wooden edge of the table. He felt a muscle twitch along his jaw and heat rising in his face. When he faced Tassie again, he saw that she had not taken her searching green eyes off of him, not for one moment.

"I don't want to talk about this," he informed her. "There is nothing to talk about."

"It's just *talking*, Brace," Tassie pressed, her voice firm. "Why can't we –"

"No!" Brace cut in. "You're always wanting to talk about things that don't need to be talked about! We don't need to dredge up my past, Tassie. The past happened, and it's over. And this... this *me-and-Yara* thing, it's nothing! It's just you and me now, Tassie. That's it. I'll have no other woman in my life, not like that."

"All I'm saying is that we need to be able to tell each other things," Tassie insisted. "We need to talk about the little things, or they will turn into big things and drive a wedge between us."

Brace felt trapped. He felt the walls closing in around him, and his throat tightened.

"I need to get out," he said shortly.

"Brace …"

He shook his head. "I need to go for a walk." He turned and left, pushing his way out through the door and crossing the street.

Tassie did not call out after him.

~

Brace went on and on, able to breathe again, but bristling with anger and frustration. Talk, talk, *talk*. Why did Tassie always want him to talk? The past was the past! He had learned to see it that way years and years ago. How else could he deal with everything that life threw at him? When his mother died, he'd had to put it in the past. When the farmer was cruel to him, he'd put it in the past, especially after he ran away from him. Whenever anything frightened him, saddened him or angered him, he simply put it in the past and went on. Why couldn't Tassie understand that?

Brace kicked at a loose clod of dirt, only then realizing that he had stormed all the way down to the southeastern garden, newly cleared of brush and ready for planting. He let out a long breath, running his hands through his hair, noticing that there were people out in the field even now, working the soil. And nearest to Brace was one of the last people he would have expected to see at the garden today – *Jordis*.

Clutching a small canvas bag in one hand, he loped along steadily in Brace's direction, dropping seeds into the soil every two steps. He was intent on his work, scarcely looking up from the task at hand. As he approached, he noticed Brace standing there, his arms crossed defensively over his chest.

"Hello," he greeted him. Didn't think to see you out here."

Brace tried to smile. "I didn't think I'd see you either. Are you working the fields now?"

Jordis smiled crookedly. "Yes, well. I was just out walking, and saw them all hard at work. Asked if I could help. I had nothing better to do."

"Well, I'm sure they appreciate the extra hands," Brace replied. His frustration simmered under the surface of his temper, clouding the gladness he felt at seeing that Jordis had shown some desire to be of help.

"Something wrong?" Jordis asked, pausing in his work.

Brace sighed. "Just ... just frustrated, really."

Jordis nodded.

Brace kept his eyes on the dirt near his feet as he chewed at his lip. "I just don't like being forced into talking about things," he told Jordis. "I feel trapped. I feel like the room is getting smaller all around me, and I can't breathe."

Jordis stood by silently for a moment. "What sort of things?"

"Past things."

"Life things?"

"Life? Yes. Things from my life. From my past. Things I'd rather just forget."

Jordis nodded, gazing out across the field, his eyes narrowing. "But you can't," he said softly.

"Can't what?"

"Forget," he replied, looking at Brace again. "When something happens, something big, you can't forget. You can try to shrug it off, but it holds on to you. It won't let you go. All you can do is act like it's not there. But the people around you, they know it's there."

"How does talking about it help at all?" Brace asked, now feeling more defeated than angry.

Jordis took a few steps, reaching into the bag he carried, and dropped two small round seeds into a hole in the soil, covering them with the toe of his boot. "When I came here," he began, "I carried a heavy burden."

"I remember."

"Right. And you came to talk to me, didn't you?"

"You seemed fearful. I wanted you to know it was all right for you to be here."

Jordis nodded, his long, thin hair blowing in the breeze. "And if I hadn't said what I did about myself, would you now be able to say you knew anything of me?"

Brace hesitated, getting at the meaning behind Jordis' words. "Not so much," he admitted. "But Tassie knows me better than this. We've known each other for nearly a year."

Jordis went on again, dropping more seeds, and Brace followed him. "Likely she wants to know you more. There's no end to how much one person can know another."

Brace sighed. He'd never expected such wise words from Jordis.

"You're right," he admitted. "That is what she wants. She told me so herself."

"It's hard to talk about some things," Jordis commented. "I know that. Some secrets don't come out easy."

"They don't," Brace agreed. He glanced back toward home. "I should go, shouldn't I? Try to work things out."

"Don't need me telling you," Jordis replied simply, dropping more seeds into the soil and continuing on his way.

~

Brace found himself back at his own front door before he was truly ready. He still had no idea what would be the right thing to say; he only knew that he had to try and make things right between him and Tassie. He hesitated, then slowly pushed the door open, stepping into the front room.

Tassie sat at the table, and looked up as he entered. She didn't have a smile for him, but she wasn't frowning either. She simply acknowledged his presence.

"Hello," Brace said lamely.

"Hello, Brace."

Brace nervously scratched at the side of his head as he made his way toward her. "I'm sorry about everything," he told her.

Tassie nodded. "So am I."

"You don't have anything to be sorry for," Brace told her.

"Maybe I pressed you too hard." Tassie took a long, steadying breath, then spoke quietly. "I understand what you were saying, Brace. And I do believe that it's true, that nothing happened with you and Yara. But I still want you to share things with me. I want to know what's going on inside you, that's all it is. I'm not accusing you of having done anything, or even that you're *thinking* about doing anything. I just want to know what is happening inside you. In your mind, and in your heart."

Before he left the house, Brace had felt himself putting up a shield, trying to block out Tassie's words. Now, he let them get in through his defenses, just enough. Feeling trapped, he let out a breath and lowered himself onto a seat across from Tassie, propping his elbows on the table and leaning his head into his hands. He sighed, shutting his eyes against the feeling that had come over him, of being caught in a corner. Was this ever going to be something he would become accustomed to? Needing to be vulnerable? He had wanted for so long to have people to share his life with, and now that he did, he found that there were demands being made on him that he wasn't sure he was ready to meet.

Brace could hear the sound of Tassie's footsteps as she came around to his side of the table, but he did not look up until he felt her hand resting lightly on his arm.

"I'm sorry, Brace," Tassie whispered.

He avoided her searching eyes, instead gazing blankly across the room.

"I didn't mean to get you so upset," Tassie went on. "I just … wanted to talk. That's all."

Brace flexed his shoulders, trying to release the tension that had built up in his muscles.

Tassie slid into the seat beside him, so close that her knee touched his. "You do understand why I wanted to talk to you about this, don't you?"

Brace nodded slowly. "Yes," he admitted.

Tassie pulled her hand away, resting it in her lap. "I just don't want us to keep any secrets from each other."

Again, Brace nodded, feeling his frustration diminish slightly.

"I'm not used to talking things over like this," he told her. "I've always had to figure things out on my own, to handle everything that came at me on my own."

"But you don't need to do that any longer. I'm here to share those things with you, Brace. Good and bad."

Brace ran his fingers through his chin-length hair, pushing it away from his face.

"Do ..." Tassie began, "do you feel like I'm only asking because I'm prying?"

Brace pondered the question for a moment. "No," he answered. "At first I did, maybe. But ..." Brace paused for a moment, but he knew he needed to go on. "I think it felt like prying because I was already feeling a little bit guilty."

"For what?" Tassie asked in a whisper, as though she wasn't sure she wanted to know the answer.

"Well, just for ... thinking that Yara is attractive," Brace replied. "And, I know she felt that way about me, at first. I don't have feelings for her, Tassie. I just noticed her looks, that's all, when we met in Erast."

A smile played at Tassie's lips. "That's all?"

"Mainly," Brace told her. He'd gotten through what he had already, and it hadn't been as painful as he'd feared. Why not take a chance and go on?

"That first night, crossing the mountains," he continued, a few words at a time, putting his thoughts together, "it was so cold. Yara – she fell asleep leaning right against my side. But," he went on quickly, "the whole time, I was wishing it was you, and not her."

Tassie's smile was fuller now, the familiar shine returning to her eyes. "Thank you."

"*Thank you?*"

"For telling me."

"You're not angry?"

"No."

"I could never have real feelings for anyone but you," Brace told her. "Not ever again."

Tassie shook her head slowly. "I know that's what you want. But people can't help what they feel."

"I would never go behind your back, Tassie. You know I wouldn't. You know I've given all of that up!"

"I do," she told him. "But I can see that Yara cares for you. I don't know if it's only because she feels responsible for what happened to you … but sometimes that's all it takes."

Brace wanted to argue his point, but he knew that Tassie was right. "Sometimes it is," he agreed. "But you saw how she was when she met you. If she does have feelings for me, she won't press it. She wants to be a friend to you, and to me. She's been lonely. She just needs a friend."

Tassie nodded and stood, picking up an empty jar from off of the table. Brace watched her as she placed it back on the shelf, alongside several others. A slight hint of tension remained in the room – Brace could feel it. It was his own fault, he knew. Should he try and do something to alleviate it, or did it just need to run its course?

"Tassie," he said, but her back was to him, and she stood on the far side of the room.

He sighed and pushed himself up, away from the table. Taking his empty mug with him, he crossed over to where she stood. Reaching around her, he placed the mug on the stone shelf lining the wall in front of him. Tassie felt him brush up against her, and she turned to look at him.

Brace searched for something to say. "I – I'm sorry," he stammered.

Tassie eyed him searchingly. "I know you are," she replied.

"It's not enough, though, is it?"

Tassie leaned back against the shelf. "I know enough about your past," she told him, "I know enough of who you used to be, and the things you were used to doing. I didn't come into this life with you blindly, Brace. I knew there would be struggles, letting the old things go. I hope you don't feel like I expect you to be … someone that you can't. Someone completely new." She smiled a little. "I fell in love with you as you *are*, Brace. Not as who you might be someday."

Brace felt more of his tension melt away, and he ran his hand along Tassie's long wavy hair. "Thank you for reminding me," he told her, and she wrapped her arms around him and held him close.

~ 29 ~

Leandra's attempt at helping Kendie make bread for that night's meal was not going well. Kendie understood everything Leandra was telling her, and she was paying attention well enough, but Leandra's mind kept wandering over to Zorix, who was pacing around the back of the room, his mind a clutter of worry and questions.

Finally, she turned away from the table to look at him. "What is it, Zorix?" she asked him aloud. "Something has you troubled, but you haven't come to me with it. What's wrong?"

The room was silent for a moment while Zorix gazed at Leandra, silently speaking to her.

"What?" Kendie asked nervously. "Something isn't wrong with the baby, is it?"

"No," Leandra replied hesitantly. "He says he heard someone thinking today, something that's upset him. It was after the meeting, though, and he's not sure who it was."

"What did he hear?" Kendie asked, stirring the dough with a long wooden spoon.

Leandra looked toward the door, as though she hoped, or expected, to see Arden come inside at that moment. "I think we need to talk to Ovard," she replied.

"Why?" Kendie asked, a sense of dread in her voice.

"Come on," Leandra told her. "We'll do the bread later. Zorix, come with me. We'll tell the others. Let's go and get them."

"*All* of the others?" Kendie asked, surprised.

"No," Leandra replied. She took Kendie by the shoulders and looked her in the eye. "Don't say a word to anyone else," she warned. "We'll get Ovard and Jair, Tassie and Brace, and Arden. No one else, do you understand? This is very important."

Kendie nodded, her eyes wide. "Yes."

"Good. Come with me."

Zorix followed closely as Leandra led Kendie slowly across the road to Brace and Tassie's home. "Don't act worried," Leandra advised. "Don't draw attention."

"All right," Kendie replied quietly, clinging to Leandra's hand.

Brace answered the door when Leandra knocked, a slight frown on his face, which Leandra noticed but paid no heed to.

"Brace, we might have a bit of trouble on our hands," she explained quietly. "Get Tassie, will you? We're going on to Ovard's."

"What is this about?" Brace asked.

"Not here," she replied. "Trust me."

Brace obeyed without further question. "Tassie," he said as he looked over his shoulder into the house. "It's Leandra. She says we need to come with her. Don't ask," he added when Tassie looked at him curiously.

As the four of them made their way silently through the empty street, they unexpectedly met Arden along the way. He regarded them with surprise at seeing them out, and all together, at that time of the evening. Leandra hushed him before he could comment.

"Come with us," she told him. "I'll explain soon."

Ovard was no less surprised when Leandra knocked on his door. "What's all this?" he asked, his eyes wide.

"It's Zorix," Leandra answered simply. "He's overheard something." She lowered her voice. "We need to talk this over."

Ovard nodded and moved aside, allowing everyone to enter. Jair watched them silently as they gathered around the front room, having heard some of what was said in the doorway.

When they were all safely within the walls of Ovard's home, seated around the wooden table, Leandra finally explained the situation fully.

"What has Zorix told you that's so upsetting?" Brace asked her, taking note of the bright red color of the animal's fur as he huddled near Leandra's feet.

"It's something he overheard at today's meeting," she replied quietly. "It was … '*I wonder what will come of what I've done. Will they come and try to force their way in here?*' Is that it exactly?" she asked, looking down at Zorix. "That's it," she said, looking up again. "*Because of what I've done,*" she added.

"Who? What have they done?" Jair asked in alarm.

Leandra shook her head. "I don't know. Zorix doesn't know. He says there were too many people at the meeting; all of their thoughts and voices were jumbled together."

"Do you mean there is someone here, in Haven, who could be a threat to the rest of us? A threat to our safety?" Arden demanded.

"It seems that way," Leandra replied meekly.

"Keep your voice down," Ovard admonished, his eyes on Arden. "This needs to stay with us alone."

"What can we do about this?" Tassie wondered nervously.

"*Try to force their way in* …" Ovard pondered over the words. "Who, I wonder? From where?"

"He heard this at the meeting, today?" Arden asked, and Leandra nodded. "Who was at the meeting?"

"Nearly everyone," Brace replied.

"Then who *wasn't* at the meeting?" Jair spoke up. "We can at least know who *wasn't* there, who couldn't have thought it."

It did not take long for the seven of them to conclude that the only people absent from the meeting were Zora and little Trystan; Torren, who had been spending quite a bit of time with the young widow; elderly Lomar, and Daris and Essa.

"That doesn't narrow it down very much," Brace remarked.

"No, it doesn't," Leandra agreed.

"Have any of you noticed any suspicious behavior among the others?" Ovard asked.

"Well, I wouldn't call it suspicious," Arden spoke up, "but Brodan's behavior has been downright insolent at times."

"Yes," Ovard agreed. "I have seen that." He looked around the room. "Any other thoughts?"

Brace mentally pictured as many faces as he could, but none of them stood out as having acted suspicious or guilty in any way. *Guilty* … One face in particular suddenly came to mind, though he hated to suspect him of anything.

"Worley," Leandra said after a moment.

"Worley?" Jair asked in surprise.

"Arden, didn't you say that Worley seemed as though he was either daydreaming or distracted, while your group was clearing the southwest garden?"

"I did," he replied.

While the others discussed Worley's character, Brace felt his muscles tighten. He did not want to pin any guilt on the man – he felt it to his very core that it would be betrayal if he spoke up. He had trusted Brace enough to talk to him. But...

"Anyone else?" Ovard asked, his voice weary.

"Jordis," Brace answered before he had time to reconsider.

"Jordis?" Jair asked, and Brace nodded. "He's been plagued by guilt, he told me, but he wouldn't say why."

"Thank you," Ovard told him, but now Brace felt pressed in by guilt himself, and he avoided everyone's eyes.

"What are we going to do?" Kendie asked plaintively. "I'm a little scared."

"It's going to be all right, Kendie," Ovard told her.

"Are you sure?" she asked. "Zorix said he heard, whoever it was, wondering if someone would try to *force* their way into Haven. What if they would try to hurt people?"

"No one can break in through Haven's gate," Arden spoke up.

"Are you *sure*?" Kendie asked again.

No one spoke.

"What *are* we going to do?" Tassie finally asked.

Ovard sighed. "We'll just need to keep a close eye on everyone," he replied. "We'll be sure not to let a word of this leak to anyone else. Unfortunately, at this point everyone is suspect." He looked at Leandra. "Did Zorix say that it was a man's voice?"

Leandra glanced questioningly at Zorix. "Yes," she replied. "It was a man, of that he's certain."

"Do you think Zorix would recognize the voice if he heard it again? Maybe he could come to the next meeting, and listen for that same voice again?"

Zorix huffed and paced around Leandra's feet, then curled up under her long skirt and hid his face.

"He says it's too much for him," Leandra spoke for Zorix. "He says he can't stand all of the voices, and he isn't sure he wants to hear any more."

"That's all right, little one," Ovard told him kindly. "I can understand that. We'll just be on high alert. But remember," he addressed the group, "this is to remain secret knowledge. No one else can know about this. If the rest of the people find out, it will be easier for the guilty one to hide the secret. Or to …" Ovard's voice trailed off. He did not want to think what the person might do, whoever they were.

Everyone agreed somberly as Ovard pointed out that it was getting late, and they should get back to their homes. Tassie held tightly to Brace's hand as they left through the front door.

"I can't believe this has happened," she muttered. "Could someone here be a threat to our safety, even in Haven?" She shook her head in disbelief. "I've come to think of everyone as a friend, even though I may not know them well."

"I've done the same, for the most part," Brace agreed. "There are some people I would never suspect of having done anything …" his voice drifted off.

"What's that?" Tassie asked.

"Sorry. I was just wondering what *'what I've done'* could mean. And who would try to force their way in? Everyone is welcome here, after all."

"Everyone with a pure heart," Tassie pointed out. "I remember what Ovard said, a long time ago. He talked about the possibility of someone wanting to rule Haven for themselves, to take it over and use its power for their own purposes."

"But can that actually happen?" Brace asked. "If those without pure hearts aren't welcome, how could they get in?"

"Someone did," Tassie replied. "Didn't they? Can whoever it is that's hiding something be of a pure heart? To be the cause of some possible danger to us, and not say anything? *They* got in through the gate, didn't they?"

Brace nodded in silence, realizing how right Tassie was.

"I don't feel safe now," Tassie muttered, leaning against Brace's side as they walked.

"Don't worry," Brace told her. "I'll be close by. And if I know Arden at all, he won't allow whoever it is to get away with this – whatever it is. It's not *harbrost* to keep a terrible secret like this, is it?"

Tassie managed a smile. "No, it isn't."

"Don't be afraid," Brace tried to encourage her. "We just need to keep our eyes open. There's nothing we can do to change what's already been done. The best we can do is be ready if something does happen."

"I pray that it won't," Tassie replied.

"So do I," Brace agreed. "Believe me, so do I."

~ 30 ~

Among the population of Haven's citizens, the mood was quite peaceful, joyous even. Life went on – the children attending school with Dorianne and the crops growing at an amazing rate, much to Dursen's surprise. Jair continued teaching Ovard and Jayla how to read the old records of life in Haven. Arden led periodic hunting trips, which Persha was now always a part of, having become quite skilled with a bow.

Only half of the chicken's eggs that had been brought back from Meriton had hatched, but Nerissa was pleased. She had been put in charge of their care, and the chicks were thriving now under her loving, watchful eye. She could be seen any morning kneeling on the ground outside her home, her cupped hands full of grain and seeds, while the tiny yellow birds pecked at them, inexpertly trying to eat.

Dursen had built a small pen for the birds, and was often at Nerissa's side. He had the excuse of helping her care for the chicks, but Brace could see right through that. It was obvious enough that he wanted to spend as much time as possible with Nerissa. Brace was glad for them. Dursen deserved to have someone to love.

Everything was coming along, more than well enough, and everyone seemed content. Brace, however, along with Haven's most recent founders, felt the tension of the unfortunate secret hanging over them. None of them wanted to become unreasonably mistrustful of any seemingly unusual behavior, but they were obligated to share anything anyone said or did that caught their attention, anything that in any way gave them reason to wonder if they could be *the one*.

Those moments of suspicion were, whether fortunately or unfortunately, few and far between. The majority of Haven's citizens were kind and helpful people, making fast friends between the two groups that had arrived separately. The lines were becoming blurred between those from Dunya and Danferron, between young and old, between the formerly wealthy or poor. This was fortunate, for this was the way life in Haven was meant to be – free from strife. It was also *unfortunate*, however, for the longer it took for the guilty one to be discovered, the closer it brought Haven's unsuspecting citizens to the unknown threat of danger that was hanging over the city.

Daris and Essa were finally married, giving everyone cause for much celebration. Shortly after that came the recognition of Jair's thirteenth birthday and the harvesting of potatoes, squash, peas and grain from the gardens. The entire city was treated to a feast, with more than plenty left over. The excess was carefully stored away in one of the empty buildings along the outside walls of the Fountain Court. Torren was put in charge of measuring quantities, of what remained in storage as well as what was given out. With the crops growing so quickly, there was no need to run out of anything. Plans were already being made for a second planting – no one living in Haven would ever need to go hungry.

Brace certainly wasn't feeling hungry after the breakfast he and Tassie enjoyed that particular morning – hot bread cakes with sliced fruit from the orchard, along with cooked eggs and thinly sliced bits of potatoes topped off with butter made from goat's milk.

"I haven't eaten that well in years," Brace commented as he sat at the table across from Tassie.

She smiled. "Neither have I."

"This was delicious. You should be very pleased with yourself."

"Me?" Tassie asked, surprised. "Why?"

"Well, you're the one who brought up the idea of having eggs," he replied.

Tassie shook her head. "One small thing," she told him. "Jair is the one who should be thanked for the rest of this."

"Well, I'll be sure to thank Jair later," Brace said in a teasing voice.

Tassie smiled as she began to clear away the dishes.

"Have we got anything we should be doing today?" Brace asked her before she turned away.

"Nothing in particular," she replied. "Why?"

"No reason," Brace told her as he heard a knocking at the front of the house. "There's someone at the door," he said as he rose from the table. "I'll see who it is."

Brace opened the door to find Kendie standing outside, smiling cheerfully.

"Well, hello," he greeted her. "More medic lessons?"

"No," Kendie replied sheepishly. "I just thought I'd come for a visit. I hope that's all right."

"Who is it?" Tassie asked.

Brace stepped aside. "It's Kendie," he told her, motioning for the girl to come in. "It seems she has nothing better to do than come and see us."

"But I *like* visiting you," Kendie protested, and Brace winked at her.

"I know that," he told her, smiling.

Kendie smiled and gave Brace a quick hug before embracing Tassie as well. These little hugs from Kendie, these undeserved gifts of hers, always caught Brace off guard. He'd felt a strange sort of connection with her, from when he had first met her in Meriton. They had both endured the same hardships, and though they never spoke of any of it, there it was, a sort of invisible bond that drew them close to one another. Brace suspected that Kendie viewed him as someone who'd rescued her, partially because he'd stood up for the idea of letting her run away from Rune Fletcher, and partially because he'd brought her over the mountains into the wondrous city of Haven. Those things may well be true, but still, he never felt that he deserved for Kendie to look up to him. Inside, he still saw himself as the man he'd been for the last eighteen years or more – a liar, a thief, and, at the root of it all, a man full of confusion and fear. No, he did not deserve for anyone to think highly of him.

"Where is Leandra?" Tassie asked Kendie as they sat down at the table, Tassie sliding a bowl of biscuits in Kendie's direction.

"She's walking with Zorix," Kendie replied, helping herself. "She says the baby is making her uncomfortable, and she feels better walking rather than either sitting, or even lying down."

"Really?" Brace asked, joining them at the table.

Kendie nodded, her mouth full of bread.

"That's to be expected, considering how far along she is," Tassie informed him.

Kendie swallowed the bit of biscuit she'd been chewing. "Do you think you'll ever have a baby together?" she asked.

Brace looked over at Tassie; he was surprised at the unexpected question, and wanted to see what her reaction might be. She was looking at him as well, her green eyes wide.

"Well," she began, facing Kendie once again, "we haven't really talked about it."

"Talked about it?" Kendie questioned.

"Yes," Brace told her. "It's a good idea to talk it over first. It's a big decision to make."

"So ..." Kendie paused, taking another bite of biscuit. "What if it just happens, even though you haven't talked about it?"

Tassie eyed Kendie for a moment. "How much do you know about having babies?" she asked.

Kendie blushed. "Everything. Leandra told me."

Brace feigned deep interest in his mug of tea. This was one conversation he'd rather not be a part of.

"Well," Tassie finally answered, "sometimes babies come when you don't plan for them, but I'm not going to worry about it."

Kendie smiled. "I hope you will have one, someday."

Brace took a big swallow of his tea. "So what is this I hear about you and Jair?" he asked, changing the subject.

"*What?*" Kendie's eyes grew wide.

"You know what I mean. You have feelings for Jair, don't you?"

Kendie chewed at her lip. "Yes, sort of," she replied. "Who told you?"

Brace tipped his head in Tassie's direction. "But she didn't need to. I've seen the way you look at him, how you try to be around him as much as you can. I couldn't help but notice."

"You're right," Kendie admitted. "But Tassie, how did you know?"

"Leandra told me. I hope you don't mind. We were just chatting one day."

Kendie broke off another piece of biscuit. "I don't mind, I guess. Just don't tell anyone else, okay?" She looked at both of them.

"You mean I can't tell Jair?" Brace asked, as though he was disappointed. "Too bad."

"No, don't tell Jair!" Kendie exclaimed in alarm. "Please don't tell Jair!"

Brace laughed. "I'm only teasing," he told her. "I wouldn't do that."

Kendie's face reddened. "Thank you."

There was another knock at the door. "Well, this is a busy place this morning," Brace commented as he rose from the table. Opening the door, he was surprised to see Leandra, who, as always, had Zorix with her. The large-eared creature huddled near Leandra's feet, his fur a deep red, revealing that he was in a fearful mood.

"Leandra," Brace greeted her in surprise. He lowered his voice. "Is everything all right?"

"I think so," she replied distractedly, tucking her pale, smooth hair behind her ear. "I mean, this has nothing to do with *the secret*. Is Tassie here just now?"

"Yes," Brace replied, "and Kendie's here too. We were all just talking. Are you sure nothing's wrong? You both look like something has you worried."

"I'm not certain," she said haltingly. "But I think – well, I think my water's broke."

"Water?" Brace asked, confused. "Oh," he said gravely when he realized what she meant. *The baby!* He turned quickly back toward the room, catching Tassie's eye.

"It's Leandra," he told her. "She says her water broke."

Tassie's eyes widened and she stood quickly, hurrying to the door.

"Leandra?" she asked, standing in front of her. "How long ago?"

"Just a few moments," she replied, smiling nervously.

"Is the baby coming?" Kendie asked, joining them in the doorway.

"It will be soon enough," Leandra told her.

"Where is Arden?" Tassie asked, hardly having noticed Kendie standing beside her.

"Out hunting," Leandra replied. "He left early this morning with Persha and a few of the men. They're planning on being out all day."

Tassie only had to look up at Brace for a moment – he saw the question in her eyes.

"I'll go and find him," he volunteered. "You take care of things here. How much time does she have?"

"There's no telling," Tassie replied. "But Arden will need to get back here as soon as he can."

"Of course." Brace pulled on his boots and grabbed his cloak – it was early still, and the Woods were cool and shaded. "I'll bring him back as soon as I find him."

"Be careful," Tassie warned him as he stopped to embrace her.

"I will," he said, glancing at Leandra, who seemed to be completely at ease, standing in the open doorway. Zorix, however, was pacing nervously. Brace grinned, and Leandra smiled back at him.

"It's finally time," she said, then caught Brace's arm as he passed her. "Tell Arden I'm all right, will you? I don't want him to worry."

"I'll tell him," Brace promised. "I'll bring him back soon."

~

Fallen evergreen needles crunched under Brace's boots as he made his way through the Woods at last. He was still in awe of the many different smells, the many different colors that overwhelmed his senses there. The deep, dark green of the mature pines was a sharp contrast to the bright, vibrant yellow-green of new-growth leaves, almost glowing in the wide shafts of sunlight breaking through to the forest floor.

Brace took a few more steps, wading through the long, narrow, feathery leaves of plants that nearly reached to his waist. He listened intently for any sounds indicating where the small hunting party might be. How far Haven's Woods stretched out into the distance, Brace had no idea, but they would not have gone any farther than they needed to.

The cool air was calm and still, quiet but for a few small birds chirping high in the trees. Arden and the others would be keeping as quiet as possible, not wanting to scare away the game. And they must be keeping *very* quiet at the moment, for Brace could not even hear a hint that they might be in this part of the Woods. He only hoped his instincts were true, and that he'd chosen to go in the right direction.

He went on a few more paces, then stopped again.

Where could they be? He looked back over his shoulder, but all he could see around him were enormous trees and patches of sun and shadow on the forest floor. Leandra was counting on him. The baby was coming! He *had* to find Arden. Brace had no idea how long it would take for the baby to come, but Arden needed to know what was happening. He hurried on again, covering a good stretch of ground before he stopped to catch his breath. He turned and looked in every direction, watching and listening for any sign that someone had been this way.

Nothing ... or was there? Brace thought he'd heard something. *A voice?*

"Hello!" he called out. "Arden? Are you out here?"

A brief moment passed in silence.

"Hello?" he called again.

"Hello!" a man's voice replied at last. "Who's there?"

Brace went on toward the sound. "It's Brace. Is Arden there with you?"

At last, as he went on, looking left and right, he spotted the hunting party through the trees. There were four of them, standing around a small pile of rabbits they'd hunted down.

"I'm here," Arden called out, a frown of curiosity on his face as he stepped forward.

Brace ran toward them, having no concern at all that he might be scaring away any game.

"Is something wrong?" Arden questioned him as he came close, catching his breath.

Brace shook his head. "No – I mean – I don't know." He took two breaths, then just blurted it out. "Leandra is having the baby."

"*What?!*" Arden exclaimed.

"Not yet, I mean," he went on, "at least I don't think so. But the time's getting closer. She'll be having it soon." Brace peered past Arden's shoulder toward Persha, Stanner and Torren, all of whom were armed with newly-made wooden bows. "She said her water broke," Brace went on in a low voice.

Arden quickly glanced back at the rest of the hunting party.

"You go on," Stanner told him. "We can handle things here."

Torren nodded in agreement.

Without a word, Arden turned back toward Brace. "Let's go," he told him, wasting no time, striding quickly back towards the city.

Brace took a breath, nodded in greeting to the others, then turned and followed after Arden.

"I hope it goes well," Persha called after them. Brace waved his hand in response, but Arden had already gone too far ahead to hear her.

~ 31 ~

Brace found it a struggle to keep up with Arden as they quickly made their way out of Haven's Woods and back into the city. All that long way, the only sounds reaching Brace's ears were his heart pounding and his own ragged breathing. Arden kept at least six steps ahead of Brace the whole way, and he did not speak a word for the longest time.

"What happened?" Arden finally asked, when they could see Haven's walls of lightstone off through the trees.

"Leandra just said she thought her water broke," Brace explained. "Nothing else."

"How long ago?"

"Well," Brace panted, trying to catch up to Arden, "she came to Tassie right after it happened, and I left to find you right after that. It must have been an hour ago, maybe a bit longer."

Arden did not hesitate in the slightest as they passed by the northwestern garden, temporarily empty of any crops. None of the homes in that part of the city were occupied as of yet, so no one lingered on the road anywhere in sight. For all the tension Brace felt, which he was sure Arden felt even more, that part of the city seemed too calm and quiet.

They turned down one of the side streets, lined with high walls of lightstone, cut across the cobblestones of the empty Fountain Court and made their way toward the clinic. When they finally came in sight of it, Arden hesitated.

"I'm sure everything is all right," Brace told him, catching his breath. "I don't think much has happened yet."

Arden nodded, removing his quiver of arrows and resting it against the wall of the clinic.

"I could go in with you, if you'd like," Brace offered hesitantly.

"Thank you," Arden replied, "but I think you should go and tell Ovard that it's happening – that the baby is coming. Will you do that for me?"

"Of course I will," Brace replied, running his sleeve across his forehead, damp with sweat.

Arden nodded, stepped aside, and pulled open the door to the clinic. Brace waited until Arden was out of sight before he turned away, heading back toward the library. He was sure he would find both Ovard and Jair there at this time of day.

Sure enough, there they were, poring over papers old and new, along with Jayla, who was writing slowly and carefully. Brace wasted no time in telling them the news, not caring that he was interrupting; he was sure they wouldn't mind, not this time.

"Wonderful!" Ovard exclaimed. "Thank you for bringing the news along to us."

"Does Arden know?" Jair asked. "He was going hunting today."

"He knows," Brace replied. "He's back, he's with Leandra at the clinic."

Jayla smiled, looking up from her writing. "Will you tell her I wish her well?" she asked.

Brace nodded. "Yes, I can tell her." He turned back to Ovard. "Will you pass the word along? About the baby, I mean. I'm guessing it will take a while. Everyone should know, shouldn't they? So they don't wonder where Leandra is, and Tassie? They'll need to go to Ronin if they need anything."

"Of course, we'll let them know."

"Thank you," Brace replied, taking a deep breath. "I think I'll check back in with Tassie, just to see how things are going."

Ovard dismissed Brace with a wave and a smile, and he hurried off again.

Brace hesitated outside the doors to the clinic, just as Arden had. He stood listening for a moment, his ear pressed to the door, but he could hear nothing. *Odd*, he thought, slowly pushing open the door.

The light inside the clinic was not as bright as outdoors, and it took a moment for his eyes to adjust enough to see clearly. The first thing he noticed was Kendie, seated across the room near the window. She was silently watching Leandra, who sat on a low, cushioned bench, leaning her arms against the bed and taking slow, even breaths. Arden sat beside her, rubbing her back with one of his large, strong hands, and looking very concerned. Brace quickly turned to face Tassie, who had seen him enter and stood facing him.

"Is everything all right?" Brace asked.

"Yes," Tassie replied. "Will you help me?"

"All right," Brace answered quickly, a bit startled by the request. He had helped Tassie with patients before, but never with anything as extreme as delivering a baby. "What should I do?"

"First, wash your hands."

"Right." Brace turned aside to thoroughly wet his hands in the basin full of stream water. He picked up the rough block of soap, looking back over his shoulder. He was starting to feel a touch of panic rising in his throat. The thought of Leandra struggling to give birth – he wasn't sure if he could bear the sight of it. She was always so strong; he'd respected Leandra, and the strength that he saw in her, even from the first day he'd met her in the wild lands outside of Bale. No, this felt wrong. He shouldn't be here. Arden belonged, of course, as did Tassie. *But not me,* he thought. *This is too personal.*

Brace caught Tassie's sleeve where she stood nearby, preparing some medicinal powders.

"I don't think I can do this," he whispered when Tassie looked at him. "Seeing Leandra like this … I just don't know if I can handle it."

Tassie's smile was amused. "It's all right," she told him quietly. "I just meant for you to help me get things ready. I didn't mean for you to stay."

Brace nodded and grinned ruefully as he rinsed the soap from his hands. "Thank you."

"I'm all right, Brace," Leandra spoke up, and he turned to face her. "I'm fine," she said, looking a little tired, "but Zorix is worried. He's outside somewhere. Will you find him for me?"

"I will," Brace replied. "I just need to help Tassie for a moment."

Leandra nodded, letting out a sigh and sitting up straighter. Arden kept his eyes on her face, concerned, while Brace followed Tassie's instructions about gathering roughspun towels from the shelves as she found a carved stone mug and filled it with drinking water.

"Arden, my back hurts," Leandra said as she leaned forward against the bed again. Arden ran his hand along her back, as he had done earlier.

"Lower," she told him.

Tassie watched them from where she stood beside Brace. "Press firmly," she said to Arden, who obeyed.

"How is that?" he asked Leandra. "Not too much?"

"No, that's perfect," she replied, stifling a moan.

Tassie lay her hand on Brace's shoulder, and he turned, startled, to look at her.

"You've helped enough, I think. We'll be all right for a while, and Kendie is here, for now. You should go and see after Zorix."

"I'll try," Brace replied.

Tassie grinned as Brace went out the door, taking one last glance back at Arden. He was hoping to try and convey a bit of encouragement, but Arden was too focused on Leandra to notice anyone else.

Outside, the sun was high in the sky, casting short, sharp shadows along the walls where they met up with the paved road and underneath the bench just outside the clinic doors.

Zorix would not have gone far, Brace knew. Was he confused about what was happening, or just worried? Where would he be? Brace glanced around, but there was nowhere for Zorix to hide ... except under the bench.

Brace leaned over and peered into the shadows. Zorix's eyes peered out at him, his large ears pressed out flat from the sides of his head, his long furry tail wrapped around his body.

"It's all right," Brace told him, kneeling on the ground. "Leandra's getting ready to have her baby. But you know that, don't you?"

Zorix blinked.

"I know you can understand me," Brace continued, feeling self-conscious. "You can hear me," he went on, "even if I can't hear you. She's going to be all right, though. You don't have to hide under there."

Zorix glanced toward the wooden doors, then looked at Brace again.

"You can feel what she's feeling, can't you? You're not feeling too great right now, are you?"

Again, Zorix blinked, then looked down at the ground.

"Well, I know I'm not Leandra, but she can't do anything to comfort you right now." Brace shrugged. "I'm the only one out here. I'm a little worried myself, but Tassie knows how to help her." He hesitated. "We can keep each other company, if you want."

Getting no response, Brace stood. Maybe Zorix wouldn't want to have Brace for company. Or maybe he just needed time.

He sat down on the bench with his back against the wall and stretched out his legs. He had nowhere else to go at the moment. Why not wait here?

Time passed, and Brace removed his wool cloak, draping it over the end of the bench beside him. The sun was high and the air was warm, and Brace was beginning to get sleepy when he felt something brush up against his legs. Only mildly surprised, he looked down to see Zorix peering up at him, his front feet grasping the edge of the stone bench.

"Do you want to come up here?" Brace asked.

Without hesitation, Zorix leaped nimbly onto the bench and situated himself halfway across Brace's lap. Brace wasn't sure how to react. Zorix had never done anything like this, not with *him*. Slowly, he reached out and rubbed behind the creature's large furry ears. Zorix closed his eyes.

"Do you like that?" Brace asked.

Zorix rumbled softly, deep in his throat.

Brace smiled. "I think you do."

Nearly an hour later, when Ronin ambled up the road toward them, neither of them had moved.

"Hello there," Ronin greeted Brace.

"Hello," Brace replied softly, not wanting to disturb Zorix.

"How is the baby coming along?" Ronin asked.

"Well enough, I think. I haven't been in there for a while. It's been quiet, for the most part."

Ronin smiled. "That's a good thing. Is this the little fellow that belongs to Leandra?" he asked, looking at Zorix where he lay on Brace's lap, apparently asleep.

"He is," Brace replied, "but Leandra might put it differently. Zorix doesn't belong to her... they belong to each other." He smiled to himself, recalling when he had referred to Zorix as "*it*" when he'd first seen him, and that Leandra had taken offence.

Ronin nodded in understanding. "He's holding up well, is he?"

"He seems to be."

"And the rest of them?"

"Arden's worried, I think. But Leandra's strong. I'm sure she'll be fine." Brace looked away from Zorix and over at Ronin, who sat down beside him on the bench. "Tassie didn't ask you to help at all?"

Ronin smiled apologetically. "No, I don't know anything about birthing babies. I'm only good for cuts and broken bones and such. I would be more of a hindrance, I think."

When one of the clinic doors opened, everyone on the bench startled a bit, Zorix most of all. He stood up, alert, when Tassie stepped out into the afternoon sunlight.

"Brace, can you do something?" she asked without hesitating.

"What?" he asked in alarm.

"Leandra says she feels hot. Could you go down to the stream and bring back some fresh water for her?"

"I can do that," Brace replied, relieved, as Zorix jumped down from his lap.

"You can go inside and see her," Tassie said, looking down at Zorix, his ears pressed forward and his dark eyes wide.

Zorix hesitated, peering in through the open doorway, then scampered inside.

Tassie acknowledged Ronin's presence with a smile as she handed Brace a large empty skin flask. "If you fill this, it should be enough for a while at least. The stream water is colder than what I've already got here."

"Of course," Brace replied. "I'll be back soon."

He made a quick trip down to the stream, enjoying the solitude, while still sensing an edge of urgency. He would have liked to linger in the quiet of the orchard, but he knew Leandra was waiting for the relief that the cold water could bring. He inhaled deeply of the cool, fresh air, took one last look across the tree-filled stretch of land, then turned and headed back.

When he arrived at the clinic, he could see that Zorix had been sent outside once again – he was pacing back and forth just outside the clinic doors. Ronin was standing nearby, watching him and speaking to him quietly, trying to give him some comfort or encouragement, though Zorix seemed to be ignoring him.

"Is everything all right?" Brace asked.

Ronin looked up. "She's coming along," he replied. "Poor Zorix. He wanted to stay inside, but Leandra sent him out when her pains started up again. He's not happy about it."

"I can see that," Brace said quietly, sympathetically. "He feels what she feels … her emotions, at least."

When Zorix looked up at Brace, it was with a scowl.

"What?" Brace asked. "Isn't it true?"

Zorix huffed and snorted, then turned his back.

Helplessly, Brace looked at Ronin. "What did I say wrong?" he asked.

Ronin shook his head. "I couldn't tell you."

Brace grimaced. "Well, I've got to get this water to Leandra. Will you … just stay out here with him?"

"Of course," Ronin replied with a nod.

Brace listened briefly at the door, but again, he heard nothing. Pushing open the door, he entered the room and saw that Leandra was still sitting on the low, padded seat, but she seemed less at ease. She gripped Arden's hand tightly and seemed to be concentrating on every slow breath she took. Kendie stood at a table nearby, making tea – or at least, she was apparently *supposed* to be making tea. At the moment, she was watching Leandra over her shoulder while absently stirring a mug of steaming liquid with a spoon.

Tassie stepped up beside Brace. "Thank you for the water," she told him quietly, and Brace nodded, his eyes catching Arden's. The tall archer's expression was full of concern as he sat close beside his wife.

They're brave, Brace thought, *both of them. For choosing to go through this.*

"Brace?" Tassie's voice broke through his thoughts.

"Hmm?" he asked, looking at her.

"The water?"

"Oh," he replied, releasing his grip on the flask. He grinned sheepishly. "Sorry."

Tassie gave him her familiar small smile, then poured some of the water into a bowl. She took a thick piece of cloth, immersed it in the water, then wrung it out. Crossing the room to where Leandra sat moaning under her breath, she ran the cloth along her face to cool it.

"Thank you," Leandra muttered, her eyes shut.

Arden looked up at Brace and forced a smile, but he couldn't hide the worry he felt. Brace could still see it easily enough.

"Are things going well?" Brace asked softly.

"I think so," Arden replied. "Are things going well, Tassie?"

"Yes, everything seems fine," she said, looking over her shoulder at Brace. "It's getting closer to time for the baby to come."

Tassie gave the wet cloth to Arden, then poured more of the water into a clean mug, taking it back to Leandra.

"Drink some of this," she instructed. Leandra let out a long breath, then took a small sip of water from the mug as Tassie held it out for her.

"Kendie," Leandra said after she swallowed, "you should leave now," she told her, looking toward the window where the girl was now seated, watching and clutching the steaming mug of tea.

"But I want to stay and help," Kendie protested meekly. "And I want to see when the baby comes."

"You can see the baby after," Leandra replied, not letting go of Arden's hand. "Please, Kendie, go on out. Tassie is here; she'll help me."

Brace spoke up when Kendie hesitated. "Zorix is out there, you know. He's not feeling too great right now. I'm sure he would like it if you would stay with him until this is over."

Kendie glanced from Leandra to Brace before she relented. "All right," she reluctantly agreed. Placing the tea on the window ledge, she leaned over and gently kissed Leandra's cheek.

Leandra smiled up at her. "I'll be fine, sweet. Don't worry."

Kendie looked at Arden for reassurance, but he only nodded, forcing a lop-sided grin.

Tassie allowed herself to look away from Leandra long enough to give Brace a quick hug. "Thank you," she said as she pulled herself away.

"Are you sure everything's going to be all right?" he asked her. "You've never done this before, have you?"

Tassie shook her head, wrapping her arms around herself. "No. I never have. But I know *what* to do. That's a start, I suppose. It's better than nothing."

Brace nodded.

"Is Ronin still out there?" Tassie asked.

"Yes."

"Ask him to stay there, will you? I know he hasn't done this either, but … it would be nice to have some help. In case she needs it."

"I'll ask him," Brace replied. "I'm sure he'll stay."

Kendie stood beside Brace, but her eyes were still on Leandra. Brace gently took hold of her arm. "Come on, Kendie," he encouraged. "Let's go take care of Zorix."

She nodded as they turned toward the door. "I can't help worrying," Kendie told him.

"I know what you mean," he replied.

"Are you worried too?"

"A little," Brace admitted. "But everything's been all right this far; it should keep on going that way."

"I hope it does."

"Come on." Brace tried to sound light-hearted. "Leandra has Arden and Tassie with her. She's not alone. Let's ask Ronin if he will stay too, in case he's needed."

Ronin stayed, of course. He was more than willing to be of help, if he could. Brace and Kendie, after some coaxing, managed to convince Zorix that Leandra would be fine, and it was all right for him to come with them.

The three of them went on in silence until they came to Brace's empty house. Kendie went inside while Brace held the door open, and Zorix followed slowly, dragging his small feet, gazing back toward the clinic as he slunk into the house.

"It's all right, Zorix," Kendie told him with forced cheerfulness. "Leandra's fine, and there will be a new baby soon."

Zorix hardly responded as he came inside, and Kendie looked up at Brace nervously.

Brace shrugged. What more could they do, if Zorix was in no mood to be comforted? As the hour passed, it was easy to see when Zorix became more agitated. His large ears remained pressed out flat from the sides of his head, his long tail twitched, and a low growl reverberated in his throat. Brace knew, at those times, that Leandra must have been in particular discomfort.

Kendie finally managed to coax Zorix into her lap. It was there that he had spent the last half hour, allowing her to run her hand over his fur – like a cat, Brace thought with a smirk – and eventually he had fallen asleep.

Brace was beginning to doze off as well, even on the hard wooden bench beside the table. He startled when he was interrupted from his thoughts by a knock at the door. Kendie and Zorix looked up when he did, all of them startled into wakefulness.

"Who is that, now?" Brace wondered aloud as he stood up and stretched out his stiff legs. "Tassie!" he exclaimed when she entered the room. "What happened?"

Tassie smiled. "The baby came," she replied simply.

Kendie leapt up from her seat, dumping Zorix onto the floor. "The baby came?"

"Yes," Tassie replied as Zorix scrambled to his feet and rushed past her, out the open door, and toward the clinic.

Brace laughed. "He's been waiting very quietly for a long while," he explained. "I'm sure he's anxious to be at Leandra's side."

"Of course," Tassie agreed as she stepped inside.

"How is the baby?" Kendie asked. "How is Leandra? Can I go and see her?"

"Not right now," Tassie replied. "She's fine, and the baby is fine. Let's just give her and Arden some quiet time alone."

"Alone, except for Zorix," Kendie pointed out playfully, but Tassie was looking at Brace.

"I'm tired too," she told him. She leaned against his side and rested her head on his shoulder, looking up at him, as he put his arms around her.

"You can rest, then," Brace replied. "Everything is all right now, isn't it?"

"It is," she said with a smile.

Kendie squeezed her way between Brace and the wooden table, coming around to where Tassie could see her. "Is the baby a boy or a girl?" she asked.

"A girl," Tassie replied. "They decided to name her Denira. They say it means 'hope'. They want her to be a reminder of the hope of the new life we all have here."

"That sounds nice," Brace commented.

"*Denira,*" Kendie said dreamily. "I have a sister!"

Brace smiled briefly, but he could not help wondering if that hope could somehow be shattered. There was still the *secret,* that someone out there was keeping, the secret that Zorix had overheard. What if there was still an unknown threat hanging over their heads? Would it ever be revealed, or would it come to nothing? Brace only hoped that the latter was true. Arden and Leandra deserved to enjoy the time with their infant daughter. The little one deserved to grow up here, in Haven, and to experience it for what it was meant to be – a refuge, a place of peace and safety, free from the troubles the outside world could inflict upon it.

Please, Brace thought. *Please, let the trouble pass us by. Let us be left in peace.*

~ 32 ~

The entire city of Haven was delighted at the birth of Arden and Leandra's baby. Word spread quickly, and by the time the sky had darkened on that first night, everyone knew the baby was a girl, and that her name was Denira – *hope*. A fitting name, everyone agreed. She was, after all, the first child born inside the city of Haven after it had stood empty for thousands of years. This was certainly an event to be remembered, and Ovard was glad to record Denira's birth in the new book of what would someday become Haven's second history.

Four days after the baby's birth, Tassie informed Brace that the new parents were at last ready for a visit.

"Are they?" he asked.

"Yes," Tassie replied. "They said we should come before we all go to Jair's meeting today. They would like to see you, Brace. And to have you see the baby. You *are* Denira's good-uncle, after all."

Brace nodded, recalling that icy day on the mountain when Arden and Leandra both had told him of their wishes. He was one of Denira's good-uncles, and though he had not the slightest idea of what would be expected of him in filling that role, he was nonetheless touched at having been all but brought into Arden and Leandra's little family.

When he accompanied Tassie to Arden and Leandra's home that day, he could see immediately that they were so happy as parents, so loving and protective of their infant daughter. Brace smiled at the sight of Arden holding Denira in his large hands, gazing at her as though she was a miracle of life, yet made of fragile glass at the same time.

"Congratulations," Brace told Arden, peering over his shoulder. Arden looked back at him, smiling as though he had discovered some treasure, some part of life that he never knew existed. And he had, after all.

"Thank you," he replied simply. "I never thought ..." he shook his head slightly. "I never thought it would be like this." Arden returned his gaze to his daughter. "She's ..."

"She's perfect," Leandra finished for him, resting her chin on Arden's shoulder as she peered down at tiny Denira.

"Isn't she cute?" Kendie asked, sitting beside Leandra, the sunlight pouring in through the window and falling across her face.

Brace grinned. "She is."

"She is beautiful," Leandra said as she stroked Denira's pale blonde hair.

Brace found himself almost in awe of the little one. She was so small, but she had eyelashes on her tiny eyelids and fingernails on her tiny fingers. She was perfect, as Leandra had said. Her blonde fluffy hair was lighter than her parents', but it was easy to see that she was taking after the both of them.

"Would you like to hold her?" Brace heard Leandra asking.

"Me, hold Denira?" Brace asked, surprised.

"You *are* one of her good-uncles," Arden pointed out.

Brace swallowed nervously. "I'd like to, but I've never held a baby."

"It's all right," Leandra told him, gesturing for him to come closer. Kendie moved aside, making room for Brace to sit on the window seat beside Leandra. Brace noticed Tassie's broad smile as he took his seat, and Arden gently lowered Denira into his arms.

"Am I holding her the right way?" he asked nervously.

"That's fine," Leandra told him.

Denira stirred, stretching her tiny arms and pressing her fists against her face before relaxing again, not waking enough to open her eyes.

Brace found himself almost holding his breath as he looked down at her face. She was warm and soft, wrapped in a blanket, and she fit perfectly in his arms. He felt something waking up inside of him, a place in his heart being touched in a way he never thought possible. *What unexpected mysteries life can bring*, he thought. He looked up and was struck by the smile on Tassie's face, at the way her green eyes shone. Here *he* was, holding a baby. The memory of Kendie's question – would they ever have a baby? He could see now, clear as day, that was something Tassie wanted. It was painted all over her face.

The idea of it – that someday, he might be holding his own infant, took Brace's breath away.

Tassie noticed Brace looking at her, and she blushed and turned away slightly. "How are you feeling?" she asked Leandra.

"I'm all right," Leandra replied. "I have no complaints, really. Thank you."

Arden cleared his throat, reluctant to interrupt. "I'm sorry, but shouldn't we be heading on to Jair's meeting?" he asked.

"We should," Brace replied, turning toward Leandra. "Thank you for letting me hold Denira."

Leandra smiled as she scooped her baby up in her arms. "Any time, Brace," she told him. "You're welcome to, any time."

Brace nodded and stood beside Tassie.

"Are you certain you feel well enough to attend?" Tassie asked Leandra.

"I'm fine, really," Leandra replied. "It's such a short walk to the Hall. I'm sure it will be no trouble."

Arden rested his arm across Leandra's back as they both stood. "I'll be with her," he said, his voice firm.

Of course, Brace thought. If Leandra seemed too tired, Arden would notice right away, and they would go back. No harm would come to Leandra, not while Arden was nearby, not if he could do anything to stop it.

Brace was silent, pensive, as the two couples, accompanied by Kendie and Zorix, made their way up the street toward the Main Hall. He was sure he could feel Tassie's unspoken thought hanging over them – *could* they have a baby, a baby of their own, someday? Was that Tassie's question, though, he wondered, or his own?

He said nothing, but took Tassie's hand as they walked. She looked up at him and smiled knowingly. Yes, Brace was sure the thoughts were Tassie's as well.

There was no time to bring up the subject, as the Main Hall stood across the square directly in front of them, as solid as it had ever been.

Another week, another meeting. Ovard insisted that Jair continue to host regular meetings, which were open to the entire city. There was always something to report on, from the progress of the latest planting of crops to any new discoveries Jair had made about Haven itself. And this subject, of making new discoveries, was the reason for today's meeting, which was soon to begin.

Zorix scurried under the stone bench outside the building and snuffed loudly enough for them all to hear. *I'm not setting foot inside*, he seemed to be saying. Brace felt awkward as they all exchanged knowing glances. More people were arriving for the meeting, and Brace couldn't help but look at them with suspicion, or at least some of them. The words still echoed in his mind – *Will something come of what I've done? Will they try to force their way in?*

He had not seen any suspicious behavior in anyone in particular, not since Zorix had overheard those troubling thoughts. Neither had anyone else, as far as he knew; no one had said anything.

He took a breath and went inside.

Kendie, Arden and Leandra seated themselves on one of the long stone benches at the back of the meeting hall, near the open door, white sunlight pouring in beside them. Beyond Haven's gate, winter ruled over the land, and the mountains in the distance could be seen covered with a thick white crust of snow. Here, however, the air was only touched with the slightest cool of autumn.

Brace and Tassie stood near the back of the Main Hall for a moment. The room was filling up quickly, and as everyone made their way into the building, they smiled and nodded at Arden and Leandra as they passed, many commenting on how sweet little Denira was.

Once again, it seemed that every person in Haven was in attendance, and the Main Hall filled up in no time.

Jair stood and cleared his throat, and everyone's voices slowly dwindled to a respectful silence in anticipation of what he might have to say.

"I'm glad everyone is here today," Jair began. "I'm sure everyone already knows, but Arden and Leandra have their new baby, Denira." Jair smiled over at them, and they smiled back. "It's a very special time," Jair continued. "She is very special. And – well, she belongs to Haven now, more than any of us do, really, and Haven belongs to her." He glanced at Ovard, who nodded, telling him to go on.

"And about Haven," Jair addressed the crowd. "Ovard and I are still re-writing the old books, and I found something new a few days ago."

Ovard slid a sheet of paper in front of Jair, and he picked it up and looked at it.

"We know that there are so many wonderful things here," he went on. "The water in the stream makes people feel stronger, the fruit in the Fountain Court heals injuries, and the crops are growing so fast. And, well, this says that the light of Haven is able to protect us, to defend us."

He set the paper down on the table and looked up. "We already know that the night screamers won't come near the lightstones. Brace and Dursen, and everyone who's come and gone with them, have been safe out there as long as they have the pieces of lightstones with them. But the text says that the light will actually fight against danger for us, to keep everyone in Haven safe from harm." Jair shrugged. "I thought everyone would like to know that."

"What exactly does that mean?" Shayrie asked, leaning forward with interest. "What does it mean, the light will fight against danger?"

"I don't know exactly," Jair was quick to admit. "The book doesn't explain it."

There was an awed silence in the room as everyone digested the new information. Finally, halfway back across the room, Lomar stood.

"How can you be certain that those are the exact words?" he asked pointedly. "What if you are not interpreting it correctly?"

A murmur spread through those gathered, but Ovard stood and held out his hand for silence.

"We have already addressed this issue," he announced. "Jair has been nothing but honest with you all, from the very beginning."

"I don't mean to say that he is lying," Lomar went on. "But what if he is simply misreading things?"

Ovard looked at Jair, gesturing for him to answer. He glanced down at the paper.

"I can just see it so clearly," Jair explained. "When I look at Haven's ancient writing, I can read it and understand it as well as our own language. I can just *see* what it means, so easily. I don't really understand this – the light defending us – I just know what it says. Haven's light will protect us. This is very good news, amazing news, and I thought everyone should know about it."

Brace felt himself glancing around the room for any sign that anyone could be ill at ease about this new declaration, but all he saw was amazement. He held tightly to Tassie's hand, not knowing what Lomar would say in response to Jair, or how Arden would react to the man's apparent mistrust. But Lomar only nodded and took his seat.

"This is great news," Ronin spoke up, breaking the tension that had begun to build up in the room. "Thank you for sharing it with us."

Brace let out his breath in relief. When the meeting ended a short time later, uneventfully, and the crowd began to leave, he and Tassie rejoined Arden and Leandra, who snugly held a sleeping Denira against her shoulder.

"How can he continue to question Jair's words?" Arden grumbled.

"Do you suspect he could be the one?" Brace asked quietly, glancing back over his shoulder to be sure he could not be overheard.

"He wasn't even at the meeting when Zorix overheard what he did," Leandra pointed out. "He can't be the one."

"Suppose there is more than one?" Arden thought aloud, almost to himself. "More than one traitor? The fact that Zorix only heard one person doesn't mean there may not be another."

Arden suddenly became silent when he saw the look of concern and worry on Ovard's face – he had been approaching them and had overheard.

"I don't know," Brace pondered. "I can't see anyone *wanting* to cause trouble here. *Wanting* anyone to get hurt."

"I don't know either," Jair agreed nervously.

"Well," Ovard spoke up. "We'll not discuss it right now, right here." He forced a smile. "It's a beautiful day. Go on and enjoy it. Jair and I will finish up in here for a bit."

Slowly, hesitantly, everyone cleared away until only Jair and Ovard remained in the large room. Dust particles drifted lazily through the shafts of white sunlight pouring in through the windows. Otherwise, the room felt dark. The inner walls were made of gray stone, onto which had been carved the figure of the frolicking deer that had become the symbol for the city. It stood out boldly against the back wall, and Jair gazed up at its face for a moment as though perhaps it could give him some much-needed answers.

"I don't know what to do about any of this," Jair complained as Ovard began to gather up the papers.

"Neither do I, son," Ovard agreed. "We're just going to take things one step at a time. There is no sense in getting the whole city in an uproar over something that might not happen at all."

"I know," Jair admitted. He began to pace along the wall behind the table, to the corner and back again. "I just feel like I should be doing something to stop this, whatever it is."

"Don't worry yourself."

"But aren't you worried, Ovard?" Jair asked as he continued to pace up and down. "Aren't you worried that … that something will …" his voice trailed off.

"Jair?" Ovard asked, seeing him gazing into the shadowed corner. "What's wrong?"

"I don't know," he replied in an odd voice. He turned to face Ovard. "I mean, nothing's wrong, but I never noticed *that* before now." Jair pointed down at the floor, and Ovard came over to investigate.

The floor of the Main Hall was made of smooth cobblestone, worn down in places, but consistent in appearance all throughout the large room. But there, just beyond Jair's feet, near the far corner, Ovard noticed a perfectly straight line cutting across the floor, nearly three feet long. That line was joined by another, and another and another, forming a perfect square.

"What is it?" Jair asked in amazement.

"I'm not certain," Ovard replied, slowly kneeling for a better look. He ran his fingers across the lines and the stones inside the square. Suddenly, he stopped, pulled his hand away, and looked closer.

"Look, Jair," he said in amazement. "Do you see that?"

Jair leaned in closer until he spotted a small, dark shape cut into one of the stones, not far from the center of the first line. "It just looks like a hole," he observed.

"A keyhole!" Ovard exclaimed, looking up at him. "In all of our time here, Jair, have you found any keys? Anywhere?"

Jair thought a moment, then shook his head slowly. "I don't remember seeing any. If I had, I would have wondered what it went to."

"You're right," Ovard agreed. "But this most certainly is a keyhole, so there must be a key."

"Where do you think it is?"

Ovard rose to his feet. "We'll search all of the side rooms here in the Main Hall," he suggested. "I would think this is the likeliest place to start."

"Right!"

The two of them spent the rest of the day in the Main Hall, searching every inch of the side rooms, full of anticipation, but there was not a single key to be found. They returned to the meeting room, feeling defeated, and stared down at the locked door on the stone floor, as though the mere sight of it could give them some insight.

"Maybe it's in one of the other buildings," Jair suggested. "Maybe the person who was in charge of the key left it in their house, even." He sighed. "It could be anywhere. Or it could be lost." He knelt down on the floor, running the tip of his finger over the keyhole. "You used to say that I was a key," he mused. "I wish I could turn myself into a real key and open this door. I feel like it's important to know what's down there."

Ovard stood pensively at Jair's side. "I think there is someone who might be able to open this," he said quietly, and Jair looked up. "Someone who could open it," he went on, "and he could do it even without a key."

～

Brace gazed down at the floor in the shadowy corner of the Main Hall. Yes, that was undoubtedly a door, as Ovard and Jair had told him.

"Can you open it?" Jair asked.

"I think so," Brace replied, "if it works the way most locks do." He scratched the back of his head, feeling strangely conflicted. He knew very well how to pick a lock, that much was certain. He had turned away from that part of his life, though – of being a thief. And now here were two of the very ones responsible for his change, asking him to "break in." He had made a promise to himself that he would give up his life as a thief, and everything that went with it. Including picking locks.

But this was different, wasn't it? After all, he wouldn't be doing this for himself. He would be *helping*, not stealing.

"I'll need two small, pointed objects to get it open," Brace finally said aloud.

"Your belt," Jair suggested. "And Ovard's. Maybe the metal prongs of your belts will work."

"Maybe," Brace replied. They chuckled as they removed their belts, and Brace tried them in the keyhole, but they were too large to fit. Ovard suggested trying tips from quill pens, but they were also too large.

"What else is there?" Brace asked from where he knelt on the cold stone floor. He was not about to give up easily. It was starting to eat at him – the wonder of what could be hidden on the other side of what seemed to be the only locked door in the entire city of Haven – and he was feeling very persistent.

Ovard sighed. "I think we're going to need more help with this. More minds, more ideas."

"But only people we know we can trust," Jair added firmly.

The three of them quietly dispersed. Finally, just as the sun was beginning to sink toward the horizon, they gathered together once again, along with Arden and Tassie, and they all stood close together in the corner of the large, otherwise empty meeting room.

Having explained the situation as best he could, Brace had thought to ask Tassie to bring along two of her small needles – the same type Ronin had used to stitch up the gash on Brace's lip.

"What are you going to do with these?" Tassie asked now, peering down at the mysterious locked door, carefully holding onto the leather pouch containing the needles.

"I'm going to try and pick the lock," Brace told her, holding out his hand.

"Just don't break them," Tassie warned. "They are all I have."

"I'll be careful," Brace replied as he gently dumped the slender needles out onto his palm. He knelt on the floor once again, and everyone gathered around closer in anticipation.

"Let's see if this works," Brace thought aloud, slipping the needles into the keyhole. Firmly but gently, with a steady hand and much concentration,

Brace worked the blunt ends of the needles into position until he heard an encouraging *click*.

He looked up in surprise to see that Jair's eyes were as wide as his own must have been.

"It's unlocked," Brace reported. Fixing his eyes on the door once again, he managed to wedge his fingertips into the crack along the front and pull it upward.

"It's heavy," he muttered. Tassie quickly removed her needles from the keyhole, and Arden joined Brace in pushing upward on the hinged door until it stopped, standing straight up, pointing toward the ceiling.

Everyone peered down into the gaping hole in the floor.

"I see steps," Jair commented. "Something is down there. More than just a small space, I mean. It's dark. What do you think is down there?"

"There's only one way to find out," Brace replied.

"I'm more than happy to go down there with you, Jair," Ovard volunteered. "We'll bring a light along."

"I'll stay here and keep watch," Arden spoke up.

"I think I'll stay with you," Brace told him. Wherever those stairs led, the opening in the floor was much too narrow for his liking.

"Will you come, Tassie?" Jair invited her.

She shook her head. "I think, whatever is down there, you and Ovard should be the first to see it."

Jair nodded. Ovard passed him a lit candle, and he slowly made his way down the stone steps, holding the light out in front of him. The small flame was just bright enough for him to see the next step, but nothing beyond that. Ovard followed closely behind him, and Jair was reassured at his presence.

Six ... seven ... eight. Jair counted each step as he went down. Holding the candle closer to the ground, he looked for the next one, but the path ran straight ahead of him.

"No more stairs," he told Ovard over his shoulder. "There is a hallway." He looked toward the far end of the hall, and looked again. Was that light he saw, way off in the distance? Yes!

"Ovard, there is a light coming from somewhere."

"I see it," Ovard replied, his voice echoing off the walls.

As Jair went on, he realized that the ground under his boots was not hard-packed dirt, as he had expected it to be. Instead, it was paved with the same smooth, round stones as the floor of the Main Hall. As he gazed downward in surprise, he realized as well that he could see light spilling across the stones from the side, coming from the base of the wall beside him.

"Ovard, look," he said, pointing at the floor.

Ovard stepped up beside Jair and, noticing the light, he turned toward the wall on his right, running his hand across it lightly.

"There is a door here," he announced. "The light is coming from behind this door."

Jair stepped closer. "Will it open?" he asked.

Ovard felt around in the dim light of the candle, then gently gave the door a push. Both of them breathed in, surprised, as the door swung easily inward, and a brilliant light fell across them.

Blinking, Jair stepped forward. A small room lay before him, the walls made entirely of lightstones. It was sparsely furnished, with only a bed and a table, but there was a door at the back.

"Someone lived down here," Jair commented, awed.

"It certainly looks that way," Ovard agreed. He crossed the room in seven easy steps and pushed open the other door. "Only a privy in here," he reported.

Jair looked back toward the hallway. "Let's see what else is down here."

Careful examination of the hallway revealed another door opposite the first, and farther down, four additional doors, two on each side of the hallway. Each door led into a room that was identical to the first – all but the last door on their right. Jair pushed open the door expecting to see another bed and table, but instead, there was a large gray stone tub of sorts, with what looked like a chimney reaching down from the ceiling, the bottom of it almost, but not quite, touching the bottom of the tub.

"What is this, Ovard?"

Ovard studied the room for a moment before answering. He stepped close to the stone tub and ran his fingers along the bottom.

"It's wet," he told Jair as he looked toward the ceiling. "How could water get in here?" he wondered. "It hasn't rained at all in Haven since we've been here."

"The fountain!" Jair exclaimed. "We've been trying to fix the fountain. They poured water down into it, didn't they? Rudge and Nevin?"

Ovard smiled. "They did. The water must have run down this stone pipe into the tub."

"But it didn't work," Jair reminded him.

"No," Ovard agreed. "I think this tub needs to be filled to the top. Maybe the water needs to be brought up through this pipe, not poured down through it."

Jair's eyes widened, and he smiled. "Then the fountain will work again?"

"I think it just might," Ovard replied, resting his hand on Jair's shoulder.

"This is fantastic," Jair breathed.

"Yes, it is, my boy. Isn't it?" Ovard glanced around, then gestured to the wall beside the fountain, at shoulder height.

"What is it?" Jair asked.

Ovard moved closer to the stone piece protruding from the wall, nearly the same width and length as his own arm. Taking it gently in his hand, he tested it until it moved up along the wall with ease.

"It's a lever," Ovard answered at last. "I believe – we'll need to test this – but I believe it triggers something inside that stone pipe that will bring the water from this basin up through the fountain above ground."

Jair gazed at the stone basin in awe.

"But there is still more," Ovard told him.

"*More?*"

"There is more light coming from the far end of the hallway."

Jair nodded. "I saw it too."

There must be twenty feet, Jair guessed, from the fountain room's doorway to the end of the hall, where they now stood. Two large stone doors faced them, intricately carved with the same image of the frolicking deer that covered the back wall of the meeting room.

Ovard and Jair eyed each other in anticipation of what might lay behind the doors. Jair felt his heart beat faster as he lay his hand on one of the doors to open it. His breath caught in his throat, and he pulled his hand away.

"What's wrong?" Ovard asked in alarm.

"Nothing," Jair whispered. "I just think this is a sacred place." He paused and took a breath. "Ovard, you open it."

"No, son," Ovard replied gently. "You are Haven's chosen. If anyone has the right to open these doors, it's you."

Jair nodded. He let out another breath, then slowly pushed open the heavy stone door.

The light was brilliant white, almost blinding at first, compared to the darkness of the hallway. A large room opened up before them, the walls again made of lightstones, as were the floor and ceiling. The room was almost round – where the corners would have been, a short wall cut across them at an angle so that the room had four long walls and four short walls. Everything was white – even the four long tables that ran down the length of the room, two along each wall.

Jair stood open-mouthed in awe at the sight of it all.

"What is this?" Ovard asked in a whisper.

"I'm not sure," Jair replied as he placed the candle on the nearest table. He ran his fingertips along its surface. "This is warm," he told Ovard. "Just like the walls outside." He turned and looked at the wall beside him, moving closer to it in awe. The ceiling reached to at least ten feet above Jair's head, and on the wall in front of him was carved a tall figure, almost the full height of the room itself. It was a man, tall and thin, wearing a long, draping robe, all in white. The hood was pulled up, covering the man's face, with only his chin visible. He held his hands out in front of him as though ready either to receive or to give something.

Slowly, Jair reached out and touched the carved figure, feeling the warm light from the stone flowing into his hand.

"Jair?" Ovard asked, concerned.

"It's all right," he replied quietly. He glanced around the room and noticed several more similar figures carved into the walls, spaced evenly apart. He could feel something forming in his mind – a sense of what this secret room had once been used for.

"Not everyone was allowed to be in here," he began, his hand pressed flat along the wall. "It *is* sacred, as I thought. The ... *leaders* ... came down here to meet, to study, to think. It's a place for quiet."

He turned and looked at Ovard, letting his hand slide away from the wall.

"What are these?" Ovard asked, nodding at one of the carved, hooded figures.

"I'm not sure," Jair replied. "I feel like it's something very good, though. Mysterious, but good."

Jair paused mid-step, turning his head toward the back wall of the large room as though something had drawn his attention.

"There's more," Jair said, almost in a whisper, as he made his way down the length of the room toward the far end of it, past the long tables and benches. Ovard followed after him.

Jair went on until he stood a mere two feet away from the far wall, which they both noticed was changing. The pure white light emanating from its surface began to grow softer, more hazy, and Ovard pulled Jair away from it until the boy spoke.

"I see something there," he said, his head tilted slightly in wonder. Ovard watched as there appeared to be white, swirling fog clearing away from the center of the wall toward the edges. There was something there, indeed! The entire expanse of the wall had changed, almost disappeared, and it was as though they were peering out across a vast landscape through a thick white mist.

"Trees," Jair said aloud. "I see trees. Don't you? And mountains beyond them."

Jair cautiously stepped forward and reached out until he felt the firmness of the wall against his fingers, though it looked as though he could have reached right through it.

"It's a familiar sight," Ovard spoke up, amazed. "I've seen this view before."

"So have I," Jair agreed. "It's … beyond the gate! That's the clearing on the outside of the stone gate, and the woods on the other side, and the mountains we crossed to get here." He turned toward Ovard, smiling broadly. "We can see what's on the other side of the gate from down here!"

"Well, that's certainly handy, isn't it?"

Jair grew reverently quiet. "They thought of everything," he thought aloud. "There's nothing lacking here, is there? There's everything anyone could need."

Ovard stepped up close to Jair, the boy's shoulder brushing up against his arm. They stood gazing at the incredible, unexpected view looming before them.

"Will this place ever cease to amaze me?" Ovard asked softly.

Jair smiled. "Probably not. But it isn't as bright in here as it was. I think the light is beginning to fade. It's getting late."

"You're right," Ovard agreed. "We should go up before it's too dark and our little candle goes out."

Reluctantly, Jair took a few steps back away from the viewing wall, and the white swirls of fog flowed together until the wall had returned to its original appearance. Jair's gaze met Ovard's momentarily before he wordlessly turned away.

Ovard rested his arm across Jair's shoulders as they slowly made their way back through the long room, taking the small candle with them. They passed the doors along the hallway as their candle grew shorter, its small golden light flickering in the darkness as they climbed up the stairs to the main floor.

"There you are," Brace greeted them, concerned. "We were about to send someone in after you."

"Someone?" Arden asked, raising an eyebrow. "Don't you mean me?"

Ovard chuckled as Brace grinned sheepishly.

"What did you find down there?" Tassie asked them.

Jair looked at Ovard, silently asking for guidance. What exactly should he say?

"Several things," Ovard answered for him. "The first of which is a way to get the fountain flowing once again, we believe. That is the easiest to explain."

"Rudge will be glad of that," Brace commented.

"As will Ben-Rickard," Tassie agreed. "He so wants to see Haven's beauty fully restored."

"What else?" Arden asked.

Jair blew out what was left of the candle. "A very special, sacred place," he answered. "It's beautiful, but strange, and full of light. Somehow, I feel like I understand more about Haven, but at the same time, I have new questions. Does that make sense?"

"Here, it makes perfect sense," Brace told him. "I've come to expect that about this place."

"I think you all should see it," Jair told them. "Leandra too. But ..."

"But this is not for everyone to know about," Ovard finished. "We still are not certain who can be trusted completely."

Arden nodded gravely as Brace and Tassie agreed.

"I'm sorry, my boy," Ovard told Jair, seeing the look of sorrow on his face at having been reminded of possible treachery. "We will get to the bottom of this," he promised. "We will find a way to solve this problem. *Somehow.*"

A heavy silence settled over each of them as they slowly, quietly, lowered the heavy door back into place on the stone floor, with a low *thud*.

"Well, everyone," Ovard said with a sigh, "it is getting late, and I suggest that we all get some sleep. We can discuss this again soon enough. Tomorrow is a new day."

~ 33 ~

Sunlight glinted on every surface of water as it cascaded down over the rimmed bowls of Haven's large stone fountain. There were many shouts of joy and happy embraces at the sight of it, even a few tears. The courtyard was packed with people – Brace was certain that no one was absent from this event.

Jair had announced at the last meeting that a door had been discovered, leading to an underground room which housed the fountain's large stone basin. Nothing more had been said – not about the door being locked, or even where it was; not about the other small side rooms or the large sacred place; not about the hooded figures carved into the lightstones.

Brace had finally seen it with his own eyes – Jair had invited him in, along with Tassie, and Arden and Leandra as well. Brace had been hesitant at first, seeing how small the space was, going down the narrow steps. He had wanted to see the large room, of course, but the thought of going down into the small, dark space made his throat close up. Reminding himself about how large and bright the underground room must be, according to Jair, he held tightly to Tassie's hand as they followed after Arden and Leandra down the narrow, high-ceilinged hallway.

The sight of it had taken his breath away – the room at the far end of the hall, past the two large stone doors, was very spacious indeed, and very white. Sacred, as Jair had told them. While Kendie held little Denira, waiting upstairs with Ovard, Leandra and Arden were free to take it all in as well. While the rest of them stood gazing around in awed silence, Leandra approached one of the carved figures and examined it closely, reverently.

It was an amazing discovery, Brace had to agree, but he was glad to get above ground once again, where it was easier to breathe.

That room, they were all given strict instructions, was to be kept secret at all cost. And so, the announcement had been made as simply that there was a way, Jair believed, to have the large fountain running once again at last. The crops had been growing fast, large and full, so there was plenty of food in storage to merit a day of celebration. And a celebration it was – joy filled the air in the Fountain Court, combined with the rhythmic splashing of the fountain as the sun shone high overhead.

Rudge was beaming – he had been waiting so long for this moment. He had even begun to wonder, Brace knew, if he would *ever* see the fountain working. Nerissa held onto Dursen's arm, smiling. Brace nudged Tassie's elbow and gestured discreetly in their direction.

"Is there another wedding in Haven's near future?" he asked with a grin.

Tassie smiled. "There could be. Essa and Daris are so very happy together; I'm sure Dursen and Nerissa will be as well."

"Well, I'm happy," he told her, leaning closer as though to kiss her.

"Not here, Brace," she scolded him, blushing.

Brace chuckled. "You're never going to get past this, are you?" he asked, smiling. "Having people see us kiss?"

Tassie grinned slightly. "I don't know … It just makes me feel uncomfortable, as though everyone is looking right at us."

"It doesn't bother me," Brace whispered, leaning in until his nose brushed her cheek.

"I know that," she whispered back before Brace kissed her.

"Excuse me," someone interrupted, clearing his throat. Brace turned to see Brodan, of all people. "I see it's not the best moment, but I just want to say what a fine thing this is."

"Don't thank me," Brace told him. "Thank Jair. He's the one who found the door to the fountain room."

Brodan tipped his head and shrugged slightly. "Yes, well, the boy has quite a bit of company at the moment."

Brace glanced around until he spotted Jair, who stood beside Ovard and was surrounded by Nevin, Shayrie, Gavin and Persha; Arden and

Leandra were close by as well, as was Kendie, who was gazing at Jair even as it was obvious that the boy still had eyes for Persha.

"I see," Brace told Brodan. "Well, I'll pass on your message to him later, then."

Brodan nodded, then lowered his gaze. "I know I can be gruff and far too outspoken," he said quietly, "but I want you to know that I respect everyone here, and all of the work that's been done. This place ... well, it's more than I could ever have imagined."

"Thank you," Brace told him, surprised. "It's good to hear you say it."

Brodan nodded again, smiling a bit, before he moved on.

Brace cringed inwardly, knowing that he had suspected Brodan of being the man with the secret. He certainly did not seem, at that moment, to be someone capable of making plans that could ruin the city and endanger everyone inside it. But if not Brodan, then *who*?

Brace looked over at Tassie and saw glad surprise in her eyes.

"That was nice to see," she told him.

"It was," he agreed. "But ..."

"I know," she said, stopping him short, resting her finger on his lips. "Not now, please? Not today." She looked out at the happy crowd. "Today, let us just have peace."

Brace nodded in reply. "All right. That sounds perfect to me." He smiled. "I wish you could hear the music," he told her. "Ovard is playing his flute."

Tassie looked ahead just as Dursen and Nerissa began dancing sprightly around the stone-paved courtyard with the fountain splashing merrily behind them. Tassie laughed. "Come on," she said. "I don't mind if everyone sees us dancing!"

~

Soon enough, it was time for the food to be served. There were sliced potatoes, fresh vegetables, fruit tarts and bread rolls brought out on trays and passed around. The stone benches filled up quickly, and many people, Brace among them, were left to seat themselves on the stone-paved ground, without complaint.

Brace sat with his back to the nearest wall, with Tassie beside him. On the bench to his left, they were joined by Leandra and Arden. Brace could not help but notice the change in each of them since the birth of their daughter. They seemed to be so much more focused, Arden in particular. For the longest time since settling in Haven, the archer had been having doubts about his purpose there. It seemed all too clear to him now; Brace could see it in his eyes. He still had people who needed his protection, and his love as well. It was easy to see, the way Arden gazed at Leandra and little Denira, that he had fully realized how deep his love for his family truly was.

Leandra was holding Denira now, the baby's tiny feet resting on Leandra's knees, on the soft fabric of her pale green dress, which flowed all the way down to the paved stone floor. Denira was just beginning to hold her head up a little, and she gazed around at the walls and the sky and Leandra's face as though everything she saw amazed her.

And Leandra – if it was possible for someone to be soft and strong at the same, she certainly was now, as she kissed Denira's tiny face. Brace found himself smiling as he picked up his bread roll and bit into it.

Maybe some day, he and Tassie would have a child of their own, as Kendie had asked if they would. How would he feel, looking at the tiny hands and feet of a child that was his own? He had already made room in his heart for more people than he had ever thought possible. Was there any limit? How much room could there possibly be in one person's heart? In *his* heart?

Brace knew he would truly be able to love his child if he had one, but would he be a good father? A former thief who was often too brash, too independent? What good advice would he give his child? *Don't do what I have done?* He shook his head slightly. That would not be enough, would it?

His thoughts were interrupted by Tassie's hand on his shoulder. "What are you thinking about?" she asked him, touching the space above the bridge of his nose. "You're frowning."

Brace managed a grin. "Just imagining the future," he told her. "Our future."

"And you're frowning?" she asked, raising her eyebrows.

Brace let out a laugh. "It's not bad. I was just ... wondering something."

"What's that?"

He thought about telling her for a moment, then shook his head. "We can talk about it later."

Tassie tipped her head as she looked at him, as she often did when she knew what Brace was thinking, even without his having to say it. Or even when she thought she knew.

"Promise?" she asked.

"Promise," he replied, looking into her eyes.

A shadow fell across his face, and he looked up to see Yara smiling down at them.

"Hello," she greeted them, nervously brushing her hands against the skirt of her yellow dress. "How are you both?"

"Very well, thank you," Tassie replied with a smile, while Brace nodded.

"This is wonderful, isn't it?" Yara went on, gesturing toward the fountain.

Brace could see that she wanted to speak with him, but she felt awkward. He sighed inwardly. Well, he *had* said he would be a friend to her, and friends couldn't ignore one another.

"It is," Brace answered, standing up with his empty plate in hand. "I think I'll take this back," he told Tassie, who nodded, understanding.

Brace walked slowly across the stone-paved ground with Yara beside him.

"I'm sorry if I interrupted," she told him.

"No, it's all right," Brace replied. "How have you been?"

"Much better," she answered as Brace added his plate to the stack. "I talked to Dorianne. She's teaching the children, you know?"

"Right," Brace commented. "Is it going well?"

"Yes, it seems to be. But I asked Dorianne if I could help in any way, and now I'll be teaching Ona and Kendie how to sew." She smiled.

"That must be great for you."

"It is," she told him. "Thank you."

"For what? I haven't done anything."

"For caring," she replied. "For listening that day, when I was upset. For encouraging me. You're a good friend, Brace. I just wanted to say thank you for that."

"Well, it's no trouble. I do care about you, Yara. I don't want you to feel alone here."

She smiled and shook her head. "I won't, not any more."

Brace nodded, looking around the courtyard, full of people. "This is a great thing, isn't it?" he asked, squinting into the sunlight.

"It is," Yara replied, but Brace was distracted at that moment by a faint rumbling sound.

"Do you hear that?" he asked.

Yara listened briefly. "I do!" She replied. "What is it? The gate?"

Brace listened again. "No, that isn't the gate."

"What is it, then?" she asked in alarm.

"I don't know." Brace looked around, and could see that many of the others heard it as well. In fact, Brace began to feel the ground vibrating under his feet. Alarmed, Yara grabbed onto Brace's arm as she looked around fearfully.

"What *is* that?" a man's voice called out.

Arden hurried over to Brace, with Tassie right behind him.

"Arden, what is going on?" Brace asked, raising his voice over the rumbling sound, over the many frightened voices carrying across the courtyard.

"It sounds like horses," Arden told him in a grave voice. "Many, many horses, and they are moving fast."

"Horses?" Brace asked in surprise as Tassie came close to his side.

"Brace, what's happening?" Tassie asked. "I feel the ground shaking!"

"I don't know," he answered quickly. "Arden, is this it? Is this what we've been worried about? The secret – the people trying to take Haven by force?"

Arden's eyes widened. "We need to get everyone to safety!"

"But this is Haven!" Brace exclaimed. "They're already supposed to be safe!"

"To the Main Hall," Arden replied. "Get them to the Main Hall. We'll see to the gate. If there is trouble, we can take them down through the door to the lower level. We can hide there if we must."

Brace turned toward Tassie. "Go to the Main Hall," he told her. "Get some of the others to go with you."

"Brace! I don't understand, what's happening?" Her eyes grew wide. "Are we under attack?"

"I don't know," Brace replied. "But please – go to the Main Hall. Take Yara with you. I'll be with Arden. We're just going to find out what's going on."

She hesitated only for a second, looking into Brace's eyes. "Please be safe," she told him before she hurried away, taking Yara's hand and pulling her along behind her.

Brace took a breath and looked around at the many fearful faces.

"What is going on here?" Brodan demanded.

"There are horses approaching," Arden replied. "It may be the sound of new friends coming – or it may not be. We don't know. But to be safe, most of you should go to the Main Hall. Some of you can join me in going to the gate. We're going to get to the bottom of this."

"Do you mean there could be trouble coming?" Shayrie asked.

"It's possible," Arden replied. "We will find out shortly, whether we're ready for it or not."

There was a bit of momentary chaos as the people began to break into groups, most of them running toward the Main Hall. Brace hurried to Ovard's side, where Jair and Arden stood close together.

"I'm going to the gate," Jair announced.

"No," Ovard told him. "Come with me to the Hall."

"No, Ovard!" Jair replied firmly. "You go with them, help them calm down. I'm going with Arden. I need to do this! If things are bad, we'll join you at the Main Hall, and we'll get everyone below ground. Please let me do this! I just need to."

Ovard looked at Jair with a mixture of sadness and respect. "All right, son," he told him. "I know it's what you should do. Just be careful."

"I will."

As Ovard left to lead more people to safety, Brace turned to Arden. "Where is Leandra?" he asked.

"She's taken Denira to the Hall," Arden replied, then turned toward those who remained in the Fountain Court. "Come with me, all of you, if you aren't going to the Hall with Ovard. There are horses approaching. We're going to the gate to find out what's happening."

There were nearly a dozen men gathered as they began to leave the courtyard, along with Persha, Jair and Kendie, who was hurrying toward them, carrying Arden's bow and quiver of arrows.

"I brought it!" she called out as she came. "I came as fast as I could."

"Thank you, Kendie," Arden told her as he took them from her. "Now go on to the Main Hall and stay with Leandra."

"No, I want to come with you."

"It might not be safe, Kendie."

"I'll be safe if I'm with you," she protested. "Everyone else has already gone to the Main Hall. I don't want to run off alone. Please let me come with you!"

"I'll watch out for her," Persha volunteered. The girl was sufficiently armed, and she had been trained by Arden himself. It was no secret that Persha had a keen eye and a resolute disposition, not likely to pull away from a potentially dangerous situation. If he could trust anyone to watch over Kendie at that moment, he could certainly trust Persha.

"All right," Arden relented as the sound of approaching hooves grew louder. "Come on."

Brace felt as though he'd joined a small army as they quickly made their way down Haven's main street toward the gate. An army, he thought. What if there was a much larger army waiting for them on the other side?

"What exactly are we going to do?" Brodan asked.

"Leave it to me," Arden replied without looking back. "There may be trouble, there may not be. We will wait and see what happens before we make any rash decisions."

~ 34 ~

The pounding of hooves was as loud as thunder by the time they reached the gate. The neighing of horses could be heard from the other side – more than a hundred of them, Brace guessed. He glanced aside, toward Arden, but the archer's face was like stone as he faced the gate.

Voices could be heard now from outside the city, as the beating of horses' hooves died away. Brace listened along with the others, trying to pick out what the horsemen could be saying.

"Ho there!" someone finally called out. "Open this gate, in the name of King Oden! Open up!"

"We will do no such thing!" Arden answered back. "Not until you tell us what business you have here!"

"We come to claim this city for the King," the reply came quickly.

"Haven belongs to no king," Arden informed him. "We will not let you enter."

There was near silence from outside the city.

"How did they get here over the mountains?" Persha asked, not seeming frightened in the least. "With all of those horses?"

"They likely came around to the west, beyond the mountains," Nevin replied. "They wouldn't need to use the pass that way."

Finally, a voice called out again from the other side. "If you will not open the gate, we will find a way to open it! Choose to open it and be dealt with peacefully, or not, and be taken as captives!"

"You will have to fight us first!" Arden challenged. Not waiting for any reply, he turned away from the gate. "Get back!" he commanded. "Everyone, back to the Fountain Court! We can rally ourselves there."

"There is no way we can fight them all off," Brace pointed out, hurrying to keep up with Arden.

"I am aware of that," Arden replied shortly.

In no time at all, the small group of Haven's citizens had reached the Fountain Court once again. The water still flowed, but its sound brought them no cheer, not this time.

"Who is responsible for this?" Arden demanded. "I know someone has been keeping something to themselves. Something they should have told – something that never should have happened. Someone knew that this might happen here today. What have you done? If any one of you knows something about this, speak up! Who is responsible?"

There was a strained silence as everyone glanced around at one another in surprise.

"It was me," a voice answered meekly.

Brace turned to look as Ben-Rickard worked his way forward.

"I am responsible," Ben continued. "I sold the information, the way to Haven. I was wrong, I was foolish." He looked around at the others' faces. Many of them were scowling, while others were dumbfounded. "I studied for so long to put the pieces together," Ben explained. "I had found what I believed would be the way to Haven – but at that time, I wasn't even sure that it truly existed!"

Brace felt the sting of betrayal, as he was sure the others did as well. How could he have done this? Ben-Rickard was the last person Brace would have suspected of harboring such a terrible secret.

Ben slowly sunk to his knees, his eyes on the ground in front of him. "I never knew this would happen," he went on, an edge of desperation in his voice. "Some of King Oden's men came and offered me a lot of silver for the information I had gathered. I didn't know *what* would happen. I thought maybe they would just want to find Haven, if it truly existed, so they could come and live here peacefully, as we did. Or maybe that's what I *wanted* to believe. Maybe I should have known something like this would happen."

He looked up. "I was greedy," he said quickly. "I never should have done it." He shook his head, seeing the look of burning anger in Arden's eyes. "I understand if you want to kill me." He swallowed. "But if you do, please do it quickly."

Ben sat back on his heels, burying his face in his hands. Arden stepped toward him, his jaw clenched in anger.

"No, don't!" Kendie cried out, rushing forward and wrapping her arms around Ben's neck. "Arden, don't! Look at him, don't you see how sorry he is? He didn't mean for this to happen. He didn't even know Haven was real when he did it! He's been helping us so much, he wouldn't want anything bad to happen to us, or to Haven."

She faced Ben, who had looked up at her in surprise. "You wouldn't, would you? You wouldn't want anything bad to happen. You weren't just *pretending* to be our friend, were you?"

Ben shook his head wordlessly, a tear running down his face.

"See?" Kendie asked, looking again at Arden. "He really means it. You won't hurt him, Arden, I know you won't. You're not horrible like that."

Arden sighed and slightly shook his head. "No," he muttered, then looked around. "Lomar, take him to the Main Hall. We'll deal with this later."

"I'm going with him," Ronin declared.

Arden gave him a nod, then turned back to Ben, who was now standing. "This *information* that you sold," he began. "Did that include the words that will open the gate?"

"No," Ben answered, shaking his head. "I knew nothing about how the gate worked."

Arden nodded briefly. "All right, then. Get him out of here," he told Lomar. "Kendie, go with them."

"But Arden —"

"No!" he replied gruffly. "Go with them, Kendie. I want you to be safe."

Kendie blinked, then nodded. "Okay," she replied meekly. "I'll go."

As Kendie followed after Lomar, Ben and Ronin, Arden turned and took a deep breath.

"Well," he began, "the King's men don't know how to get in through the gate, and I don't know if it's possible to break it down or not. But I don't think they will give up and leave. How many of them there are, I'm not certain, but I know they outnumber us." He paused to gather his thoughts. "Persha, how many arrows do you have?"

Persha looked quickly at her supply. "Eight," she replied.

"I have ten," Arden thought aloud. "If it comes to it, we'll need to make every one count."

Persha nodded gravely.

"The rest of you," Arden went on. "Do you have any weapons at all?"

Many blank expressions were the only response.

"I have a knife," Brace replied lamely.

Arden's face was grim as he realized how desperate the situation had become. "Well, gather anything you can, the rest of you. We're not going to go down without a fight."

A heavy silence fell over them. Was this really happening? Brace wondered. Could this be their last day in Haven? This perfect place, where nothing should ever go wrong? Would they die today, in defense of the city they had all come to love so much? Brace looked aside at Jair, wondering what the boy could possibly be feeling at this moment.

Jair's face revealed fear, sorrow and desperation all at once, as though he was somehow hoping against hope that this couldn't *possibly* be happening. Brace wished he could somehow tell him that things would be all right, that he did not need to worry, but it would be an obvious lie, and Jair would see right through it.

Brace could hear, faintly, evidence that the King's men were still there, outside Haven's gate, making plans of their own. He closed his eyes for a moment, taking a breath. He ran his palms down the legs of his trousers, trying to calm his nerves. *Tassie*, he thought. What would he say to Tassie right now, if he was given the chance to have one last word with her? He would tell her that he loved her, that he wanted with all his heart to spend the rest of his life with her. To have and to do everything, the things that he never thought he would be able to – to have a family, to have children, to lead a good long life of peace and decency, of *harbrost*, with her always at his side.

He slowly became aware of a new sound – a faint, ringing hum. He opened his eyes again, unsure if he was really hearing it. When he caught sight of Arden's face, he knew the archer was hearing it as well.

"What is *that* now?" Brace asked. Arden shook his head, looking all around.

Brace turned to look at Jair, whose eyes were wide in wonder as the sound grew louder.

"Something's happening," Jair announced as everyone crowded together.

Arden and Persha had readied their bows and stood ready to fire.

"Something – like what?" Brodan asked in alarm.

"I don't know," Jair replied as the ground beneath their feet began to rumble once again. "But it's something good!"

Brace stood close at Jair's side as the faint humming increased in volume, now sounding out as loudly as the call of many trumpets.

The light from Haven's glassy stone walls suddenly grew piercingly bright, so much so that Brace had to look away. He pulled Jair closer to him as everyone pressed in together, moving away from the lightstone walls. Even Arden was backing up into the huddled group, slowly lowering his bow. Brace startled when bright shafts of light burst upward into the sky. He was suddenly reminded of something Jair had said at one of the meetings – that Haven's light would defend them, protect them. Was that what was happening now, right before their eyes?

He could only stare in awe as there rose up, within the beams of light, white hooded figures, like wisps of smoke. Their faces were hidden, just like the carved figures on the walls of the large underground room. They drifted upward into the sky, higher and higher, over their heads, their robes flowing in some unseen wind. Slowly, slowly, they lifted their arms upward.

Suddenly, a blast of light burst outward, across the city streets in every direction. Brace felt it pass over him, through him; he felt its piercing heat as it rushed quickly toward the gate. Nothing could stand in its way – no person, no wall; the light went right through everything in its path, including Haven's large stone gate.

Startled cries and shouting reached Brace's ears from beyond the gate, followed by the frightened shrieking of horses. Brace stood, clutching Jair's arm in amazement, surrounded by the others. No one spoke – they were all frozen in wonder at what was happening all around them, at the sounds of the horses neighing and running, the loud ringing sound filling the air, and the rushing of bright light all around them.

And then, just as suddenly as it had all began, the light vanished in one instant, and all was silent inside the city. The pounding of horses' hooves could be heard retreating into the distance, and now Brace could hear as well the rapid beating of his heart and the sound of his own breathing.

Brace stood still for a moment – what felt like a long moment, then slowly turned to face Jair, whose face revealed his amazement.

Jair swallowed. "Haven's light," he said at last, and all eyes were on him. "It came to our defense. It protected us, just like the ancient books said it would."

Worley's legs buckled and he stumbled against Brace, who managed to catch him. "Are you all right?" he asked.

Worley took a few breaths and managed a weak smile. "I am," he replied. "That – that was so …"

"Amazing," Jair whispered.

"There are hardly any words," Arden added, putting away his arrow.

"The men," Brodan spoke up. "The King's men. What happened to them?"

"I will go and find out," Arden volunteered.

"I'm coming with you," Persha told him.

"Right," Arden replied with a nod. "Are you all coming?"

Worley, still feeling faint, shook his head. "I don't think I can make it."

"I'll stay with him," Stanner volunteered.

"Well enough," Arden replied, then hurried forward toward the gate, with the remaining seven of them following after him. He wasted no time as he rushed up to the square stone plate that would open the gate from the inside. He reached up to press it, and only then did he hesitate.

"I don't know what we will see out there," he said, looking back over his shoulder.

Brace nodded.

Beside him, Nevin cleared his throat. "We understand. We're ready."

Arden nodded, then pressed the stone plate. The gate groaned and creaked loudly as it slowly began to swing outward. Brace found himself holding his breath as the view opened up before him, noticing that temperature of the air all around them instantly grew colder, a wintry chill settling over him.

Evergreen trees loomed tall and straight in the distance, as they always had, now dusted with snow. The horses were all gone – hardly any sign remained that they had been there. Brace was relieved that there were no signs of any riders having been there, either. What had happened to them? Had they been killed, destroyed? They had vanished, that much was certain.

"They're gone," Jair said in surprise. "They're all just *gone*."

"Not all of them," Arden replied. "Look."

Brace peered across the open land outside Haven's gate toward the forest, where he spotted a man in thick leather armor– no, two of them, looking out from behind the large trees.

"You there!" Arden shouted. "Come out here. We see you, and we are armed. Do not try and run!"

Slowly, fearfully, not two, but four men came out from behind the trees and stood at the edge of the woods. Arden and Persha had readied their bows once again, but the men did not look at all prepared to attack, even if they had wanted to.

"What happened out here?" Arden demanded.

The men glanced at one another, then one of them stepped forward. "It was the light," he said, his voice carrying across the open land. "Some strange, bright light just swept across everything, and – and, well, they just disappeared."

"Who disappeared?"

"All of them," the man replied with a sweeping motion of his arm. "The other riders."

"Why didn't you disappear?" Brace asked.

The remaining King's men looked at each other once again, shrugging and shaking their heads. "We don't know."

Jair stepped forward slowly until he stood between Brace and Arden. He was silent, pensive, for a moment before he spoke. "They didn't want to come here," he said slowly. "They didn't want to attack the city. They only came because they *had* to."

Arden kept his eyes on the King's men, frowning in thought. "This is what happens when Haven comes under attack," he spoke loudly. "You go to King Oden – tell him what happened. It wasn't our doing; it was Haven itself. No one will ever be able to take this city by force. You tell King Oden! The rest of those men did not need to die today. If the King has any sense, he will listen to you. You can stop this from ever happening again!"

"We have no horses," one of the men protested.

"And those beasts," another spoke up. "They come out at night. We've heard them, we've *seen* them!"

Jair grabbed hold of Brace's arm. "Do you have the pieces of lightstones?" he asked.

Brace shook his head. "I gave them to Dursen," he replied.

Jair glanced around quickly, back toward the city. "Are there any more?" he wondered aloud. He hurried over to the nearest wall of lightstones and ran his hand along the end, searching for any breaks. Brace watched as Jair rested his hand on the wall and looked at it, then quickly ran back to them. He passed Arden, stepping into the clearing, holding out his hand. Brace could see a large piece of lightstone in Jair's palm, and he blinked in surprise. Where had he found *that*?

"Here," Jair called out to the men. "This will keep you safe from those creatures."

"What is it?"

"It's made of stone, but of light as well," Jair told him. "It keeps the night screamers away. That's what we call them – night screamers. You'll be safe from them as long as you have this with you."

"Don't get too close to them," Arden warned as Jair took another step.

"They won't hurt me," Jair told him.

Arden kept his bow ready all the same, as Jair crossed the clearing. The man nearest him slowly came forward to accept Jair's gift, gazing at it in wonder. Misty puffs of air lingered momentarily before him with every breath he took, his hand lingering just above the piece of lightstone as though he feared to touch it.

"It's all right," Jair told him as he placed it in the man's hand. "It won't hurt you. It will keep you safe."

The four remaining men gathered together, gazing at the lightstone, as Jair hurried back to rejoin the group.

"Go on now," Arden told the men once again. "Go, and stop this from happening again."

"We will," came the reply. "Thank you."

Arden turned and gestured for everyone to go back into the city. Brace caught Jair's arm and pulled him along as they went. The boy seemed unable to take his eyes off of what remained of King Oden's men, who watched the rest of them retreat behind the gate as it slowly began to swing shut.

"Where did you find that piece of lightstone?" Brace asked Jair when the King's men were finally blocked from view.

Jair smiled. "There weren't any broken pieces," he replied.

"Where did you get it, then?"

"I needed it, and the wall gave it to me."

"What are you talking about?"

Jair shrugged. "Just that – that's what happened. I put my hand on the wall, and thought about how much those men needed a piece of it to be safe, and there it was, in my hand."

Brace let his mouth fall open in surprise.

"Don't ask me any more, please," Jair told everyone. "I just want to get to the Main Hall and make sure everyone's all right."

Arden nodded. "Let's go, then. We'll have no more trouble from the outside, we know that now. There's no need to fear another attack, whether one ever happens again or not."

~

When they pulled open the doors to the Main Hall, they were met first with gasps of fear and surprise, then cries of joy and relief. Brace watched as Leandra, holding Denira tightly, hurried to Arden's side. He watched as Arden dropped his bow and wrapped his arms around his family. The large room was filled with a jumbled chaos of voices as everyone began talking at once, some asking questions while others gave assurance that they were all right, that everything was all right.

Brace could see Tassie pushing her way through the crowded room, and he ran to her and held her tightly.

"Brace, what happened?" she asked, pulling back just enough to see his face. "That light! Did you see that light?"

"We saw it."

"It came right in through the walls," Tassie went on. "I could feel it, Brace. I could feel it going right through me!"

"I know," he told her. "I felt it too."

"What was it?"

Brace looked past Tassie for a moment, to where Jair stood, surrounded, as he answered the questions being thrown at him.

"Haven's light," Brace answered Tassie's question. "It was Haven's light protecting the city. I think it was … searching."

"Searching?" Tassie asked.

Brace nodded. "It was searching hearts. *The pure in heart*," he continued, remembering the words Jair had read on Haven's wall so long ago. "The pure in heart were left untouched. And the others … well, they're gone."

Brace suddenly remembered Ben-Rickard, and the secret he had kept to himself. He had been the cause of the King's men coming here!

"How is everyone here?" Brace asked Tassie quickly. "Did anything happen to anyone? Is everyone all right?"

"Everyone is fine," Tassie replied, tilting her head. "Why?"

Brace hesitated, unsure whether it was his place to say anything.

"It was Ben-Rickard, wasn't it?" Tassie asked. "He's the *one*. The one whose thoughts Zorix overheard. I saw Lomar and Ronin bring him back here, but no one said why. I only noticed that he seemed … sad, or something." Tassie looked around the room, still leaning against Brace's side.

"But he's all right?" Brace asked, seeing Ben seated at the back of the room, with Stanner and Ronin beside him. He had his head in his hands, looking down at the floor, but he was there. He was alive.

The pure in heart … the King's men had been destroyed because they had come to threaten the city. But the light had let Ben live. He must have truly meant what he said, that he hadn't intended to bring any trouble here.

Brace reached up and put his hand on Tassie's cheek, and she turned toward him again.

"We're safe, Tassie," he told her, finally feeling relief sweeping over him. "No one will *ever* be able to attack Haven. The light will protect us."

Tassie smiled and held Brace tightly.

"We're safe," she sighed. "We're *safe*."

~ 35 ~

Brace leaned on the window ledge and looked out into the morning sunlight as it reflected off the lightstone walls. It was bright, but nowhere near as bright as it had been three days ago, when the light had come alive to defend the city against would-be invaders. Brace had always been in awe of the lightstones, but now that he knew what power was hidden dormant within them, he saw them very differently. He had a strange sense of respect for them now, often wondering, as he walked past them, if they were somehow looking back at him.

Three days, and things were just beginning to settle down once again. There had been so much to work out after the dramatic events that had occurred, that everyone had spent almost two entire days in the Main Hall. The first task had been to discuss what to do about Ben-Rickard. Word had spread quickly about Ben's confession, that he had been the cause of all the trouble. It was obvious that the man was overwhelmed with guilt about what he had done; that was easy enough to see.

From the day he had set foot in Haven, he had been nothing but kind, hard-working and encouraging. Until now, no one would have had any unfavorable opinion of him. As Ben stood before Haven's people in the Main Hall, verifying that he was indeed the guilty one, this was no longer the case. It was because of him that they'd all feared for their safety, or even their lives. Needless to say, the news had come as quite a shock. For the longest time, silence had filled the Main Hall. What could anyone possibly say in response to Ben's confession? Nothing could adequately describe the sense of betrayal felt by so many.

Finally, unable to bear the heavy silence any longer, Brace had spoken up in Ben's defense. He reminded everyone of how much Ben had done to help make Haven as beautiful as it could be, of his giving, caring nature. He had known Ben-Rickard as a kind-hearted person, even before he'd come to Haven, remembering how he had been there with Ronin and Torren to help him in Erast. Brace asserted that even good, honest people were capable of making mistakes. He had only paused slightly before going on to tell everyone, reminding many of them, that he himself had made many more mistakes than Ben had, he was sure.

Brace had been thankful when Jair stood beside him to speak up for Ben as well. The boy pointed out that everyone who had anything less than a pure heart, as far as Haven was concerned, had been destroyed by the light from Haven's walls. Ben could not possibly be lying about his intentions – the light had revealed the truth, and he remained standing. If Ben had tried to enter Haven with thoughts of taking it away from the people, he would not have survived.

These words of Jair's seemed to make the most impact on everyone gathered there that day. This was an undeniable fact. Haven had declared Ben to be innocent, and the city could, it seemed, look right into each person's heart, something that none of them could ever possibly be capable of.

Whether or not every heart had fully forgiven him, Ben-Rickard was declared to be upright, free from any lingering guilt. He was officially pardoned that day.

Kendie, at least, had completely forgiven him – that was certain. As soon as the meeting was over, she had run to him and hugged him tightly.

Arden, on the other hand, Brace was not so sure about. He was not a cruel man, and he never would have killed Ben that day, as Kendie had feared. But he certainly did take his time when it came to changing his mind about a person. Brace could attest to that firsthand.

The second meeting at the Main Hall, on the following day, had been concerning the light itself. Everyone had experienced it in one way or another – either seeing it from outside in the Fountain Court, or simply feeling it flow through the large room of the Main Hall. That being the case, everyone needed to hear what Jair had to say about it. The incident had reminded them of what Jair had said some time ago, that Haven's light would protect them. Now, his words made perfect sense.

Jair had decided that this was the time to tell the people everything. He told them that he had a sort of strange kinship with the city of Haven, that he could understand its ancient language and was constantly becoming aware of its secrets. It was as though the city of Haven had been waiting for Jair to arrive, and it had so many things that it needed to tell him, and him alone.

Neither Brodan nor Lomar had any lingering doubts about what Jair had to say, whether they understood it or not. They had seen one of Haven's mysteries come to life with their own eyes, after all. There was no question that Haven's light was alive indeed.

Ovard had something to say as well, although Jair seemed a bit reluctant to have him say it. He told the people that Jair's ancestor had been a close relative of Haven's last living overseer, so many thousands of years ago, and that now, Jair would be taking up that position himself. He told them that this was not something that he, Ovard, had decided, nor had Jair. The city itself, and not only the people there, had chosen Jair as its new leader.

That had been only yesterday, and now, everyone would gather in the Fountain Court once again, for a celebration to commemorate the day of Haven's victory.

Silently, Tassie slipped up to the window and stood beside Brace, her arm brushing up against his.

She smiled faintly. "You're thinking about the light again, aren't you?" she asked.

Brace nodded. "I can't get it out of my mind, Tassie. I wish you could have seen it! It just came right up out of the lightstone walls, like ... well, just like those figures carved into the walls in the white room underground. It was unbelievable, almost."

"You've told me so many times," Tassie told him, amused, "that I almost feel like I *did* see it." She leaned her chin on Brace's shoulder and looked out through the window. "I can close my eyes and imagine it, just the way it must have happened."

Brace nodded. "I guess that will have to be enough, won't it?"

Tassie stood up straight. "Did you say something?"

"No," Brace replied with a grin.

Tassie gave him that smile that said she wasn't sure she believed him, but she let it go. "Well, we should head out now, don't you think? The celebration will be starting soon."

~

Brace and Tassie walked hand-in-hand into the Fountain Court, where a crowd was already gathering. Ovard stood beside Jair in front of the gurgling fountain, looking out at the people who had gathered. Although the courtyard was quickly becoming just as full as it had been at their last celebration, today, the air was calm and quiet. People were conversing in soft voices; there was no lively music or clattering of spoons on serving dishes, not this time. Everyone was in awe of their great city, of its ability to come alive and fight for them. It still seemed odd to Brace, looking at everyone's faces and seeing the change in them. Three days had passed, and there was still reverence, awe, and fear to be seen in their eyes. Brace noticed Yara standing beside Dorianne, a short distance ahead, and he slowed his steps, hesitating. He held Tassie's hand tightly as Yara looked in his direction, giving him a small, friendly smile.

Tassie pulled Brace close to her side, and he turned his gaze to look into her eyes. She smiled an encouraging smile, then slipped her hand out of his and stepped toward Yara purposefully. What could she be doing? Brace wondered. Would she confront her, here, now? He wondered whether he should follow her, or pull her away.

He took one step forward, then stopped when he saw the two women pull each other close in a warm embrace. He smiled to himself and turned away. He should have known better – today was not a day for confrontation. Today was a day for all things to be made right. This was their moment, a moment for Tassie to let Yara know beyond all doubt that she held no hard feelings toward her.

His eyes scanned the crowd until he spotted Jordis coming slowly toward him.

"Hello," Jordis said quietly.

"Hello," Brace replied, feeling fresh regret over ever having suspected Jordis of plotting any harm, and relief that he hadn't. "Amazing day, isn't it?"

Jordis nodded. "This is an amazing place."

"I'm glad to know we're all safe here," Brace commented, and Jordis nodded. He seemed uncomfortable, surrounded by so many others, but he was *here,* in the courtyard. It had taken time, but it was evident that Brace's words had stuck with Jordis, and they had begun to chip away at him. He still often hung back, but he had stayed. And from time to time, he even smiled.

"Jordis?" Brace asked before moving on through the crowd. "I'm glad you found your reason to stay." Brace smiled, and Jordis smiled in return.

"Thank you. As am I."

Jordis went on, giving Brace a nod, and Brace noticed Torren standing against the far wall of the courtyard. Ben-Rickard sat beside him on one of the stone benches, his head bowed under the load of shame that he still carried with him. Brace glanced aside, but Tassie was still talking with Yara. Well, he told himself, if he could speak up in Ben's defense at the meeting, he could certainly go and talk to Ben himself, here in the Fountain Court.

He had no idea what to say, he realized, as he weaved his way through those standing nearby. Torren noticed Brace approaching, and he nodded in greeting.

"Mind if I join you for a bit?" Brace asked for Ben's benefit. Torren, he was sure, already knew what was on Brace's mind.

Ben looked up, his eyes tired and full of regret. "Are you sure you want to do that?" he asked quietly.

Without a word, Brace sat down beside him on the cool stone bench.

"I wouldn't have come over here if I didn't," he replied matter-of-factly.

Ben looked at him, a hint of a smile showing in his eyes, but not so much on his face.

Brace crossed his arms over his chest. "Don't know why you're hiding over here to begin with," he told Ben. "You've been cleared of any guilt. By the people, and by Haven itself."

Ben nodded slowly. "That's so," he agreed, his voice cautious. He glanced around the courtyard, which was quickly filling with new arrivals who were waiting for the celebration to begin.

"Ovard and Jair declared me pardoned," Ben went on slowly, "but I don't know about everyone else. They're holding on to something. They don't know if they should trust me, if they should forgive me." He shrugged. "I don't know if I should forgive myself."

Brace nodded, understanding. "I know how you feel," he told Ben. "But no one was hurt. No one can get into Haven intending to take it by force. No one can attack us here. We're safe."

"But I didn't know that when I showed the King's men how to get here."

"You didn't even know Haven was real when you did that," Brace reminded him.

Ben sat in silence for a moment, then nodded.

"That's true," he admitted. "I don't know if it makes a difference, though. No one's really spoken to me for the past three days. They've hardly even looked at me. I don't think I really belong here after all."

"Give them time, Ben," Torren spoke up. "They just need to get over the shock, that's all."

It was easy for Brace to remember how he had once doubted whether he belonged in Haven himself, as had Jordis. What words had he wanted to hear then? Finally, he looked at Ben-Rickard once again.

"Do you want to stay here?" he asked him bluntly.

Ben straightened up in surprise. He let Brace's question sink in, and he looked around, recalling the wonders of the city that lay all around them.

"Yes," he answered slowly, softly. "Yes, I do want to stay. Very much."

"Then stay," Brace told him. He smiled when Ben looked up at him, then gave him a friendly clap on the shoulder. Nodding at Torren, he went to rejoin Tassie, who now stood alone, waiting for him. She slipped her arm around his as he stepped up beside her.

"Is everything all right?" she asked.

"Well enough, I think," he replied. "It's Ben. He's tearing himself up over what happened, pulling away from everyone."

Tassie peered at Ben-Rickard over Brace's shoulder. "I think we should have him over for a meal tomorrow, then. Don't you?"

Brace smiled and looked into Tassie's deep green eyes. "Sure," he replied. "I think Arden and Leandra should join us too."

Tassie's eyes shone with joy as she smiled at him. "That is a very wise idea."

Ovard's voice calling out over the crowd drew Brace's attention. "Welcome, everyone, welcome!"

Brace nudged Tassie, making her aware that her uncle was speaking. As the crowded Court grew quiet once again, Ovard continued.

"Thank you all for coming here again. In remembrance of what has happened here – in Haven, in our city – Jair and I have decided to commemorate this day as sacred, never to be forgotten. The living light of Haven has risen up to defend itself, and us, its citizens, against any outside attack. We are truly safe here, in our new home. Let us never forget that fact. Let us never forget the amazing events that took place, nor let us forget what a truly miraculous place that Haven is."

When Ovard paused to take a breath, the people were all silent. Brace could not hear a single cough or whisper. Ovard took a moment to look all around him, then smiled and looked aside at Jair. "What would you like to say, young man?" he asked him. "You are our leader, after all."

Jair glanced around at the many faces, the many pairs of eyes that were on him.

"Well," he began uncertainly, but Ovard nudged him and gestured for him to speak louder.

"I just don't want anyone to forget what happened," Jair went on, his voice carrying across the stone-paved courtyard. "We need to always remember, and to tell new people who come to live here, and tell the children who will be born here." Jair looked over at Arden, Leandra, and little Denira. "And the one who already has been born here." He smiled, then grew pensive. "It might never happen again," he went on, "the way the light rose up to defend us. It might never need to happen again, but we can't forget what it can do." He paused, started to shrug, but stopped himself. Brace noticed when Jair blinked, noticed the realization that came into his eyes. He was no longer a *child*. He was Haven's leader. He did not have any reason to feel unsure while he was speaking to his people.

Jair's surprised expression grew into a smile.

"When we found the room that makes the fountain work," he went on, "we also found a special place that lets us see what's on the outside of the gate. It's a place where we can keep watch. I've decided to put together a team who can share that special duty." Jair smiled. "I hope you will all accept it. Please come up here when I call your name. Arden?"

The archer's eyes widened for a moment, then he smiled and stood at Jair's side, bowing slightly, a gesture of thanks and respect. "Persha?" Jair went on. "Stanner? Brace?"

Brace's breath caught in his throat. *Watch the gate?* He thought. *Go back down into that small space? You've got to be joking.*

He quickly considered the offer, the request, and realized what an honor it was to be asked. Serving in the White Room was an honor he did not deserve.

"Did he call your name?" Tassie whispered in Brace's ear, and he nodded. "You'd better go on up there," she told him, smiling proudly.

Brace swallowed and, holding Tassie's hand, bringing her along with him, he made his way to join the others.

Arden clapped him on the back as Jair smiled at him.

"You've earned it," Arden told him, and Brace managed a half-hearted grin.

"Ben-Rickard?" Jair called out, and a murmur swept through the crowd.

Ben's face paled and he stood his ground near the back of the courtyard. Kendie ran to him, grabbing his hand to pull him forward.

"Come on," she said, smiling. "Jair wants you on the team."

Ben started at her, dumbfounded, and shook his head.

"Please," Jair told him. "I trust you, Ben."

"I trust you," Brace repeated.

One by one, others repeated the phrase, bringing tears to Ben-Rickard's eyes.

"I trust you," Arden told him at last.

At Arden's words, Ben straightened up and came to join the others, allowing Kendie to pull him forward.

Jair smiled broadly. "Thank you," he told the group who had gathered beside him. "You are now Haven's Watch. I know you will do your job well. Kendie," he added, facing her, "why don't you sing your song now?"

Kendie nodded and stood beside Jair in front of the gurgling fountain. The girl's black wavy hair flowed freely down around her shoulders as she stood straight and tall, her hands clasped together in front of her. She looked up at Jair for a moment, her eyes full of something more than respect, and Brace had to stifle a chuckle.

Kendie coughed to clear her throat as she turned to face her audience. "I've been working on this song for a while," she began. "After what happened the other day, I changed it a little. But … anyway … I hope you like it." Kendie lifted her chin a little, smiled at someone in the crowd, then began to sing out clearly.

> "When the world weighs heavy on your shoulders,
> If you feel like your heart might break,
> There's a beam of light
> That bursts through the night
> And you can find your way home.
> In Haven there is a beginning
> And life starts again, fresh and new
> Come find safety and friendship
> Its arms are open to you.
> Hope for weary hearts
> Hope for weary souls
> Haven is waiting for you."

Kendie took a breath and stepped back as she finished, looking over at Jair for approval. He smiled and nodded, and Brace could hear a few sniffles around the courtyard, noticed Shayrie brushing away a tear.

"This is Haven's song," Jair addressed the people once again. "This is our song. It's everything Haven is, what it was always meant to be. We can learn it and remember it, and it can bring us all together. Haven is our home. Here we can all find friends, and light, and safety and hope. For now, and for years and years to come, and forever."

Brace took Tassie's hand and pulled her close beside him. She looked up at him, her deep green eyes shining. "Forever," she said with a smile.

"Forever," Brace agreed. "No matter what the future holds."

~

Theon hurried into the spacious, richly furnished room, his red brocade cloak flying out behind him.

"King Oden, sir! Your Majesty!" His words flew out faster than he could put his thoughts together, the hard soles of his boots echoing off the smooth stone floor. He hurried to a stop a respectful distance from the throne of the surprised king, going down to one knee and taking a full breath.

"What is this?" Oden demanded as he stood, rising and taking a step forward.

Theon paused, catching his breath.

"I apologize, Your Majesty," he began, standing. "It's the men, sir. Your army – some of them have returned."

"Well?" the king asked, his arms spread wide. "Where are they? Bring them in. Let them report."

"Forgive me, Your Majesty." Theon bowed his head, fixing his gaze on the floor, "But there has been some trouble."

Oden stepped closer, his large heavy boots coming into Theon's view. "Are the men here, or are they not?" he asked impatiently.

"Yes, my King," Theon replied, daring to lift his eyes slowly. The king's scowling, bearded face loomed before him.

"Send them in, then! Let them report!"

"Yes, my King." Theon rose to his feet, bowed, then turned and hurried back toward the door. Flinging it wide, he frantically gestured to the four bedraggled men who stood waiting. Obediently, but hesitantly, they entered the king's throne room and approached, their eyes averted.

Oden remained standing as, one by one, his men touched a knee to the hard stone floor before him.

"Tell me, then," Oden addressed them, folding his arms behind his back. "What news? Is the city ours?"

An uncomfortable silence lingered, filling the enormous room with an unease that was almost tangible.

"No," one of the men finally spoke, keeping his eyes on the floor.

"*No?*"

"No, Your Majesty."

The king's voice rose in volume. "What, then? Tell me, what has happened?"

The four leather-clad men exchanged glances, but none spoke.

"Tell me!" Oden bellowed.

The men flinched, quickly returning their gaze to the floor at the king's feet.

Finally, one of them dared to speak. "Forgive us, my King, for bringing you this news of our defeat. There was nothing we could have done. We couldn't even get in through the gate."

Oden's scowl deepened. "No?"

"No, Your Majesty," the fourth replied. "But ..." he hesitated, then went on. "But, although the city was already occupied, it was not the people who live there that gave us the trouble."

"What, then?"

The first man lifted his gaze, ever so slightly. "I can't really say, Your Majesty. One moment, we were all gathered there in the clearing before the gate, and the next moment, they just... disappeared."

"Who disappeared?"

"The other men. The commanders, everyone."

"Everyone but the four of us," another agreed.

"Disappeared?!" Oden exclaimed. "Disappeared?! *Disappeared?!*" He repeated, grabbing a fistful of the nearest soldier's shirt and pulling him to his feet. "No one simply disappears!"

The man's eyes were wide as he now stared fully at his king's angered face. He shook his head.

"No, Your Majesty. I know that, Your Majesty. But it's true. I'm sorry, but it's true. They were there, and then they were gone!"

"Gone!" King Oden shouted. "What is it you're hiding from me? What really happened out there? Two hundred men don't disappear! Do you take me for a fool?"

"No! No, Your Majesty!" the soldier replied, shaking his head.

"He tells the truth," another spoke in his defense.

King Oden looked sharply in his direction, releasing the man's shirt with a shove that sent him sprawling on the floor.

"Does he now?" the king asked, turning his wrath on the other three men, who kept their heads low.

"The horses fled in fear," the second soldier went on. "There was this … very bright, hot light. It came from the city, it swept over everything. And then, they were gone. Just *gone*."

"Bright light?" Oden asked in a voice of anger mixed with confusion.

"Yes, my King," the third replied. "I felt it myself. We all did."

"It was the light," the soldier spoke up, lying on his back, his arms held protectively over his face. "The light made the others vanish."

King Oden tugged at his grizzled beard, frowning deeply.

"You're certain?" he asked.

"Very, my King. Very certain."

Theon wrung his hands nervously, standing behind the kneeling soldiers. The king slowly paced in one direction, then the other, then lowered himself onto his heavy golden throne.

"This is quite unfortunate. Unbelievable!" he exclaimed. "Gone? All two hundred of the men I sent, all but four? *Gone?* Just like that, without any explanation but some mysterious *light?*"

"That's exactly the way it happened, my King. It was like the city just …came alive and destroyed them."

"Why them, and not you?"

There were more nervous glances.

"I don't know, my King."

Oden pounded his fist on the arm of his throne. "What is to be done now?" he asked aloud, to no one in particular. "All of those men, gone to their deaths, with nothing to show for it. *My* men – and I'm the one who sent them. This is no small loss. Everyone in Dunya will know of their deaths in no time at all! I can hear the people now – 'King Oden has sent them to their doom!'"

He glared at the soldiers, at Theon.

"What is to be done now?"

Theon tugged at his sleeves, putting his thoughts in order.

"Pardon me, my King," he spoke up. "But I believe I know a way for this situation to be redeemed, to your benefit …"

Tia Austin lives in Northwest Washington, where she enjoys spending time outside, walking the forest trails and along the rocky beaches. She has been writing fiction and poetry from a young age, with some poems published in anthologies. Haven's Light is her second published novel. Her favorite genres to write (and read!) are fantasy and historical fiction.

Printed in the United States
By Bookmasters